THE DOUBLE

Stephanie was staring at President-elect Newell with a strange look of sudden revelation in her eyes. "That's what my sister, Eva, was doing, isn't it?" she said slowly. "She was with your intelligence operation."

Newell nodded affirmatively. "But there was more than just that," he said. "You see, Eva had infiltrated a part of the Opposition . . ."

"Do you mean she was a spy?" Stephanie said.

"Yes," Newell said candidly. "But what made her so valuable was that *they* thought it was themselves who had infiltrated us—that Eva had turned and was working for them."

"You mean she was a double agent," Stephanie said.

"As far as they were concerned," Newell agreed. "But in reality she was a triple. Can you see what a priceless asset she represented to us?"

"Irreplaceable," Mel said mechanically.

Newell nodded. "But then, not *quite* irreplaceable. You and your sister have been mistaken for each other twice already." Stephanie started to say something, but Newell raised a hand. "You see, what we want you to do is become Eva. We want you to take your sister's place. . . ."

Books by James P. Hogan

The Code of the Lifemaker
Endgame Enigma
Genesis Machine
Gentle Giants of Ganymede
Giants' Star
Inherit the Stars
Minds, Machines and Evolution
The Mirror Maze
The Proteus Operation
Thrice upon a Time
Two Faces of Tomorrow
Voyage from Yesteryear

THE
MIRROR
MAZE

James P. Hogan

BANTAM BOOKS
TORONTO • NEW YORK • LONDON • SYDNEY • AUCKLAND

To GRACE and BILL,
and in memory of NICKY

THE MIRROR MAZE

A Bantam Spectra Book / March 1989

All rights reserved.
Copyright © 1989 by James P. Hogan.
Cover art copyright © 1989 by Tony Randazzo.

ISBN: 0-553-27762-6

Published simultaneously in the United States and Canada

Bantam Books are published by Bantam Books, a division of Bantam
Doubleday Dell Publishing Group, Inc. Its trademark, consisting of
the words "Bantam Books" and the portrayal of a rooster, is
Registered in U.S. Patent and Trademark Office and in other
countries. Marca Registrada. Bantam Books, 666 Fifth Avenue, New
York, New York 10103

PRINTED IN THE UNITED STATES OF AMERICA

KR   0 9 8 7 6 5 4 3 2 1

ACKNOWLEDGMENTS

The help and advice of the following people is gratefully appreciated:

David Robb, Lynx Crowe, and Rod Hyde, for thoughts on breaking and entering computer systems.

Cheryl Robinson, who supports free enterprise and individualism.

Steve Fairchild, for needing a lot of convincing.

John J. Woods and Gary Dambacher, attorneys at law, Sonora, California.

Kevin Magee, Lyn Hogan, Petr Beckmann, Larry Cornish, Ashley Grayson, Brent Warner, and Deborah Bigbee for help with local information and geographies.

Kathleen Vlahakos of Sacramento, and Laura Synhorst of the Sacramento County Coroner's Office.

Juanita Leapheart, for help with languages.

Ken Bell of NBC, New York, for clarifying some of the mysteries of the American electoral system.

Andrew Corbett of Aer Lingus for information on airline practices and air traffic control.

Jerry Fitzgerald of Dublin Airport, for aeronautical information.

Shawna McCarthy of Bantam Books, for not being too easy to please.

And Jackie and Dorothy, for letting me become the recluse I needed to be.

PROLOGUE

She was tall and slim, with silky, platinum hair sweeping across one side of her face to her shoulder. Her eyes were a vivid green, which in strong light seemed to take on an inner iridescence of their own, like those of a nocturnal predatory animal. Her penthouse looked down over Madison Avenue just south of New York's Central Park. In the select, anonymous circles that engaged her professional services from time to time, she was known as "The Lynx."

Outside, the evening was cool. It had just turned November. The Lynx sat as she had for the last fifteen minutes, gazing at the eight-by-eleven-inch picture propped on the red leather top of the fitted desk unit at one end of the sunken lounge area. Around her lay the notes and instructions that she had studied, and to one side, the large yellow envelope that the dossier had arrived in earlier that day by special courier. She sat, slowly allowing her mind to blend the information with the face and to absorb the personality that she felt emerging. "Yes, now I think I'm starting to know you," she murmured.

She got up and crossed the room to mix herself a martini, very dry—just enough vermouth to wet the olive—at the bar by the window. Then she tapped a command for a Mahler symphony into the pad lying on the bar, and stood for a moment watching the evening traffic below as she took her first sip. As the opening bars of the music swelled to fill the room, she returned to the couch and sat down again to resume contemplating the face staring back at her from the photograph.

It was a pretty face, of a girl in her mid-twenties, with long, straight, fair hair, lean, nicely proportioned features that showed her cheekbones and accentuated her straight nose, a wide mouth with soft outlines, and pale skin. "A pity," the Lynx murmured aloud, and sipped her drink again. She took in the soft curve of the chin and innocent roundness of the eyes, brightening with the beginnings of a smile. "I think I would rather have enjoyed seducing you instead. Have you ever had a woman as a lover, I wonder?" The Lynx wondered idly who would pay fifty thousand dollars to kill a physicist, and why.

Some people who didn't understand the business thought that it wasn't good to get involved emotionally with one's assignments or to know too much about them. But the Lynx liked to know everything about them. Somehow the intimacy made the eventual finale not so much an execution as a consummation. The ability to keep the professional aspects of the job in a separate compartment of the mind was one reason why some of the best assassins were women. Another, of course, was the comparative ease with which they could lure many of their victims into secluded and vulnerable situations. But that was really ancillary. The main reason was that men were too emotional.

Originally from East Germany, she had been trained and taught how to kill by the East German military intelligence service, in effect a local subsidiary of the KGB. By supplying her with false papers and a carefully prepared cover identity to reside in the West, they had provided the perfect opportunity for her to vanish and put as much distance between herself and the eastern frontier as possible. Now she was safely ensconced in the West under a new name and, following the precepts of her new host country, dutifully devoting her talents and her training to the cause of private enterprise.

The phone rang. She stretched out an arm and lifted the handset. The video circuit was already switched out. "Hello."

"Hilda?"

"This is Hilda."

"Hey, baby! It's Max."

"Max, darling. So good to hear from you."

"Look, I've still got those tickets. I said I'd call you the day before the show, remember? So this is the night. How are you fixed?"

"The show is tomorrow?"

"Don't tell me you forgot."

"No, I didn't forget. But I must have got the weeks confused."

"You're not saying you can't make it? You'll break my heart. I'll jump off a bridge."

"Oh Max, you idiot!"

"No, seriously, you're not tied up, are you?"

"Something has come up, I'm afraid. I have to go out of town for a few days, maybe a week."

"Oh no. . . . What am I supposed to do?"

"Come on. I'm sure you have a black book full of numbers of pretty girls who'd love to keep you company."

"There's no way you can put it off?"

"I'm sorry, Max. No, there isn't."

"How about dinner next Friday, then?"

"Make it the Friday after. I said I might be away for a week."

"That's firm? No maybes."

"It's firm. I promise."

"Okay. I'll call in the meantime, just in case you get back sooner."

"You're a sweetie."

"So long for now, then, eh, beautiful?"

"I'll see you in a week, Max. Behave yourself."

"Huh? What the hell for? What kind of a life would that be?"

"Take care, then. Good-bye, Max."

The Lynx hung up the receiver, but kept her hand on it, thinking to herself for a few seconds and glancing at the papers from the dossier, strewn around her on the couch. Then she picked the receiver up again, called a directory page onto the screen facing the couch from beside the bureau, and tapped in a number.

"United Airlines ticketing. This is Mavis. Can I help you?" a voice answered.

"Hello, Mavis, yes. I'd like to book a flight to Denver as early tomorrow as you can manage, please."

CHAPTER 1

"Mr. Bracey just called from downstairs, Mr. Gilman. The ILC people are leaving. He thought you might want to put in an appearance before they go."

"Oh, thanks, Ruth. Yes. Tell them I'll be there in a couple of minutes." Ed Gilman, president of the General Plasma Dynamics corporation of Denver, Colorado, flipped off the desk intercom and returned his attention to the correspondence that he had been checking over and signing.

Regulations!

He stared exasperatedly at the next sheet in the pile. Why did it require the permission of no fewer then five different branches of the federal government to install a couple of showers in a staff washroom? There had been a time when even a large-scale heavy industrial plant could be built and in production in less than two years. Now it took twice that time to get the permits—involving over twenty different agencies— just to begin breaking ground. The site across the river from GPD was bare, and would be for some time now. After four and a half years of battling, and an outlay of five million dollars to obtain six of the eighty-two permits that would be required, the Hydroline company had abandoned its plans for an experimental plant to produce a hydrogen-based liquid synthetic fuel from the high-temperature "cracking" of water. It would have employed three thousand people and trained scores of invaluable engineers and technicians. Now they were either on the dole or pumping gas instead of creating it, and the venture was going ahead in Taiwan. The Energy Policy Implementation Agency, a reorganized and restructured version of the former DOE, now employed somewhere around forty thousand bureaucrats, busily compounding and contradicting the requirements of all the other agencies as well as each others'. Its annual budget of twenty-five billion dollars exceeded the earnings of the eight largest oil companies combined. The Federal Register, the official list of regulations, ran to well over one hundred thousand pages and took up thirty-two feet of shelf space—the Ten Commandments fitted easily onto a single sheet. As Gilman finished reading the final letter and signed it, he wondered how many army divisions the Soviets would have sacrificed readily to achieve the same results that America was inflicting upon itself.

He carried the correspondence folder out to Ruth in the front office, where a babbling voice from a radio turned low by her elbow was bringing news of another election result. "Where's this?" he asked her.

"New York."

"Did the Constitutionals take it?"

"Yes. A landslide."

Gilman raised his eyebrows and pursed his lips in a silent nod of approval, then left. Outside, he went down two stories to the conference room where the meeting with the people from the Industrial Liaison Commission had taken place. He didn't expect to find the atmosphere particularly cordial. Why it should take four ILC officials to deliver a simple message or read a list of regulations was beyond Gilman. Only a government department could have afforded it. Perhaps numbers enhanced their power to intimidate.

The meeting was just breaking up as Gilman entered. Gus Thornton, GPD's vice president for administration and personnel, was sitting tight-lipped as he finished some notes, while beside him Stan Cray, from the legal department, tidied papers together. Heading the ILC group was a man called Roth from the local office, whom Gilman knew from previous encounters. They were already putting folders back into briefcases, standing, and making to leave. Gilman sensed that, as he had anticipated, the exchange had been acrimonious.

"So, how are we doing?" he asked, resting his hands on the back of one of the unoccupied chairs at the table.

Thornton answered without looking up. "They're not going to ease up on the quotas. It's national policy. Firm from Washington."

It was what Gilman had been expecting. "Don't your people have any concept of what it takes to run a project like this profitably?" he asked Roth exasperatedly. "Look, *we* can't simply stretch out a hand and dig deeper into the public's pocket if we go over the limit. We have to perform. What are we supposed to do with people we're forced to take on, who aren't any good to us? We can't even start up until we get the revised EPIA license, and they've just called another delay on that. Our stockholders are pulling out. Where do you imagine the money's going to come from to pay them?"

The answer, of course, was from the government. Mandatory hiring quotas had become an automatic prerequisite for receiving federal funding—a social obligation that industry owed society. Whether or not the company was owed anything in return was irrelevant, and the damage and losses caused by the incompetents force-hired in this way were its problem. In effect, it was a way of getting industry to pick up part of the unemployment tab, and smaller numbers needed to be admitted officially. Also, the government could point to its contribution as a "research grant."

Roth was a sharp-faced, gnomish little man with patches of wiry hair fringing a balding top. "We've been through all that before, Mr. Gilman," he retorted. "I would have thought that the federal allocations to this establishment were more than sufficient to meet requirements."

"My understanding when that was agreed was that it was for research. Nobody told us it was a camouflaged welfare scam."

"I don't think such terms are necessary."

"What would you call it?"

"You can't conduct research without people."

"I'd like to have some say in the kind of people I get."

Roth stood up and closed his briefcase with an air of finality. "There is a national situation of need which you seem unable or unwilling to acknowledge, Mr. Gilman," he said. "I can only conclude that this company is not disposed to fulfill its obligations under the grant agreement, and I shall be forced to file my report accordingly."

Gilman's color deepened. "Whatever the national situation is, it isn't of my making. If you're really interested in looking for a cause, I'd suggest that you examine your own policies. And I am not aware of having contracted any obligation to relieve you of the consequences of them. If the only purpose of the grant was to fund dole checks, then take it back. All of it. We'll make other arrangements."

"What other arrangements do you think you have left?" Roth sneered.

"After three years of delays and harassment, not a lot," Gilman replied candidly. "But that's my problem and I'll handle it. You've got problems of your own. Have you forgotten that there's an election going on out there today? The Constitutionals are running away with it. When the twenty-eighth goes through, all this will be irrelevant history. Then, maybe, the only people in the dole lines will be washed-up bureaucrats."

"We'll see," Roth replied acidly. "But for now the matter is pure conjecture. In the meantime, the department's requirements are clearly spelled out, and they must be met. Good day." With that, he led his delegation out of the room. Cray went with them to escort them from the building.

Thornton tucked his folder of papers under his arm and moved over to join Gilman by the door. "There were a few other points, too, Ed. Want a rundown on them?"

Gilman looked at his watch. "Oh, it's late. Let's do it tomorrow. Besides, it's a big day. Things are happening in the big wide world out there." They began walking back along the corridor toward the stairwell.

"Were you serious about telling them to shove their funding and looking around?" Thornton asked.

"Maybe. It's a nice thought, isn't it?"

"Wonderful. What's the latest on the election?"

"Newell's got New York and Florida."

"New York!" Thornton emitted a low whistle. "This *is* a big day. I mean, they're going to do it. It's going to happen."

"Let's hope so."

At the stairs, Thornton started to ascend. Gilman stopped by the elevator. "Not coming back up?" Thornton asked.

"I think I'll take a look around the rig."

"Well, I'll be leaving in about ten minutes. Good night in case I don't see you again. And let's see those results keep rolling on in, eh?"

"'Night, Gus. Yes. I'll call you later this evening."

As Gilman stood waiting for the elevator to arrive, he thought about the excitement sweeping the country—Ruth had been updating him periodically with details since morning. This was not just another presidential election year, but presidential election year 2000—the year in which America would choose its first administration of the new millennium. The occasion was symbolic, and the nation—indeed the whole world—had been watching for a sign of changing tides and a fresh course being set into the new era. That made it all the more significant for a newly created party to have appeared out of nowhere to challenge the traditional two-sided balance. Ten years ago, nobody had heard of the Constitutionals. Now, seemingly, they were about to take over the country. Yes, times were a-changing. . . .

He took the elevator down to the basement level and emerged into a wide corridor with a concrete floor, yellow-painted brick walls, and doors opening into rooms filled with electrical machinery and rows of instrumentation cubicles. As he began walking toward the reactor hall where the hybrid prototype was being constructed, two technicians who were finished for the day passed him, heading the other way.

"Good night, Mr. Gilman," one of them called. Gilman acknowledged with a nod and a faint smile.

"Is the election good news for the company, from the way things are going?" the other inquired.

"Hopefully. Let's wait and see."

At the end of the corridor he went through a set of double doors and came out beneath a tangle of steel structural work built around pump housings, transformers, and banks of superconducting windings, with access ladders leading up to overhead catwalks. Beyond was a vaster space, lit by batteries of overhead lights and a line of window panels high in the building's girder-braced walls. In the center stood the partially completed bulk of the prototype reactor itself—a curving, thirty-foot-high wall of stainless steel, supported by a sturdier framework and barely visible through the labyrinth of cabling and pipework clinging to its side.

Gilman walked slowly through the clutter of equipment and test benches in the surrounding space, his eyes checking unconsciously for signs of sloppiness—tools not put away, equipment not switched off that should have been, spills that hadn't been cleaned up. Everything that he could see was in order. He came to the base of the reactor housing and stood for a while looking up at it. It had cost him and the backers whom he had persuaded to come in on the venture all their liquid capital and credit, and over ten years of their lives. Here was a solution to most of the problems that the world had been cringing before in superstitious dread for over a quarter of a century. But the powers that were in control, it seemed, didn't *want* solutions. Fear and insecurity produced more controllable populations than affluence and independence did.

As he moved on around the reactor vessel, a light caught his eye from inside the partitioned room where the instrumentation computers were located. Through the window facing the reactor area, he glimpsed a white-coated figure with long, straight, fair hair, poring over a desk and tapping intermittently at a keyboard below a screen to one side. He shook his head. Typical: Stephanie was working late again. Gilman walked over and stuck his head through the door. "Hey, don't you ever give it a break? Come on. Time to quit."

Stephanie looked up, startled for an instant. She was in her mid-twenties, with lean, sensitively formed features that accentuated her cheekbones and the straightness of her nose, a wide mouth with a soft outline, rounded eyes, and pale, unblemished skin. It was an attractive face, though somewhat drawn. "Oh, I didn't realize there was anyone here." She paused awkwardly, and then to break the silence gestured quickly at the screen in front of her. "I was just finishing the calibration corrections on the neutron flux analyzers."

Gilman came inside and perched himself on the edge of a desk by the door. "How are they looking?"

"Pretty good. I think there's a detector that's going to have to be replaced, though."

"Hum. Anything that can't wait until tomorrow?"

Stephanie conceded the point with a tired smile. "I guess not." She glanced at the clock above the supervisory panel. "I should be getting along, anyway. I have to meet someone later."

"That's right. Get yourself out and about. Don't retreat into a shell and get trapped there. I know it's easy for me to say, but life has to go on. You have to go on."

There was concern in Gilman's voice as he spoke. Stephanie's boyfriend, whom she had lived with and seemed very close to, had been killed in an accident three weeks previously. She had taken the shock badly and gone into a state of depression that was only now showing its first sign of easing. Gilman had urged her to take time off and rest, but she had insisted that she would rather be at work and among people she knew.

"We should have it cleared by the weekend, anyhow," Stephanie said as she began flipping switches to shut down the system. "It should be okay for the start-up next week."

"You don't have to worry too much about that," Gilman said. "EPIA has delayed the license again."

"Oh no. . . . What for, now?"

"Some legal point. Even I don't pretend to understand it."

Stephanie shook her head protestingly. "It's criminal, after everything that's gone into this project. . . . And none of them really understands it, even. I've seen some of their reports."

"Maybe we'd have thought better of it if we'd known ten years ago what we were up against. Anyhow, they're my worries, and you've got yours." Gilman stood up. "Come on. I'll walk you back to the elevators."

They came out of the room and started in the direction that Gilman had come from. "What's the latest on the election?" Stephanie asked.

"It sounds as if the new kid on the block is running away with it."

"Really? The last I heard was at lunchtime. It sounds too good to be true. People are saying it's the only hope for GPD and the program. Is that true, do you think?"

"Oh, don't be too influenced by everything you hear." Gilman held the door open as they came to the corridor that led back to the elevators. "Maybe our problems aren't as bad as some people say. But at any rate, let's wait first and see if Henry Newell gets in."

"It will have to make a difference if the twenty-eighth amendment gets passed."

They came to the elevators. Gilman punched the call button. "Let's hope so. I've got a feeling that a lot of things are going to be changing before very much longer, so I wouldn't worry too much about sending your résumé around just yet if I were you." The doors slid open. "Anyhow, I'll leave you here. There are a couple more things I want to look at down here."

"Good night, Mr. Gilman. And thanks for the help. I appreciate it."

"'Night, Stephanie. And you take it easy, now, d'you hear?"

CHAPTER 2

Sage Street was in the older part of Denver, an area consisting of ornate but tired-looking two-story homes warding off time with barricades of overgrown shrubbery and rose-tangled fences. For the past two hours, the Lynx had sat watching from an inconspicuous gray, unmarked Dodge van with changed license plates, which she had rented from a small auto repair shop after arriving from New York. She had not parked near the house where she had left the flowers late that afternoon, but on the far side of an intersection, where a slight bend in the street gave an unobstructed view of the driveway from a distance. From her observations of the house during the three previous evenings, it was already more than an hour past the time that Stephanie Carne normally got home from work. Not that it made much difference. The Lynx had intended to wait until well after dusk, anyway.

From the radio, interleaved with passages of a piano recital on the channel that the Lynx had selected, the excited voice of an announcer brought updates on the election news that had been stunning the country all day. "And with the result from Minnesota now in, it just about ties up the Midwest for the Constitutionals. We've got them with . . . it looks like somewhere around thirty-seven percent of the vote up there, with the other two biggies trailing in at Democrats, thirty-two percent, Republicans, twenty-seven. What a day this has been! What a way to start out on a whole new thousand years! It's beginning to really look as if we'll see the unprecedented spectacle of both presidential candidates from the traditional parties conceding before the night is out. Boy, Henry Newell must be a happy man right now! In fact, I've just received a flash that we'll be going over to Washington in a few minutes to hear some of his thoughts at this time. . . ."

The evening darkened, and the street became a patchwork of isolated lights and shadows. People passed occasionally, talking, walking dogs, or just strolling. Every now and again a car arrived or went. The intervening crossroad, intersecting Sage between the house and the place where the Lynx had parked, was busier, forming a psychological barrier that would screen the van from the attention of the house and its neighbors.

Then, a car appeared, positioning to make a left turn onto the far section of Sage, and stopped to give way to an oncoming pickup. In the light of the intersection lamp, the Lynx identified it as Stephanie Carne's midnight blue 1994 Toyota. She switched off the radio and watched as the Toyota completed the turn into the narrow street cluttered with vehicles and drove into the front yard of the house, half of which had been turned into parking space. The other slot was empty, indicating that the couple who lived in the lower of the two apartments into which the house had been converted were out—which eliminated that possible source of complications.

The Lynx watched as Stephanie Carne got out and walked around to open the trunk of her car and take out a bag. Her hair was gathered in a band, falling in a ponytail to the center of her back that day, and she was wearing an orange coat. She ascended the steps to the front porch, where she paused to find her key. As she did so, she noticed the cellophane-wrapped package of roses, carnations, and chrysanthemums against the wall by the door. She stooped and picked up the bouquet, turning it to read the attached card in the light from the corner streetlamp. She hesitated for a moment, and then disappeared inside, taking the flowers with her.

The Lynx waited another fifteen minutes. Then, choosing a moment when the street was empty of passersby or moving vehicles, she eased the Dodge out of its parking slot, crossed the intersection, and drew up in front of the house. She checked one last time the contents of the pockets of the brown warehouse coat that she was wearing, slipped on a pair of pink silk gloves, and climbed out. There was nobody on any of the porches in the vicinity, and no curious faces watched from windows. The Lynx went up the stairs to the front door and pressed the bell marked "S. Carne." A few seconds passed. Then a woman's voice squawked from the intercom grille. "Hello?"

"Hello. Look, I'm sorry to bother you, but I'm from the Flower Basket florist's, in town. There's been a mix-up. I left some flowers here earlier, but it's the wrong place. Have you seen them?"

"Oh, so that's what they were. I was wondering. They're addressed to a Susan *Crane*. I've never heard of her."

"The names were similar. Somebody back at the store made a mistake. Can I pick them up?"

"Sure. I'll let you in. It's the upstairs apartment."

"Sorry to be a nuisance like this."

"No problem."

A buzz sounded from the door. The Lynx pushed to disengage the lock, and stepped inside. The hallway was dimly lit by a night-light, with the door to the downstairs apartment on one side, a bicycle propped by a hall stand on the other, and in front of her, across a square of tiled floor covered by coarse fiber matting, a carpeted stairway with a polished wooden banister, leading up to a landing. After pausing to listen outside the door to the downstairs apartment, the Lynx moved on up the stairs.

At the landing, she felt inside the pocket of her coat and released the safety on the gas pistol. As she turned to continue up the second flight, a light at the top of the stairs came on, and the upper apartment door opened to reveal Stephanie Carne, waiting with the flowers in her arms. She had taken off her coat and was wearing a blue sweater with black slacks. From close up, the Lynx recognized the face that she had memorized from the photographs: lean, sharp-boned features, straight nose and wide mouth, pale complexion warmed with powder and a hint of rouge, makeup a touch heavier around the eyes—as attractive as her image had suggested. But regret formed no part of the Lynx's feelings now. It was time for business. Sentimentality remained firmly locked in a separate compartment of her mind.

"You work late," Stephanie remarked.

"Not usually this late." The Lynx came to the doorway. "But tonight we've got an irate customer. It's worth the hassle to keep the peace."

"You were lucky. I was about to take them out and put them in water." Stephanie extended her arms to hold out the bouquet. "It would have been a shame to waste— "

The movement had uncovered her midriff. The Lynx jabbed low and swiftly with the fingers of her straightened hand, below the flowers and into the V below Stephanie's breast-bone, hard enough to paralyze the breathing momentarily but not enough to bruise. Stephanie gasped, and as a reflexive reaction made her draw in deeply, the Lynx raised the pistol with her other hand and discharged a puff of a nerve-toxin aerosol into her face. Stephanie recoiled, choking, and the flowers fell to the floor. Her eyes became glassy, and she tottered back against the wall, but retaining enough awareness to put up her arms in an effort to resist as the Lynx closed after her. But her strength was failing quickly. The Lynx clamped a hand over her mouth, stifling any sound before it could form, and held her firmly while she raised the pistol again and released a second whiff of gas just below her nostrils, keeping her own face well back—slowly this time, just the minimum to induce unconsciousness and leave no detectable residue by the time the body's metabolism ceased functioning. The Lynx held her until her struggles became feeble and died away. When the body went limp, she let it slide down to the floor. Then she closed the door, put the pistol back in her pocket, and reconnoitered the apartment.

In the kitchen she found a cabinet containing drinking glasses, and took one through into the bedroom. There, she ruffled up the covers on the bed and stacked up the pillows before going back into the hallway to carry in Stephanie's unconscious body. She laid it along the bed, sat down on the edge, and from another pocket produced a hip bottle of bourbon and opened it. Using one hand to support Stephanie's head, she raised the bottle to her mouth with the other and coaxed the liquid between her lips. Stephanie gagged at the first sip, but swallowed automatically as the Lynx persisted. The Lynx continued until she had infused the equivalent of four or five shots. Then she took the bottle into the bathroom and flushed half the remainder of its contents down the toilet, then brought the bottle back into the bedroom and half filled the glass which she had found in the kitchen. She imprinted the bottle from Stephanie's fingers and stood it on the night table, then repeated the procedure with the glass, splashed some of the bourbon on the bed, and lodged the glass in Stephanie's hand.

Stephanie's breathing was more regular now. The Lynx allowed a further fifteen minutes for the alcohol to circulate and break down the last traces of the toxin. Then she took a .38 caliber single-action revolver from inside her coat—unmarked, unlicensed; it could have been obtained by anyone, anywhere—pressed it into Stephanie's other hand, lifted the hand to bring the muzzle against her temple, and squeezed the unresisting finger against the trigger until the gun fired. She left some ammunition in the night-table drawer and, as a finishing touch, turned on the bedside radio. After one last check around the apartment, she picked up the flowers in the hallway and let herself quietly out.

A small item in the evening edition of the following day's *Denver Post* reported that twenty-four-year-old Stephanie Carne, a physicist at the nearby General Plasma Dynamics corporation, had been found dead in her home, killed by a gunshot wound to the head. The coroner would later return a verdict of suicide following severe depression.

CHAPTER 3

Walking briskly in the chill air of approaching winter, two men and a youth followed a bridle path between grassy meadows bordering a stream, and a copse of elm and larch. Above the trees, a cluster of roofs hemmed in by carved gables and sprouting irregular groves of redbrick chimneys marked the center of the grounds of the Vandelmayne estate, in Montgomery County, Maryland.

Jordan Vandelmayne, prominently listed in *Who's Who* and *The American Social Register,* chairman of the board of stockholders of the Vandelmayne-Myer international merchant banking group, with directorships in several dozen of the major financial institutions which it controlled, was in the middle. "So, what was Ponchillez's reaction to the deadeyes?" he asked. "Will he meet our price if we include them as part of the deal?"

He addressed his words to the older of his two companions, an official with the State Department, who had recently returned from political talks in Mexico. The "deadeye" was an air-to-ground, laser-guided cluster bomb that had proved effective elsewhere in the kind of operations that the Mexican government was waging against the communist-inspired "Frente de Liberta" insurgency movement. The collapse of the OPEC cartel in the eighties had brought a temporary decline in oil prices, but the short-term benefits had been more than offset by the consequent removal of incentives to develop remaining U.S. domestic supplies and more advanced technologies. With access to the Middle East's reserves now restricted again, all the old problems had returned with a vengeance.

Mexico's potential put a new slant on things, however. If adequate supplies could be guaranteed at the right price from that direction, then a significant proportion of Alaska's production could be diverted to Japan at the going market rate, which would relieve the U.S.'s situation considerably. But Mexico was being courted by other suitors, too, and Mexicans had a traditional fear of becoming too dominated from the north.

"It's tough," the man from State replied. "He's still holding out, but he won't come out in the open and say officially what they want. However, I did get a chance to talk to a couple of his people off the record."

"And? . . . Is it as we expected?"

"Yes—more leeway on the Peruvian channel."

In other words, there would be little to gain from being paid American dollars for oil if the dollars went straight back to the U.S. again to buy weapons. But if the U.S. authorities could be persuaded to reduce their zealousness in interdicting the flow of Peruvian cocaine and other narcotics across the Mexican border, the increase in percentages changing hands as a consequence would mean, in effect, that the weapons would be subsidized out of the pockets of American users. That would change the economics, and hence the appeal, of the whole proposition appreciably.

Vandelmayne shook his head. "I've been thinking about it, and I don't like it, Milt. Too sensitive. Too much risk of it backfiring publicly. It would be risking Watergate and the Contras all over again."

"What alternative are you proposing?"

Vandelmayne paused just long enough to convey the appropriate shade of delicacy. "Perhaps if the value of 'security' were increased somewhat in Ponchillez's eyes, we might find his attitude a little more accommodating, don't you think? . . ."

"You mean if the Frente situation were to become more threatening to him, for example?"

"Exactly."

"I take it we're talking about an enhancement in their capabilities equipmentwise."

"A modest one. The CIA already have some caches down there of AK47s with Cuban markings."

"Hmm . . . Don't you think it would be better to wait and see how the election result will affect things?"

Vandelmayne shook his head. "In the long run, it won't make any difference. Take my word for it."

The young man on Vandelmayne's other side, Edgar, his twenty-year-old son, looked across uncertainly. Before entering professional life, he would marry the daughter of a New York commodity-broking family, currently attending Vassar, with arrangements for finishing school in Europe already finalized. "Have I understood correctly?" he said. "It sounds as if you're talking about supplying arms to the *communists*. How could that help anything?"

Jordan explained, "In a situation like this, you destabilize things a little—enough to make the government feel insecure, but not enough to really threaten the country. That makes them feel more dependent on us for aid, which strengthens our bargaining position. One of the things you have to realize, Edgar, is—" The communicator in Vandelmayne's pocket began beeping suddenly. "Excuse me." He stopped to take the unit out, and held it near his face. "Yes?"

The respectful voice of Partridge, Vandelmayne's private secretary, answered, calling from inside the house. "The message that you wished to be informed of has come in, Mr. Vandelmayne. It reads, 'Esmeralda.'" The code word had been received from Denver. It meant that a potential threat to the security of a highly sensitive operation had been removed.

Vandelmayne remained silent for a few seconds. Then he said, "Thank you. That is satisfactory."

"I take it there has been no change of plan, then, sir?"

"None. Proceed as agreed." Vandelmayne switched the unit off and returned it to his pocket. He slipped an arm lightly around his son's shoulder as they resumed walking. "One of the realities of this world that you have to come to terms with, Edgar, is that . . ."

In the house, Partridge returned a file to the safe in his office, next door to Vandelmayne's. Although Vandelmayne was aware in a general sense of the significance of the package that had been sent to New York by courier a week previously, he was not acquainted with the specific details of the contents. And that, after all, was as it should be, Partridge reflected as he closed the safe. It was on occasions like this that intermediaries such as himself earned their not inconsiderable remuneration and other benefits.

Some tasks were unbecoming of gentlemen to perform.

CHAPTER 4

"These are the plating baths and metallizing tanks," Alan Dray, president of Platek Electrical Inc. said, gesturing, as he led his visitor from the chemicals storage area, with its vats of acids and solutions, up a short flight of steel stairs and through a doorway into a wide corridor. Windows on either side looked into bays where technicians in protective smocks and caps, some wearing respirators, attended baths of bubbling liquids, cluttered with pipes and gauges. The air smelled faintly vinegary. Dray was a solidly built man in his early forties, with a ruddy, rounded face and straight, yellow hair, combed flat. He walked with the kind of jerky, determined gait that seemed to seek obstacles as challenges. "Do you know anything about this kind of thing, Mr. Shears? Do you have any technical background?"

Melvin Shears shook his head, "Not really. I did do a few years of computer science back at university, before I decided to switch to law."

"Computers, eh? Where was that?"

"West Florida, Pensacola—up on the panhandle. But these days I'm strictly a lawyer . . . or at least getting there, anyway." His card described him as an associate at the small Boston law firm of Evron and Winthram. Approaching twenty-seven now, he was of medium height and slimly built, with dark, wavy hair and sensitive features that wore an expression of exaggerated seriousness just at that moment from trying to look as if the things around him made more sense than they did. His skin had the vaguely pinkish hue that went with good health and vigor, and despite his modest bulk, his firm, easy stride and the mobile contours beneath his suit hinted of a body that kept itself in good shape.

They stopped to look into a bay where a woman in a pink smock was positioning a wire basket loaded with components in one of the baths. "That's where we plate gold onto the contacts of printed circuits," Dray said. "In the room next door, they're putting silver and rhodium onto connector parts. Across the way there is one of our electroforming tanks—producing a shape by depositing metal on a former."

"That's interesting. I didn't know you could do that."

They resumed walking, and Dray went on, "All of these techniques follow from the same basic principle: the ability of electric current to reduce metal salts to metal. In the early days it helped make beautiful things. There were masters who learned how to coax attractive coatings from unpleasant solutions."

"You make it sound more like an art than a science."

"But it is . . . or maybe it's both. You can't exclude personality from this business. Is silver plating best done with one strike, or two, or three? I prefer one, but I've a friend in Chicago who swears by three. So are we talking about formulas or recipes?"

At the end of the corridor they stopped to look through an open door into a noisier room filled with machinery and ducting. "The fumes and released gases from the processing rooms are drawn off and piped through to here for disposal," Dray said. "This is what the trouble is all about. It began a long time ago. In my father's time back in the sixties, they didn't have any of this. The stuff was just blown out of the building by big fans. But things changed, and they were told they had to install washers to take out the acids and so forth."

"Not so unreasonable, maybe," Shears commented. "The population was probably growing. And you're not exactly next to the ocean here. . . ."

"You're right; they probably had a point. . . . So we put in several hundred thousand dollars worth of washers, and that was when everything started getting really stupid. You see, the first part of the process involved neutralizing the acidic fumes with sodium hydroxide. Do you know what you get when you treat acid with a strong base like sodium hydroxide?"

"What?"

"Salt water. We were simply going to run it through the main sewer into the bay. But the EPA, as it was back then, said we couldn't. They wouldn't let us dump salt water into the ocean."

"But the ocean *is* salt water."

"I know that, you know that, and any six-year-old kid knows that. But according to their regulations, it was from a toxic process, and therefore a toxic by-product. It had to be hauled away by truck to a certified dump. But since no one would certify any dumps anywhere near here, that meant New Jersey."

"You were trucking salt water from Boston to New Jersey."

"Right. It was so ridiculous that I got together with one of our engineers and a chemist that I know from MIT to figure out a better way." Dray raised an arm to indicate the machinery room in front of them. "We decided to distill the water out and leave only the salts to be carted off—it's no less ridiculous, but at least there's a lot less of it."

Shears nodded. "That makes sense."

"You'd have thought so. But it's been a long time since anything needed to make sense. This is a vacuum still. We chose a vacuum process because it doesn't use heat for evaporation, and is therefore relatively cost-effective. But now the Compliance Board is telling us we have to tear it all out and put in a thermal still." Dray shook his head and sighed wearily. He turned and steered Shears out of the door at the end of the corridor, onto a pathway running beside the loading dock outside.

"How come? Isn't your system as good as a thermal still?" Shears asked.

"It's *better*," Dray replied. "But that's the way things are now. They don't just set the results you're supposed to achieve; they have to specify every nut and bolt of how you're supposed to achieve it—except that none of them know what they're talking about. They have certified and approved thermal equipment, but not vacuum equipment. That's what it's all about. The real problem is that I'm either going to have to go way into the red or start laying people off to pay for it. And none of it will do anyone a penny's worth of good. Not a penny's worth."

They came back to the office building at the front of the plant and entered through the rear door. A flight of stairs covered by a worn carpet brought them to an office area where a half dozen or so people were working at desks and keyboard terminals. Dray led the way through to a short passageway on the far side where a row of doors opened into private offices, and entered an unostentatious one at the end, standing ajar, which was marked ALAN J. DRAY. PRESIDENT. In the outer room, his graying, middle-aged secretary handed him a thick folder full of papers and tied around with tape. "There's a full set, with the letters from ACS," she informed him.

"Thanks, Ginnie," Dray said, passing the folder to Shears.

Dray and Shears went through into the inner office, and Dray sat down behind his desk. It was cluttered with pieces of mechanisms and electrical devices among the files and papers. A periodic table of the elements and various physical and engineering charts adorned the walls, as well as graphs of sales and production schedules. The shelves behind the desk carried as many volumes on chemistry, electricity, and metallurgy as on marketing and regulations. It was a "doer's" office, not a showplace—an expression of a mind dedicated to knowledge and competence. Shears wondered what the offices of the bureaucrats who wrote the regulations looked like.

"Those are copies of all the relevant papers," Dray said, nodding across the desk as Shears sat down in the chair on the far side of the desk and lifted his briefcase onto his knee to put the folder inside. "As I told Robert yesterday, there are some strong hints in there that the consultants hired by the Compliance Board as good as wrote the regulations into their report, and we're pretty certain they were being paid by Kerring, too. Kerring's Industrial Division makes a line of thermal stills, but they don't make vacuum stills. Get the picture?"

Shears nodded as he closed the lid of the briefcase. Robert Winthram was one of the senior partners of the law firm that Shears was from, and had handled Platek's legal affairs for years. The Kerring Corporation's Industrial Division was based in Springfield, and the parent group had strong political connections. Dray was alleging that the company had colluded with state officials to prevent its rivals from competing by having its own equipment effectively specified as a mandatory requirement by law. Shears had come to collect the evidence to begin assessing what kind of a case might be built against it. "Well, we'll look into it," he promised. He stood up and began putting on his coat. "Is there anything else?"

Dray sat back and contemplated the things on his desk for a moment. "Just hope that the Constitutionals can get the twenty-eighth amendment passed," he said, looking up finally.

CHAPTER 5

Winter had come early that year in Boston. There was snow on the streets when Melvin Shears came out of Platek's front entrance, which a watery sun, strained through a layer of low overcast, had done little to soften after the previous night's freeze, even by lunchtime. He turned up his overcoat collar and walked as briskly as he dared on the slippery sidewalks, heading westward from the waterfront area and crossing between the green-painted steel pillars supporting the elevated traffic jam misnamed the Fitzgerald Expressway, toward Quincy Market. Ahead, the towers of the downtown area looked shabby and weary of it all. The windows in some of the blocks still showed rows of neon lights inside, keeping up a face of business as usual, but others stared sightlessly out across the city. Several of what had originally been built as office buildings now resembled lower-grade apartment blocks, with cheap drapes and blinds and a sprinkling of crudely patched broken panes. They had been taken over by the government and converted into low rentals for dependent groups, who flocked in from all over the state because benefits in the city were better. Shears could see the lines of people waiting to collect checks, and the huddles of unemployed standing around in the forecourt outside the Government Center behind Faneuil Hall as he crossed Union Street.

He turned the corner into Washington Street, where a couple of unkempt, bearded youths were pestering Asian tourists to buy handmade trinkets, probably from one of the folk-art communes across the Charles River. He wondered what induced Asians to take their vacation in a place like Boston in midwinter. Maybe it had something to do with Christmas and New Year's, which were not far away. He could imagine the poster in the Tokyo travel agent's window: *WINTER IN AMERICA THIS YEAR—the season of ancient*

Western pageantry and celebrations. "You buy pletty beads? Velly good, velly cheap. . . ."

A few blocks farther on, he stopped at the post office to drop off a package to Philadelphia that needed to be on its way that afternoon. Predictably, since it was lunchtime and most of the customers could get away only during their break, most of the clerks had gone to lunch and the lines were long. Shears groaned inwardly as the overweight woman at the head of the line he had joined waddled purposefully up to the window, deposited a bulging purse on the counter, and only then began rummaging through its seemingly innumerable pockets and pouches while the clerk looked on indifferently. The lines on either side, of course, proceeded to rattle through like machine-gun ammunition. Shears opened his briefcase and took out the package to have it ready. Ahead, the woman was pushing a heap of papers and passbooks across the counter. Then she set the purse to one side and spread her elbows to settle herself for the coming fray.

One of the great mysteries of life that Shears had never fathomed was knowing what went on at the front of all the lines he stood in. The elbows planted themselves solidly along the edge of the counter to provide a solid fire-base, and her obscene behind quivered from the recoil as she delivered her return salvo to the clerk's ranging shots. Papers were scrutinized; figures were pointed at. Then the clerk hoisted down from a shelf a tome the size of the Domesday Book, turned pages, and then froze slowly into catatonia as the realization dawned that he was going to have to make a decision. He chickened at the last moment, and went to consult a supervisor.

The supervisor, however, was engaged in a dispute involving a clerk at another window, a mail carrier, and a frail woman in a green coat. "We aren't general delivery. I can't hand you your mail," the clerk said.

"But I haven't seen any for almost a week. Why aren't you delivering it?" the woman in the green coat asked.

"I told you, there's a problem with unshoveled snow on the sidewalks around Pearl Street," the carrier said. "We're not required to deliver through snow."

"But, I don't understand. . . . It's an apartment house. The sidewalk in front is clear. Could you look and see if I have any mail?"

"Yes, you have," the clerk informed her.

"But I'm expecting a check. It's important. Can't I have it?"

"No. It has to be delivered."

The woman in the green coat looked confused. "But you've just said you won't deliver it. What am I supposed to do?"

"I guess you're going to have to clear your street," the supervisor told her.

"It is clear. I've already told you."

"If it was clear, we'd have delivered your mail," the supervisor replied.

The carrier interjected, "The problem there is farther along the street."

"So no mail can be delivered on that street," the supervisor said.

"You mean I can't get my mail?" the woman asked again.

"Sure. You can get it anytime you can get the city or your landlord to clean the street."

As he came out after finally consigning his package to Philadelphia, Shears thought about the crowds of unemployed that he had seen outside the Government Center. A city that couldn't clear its streets was paying thousands of able-bodied people for doing nothing. He wondered why it was better to be unemployed and not getting seven dollars an hour, which was the minimum, even for casual work, than to be employed and getting five. And with people employed at five dollars, the bottom rungs of the employment ladders wouldn't have been sawn off. And people would be able to get their mail, too. Another of life's mysteries, which only a bureaucrat could understand.

After stopping for a coffee and sandwich in a steamy snack bar around the corner, Shears reached the offices of Evron and Winthram a little after one-thirty, located in the maze of backstreets and alleys behind Tremont Street, across from Boston Common. The premises stood behind a dignified door of polished oak with a brass sign, atop stone steps flanked by wrought iron railings that raised it above the mundane world of the sidewalk's scurrying anonymities. Ascending those steps from the street always gave him a mild feeling of entering a higher, more rarefied, plane of existence—probably the reason why so many houses of the previous century had been built that way.

Ursula, the firm's receptionist, treated him to a smile from behind her desk in the entrance hall. She was tall and lean, dusky-skinned with high-cheeked features that hinted of a trace of Amerind, and had her long hair braided in a pigtail that day. "Hi, Mel. Is it any warmer out there yet?"

"Not that you'd notice. I have the suspicion it's going to be one hell of a winter."

"You've got these messages, and Robert had to go out." Ursula handed across a sheaf of slips of paper. "He said to leave the papers from Platek with Carol."

"Uh-huh." Shears glanced through the messages briefly. "Anything else?"

Ursula rested her chin in her hands to stare at him. The look in her dark eyes, their lashes heavy with mascara, was shamelessly frank. "Well, now that the election is over and you've won, we could have that date to celebrate." Gentle subtlety had never been Ursula's forte. She was definitely the kind that mothers warned their sons not to get mixed up with, and which every son went through life praying that he would.

Shears smiled. As an active supporter of the Constitutional party, all his spare time had been devoted to campaign work in the lead-up to the November election. For months he had been promising playfully that they would paint the town together when it was over if the Constitutionals won. "I still have to tidy up the loose ends."

Ursula sighed. "Do you know, I sometimes get the feeling that you're not really sincere about this."

"You're just too suspicious. It comes from working with lawyers."

He went upstairs and delivered the dossier from Platek to Robert Winthram's secretary, Carol. Then he continued to his own office, which he shared with another associate, Chris Rhodes. Chris had his coat on and was sorting through papers when Shears entered.

"Going out?" Shears said unnecessarily as he tossed his briefcase down on the desk and peeled off his gloves.

"Framingham," Chris muttered.

"Snead versus Rawlinson, I presume."

"How'd you guess?"

Shears took off his coat and hung it on the rack beside the door. "How's it going?"

"Oh, we need to move fast. They're trying to oppose any pretrial discovery in the case. The usual procedural motions: bury the plaintiff in paper; move to dismiss; ask for a change of venue; ask for a summary judgment. Whatever they can think of to tie us up."

"It figures."

"What's new at Platek?"

"It sounds as if there's a case of collusion all right, maybe corruption. We'll see what Robert has to say when he's had a chance to look at the material I brought back." Shears watched as Chris began transferring the papers he had selected into a briefcase. "Also, they've achieved the ancient alchemist's dream—how to make gold."

"You mean by transmuting base metals?"

"Hell, no. Better than that. I mean actually creating it—out of nothing."

Chris glanced up with an oh-yeah? look on his face. "And how about bridges for sale and good rice-growing real estate near Okeechobee?"

"No, really."

"Okay, Mel, I'll buy it. How?"

"They took on a new chemist a few weeks ago, under the new quota law. He's black."

"Uh-huh." That in itself meant nothing. Bill Evron, Robert Winthram's partner at the firm, was also black.

Shears went on. "Platek has to keep a strict account of the gold it uses—how much comes into the place, how much is in storage, what goes into the plating, what goes down the drain, and so on. Well, from the tests this guy was running, it appeared that they had more gold in solution in the tanks than came into the building."

"That's a neat trick," Chris agreed. "How did they manage it?"

"Alan Dray couldn't figure it either. So he asked to see the raw data that this new chemist had been working from. Then it was obvious: he was using grams and ounces interchangeably."

Chris looked up incredulously. "You're kidding!"

"No. . . . Then Alan had a talk with him. It turned out that he didn't know about systems of units and had no concept of conversion between them. Also, he'd never heard of pH number or what valency is."

"But I thought he was supposed to be a chemist."

"So did Alan—the quota spec listed him as holding an MIT degree. But when Alan called MIT and finally got ahold of somebody there who knew about it, you know what the story was?"

"What?"

"If you read the small print on the certificate carefully, it says awarded *at* MIT, not awarded *by* MIT. It's a federal program run by the Employment Protection Agency to train minorities. They use part of a building at MIT, and that's what's printed on their degrees. The professor that Alan talked to said he wished they wouldn't do that. A lot of other firms have been getting mad about it, too. He said he finds it embarrassing. Isn't that nice? He finds it embarrassing."

Chris shook his head as he snapped his briefcase shut and stood up. "Anyhow, I have to be moving."

"Will you be back later?"

"Probably not. I'll catch you tomorrow, then, okay?"

"Sure. Good luck on the case."

"Thanks."

Shears pulled across the file of a deposition that he was preparing. As he opened it and shuffled through the contents, he wondered at the thought of the greatest production economy the world had ever seen, dismantling itself and astounding its rivals and enemies overseas, even as they looked on and applauded. Hopefully the new political scene would change things.

He had been working for about twenty minutes when Ursula put a personal call through to him.

"Yes, hello? This is Melvin Shears."

A woman's voice answered, speaking in little more than a whisper. "Mel, this is Stephanie."

"I'm sorry, who? Ste—" He caught himself as his mind returned fully to the immediate present. "Not Stephanie Carne?"

"Yes."

He grinned and leaned back in his chair. "Hey, it's been such a long time! It's great to hear from you. You won't believe it, but I was thinking only the other day that—"

"Mel, I don't have a lot of time."

That was when the strain in her voice registered. His manner changed at once. "Steph, are you okay?"

"I can't go into it now. Look, I need to talk to you. I'll be arriving at Logan airport at seven-forty tonight. Can— "

"You're coming *here*, tonight? . . ."

"There isn't anywhere else I can go. Can you pick me up? I'm sorry to dump it on you like this, but it's important."

"Well, of course I'll be there, Steph. . . . But can't you tell me what it's about? Is it something to do with you and Brett, something that maybe—" There was the sound of a quick intake of breath that could have been the beginning of a sob, and the line went dead. He looked at the phone in his hand bemusedly and replaced it on the hook.

Then he realized that she had hung up without giving him the airline or the flight number. He bit his lip for a moment, then glanced at his watch and reached for his phone book. She had moved from California to Denver almost a year ago, now. It would be noon there—just time to catch her before lunch, if he had a note of her number at work. He opened the book at *C* and scanned back through the entries. . . . The number wasn't there, but he did have a note of the name of the company she had gone there to work for. He picked up the handset again.

"Urse, find the number of General Plasma Dynamics in Denver, would you? I want to speak to somebody there called Stephanie Carne. She's a physicist. I don't have the department. Quick as you can, please."

"I'll call you back."

"Thanks."

He stared down at the flight arrival time he had noted on his pad, then across at Chris's empty chair on the far side of the desk facing his. It wasn't at all like Stephanie. She had always been so clearheaded and meticulous. He drummed his fingers on the desk and fidgeted in his chair, imagining faceless people who were tying up GPD's lines and hating them for it. Why did this always happen? In post offices, in supermarkets, at airport check-ins, at toll booths . . . every time he was in a hurry. "Come on, come on," he muttered. He could picture Stephanie closing a suitcase somewhere, with a cab waiting outside. Maybe he could have her paged at Denver airport. . . . Damn! He didn't even know if she'd called from Denver. . . .

Finally the phone rang.

"Melvin Shears."

"There seems to be some kind of problem, Mel," Ursula's voice said. "They want to talk to you personally. Shall I put you through?"

"Yes please."

Click, pause, click click. "This is Julie Sechel in Personnel," a woman's voice said. "Can I help you?"

Since he'd been put through to Personnel, he assumed that Stephanie had left the company. "My name is Shears. I'm trying to get in touch with somebody called Stephanie Carne, who used to work there."

"Can I ask what it's about, Mr. Shears?"

Shears adopted a tack that usually worked. "I'm with the law offices of Evron and Winthram in Boston. It is a private matter, I'm afraid, but very urgent. Do you have a number where she can be reached, please?" I talked to her a little while ago and I need to get back to her."

"Er, Stephanie Carne?"

"That's right."

"I think I'd better transfer you to the manager. One moment."

"Mr. Shears? My name is Thornton. You're with a law firm in Boston, I understand. Can I help you?"

"Yes, the firm is Evron and Winthram. I'm trying to get in touch with Stephanie Carne who used to be with your company. Do you have a record of where she went, or how she can be contacted? I need to talk to her right away."

There was a pause, as if Thornton was perplexed about how best to put something. Finally he asked, "Are you calling on behalf of a relative of hers, Mr. Shears?"

The question took Shears by surprise. He answered automatically. "No, it's a personal matter. . . . I'm an old friend of hers. Look, she called me from somewhere, but forgot to leave her number. I need to call her back." There was a long silence, until Shears began to wonder if Thornton was still there. "Hello?"

"You say that she talked to you? When was that?"

"Just a few minutes ago. She called me right here. What is this?"

When Thornton answered, his voice was very quiet, with a note of skepticism that he made little effort to disguise. "Stephanie Carne is dead, Mr. Shears. She committed suicide two days ago."

CHAPTER 6

It had all started six years ago, while he was at university in Florida—when he'd shared the apartment with Brett. . . .

"Sure, wait a sec. I'll see what he says." Brett Vorland appeared in the doorway from the kitchen, barefoot and wearing tan shorts with a gaudy beach shirt. He was holding a can of 7-Up in one hand and trailing yards partly uncoiled phone cord from the other. "It's Marty," he called across the lounge. "The gang's organizing a boat party over on one of the islands tonight. He's looking for a partner for Celia. You wanna come along, Mel?"

Melvin Shears stopped tapping at the keyboard lodged on a corner of the scarred walnut dining table, which also served as the apartment's office and general workbench, and looked away from the monitor on its shelf above. The place looked a students' apartment, with unframed prints and travel posters brightening the walls, improvised board-and-breeze-block bookshelves sagging under their loads of college texts and paperbacks, and partly dismantled appliances and other electrical devices lying around in shoe boxes or on shelves, in various stages of disintegration. An Eric Clapton number from the seventies was playing on the reel-to-reel tape player rigged in one of the niches next to the computer monitor. At the far end of the lounge, a picture window looked out over a balcony across Pensacola Bay, where sailboats and seagulls idled languidly, each in its own kind of way, under the Florida sun.

"Not really," Mel answered. "I guess I'm not in a party mood today. Tell 'em some other time." He resumed tapping at the keyboard.

Brett stepped farther into the room to put the can down on the coffee table by the recliner and clapped his free hand over the telephone mouthpiece. "Aw, come on, Mel. That's letting the team down. It'll be great out there. Nice cool

31

breeze after the sun goes down, get a fire started and cook some oysters, a few cold beers . . . And you could do a lot worse than Celia, too."

Mel sighed and sat back from the keyboard. "Look, Brett, you know how it's going to be."

"How do I know how it's going to be? So, how's it going to be?"

"It'll end up a circus. First, they'll all be in hysterics by this evening, before they've even left, because the logistics will have gotten screwed up. When they get there, Harry and Jeff will get in a fight over Marge. The only thing that Gary and Lisa will be interested in will be sneaking off to find a place to get laid, and that will get Sylvie upset. Then somebody will start throwing cans and shit all over the beach, and there'll be a row over that. . . . It'll be a circus."

Brett held up his hand in a resigned gesture and raised the phone back to his ear. Mel could hear his voice retreat as he was reeled back into the kitchen on the cord. "Sorry, Marty, but Mel says some other time. . . . How do I know what? He's doing something on the computer. . . . Right. . . . You want me to do what? . . . Hang on while I find a pen. . . ."

Mel returned his attention to the monitor screen. There had to be some way of getting past the troll guarding the bridge, without losing one of the treasures. . . . He reached up over the table and turned down the volume of the tape player a fraction. One of Brett's inexhaustible supply of girlfriends had said once that she thought Brett looked like the picture on one of the old Clapton album covers, with his neck-length mane of blond hair, shaggy beard, and the general lean-bodied, laid-back look about him. Maybe that was why Brett had included so many Clapton tracks when he put the tape together.

Mel and Brett had been pacing each other through the University of West Florida's computer-science curriculum and sharing lodgings for over a year now. Brett was the hardware tinkerer responsible for the decomposition of their electronic possessions and half the apartment's appliances. He was like some kind of digestive enzyme, programmed irresistibly to attack and dismantle anything with buttons on the outside and chips on the inside—always with the noblest of intentions, but invariably to be sidetracked by some yet higher priority before he got it together again. And so they listened to museum-piece tapes while parts of the laser disk player languished in at least four different places, and they watched VCR movies until the network terminal's mass storage array was working again.

Mel stared at the portion of classical "Adventure" showing on the screen. What if the magic word sent the golden eggs back to the nest at the top of the beanstalk *after* you'd given them to the troll? . . .

Brett padded back in from the kitchen and sat down in the recliner to finish his drink. "You wanna know how to get past the troll?" he asked, eyeing the screen and taking in the situation.

"I already know how to get past the troll."

"I mean without losing a treasure."

"There is a way, then, eh?"

"Of course there's a way."

"No . . . don't tell me. I'll figure it out. What happens if I try giving him the eggs and zapping them back to the nest after I'm back over the bridge?"

Brett shrugged. "Try it and see." He crumpled the empty can and tossed it through the kitchen doorway into the trash bucket. "So what are your plans?" he inquired.

"Oh, this afternoon I'll probably get some groceries in for the weekend. Then tonight I might go into town, see who's around. Or I might do some work on my project. . . . It depends."

"Hey, if you're going to the supermarket, does that mean you'll be driving past Obee's?"

"I could. Why?"

"They called yesterday and said they've got the part I need for my carburetor. Could you stop by and pick it up? Then I could have the car running right by tonight."

"Any idea how much it's likely to cost?"

"Aw, thirty or forty, maybe. I'll pay you when you get back."

"No problem. . . . Oh, and I'll include some bug-bite lotion when I get the groceries. You'll be needing it."

There weren't as many clerks at the checkouts in Albertson's as there used to be. As a protest at the legislation that forced them to cut their payroll, the management had placed signs at the vacant checkout desks reading CLOSED BY ORDER U.S. GOVERNMENT. Therefore the lines at the remaining desks were long. Mel watched despondently while the woman ahead waited until she had reached the till before producing wads of discount coupons from her purse and sorting among them. The clerk looked dubiously at the ones she finally proffered, and produced a binder from under the counter. These had expired; those weren't on special offer this week. Pages were searched, entries were pointed at. Well, this was *like* the one on offer. A manager was summoned to arbitrate. Then she couldn't find her checkbook. . . .

It was like walking into a wall of heat when Mel finally emerged from the air-conditioned cool into a Floridian mid-afternoon, trundling a cart holding three grocery bags. He loaded the bags into the trunk of his battered maroon 1987 Chevrolet, disposed of the cart in the retrieval area on the side of the parking lot, and climbed into his car. Brett had received a panic phone call from Donna just before Mel left, asking Brett to get some mushrooms, sweet potatoes, onion dip, and a list of other things that she'd forgotten to put on Harry's list before he went roaring off. So Mel had added them to his. It seemed that the logistics problems were starting early.

He pulled out onto the boulevard heading east, flipping on the radio as he moved across into the middle traffic lane. The music that had been playing ended, and without warning a man's voice began speaking in strident tones: "I was talking the other day to a man who made over a hundred thousand dollars last year from a business that he thought was about to go under. Why did his business suddenly turn right around like that, when all the time we hear about hundreds of others that are going belly-up? Well, I'll tell you why. Because he had faith in the Lord, that's why. A year ago that man sent me his last thousand dollars. He said we might as well take it as anybody, since he was about all through, anyhow. Said if the Lord thought he could work some kind of a miracle out of it, he was welcome to try. And he got a miracle, folks—one hundred thousand dollars worth of miracle! Now that *proves* that if you really believe, then the Lord will return one hundred dollars for every dollar that you send in. Yes, that's what I said—*one hundred dollars* for every *single* dollar that you—"

"There's a sucker born–again every minute," Mel murmured, and switched to a soft rock channel.

Ten minutes later he parked in the forecourt of Obee's Auto and Truck Repair shop. Sam Obee's tow truck was in front of the workshop door, and Nick, one of the mechanics, was unhitching a midnight blue Toyota that had evidently just been brought in. Mel stopped for a moment to watch.

"It's like they say, no rest for the wicked, eh, Nick?"

"Hey, Mel, how's it going?"

"Not bad." Mel inclined his head toward the Toyota. "What's wrong with it?"

"Oh, something dud in the electronics, I'd guess. We'll check it out."

"It looks brand new."

"It is—less than two hundred miles."

"New improved model?"

"It happens."

"Well, don't work too hard in the heat."

"I'll watch it. You take care, now."

Mel sauntered on into the office. Sam was behind the counter, making out a worksheet, watched by a girl standing on the customer side. Mel guessed her to be the owner of the Toyota. She was around twenty, maybe, tall and lean, with straight, fair hair tied in a band. She was wearing a white tank top and pink jeans. "Hi, Sam," Mel greeted. She was also at the university. He had seen her around the campus but never had reason to talk to her.

Sam glanced up as he wrote. He was gnarled and wrinkled, with wiry gray hair and gorilla hands—one of the old-school breed of auto mechanics who inspired confidence, giving the impression that he could take any car ever made apart and put it together again blindfolded. "How're you doing there, Mel? I'll be with you in a second. What can I do for you?"

"Brett says you've got a part in for him—something to do with his carburetor?"

"Yeah, the cutoff assembly. Came in yesterday." Mel caught the girl's eye and grinned. She flashed a quick, nervous smile back—probably anxious about her car.

"So, is life in general treating you well?" Mel asked, looking back at Sam.

"It'd be better with less damn papers to fill in all the time," Sam muttered as he scrawled. "Forms, questions, all the time goddam papers. Do you know I threw out the coffee machine because the last ass of a state inspector who was here decided that it classified the place as a restaurant? A restaurant, this place? I ask you!"

"You're kidding." She wasn't that bad looking, Mel saw, stealing another glance, with her clear, sharp-angled features and straight nose turning up just a fraction at the tip. And despite the sun, her skin had a light tone that made her look appealingly delicate.

"And the taxes!" Sam grumbled. "Do you know, they said I owed 'em another one-fifty on my last return, and they goddam went and had it lifted straight outta my bank account—just on their say-so, without even telling me! I didn't even know about it. I mean, what's it all coming to? If anybody in business thinks I owe them something, they have to go to court and get an order, right? And I get a chance to present my side, too. But who are these guys that can just go in and take your money, and you don't even know about it? Even the Mafia don't do that to you. I mean, it's at least as if you've got a choice in the matter, right? Like, if I'm into gambling, or drugs, or girls, or what have you, I *know* a slice of the action goes to the firm. But it's my choice, right? If I don't deal with them, they leave me alone. They don't send guys with guns round to my front door to take what they figure I owe them, and I don't have any say. But it ain't like that with the feds. So for my money, if you look at it on a scale of ethics from one to ten, the Mafia scores higher."

The girl interrupted. "It looks as if I'm going to be a while anyway. If this gentleman's just in for a part, why don't you take care of that and he can be on his way?"

"Thanks," Mel acknowledged.

Sam finished what he was writing on the worksheet and turned to take a cardboard box from one of the shelves behind. "Sixty-eight dollar and fifteen cents. Are you paying, or do you want me to charge it to Brett?" he asked, dumping the box on the counter.

"I'll pay for it," Mel sighed. He pulled his wallet from a hip pocket and took out a Visa card.

"Do you know how long the car will take?" the girl asked Sam.

Sam took Mel's Visa and inserted it into a card-reader slot. "Could be a while. If we have to get a replacement chip, it mightn't be till after the weekend. No use hanging around. We'll call you as soon as we know."

"Oh . . . I see." The girl looked perplexed. She hesitated. "I have to get back to Garcia Street, down near the bay. Is there any chance of a ride?"

Sam shook his head. "'Fraid not today, ma'am. Normally we'd be happy to oblige, but one of my mechanics is out this afternoon, and Nick has another emergency call waiting. I can't leave the place unattended. Be happy to call a cab for you, though."

"I'm going that way," Mel said. "What part of Garcia are you on?"

"The east end. I'm in the university flats there."

"Then we're only about four blocks away."

"Thanks. That'd be just great. . . . You know, this is embarrassing. It's a brand new car. My folks got it for me as a graduation present."

"It happens," Mel said. He nodded at Sam. "Thanks, Sam. See you around."

"Yeah. Take care."

Mel held the door open and followed the girl out. "I have to stop off at our place to unload some groceries before they melt," he said as they walked over to his car. "And Brett needs this part right away. He's going off with a group to a boat party out on one of the islands tonight."

"Brett?" The girl climbed in while Mel held the passenger door. "Is he your roommate or something?"

"Yep. We've got a place down by the water."

"Are you both with the university, too?"

"Yes. Oh, and I'm Mel, by the way."

"Hi. My name's Stephanie."

Pensacola had a long-running feud with Saint Augustine over which was truly the oldest city of the nation, and its sixteenth-century foundations gave it an excellent claim to the title. Originally founded as a Spanish mission, the city also had a turbulent, as well as long, history, having flown five different flags and changed hands thirteen times. It was a product of an age of elegance, and much of its past had endured alongside the signs of its progress toward the twenty-first century to endow it with a flavor that was unique. Between its wide, sun-drenched boulevards and modern office towers were lazy streets of tall live oaks draped with gossamer films of Spanish moss, shading rambling mansions that had been built by the timber barons of a century before, with bay windows and tall chimneys, wraparound verandas, turrets and gables, and ornate gingerbread trim.

It was Mel's hometown, too. His family lived in Warrington over on the west side, and he visited from time to time to pay respects and be sociable. But the truth was that as he'd come to the end of this teens, his interests and concerns had diverged steadily from those of his parents, and while a natural affection remained at the filial level, the range of things they had in common to talk about shrank as his horizons broadened. So, eventually he had moved out, and he now spent most of his time with his own kind of friends in his own world, while they stayed contentedly in theirs. The arrangement suited him, and the family was happy with his proximity. Life in general was pleasant. And one of the things that added distinctly to its quality from time to time was finding himself driving through the city on a sunny weekend day with nothing pressing to do, with a new, attractive girl sitting next to him, and the prospect of all the getting-to-know-you excitement which such a situation implied.

Houses and palm trees flowed by, with the bay glistening in the background off to the right. Stephanie sat back loosely in the seat, an elbow resting on the ledge of the open window and her hair billowing in the wind.

"So what are you taking?" Mel asked her. She had narrow, feline eyes with a light blue-gray tint that moved inquisitively all the time. One of the things he liked about her already was that if she had been watching him, too, she didn't make it obvious.

"Physics. I'd like to end up doing something in the nuclear field. But that's some time away, yet. I only started here a week ago. That's why I'm in the flats. I plan on moving out into a private place when I make some friends and get to know the city better."

Mel gave her a puzzled glance. "A week? But I've seen you around the campus on and off for a long time. I'm sure I have."

Stephanie smiled. "That was probably my sister. She's been here for about a year now. A lot of people get us confused."

"Twins?"

"No, but we're often taken for twins. Eva's a couple of years older than me."

"That's her name, Eva? What does she do?"

"Philosophy and political science, mainly. We're alike outside, but quite a bit different inside."

"I see. Brett and I are both in computer science—just finishing second year now. Where are you from?"

"California—the northern part, near San Francisco. I was thinking of going to Cal Tech-Berkeley, but the standards these days aren't what they used to be. Everything's so socialist there now. So I came here, to be near Eva, mainly. We're very close. How about you?"

"Oh, I'm just a regular ol' southern boy from right here in Pensacola. Never did stray too far from home." Mel hesitated for just a second. "So if you're ever looking for someone to show you around the town. . . ."

"Well, Eva knows the town pretty well already. . . ." Stephanie began automatically. Then she checked herself and looked across the car curiously. "Well, why not? As a matter of fact she and I were going to go to a party tonight with some of Eva's friends over on Santa Rosa Island. How would you like to come along? It looks as if I won't have a car, anyway."

"Well, sure. . . . I mean, if I wouldn't—"

"It's not really a party—more just a kind of get-together over a few drinks, and a lot of talk. They're quiet types, really. At least, that's what Eva says."

"What do they talk about?"

"Probably politics and economics."

"Sounds like a wild evening."

They turned off the avenue, and after a couple of blocks halted in front of the apartment building, a brick-built duplex with cream-painted wooden veranda and trim. The hood of Brett's Ford Falcon was raised, and Mel could see him fiddling with something on the far side.

"You weren't kidding," Stephanie said, looking around as they got out. "It's right by the water. I love it. How did you find it?"

"Years of playing the market," Mel answered, going back to open the trunk. "We're upstairs."

Brett came around from the front of this own car and eyed Stephanie up and down with a knowing nod. "Oh yeah?" he said, looking at Mel. "Going into town tonight to see who's around, huh? Or maybe gonna work on my project."

"Stephanie, meet Brett. Brett, this is Stephanie. She had to be towed and I gave her a ride back from Obee's. She lives in the flats over on Garcia."

"Hi."

"Hello, Brett. I've heard a lot about you already."

"From him? Don't believe any of it."

Mel tossed across the box he had collected. "There's the part for your carb. Now quit staring like that, Brett, and grab one of the bags. The ice cream will be vanilla sauce already."

They went upstairs, and Mel began unpacking the bags

while Brett stowed the items away. Stephanie went through the lounge to the picture window. "Oh, I love this place," she called back. "You've got such a great view of the bay from up here. I wonder if Eva and I could find something like this."

In the kitchen, Brett caught Mel's arm as he was about to place a jar of grape jelly in the refrigerator. "Who's Eva?" he hissed.

"Did you grow these plants over by the window?" Stephanie's voice asked.

"They were here when we moved in," Mel called back. He lowered his voice. "Her sister. Maybe you've seen her around. They look the same." He saw the mean look coming into Brett's eye and couldn't resist it. "As a matter of fact, I'm going to a party with them tonight across on Santa Rosa—It's a pity you're tied up."

Stephanie's voice called again, "What's this? It looks like a part of something optical."

"I'll be there in just a second." Mel closed the refrigerator door and began walking toward the door.

Brett grabbed his shirt and jerked him back again. "*What!*" he whispered. "There's another one that looks just like *her*? And you're taking both of them?"

"Well, it's more like they're taking me—"

"Now wa-a-a-it, a minute. I thought we were supposed to be buddies. You're right. This other thing will turn into a circus. I've been thinking about it."

"Oh, come on, now, Brett," Mel taunted. "Wouldn't that be letting the team down?"

Brett glowered maliciously. "How many times have I fixed you up?" he said rapidly, keeping his voice down. "You could drop off the groceries that Donna wanted when you take Stephanie home, and I'll call Marty and tell him something's come up."

"What am I supposed to do with the bug-bite lotion?"

"Hell, I'll pay you for the goddam—"

Mel laughed and went back into the lounge. "Do you think Brett could come along too, maybe?" he asked Stephanie. "He's at a loose end and doesn't have anything to do tonight. How would Eva feel about making it a foursome?"

Stephanie looked at Brett thoughtfully for a few seconds, then smiled. "I think she might like it," she replied. "Where's the phone? I'll call her, and we'll see what she says."

CHAPTER 7

The terminal at Boston's Logan airport was crowded and noisy, with flight delays adding to the confusion. As had come to be the case everywhere, the service at the desks was for the most part indifferent. Under the year-old Inflation Control Act, pay raises couldn't be awarded without government approval to staff who did a good job, while the earlier Occupational Security Act prohibited their being fired if they did a bad one. The result was what it could only be when whatever people did or didn't do no longer made any difference to their future.

After his call to General Plasma Dynamics that afternoon, Mel had called all the airlines in turn and established that the only arrival scheduled for 7:40 P.M. was United Flight 86 from Denver, which was the right city and sounded promising. The name Stephanie Carne was not on the passenger list, but considering the circumstances likely to surround somebody who was supposed to be dead, that hadn't really surprised him. As he made his way across the floor toward an arrivals indicator, he was assailed by the usual mix of fund-raisers, activists, and crazies.

"Would you like to give something for starving children?"

"Thank you, but no."

"Could you spare a minute for Jesus?"

"No, thanks."

"Help save the cheetahs?"

"No."

"Electricity is poisoning the atmosphere."

"I'm not interested."

"Spare a dollar for a cup of coffee?"

"Go away."

"Are you for strong government?"

"Fuck off . . . please."

Amazingly, the indicator showed the flight to be due on time, arriving at Gate 14. That still left him with over twenty

minutes to kill. After the cold outside, he decided that a stiff
brandy would be in order.

There was a packed bar at the end of the concourse. Mel
squeezed through the throng at the counter to order himself a
double measure of Courvoisier, and carried his glass over to
the last remaining empty seat at one of the tables by a wall.
The others around the table were a young couple with a
sleeping baby and a pile of bags by their chairs, looking tired;
a man absorbed in a book; a middle-aged woman staring
determinedly into the distance; and a man in a black felt hat
and heavy overcoat, with a bulbous nose lined with a network
of fine purple veins. He looked like what Mel thought
bookmakers at racetracks ought to look like, even down to the
eyes that were shifting constantly, as if weighing up the
situation and calculating odds. Mel kept his gaze on his glass as
he sat down, not being in a mood to invite attention.

He had needed the brandy for more than just warmth. The
shock of what had happened that afternoon still hadn't left
him.

After getting the flight number from United, he had called
the coroner's office in Denver. A deputy corner confirmed that
Stephanie Carne had been found dead in the bedroom of her
home, two days previously on November 7, a Tuesday. She
had been shot once in the head. The death certificate had been
prepared but not issued yet, and the final report would take a
while. However, no indication of foul play had been found,
and the woman that Mel spoke to had sounded confident that
the verdict would be suicide while the balance of the mind was
disturbed. But he, on the other hand, was equally confident
that it was Stephanie who had called him. And yet somebody
identified as Stephanie had been found dead in Stephanie's
home. He could only guess that the body had been Eva's. If so,
what had Eva been doing in Denver—on election day of all
times? She had become so immersed in her work with the
Constitutional party in California that Mel had practically lost
touch with her for almost a year. But strangest of all, if Mel had
been asked to choose from all the people on earth, Eva would
have been the last person he'd have picked as a candidate for
committing suicide.

"Who found the body?" he had asked the deputy coroner.

"The people downstairs called the landlord after they had
heard the radio playing all day but hadn't seen Ms. Carne at

any of her usual times. The landlord came to check, and he
called the police."

"And he identified her?"

"Yes, Mr. Shears. So did the medical supervisor from the
place where she worked."

"None of her family members were brought over from
California?"

"That didn't seem necessary. Also, it wouldn't have been an
exactly pleasant experience for them . . . if you understand
what I mean. The gun was fired in contact with the head."

"Yes, of course. . . ."

"As I said, there is no reason to suspect anything irregular.
She was very depressed and had been showing signs of stress,
apparently. . . . Hello, Mr. Shears, are you still there? . . .
Mr. Shears?"

"I'm here."

"Is there anything else I can tell you?"

"Er . . . no. That's all."

"You're welcome. I'm sorry about the news."

"Yes, thank you."

Mel gulped his drink as he found himself able to think
coherently for the first time since the afternoon. The delayed
reaction that had been numbing his mind was wearing off, and
the full realization was finally getting through to him. Eva
dead? His mind began wandering back over the years since
that day he first talked to Stephanie. He had met Eva that
same evening. . . .

"Can I interest you in some economy merchandise?" a voice
murmured close to his ear, bringing him back from his reverie.

"Pardon?"

The bookmaker was leaning across in his chair at Mel's
elbow. Mel noticed that he was wearing a tortoise lapel
pin—the Constitutional party emblem. "I can always tell an
okay face. Economy merchandise—strictly cash, no receipts,
no taxes. We got toiletries and cosmetics. We got menswear.
We got jewelry. We got electronics, appliances, kitchenware,
tools. . . . There's a van out in one of the parking levels with
samples. Care to come over and take a look? Top quality. Get
you thirty percent off the best retail."

"Not now . . . thanks. I have to meet someone. Maybe
some other time?"

"You from around here?" the bookmaker asked. Mel nodded. "There's a whole warehouse, in the city. We deal direct

with the public. Know what I mean?" The bookmaker winked and pulled a card from his pocket. "Give us a call some day when you're not too busy."

Mel looked at the card. "Thanks, er, Barney. I might do that."

"We take care of our customers. It's a straight deal." The bookmaker sipped his whiskey and savored the taste with a smacking sound from his lips. "Life's strange, isn't it? I used to run an importing business that employed fifty people. We all paid our taxes, it was honest and legal, but tariffs and quotas wiped me out. Today I deal in the same stuff, but I charge lower prices, I keep more people in a living, and I still make more for myself. So the customers are happier, my people are happier, and I'm happier. But it's criminal. I could go to jail. Now, you tell me where the sense is in that."

"I can't tell you, Barney, and I'm a lawyer."

"Oh, shit. . . ."

"Don't worry about it—I can probably send you a lot of business." Mel drained his glass and stood up. "But for now, I gotta go."

"So maybe we'll be hearing from you, eh?"

"You bet."

Mel left the bar and followed signs for Gates 10 to 22. According to the indicator, United Flight 86 from Denver had already landed. He continued on, and by the time he joined the gaggle of people waiting in front of Gate 14, the first arrivals from the flight were beginning to trickle through from the jetway.

Normally he liked airports. He liked watching people hug, kiss, cry, and give vent to emotions which custom and their own uptightness made them suppress for most of their lives. The world would be so much more livable if people would let themselves be themselves for more of the time, he thought. But he had been as bad himself, once. Finding out how to think and feel differently about himself was one of the things he'd learned from Eva. Freedom's child, if ever there had been one. . . . He forced back the emotions rising inside him and scanned the oncoming faces.

Then he spotted her in a blue-green raincoat and carrying a brown case, behind two men in business suits. She didn't see him until he stepped in front of her and she almost collided with him. She stopped, recognized him, and without saying anything threw her arms around his neck and clung. He held her close, sensing her need to feel secure if only for a few seconds, and after a while when she stayed put, trembling, he slid a hand up her back to stroke her hair. Finally she released her grip and stood back, trying to muster a smile, but too wan and exhausted. Mel stared at her face for a moment or two longer than would have been normal, just to be certain. It was definitely Stephanie. But at least there were no tears. From the look of her that might well have been because she didn't have any left. "It's been a long time, Steph," he said. Hardly original, but what else was there?

Stephanie nodded and closed her eyes. She seemed to be trying to summon the strength for something she had been composing herself to say. "Mel, so much has happened . . . I don't really know where to start, but . . ." She faltered.

He did it for her. "I know," he said gently. "I'm sorry."

Stephanie's eyes widened in confusion. "How could—"

"You didn't give me any flight details, so I tried to call you back at GPD. Thornton in Personnel told me. . . . It was Eva, wasn't it?"

Stephanie released a long sigh, closed her eyes for a moment again, and nodded. "But that's not all of it. You see, there was . . ." She swallowed and couldn't finish. Before she could resume, a man lugging a bulging garment bag through the crowd jostled her from behind. Mel took her bag in one hand, her elbow with the other, and steered her away from the gate. "Do you have any more bags to pick up?"

"Just one case."

"Then let's collect it and get out of here to somewhere quiet." They began walking. "Could you eat?"

Stephanie nodded. "We had a snack on the plane, but it was the first I've touched for days." She glanced at him. "I've kind of assumed you can put me up for a while, Mel. Would that be any problem?"

They came to the escalator going down to the baggage-claim level. Mel's head was whirling with questions: How had Eva come to be there? Where did Brett figure in all this? He had wondered if Stephanie and Brett's getting back together had turned out to be a lost cause after all, and if Brett was no longer around . . . but at a time like this he didn't want to cross-examine her. Right now, he could see, she needed rest. The talking could wait until tomorrow. They came off the bottom of the elevator. Finally, to break the silence, he said, "It just . . . didn't seem like Eva to go and do that, somehow."

Stephanie walked a few paces farther, then halted. Mel stopped with her, uncertain what he had said wrong. She drew a long breath, then turned toward him and drew him aside, out of the tide of people. Her face was different now, still showing the strain, but underneath it had acquired a firmer set of determination. "Mel, it isn't just Eva. Brett's dead, too. He went back to California about three weeks ago, in the middle of October. There was an accident. . . . Except I don't think it was an accident. And Eva didn't kill herself, either. You're right—she wasn't the type, and she didn't have any reason. But besides that, I was the only person who knew she was in Denver. You see what that means? It wasn't suicide, Mel. She was murdered—by the same people who killed Brett. She was murdered, by somebody who thought she was me.

CHAPTER 8

The "party" turned out to be at the home of Eva's tutor, Dr. Paul Brodstein, a professor of political science at the university. His wife, Martha, also taught there, her subject being modern European history. Their house lay across the Pensacola Bay bridge on the seaward side of Santa Rosa Island, facing the Gulf. It was a sprawling, two-story affair of split-level decking and stained redwood, with a hodgepodge of cheerfully uncoordinated extensions that appeared to have evolved as afterthoughts, and stood comfortably removed from neighbors above dunes of white sand and crabgrass lining the shore.

There were a dozen or so vehicles parked haphazardly around the house when Stephanie arrived with Mel and Brett. There had been a slight modification to the arrangement they had contemplated earlier in the day. Eva, it turned out, would be making her own way there with a boyfriend of hers who was visiting for the weekend from Washington. Mel had known Brett for too long to hope that any sense of fair play might induce him to back off and go to the beach party as he'd originally intended, and even before they arrived at the Brodsteins', he was becoming uncomfortably conscious of an immediate attraction between Stephanie and Brett. They didn't go out of their way to flaunt it, and Stephanie was obviously trying hard not to injure Mel's feelings unduly, but it was there. He felt awkwardly as if it was he and not Brett who should have been finding something else to do.

Paul Brodstein greeted them at the door. He turned out to be a lively, expressive man, with dark, bushy-browed eyes, a full head of curly black hair, and a graying beard. He was wearing jeans and a Pendleton plaid shirt, with a striped apron over the top. "Three more. My word! If this goes on, we'll have to sell the house and buy a hotel or something. . . ." He shook hands vigorously and scanned the faces of the arrivals. "Well, at least that face isn't exactly new. You have to be Eva's sister. She's here already somewhere. . . . Anyhow, glad to see you all here. Come on in. Martha will fix you up with drinks, if you can find her. Otherwise help yourselves— they're through there. I'm just about to get some chicken going out back."

The interior was as lacking in formality as the outside had suggested, with walls predominantly of bare timber, adorned with souvenirs that ranged from a South African assegai and a Japanese Space Agency astronaut's cap, to a human skeleton and a stuffed skunk. The furniture was well seasoned and chosen for utility and comfort, not show; the housekeeping was sufficiently minimal to put guests who worried about the adequacy of their own efforts in that direction blissfully at ease; and of course, with two university professors in residence, there were books, papers, magazines, and journals crammed on shelves in every room and in the hallways, on window ledges, mantelpieces, and stacked on any other horizontal space that could be found.

After ushering the new arrivals into the living area, where numerous people, mainly students by the look of them, were drinking and talking in groups, Paul brought Eva in from an adjacent room and let Stephanie introduce her two companions. Then he excused himself and hurried out to the deck at the rear of the house, just as Martha appeared. She was a plump, jovial, bespectacled woman, like Paul in her forties, at that moment too busy taking care of everyone to exchange more than a few pleasantries. She asked what they wanted to drink. Mel and Brett settled for beers from an ice-filled tub in the corner, while Eva asked for another vodka tonic with a touch of lime, and Stephanie for a white wine. Martha bustled away back to the kitchen.

Stephanie and Eva were indeed virtually images of one another. It was no wonder that they were always being mistaken. Only when they were side by side could Mel discern Eva's face to be a shade more womanly, with less of the girlish freshness of Stephanie's, and her body to be slightly fuller. And the similarity would in all likelihood become closer with time, as the two years that separated them became proportionately less. The difference in personalities was more apparent. Eva was wearing a pale green button-up dress, simple but smart, which contrasted with Stephanie's beige top and blue jeans. Stephanie, bright-eyed, exuberant, eager to fit into her new role and be accepted, was all freshman student; Eva, was less talkative and impetuous, more restrained, a listener and a thinker. And while she listened, she watched people's faces, hearing not only their words, but also the things they didn't even know they were saying. As he stood, watching her, Mel was unable to recall anyone who had struck him in such a short space of time as so fascinatingly . . . *deep*.

A conversation going on to one side was about environmental scares. "The whole business about DDT was a fraud," a fat man in a gray sweatshirt was saying. "None of the claims had any basis in scientific fact, but they've all been so absorbed into the popular mythology that nothing will change it now."

"I thought there was a scientific panel on it," a tall girl in a black dress said.

The man in the gray sweatshirt snorted. "There was a panel all right, but it recommended unanimously *not* to ban it. But the EPA secretary at the time didn't bother to read the report and hadn't attended any of the hearings. The decision had already been made for political reasons, regardless of what the evidence said."

"What reasons were they?" Brett asked, moving forward to join in.

Mel watched as Brett was drawn into the circle and Stephanie squeezed in next to him. Not that Mel was that surprised—or especially perturbed, since he had hardly known her long enough to have a claim to ownership rights . . . but hell, he'd found her, after all. . . .

"You win a few, you lose a few," a voice said near him. He

looked around to find Eva watching him, a faint smile playing on her face.

"Do you read minds, too?"

"When Stephanie called me earlier, she said she'd found a tall, blond date for me, with a beard. So she must have been supposed to be yours."

Mel shrugged and grinned resignedly. "If you really want to know the truth, you win a few, and you lose a hell of a lot."

"I know, but most guys wouldn't say so."

"I don't know why. If you've never failed, you've never tried."

"But it's not the way to hold your own in locker-room talk."

"Well, that's the problem with everything these days," Mel said. "It isn't knowing what you're talking about that matters, but knowing how to sound as if you do."

"You mean you're not going to try and impress me by being all man and macho? Oh, I think I like you already."

"If that's the case, then I guess not."

Eva looked him up and down. "You keep in good shape, though. What do you do?"

"Oh, I like to swim a lot . . . work out at the gym sometimes. But if you mean classwise, I'm taking computer science. So's Brett, my roommate. He's the guy who just walked off with my date."

"Real close buddies."

"Yeah, right . . ."

"She's going to be a physicist," Eva said. "She wants to work on nuclear things."

"She told me."

"How do you feel about it . . . with all the controversy and so on that you hear?"

"Nuclear stuff, you mean?"

"Yes."

Mel scratched his head. "Well, I guess if God had meant us to build nuclear plants, he'd have given us brains."

Eva laughed. "Good for you."

"Sure . . . I think they're okay," he said, relieved to find they were on the same side. "People get it all out of proportion."

The initial attraction that Mel had felt was already growing into something more. She was interested and interesting, which was enough in itself to make her different—the kind of person who would have thoughts of her own. He couldn't imagine her chattering verbal styrofoam for an evening, which filled space but had no substance, leaving only the thought that the time would have been spent better with a good book. Already he found himself searching inwardly for ways to suggest getting together again, on their own somewhere. But then he remembered that she was already with a guy, the one who had come down from Washington.

As if on cue, a man sauntered in from the door leading out to the rear deck and crossed the room toward them. He was older than Mel had expected, maybe in his early thirties, with tanned, clean-shaven features and dark hair, neatly trimmed and brushed flat, which, with his white shirt and casual tan slacks, singled him out from the generally more hirsute company of students and academic staff members. Eva smiled and slipped an arm easily and naturally through his as he joined them. The simple physical act caused Mel to experience a sinking feeling inside, even though he had no business to.

"Having fun?" the newcomer asked. "The chicken's cooking outside. It's good. Be warned, though, that the conversation out there is politics."

"Dave, this is Mel," Eva said. "He's a computer expert at the university. Dave Fenner, a friend of mine from Washington."

"Hi." Dave gave Mel's hand a firm shake. His manner was frank and genial.

"A long way to come for a party," Mel said.

"Not too far to see Eva, though. Are you from near here, Mel?"

"Right here. Pensacola's my hometown."

"It's a nice place."

"I like it. . . . Not sure if I want to stay here forever, though. You're from California, is that right?" Mel said to Eva.

"San Mateo, south of San Francisco. Wherever you're from, it's nice to have a change to somewhere different."

"I guess so." Mel watched Eva's long nails tracing lightly on Dave's forearm while they spoke. Dave stood easily, his relaxed poise and confidence affirming status far more effectively than any overt male-rivalry ritual could have. It said, simply, that he didn't need to compete. Mel had the feeling of being hopelessly outclassed. He didn't want to make a long, drawn-out issue of proving it. It just wasn't his day today. "Anyhow, I guess I'll take a look outside," he said. "Maybe try some of that chicken."

"Catch you later," Eva said after him as he moved away.

The sun was bleeding into the ocean off to the west when he came out onto the deck. A few hundred feet away across the sand below the house, lines of white-capped breakers were rolling lazily in from the Gulf. Paul Brodstein was piling breaded drumsticks and portions of breast into a tray from a grill of glowing coals, while people helped themselves and added bread, sweet corn, sauce, and potato salad from a side table. The aroma reminded Mel that he hadn't eaten since lunchtime. Without further ado, he picked up a plate from the stack and piled himself a generous serving.

"The conventional wisdom about the robber-baron era is a load of bunk," Brodstein was saying to the company in general. "Most people think of the excesses of the nineteenth century as the inevitable result of unrestrained laissez-faire capitalism, and that only when the public demanded regulation were the laws and controls implemented to force the economy to serve the many rather than the few." He looked up challengingly. "Isn't that the way it's taught in the schools, acted upon in Congress, and what's believed by the man in the streets?"

"Well, isn't it true?" one of the listeners asked, a heavily tanned student with blond hair, wearing shorts and a green windbreaker, perched on a corner of the rail.

"No, it couldn't be more wrong, Jack," Brodstein replied. "*Every one* of those evils happened not because of capitalism, but because of *interference* in it, by the government. This nation has never had a genuine free-market economy at all."

"What about the big railroad scams?" another voice asked. "Wouldn't you call those exploitive monopolies?"

"But that was precisely *because* of intervention in the free market," Brodstein replied. "You see, except for a few, very rare cases, in a genuine free market, a monopoly *cannot* survive. Monopoly privilege can be sustained only by force— either of the criminal kind, where you blow your competition away with bombs and bullets, or the legal kind, where the government does it for you. The only exception is when the monopoly exists through genuine excellence of the product, where it's impossible for anyone to offer the customer a better deal—and in that case there's nothing to complain about, anyhow."

Brodstein looked around to invite comment, but the listeners preferred to hear him out. He went on, "Take the great Union Pacific fraud. It was given twelve million acres of land by the feds, and twenty-seven million dollars in six-percent, thirty-year bonds. The Central Pacific, which built eastward to meet it, was given nine million acres and twenty-four million dollars. That was how they got their capital—not by private investment, which is how real free enterprise works, but by government subsidy. The men in control of policy subcontracted all the construction to themselves through an operation called the Credit Mobilier, and the costs mysteriously skyrocketed. They weren't interested in building a railroad; they were out to milk it dry."

"The really big-time crooks don't break laws," one of the faculty members chipped in. "They make them." Some of the others laughed.

Martha came out onto the deck with an ice bucket containing bottles. Other figures, attracted by the scent of food, were drifting out of the doorway behind her. Brett was among them, still with Stephanie in tow. They came over to join Mel. "What's going on out here?" Brett asked.

"Paul's talking about interference in the free market," Mel told him.

"I did warn you," Stephanie said.

". . . because the basis of government is coercion, and coercion isn't a very good way of finding out what people want," Brodstein was saying.

"What people want might not always be what's best for them, though," one of the students pointed out.

Brodstein showed his teeth in a smile, as if he had been waiting for that. "And who are you to decide what's best for them? And who is anyone else, for that matter?"

Brett had wrinkled up his face and was shifting his head in the way he always did in response to challenge. Typically, he pitched straight in. "What about the Depression, back in 1929? That wasn't a terminal case of laissez-faire going belly-up?"

"I thought boom and bust cycles were endemic to capitalism." The speaker was the girl in the black dress whom Mel had seen inside earlier.

"That's another myth," Martha said. Evidently this was a husband-wife double act. "In fact a free money market provides the perfect economic stabilizer: the interest rate." While Martha was talking, Paul excused himself for a moment and disappeared into the house. Martha continued, "It's a price— the price of capital—and prices are signals that tell you things . . . if you don't distort them. They tell you what investments are sound. The Federal Reserve system, which was set up in 1913, provided cheap credit by inflating the money supply, which reversed the signals and created huge malinvestments. Eventually bad investments have to liquidate, which is what a depression is."

With growing resentment at the steady encroachment of more rules and regulations into everybody's life, there had been a lot of this kind of talk going around in recent times. Mel had been too preoccupied with his own studies to pay a lot of attention to it, but tonight he found it a welcome change from the things he spent most of his time thinking about.

"What you're saying is, you'd like to see complete economic freedom, then," a young man in a blue turtleneck said, sitting munching on one of the sun lounges.

"Exactly." Heads turned as Paul Brodstein came back out from the house, carrying a rolled poster-size sheet. "Once you control a person's right to make a living, what other freedom does he have left? That's where the American concept has gone wrong, and what we're aiming to put right."

"We?" Mel queried.

"The Constitutional movement," Paul said. Mel looked at Brett. Brett shrugged and looked at Stephanie. "I take it you haven't heard of us yet," Paul said. They shook their heads. "I thought that was why Eva invited you."

"It was more me that invited them," Stephanie said.

"Well, the more, the better," Paul said. "We need all the new faces we can get." He went on to explain, "Briefly, it's a political movement that's catching on across the country, especially among younger people who've come to despair of both the established parties. So we're forming a new one."

"A new party?" Mel echoed.

"Wait a minute, I think I've heard about it," a man near Brett said. "Isn't it do with that guy, what's his name? . . . Newell, or something?"

Paul nodded. "Henry Newell. Basically, we've come to the conclusion that the first amendment, separating church and state, is all very fine, but it doesn't go far enough. It only does half the job. We want to finish it: by completely separating the power of state from economic affairs."

Mel frowned as he tried to visualize exactly what that meant. "You mean *all* kinds of economic affairs?" he said. "Personal? Corporate? International? Everything? . . ."

"Everything," Paul replied simply.

Eva's voice came from the direction of the doorway. "The analogy to the separation of church and state is a good one." Mel looked around to see that she had come out from the house, too. Dave Fenner was standing behind her, holding a glass in one hand and a cigarette in the other. She continued, "The average citizen in the Middle Ages would have been unable to conceive of a society in which his religious life was none of the state's business. The approved faith was enforced, and any deviation from it was savagely punished. But today anyone is free to worship whatever god he chooses, or none at all. The state protects that freedom. The citizen has become a beneficiary of state power instead of its victim." She spoke clearly and firmly, but with a calmness that sought to persuade, not to pontificate. Mel guessed that she was one of the long-time attendees at these get-togethers of the Brodsteins. "What we're saying is that the power of the state should no more be available to secure economic privileges for one group at the expense of another, than to impose a favored religion."

"You mean that its role should be to protect your freedom to make a living any way you choose," somebody said.

"Exactly," Eva said. "And to keep what you make, and to spend it as you see fit."

Martha elaborated. "Government shouldn't have any say in how you trade our own services or property—to whom, under what conditions, or at what price. Its only function should be to enforce contracts that were entered into freely. So all the laws that result in some kind of enforced privilege should go: all forms of protectionism—export subsidies, import tariffs, preferential regulations; and all the laws that coercively subsidize one group at the expense of another—wage laws, union laws, hiring quotas, compulsory social programs . . ." She waved a hand to and fro in front of her face. "Poof! Gone. The Constitution guaranteed the right of opportunity to compete on equal terms, without discrimination. It never guaranteed equality of result, or the right to be given what has been taken away from somebody else."

"That's why we're called the Constitutional movement," Paul said. "Taking away by force what a person has earned is theft—however else you try to disguise it with words. This country was not founded upon principles like that. And we won't get out of the mess we're getting into until we get back on the tracks we began on. The law shouldn't legalize for government what would be considered criminal if done by anyone else."

"Hear, hear!" somebody threw in from the back. Approving murmuring broke out in support.

Paul had a talent for inspiring, Mel realized as he listened. He could see what had made Paul the focal point of this local nucleus for action that was forming. Paul chose his moment well. Stepping forward to the center of the deck, he held up the rolled poster that he had brought from the house. "And, I have something to show you all," he announced. An expectant hush fell. "In keeping without avowed intent of forming a full-fledged party apparatus to challenge the incumbents, we now have an official party animal." He unfurled the poster and turned first one way, then the other to let everyone see it. "The Constitutional Tortoise," Paul announced. "Starting from the back and just plodding along at its own steady pace . . . but you all know where that gets you in the end." He grinned broadly, and was rewarded by applause and approving shouts from all around the deck.

Through it all, Brett was staring at Paul disbelievingly. "You people are serious?" he said. "I mean, do you really think you can change anything? . . . You're gonna upset one hell of a lot of people."

Brodstein looked back at him unblinkingly. "Oh yes, Brett. We're quite serious. In fact, we intend fielding a presidential candidate for the year 2000 election, six years from now—very probably, Henry Newell himself. The election that will choose the country's first administration of a new millenium. Very significant, symbolically."

Brett met Brodstein's gaze and shook his head slowly. "Not a prayer," he declared bluntly. "Six years from now? No way. Not even in another thousand."

CHAPTER 9

It had been bad enough to be told that Stephanie had killed herself, and then to have worked out that it must have been Eva. But then to learn that someone who had been so close to

all of them, and a sister to Stephanie, had not only been killed
deliberately, but in the brutal manner that the deputy coroner
at Denver had described. . . . The thought filled Mel with
such horror and helpless outrage that he was unable to bring
himself to speak for the rest of their journey away from the
airport. And then Brett, on top of it? . . . It was only as his
own numbness and the sick feeling in his stomach began
wearing off to allow coherent thought to form again that he was
able to realize fully what Stephanie had been going through for
days.

They took a cab underneath the harbor through the Sumner
Tunnel and across downtown to a steak-and-pancake restaurant on Beacon Hill, which was one of Mel's regular eating
places. He could manage no more than a black coffee, while
Stephanie nibbled at a sandwich and then pushed it aside. Her
exhaustion after the flight and all that had happened was
catching up with her, and despite all, her conversation was
sparse. As far as Mel was concerned, that was just as well.

Snow was falling again when they left. After a thirty-minute
wait they despaired of getting another cab, and deciding to risk
the elements, walked and slithered the seven blocks to where
Mel lived in the Back Bay area, south of the Charles River
Basin. The apartment was on the second floor of a solid, once
imposing but now aging, Victorian town house, smelling of
cats, dusty drapes, and the accumulated odors of four gener-
ations of living.

When they were halfway up the stairs, the power went off.
They completed the climb in darkness, and Mel let them in
the front door of the apartment by touch until he located the
flashlight which he kept strategically on the hall table for such
eventualities. By its light he lit a kerosene lantern in the living
room, and then led Stephanie through to the single bedroom
and left the lantern for her to unpack her things. He went back
into the living room with the flashlight and started a wood fire
in the stove fitted inside the original fireplace—nobody with
any experience of Massachusetts winters relied on the power
companies alone for warmth these days. When the logs had
taken, he augmented the blaze with a shovel of coal from a
stock that he kept in a bin beneath the sink in the cooking area,
and put a pot of water for coffee on top. Stephanie, now
wearing a bathrobe of his which she had found in the bedroom
closet, came back out with the kerosene lantern and sat down
in the leather armchair by the stove, and Mel got a blanket for

her to wrap around herself while the room was warming up. Then he went into the bedroom to change into some dry jeans and a sweater. By the time he came out again, the water was hot. He made two mugs of instant coffee and settled down on the couch facing the stove. The warmth and the drink revived Stephanie's spirits, and at last she was able to begin relating her story.

"I never did tell you the real reasons why I left California and moved out to Denver, did I?" she said. Her voice was strained and shaky, but determined to see it through.

Mel shook his head. "Not really."

Stephanie and Brett's mutual attraction had developed quickly into a steady relationship that lasted through the rest of their time at the university. When Brett and Mel graduated, and Mel reset his vocational sights to go to law school at Chapel Hill in North Carolina, Brett had stayed on for a year of postgraduate work at Pensacola to be near Stephanie while she completed her own course of studies. Then the two of them had moved to her home state, California. Stephanie had fulfilled her ambition by taking a research position in nuclear physics at Stanford, while Brett, who excelled in programming intricate real-time systems, had first spent a year with one of the Silicon-Valley-based defense contractors, and then gone to the national laboratory at Livermore to work on the development of battle-management software for the strategic space defense system. That was when Mel, absorbed in a new field of his own, had lost regular contact with them. Life had followed the standard pattern: they would call each other with diminishing frequency, and he had visited once or twice to reminisce about the old days; but those times could never be relived or entirely recaptured, and the present had displaced it all with its own relentless and more pressing demands.

Then, one day, Mel had learned to his surprise that she and Brett were having problems. Soon after that, Stephanie had moved on her own to Denver—to clear the air and give herself time to think, she had said. She hadn't been more specific. In his own mind, Mel had regarded it as one of those temporary things that would straighten itself out, and he had left them alone to work it out in their own time. And sure enough, by spring of the current year, Brett had quit his job in California and moved out to join her. Everything had sounded fine again. . . .

And now this.

Stephanie went on, "You know how Brett used to feel about far-right religious fanatics back in Pensacola?"

"Tell me about it. I lived with him, too, remember."

"Well, it got worse after you went to Carolina. Did we ever tell you about that time he got arrested?"

"Didn't he break someone's arm or something?"

"A bunch of them were demonstrating in the library over some books they wanted taken off of the shelves. Brett hauled one of them out and threw him down the stairs."

Despite the circumstances, Mel couldn't contain a thin smile. "Who was it? Anyone I knew?"

"Oh sure. He'd been a pain all over the campus for months. Even the cops who came to pick Brett up thought it was funny. Do you remember a thin, weedy guy called Rudshaw?"

"Oh, *him*! . . . He was one of the ones who used to start quoting the Bible in biology classes when anyone mentioned evolution. . . . They sent letters to the parents of anyone they thought was screwing around."

"That's him. Anyhow, he was giving that little Cuban girl who worked in the library a hard time. . . ."

"Maria?"

"Yes. He kept preaching at her until she was in tears, and that was when Brett went over and threw him out."

Mel nodded but was looking puzzled. "Okay. But what did that have to do with you and Brett splitting up, and you moving to Denver?"

Stephanie sipped from her mug and sighed. "Oh, that was the beginning of the problem, I guess." She looked across at Mel from the armchair. "Have you any idea how crazy some of those people are?"

"Fanatics? They're all crazy if you ask me."

"I mean the way-far-out-right religious ones."

"You mean about Armageddon and the Second Coming? How they think God wants us to have a nuclear war with the Russians?"

"Yes."

Mel nodded. "I told you, I lived with Brett, too. He told me all about it at least a dozen times."

"Didn't it ever strike you as strange that Brett should have ended up working in the defense industry, considering how he felt about things?"

Mel shrugged. "I always assumed he did it for the intellectual kick. It happens like that sometimes."

"Yes, at first I thought so too," Stephanie said. "But now I think there was more to it." She paused, but Mel drank from his mug and stared at her without interrupting. "He got more active politically in that year after you left. I know that's not uncommon among students . . . but you know how intense Brett could be once he got into something."

"How do you mean? He never really got into becoming a Constitutional the way I did with Eva. And I couldn't see him marching around with placards or sitting down in the middle of the road. He wasn't that type of guy."

"No, it wasn't anything like that. But more. . . . Do you remember that group called the Socratics?"

"A sort of political debating society, wasn't it?"

"That's what they called themselves. But there was a core of people in it who had interests that went beyond talking. They had other connections outside the university."

"Okay . . ."

"Well, they didn't just go away after we left Florida. Brett carried on his involvement with them after we moved to California—or at least, another group that was part of the same organization."

"Go on."

"Only the involvement got deeper. Brett seemed to . . . to change. He was turning into a different person."

"In what way?"

"Moody, secretive. . . . He'd stay out late, and then not talk about where he'd been . . . Going off to keep strange appointments . . ."

"You're sure it wasn't another girl?" Mel didn't really think so. The lawyer part of him asked the question automatically.

Stephanie shook her head. "I'd have known. Besides, none of us was exactly uptight about things like that. He'd have said so if that was what it was."

Mel nodded. "Sure. So?"

Stephanie made a throwing-away gesture. "The routine that you always think only happens to other people, but won't happen to you because you're so much smarter than they are. I wanted to know what was wrong. He said nothing was wrong. I said he had to think I was stupid. We ended up fighting or not talking. . . ."

"Which was when you moved to Denver . . ."

"And started at GPD."

"But I thought that worked out okay in the end. Brett followed you out there after a while."

Stephanie sighed. "I thought it had worked out, too. But then it started all over again. He began getting phone calls. . . . Then one day, sometime early in October, he said he had to go back to California—just for a few days. He promised that it was over—he was going there to wind things up, and one day he'd tell me what it had been all about." Stephanie's voice caught, and she gulped her coffee hurriedly.

Mel hesitated before saying it. "And that was when? . . ."

"The car he rented was found two days later, at the bottom of Devil's Slide—a cliff on the coast a few miles south of San Francisco. The verdict was accidental death, but . . ."

"You don't think so."

Stephanie shook her head again, this time with a short, firm motion. "I had my doubts at the time, but what can you say? You can't prove anything. But this latest thing with Eva has convinced me."

"When did it happen exactly?"

"A little over two weeks ago. October fifteen. A Sunday."

The lights came on again suddenly.

Mel got up from the couch. "Ah, perhaps we'll get a hot breakfast after all. Thank God for Canadian nukes. Do you know we're having to buy power from them now, here, to keep going through winter?" He went over to the kerosene lamp and raised the glass to blow it out. "Was there anything about the body that seemed suspicious?" he asked over his shoulder.

"They never found it. It must have been washed out to sea. Apparently it's happened there like that before."

"Oh." Mel turned on a table lamp, put another log in the stove, and sat down on the couch again.

Stephanie leaned forward and touched his arm to hold his attention. "Brett would never say anything about who he was dealing with or why. But listen to this. Some mail came for him a couple of days after the accident, from an outfit called the Western Peace Initiative. And more turned up in his mailbox in Denver this morning. I did some checking after the first batch. WPI turns out to be a subsidiary of the World Peace Council. Does that mean anything to you?"

Mel frowned. "I thought that was a Soviet propaganda front."

Stephanie nodded. "It emerged in Paris in 1950 to launch a Western ban-the-bomb movement at a time when the Soviet

weapons program was lagging. It was thrown out of France for
subversion in 1951, moved to Prague, and then to Vienna,
until the Austrians evicted it in 1957. It finally established a
headquarters in Helsinki in 1968, followed by another European branch in Geneva in 1977. And it's still true today that
the Soviet International Department and the KGB both assign
representatives to the permanent WPC Secretariat in Helsinki." Stephanie drew back her hand and looked at Mel in a
way that invited him to draw the conclusion for himself.

Mel was rubbing his forehead in consternation. "What the
hell are you saying?" he breathed. "No, Steph." He shook his
head. "I don't believe it."

"You're the lawyer," she said. "Let's go through the evidence step by step."

Mel licked his lips. "Now, let's get this straight. First Brett
develops an obsession. . . . What would you call it?"

"Paranoia."

"Okay, over the danger of conservative extremists starting
an all-out war because they think it's God's will."

"More than that," Stephanie said. "He figured that the
biggest risk was right here: us, the West."

"He really thought that?"

She nodded. "And you can see how a guy might think that
way. . . . With our policy-making in the hands of born-agains
who think God's talking to them, it would be easy to arrive at
the conclusion that by comparison the Soviets might not be
perfect, but at least they're rational—a step forward from the
Middle Ages. So maybe you could end up believing that one
way to stop the crazies would be to make sure the situation
stayed stable—which you do by preserving the balance. But if
we went ahead and deployed the space defense system, the
balance would be destroyed." Stephanie was speaking rapidly
and nervously now, as if she didn't want to believe it either,
but could see no alternative.

Mel took it from there. "So, in a way that at first seems out
of character, he ends up working in the defense program. At
the same time, he's getting involved with people he won't talk
about, and acting strange. The strain gets worse, and eventually you split up. Then, one day he quits his job, comes out to
Denver, and seems to be his old self again. But then he gets a
call and has to go back. And two days later he's dead."

He stared hard at the stove, unwilling to meet her eyes just
at that instant. What it seemed to point to was too clear to need

voicing: Brett had been passing information on the top-secret strategic battle-management software to the Soviets— information that would be priceless in enabling them to devise countermeasures. Then, when his personal life came apart as a consequence, and maybe after he'd had second thoughts, he had tried to get out. But by then there could be no getting out. He had known too much.

That left only one question unanswered. Mel brought a hand up to his mouth and drew a deep breath. But there was no way to avoid it. "So, how did Eva come into it?" he asked somberly.

"She called me less than a week ago."

"You mean she'd heard about Brett somehow?"

"No . . . but it wasn't just a social call, either. She wanted to come and talk to me about something. Then when I told her about Brett, she decided to come out to Denver straight away."

"And did you find out what she wanted?"

Stephanie shook her head. "I met her after work on the day she arrived. We went out to eat dinner before going home, but she wanted to hear about Brett, so we didn't go into it there. She was planning on staying for a few days, and I'd bought a dresser and some other things for the spare room from some people across town, but hadn't had a chance to collect them yet. Her car was bigger than mine, with a rear door. . . . So we traded cars. She went on ahead in mine to the apartment, and I took hers to collect the things. . . . And when I got back . . ."

Mel was staring at her with a horrified expression. "Oh my God! Then it was *you* that found her. . . ."

Stephanie closed her eyes and nodded. "It was awful. There was blood everywhere, and . . ." She raised a hand to her face as she struggled to maintain her composure.

Mel leaned across and squeezed her arm. "Don't think about it, Steph."

She swallowed hard and went on. "They must have had some reason to think that Brett had told me more than he did about what he'd been doing. Or perhaps they just weren't taking any chances. Under the circumstances, who would have been suspicious of an apparent suicide? But they got the wrong one. It was supposed to be me."

Mel was still shaking his head helplessly at the enormity of what Stephanie had been through. "And . . . you just left."

It was simply a statement, not an accusation. "You didn't report it or anything?"

"My sister had been killed, Mel. Her head was . . ." She shook her head violently, as if trying to rid herself of the memory. For a moment Mel thought she would break down. "And it was supposed to be me. . . . They could still be there . . . anywhere. I didn't want to be visible. I checked into a motel. I'm still panicking. I just wanted to get out."

Mel slumped back and looked across at her. "Why three weeks?" he asked. "After Brett's accident, why did you let three weeks go by without calling me? You know you could have called."

"I don't know. I was confused about the things I'd begun to suspect . . . disoriented. I went back to California to my folks for the first week. I meant to call you. I just kept putting everything off." Stephanie pulled the blanket more tightly around her shoulders and stared numbly at the mug in her hands. Evidently she was through.

Mel had no real idea what to do in a situation like this. Stephanie was watching him with tired but waiting eyes. But what was there for him to say? He got up and rested a hand on her shoulder. She brought her hand up and gripped his fingers instinctively. "We'll work something out, Steph," he said, squeezing her hand. "Anyway, you'll be all right here for a while. First, you've got more than a few days of sleep to catch up on. We'll leave worrying about the answers until morning."

CHAPTER 10

Melvin Shears sat at a terminal in one of the university's computer science labs, reading the message that had appeared on the screen in front of him. It meant that the program he had been modifying, testing, fixing, and remodifying all morning had at last compiled without errors. He stared at it for a few seconds, savoring something of the feeling of a conqueror's triumph, then leaned forward over the keyboard again, defined a prepared datafile as a test input, and tapped in the command RUN. Then he sat back to await the result.

Since the evening at the Brodsteins', he had been thinking more about economic ideas and catching something of the infection becoming noticeable all over the campus—which by all accounts was happening nationwide. As Martha had pointed out, prices telegraphed information. The trouble with the idea of a centrally directed economy was that there was no effective way for buyers through the various levels of the system to tell suppliers what they needed. So the best the planners could deliver instead was what they thought people ought to have. And that tended not to work too well. It had been ruining economies around the world for half a century. The only thing that such systems *did* provide an effective means of control over—was people.

The ironic part was that people should talk about "planned" economies as if what happened in a free market wasn't planned. But in truth, in all the countless interactions that went on daily to form a free-trading system, there wasn't a product made, a price set, or a new market chosen without extensive preparation and planning—all done by professionals with years of accumulated experience. Yes, true, they sometimes made mistakes, nevertheless; but did anyone seriously imagine that a handful of bureaucrats, who had never run a business and never risked a dollar of their own money, were likely to do better?

And it simply wasn't true, despite all the claims, that private enterprise defeated the spirit of human cooperation. The various activities involved in bringing materials together from all over the world to equip an airline, say, or to build and operate a hotel chain required contributions of knowledge and skill and a degree of cooperation among countless individuals—most of whom knew nothing of the others' existence—that was staggering.

"Figure you've cracked it, then?" Brett's voice said over his shoulder. Mel looked up from his chair. Brett had wandered across from the graphics terminal that he had been working at on the far side of the lab, and was looking critically at the lines of code still displayed on Mel's screen. About twenty other students were busy at keyboards, printers, and plotter tables around the room.

"I'll soon find out," Mel said.

"What d'you figure it was?"

"One of the subroutines could get into a loop and never exit back to the main program."

"Uh—huh." Brett's tone was noncommittal. They carried on staring at the screen.

"You know, I've been thinking," Mel said. "I might sign up for one of Brodstein's classes over in Economics. I thought that some of the stuff they were talking about over at his place the other night was interesting. I'd like to know more about it."

"You just wanna get closer to Eva's pants," Brett said flatly.

Which was true, but not all there was to it.

Mel gestured at the terminal in front of them. "Do you realize how much misplaced faith there is in these things by people who make decisions that affect the whole world, but who don't understand the first thing about them?"

"Misplaced faith in what things?"

"Computers—computer systems generally. I mean, it doesn't matter how simplistic the model is, or how unreliable the data, or how shaky the assumptions, once they've got an output in black and white, it becomes infallible and takes precedence over reality. . . . Worse than that, it *becomes* reality. GIGO with a new meaning: Garbage In, Gospel Out."

"We already knew that," Brett said.

"Yes, but we're not running the world."

At that instant the pattern on the screen vanished, and a series of columns of numbers appeared, terminating with the words RUN COMPLETE. Mel gave a satisfied grunt and leaned forward to compare the results with a printout in a folder lying open beside the keyboard.

"How is it?"

"Looking good . . ."

Brett glanced at his watch. "You'd better start clearing up. We're due out of here in a few minutes."

Mel ran a hard copy of the program on the printer beside him, folded it, and put it in the folder along with the other sheets that he wanted to keep from the papers strewn over the worktable. He stuffed the folder into the canvas bag propped by his chair and logged off from the system. They walked back to the far side of the lab to pick up Brett's bag, and then headed for the doors leading out of the lab. Stephanie was just arriving from the direction of the main entrance-hall as they came out into the corridor. She began walking back with them.

"How was class this morning?" Brett asked her.

"Fine."

"What was it about?"

"Fields and forces on conductors."

Brett looked down at the purse hanging from her shoulder. It was black leather, worn and faded, and too old for her years. "You still hauling that around? I'll buy you a new one. When's you birthday?"

"June twenty-three. Promise?"

"He'll forget," Mel said. "I'll get you one."

"Still coming over to watch the movie tonight?" Brett asked Stephanie.

"Sure."

Brett glanced at Mel. "You ought to ask her," he said. "

Ask me what?" Stephanie looked from one to the other.

"Mel's getting a crush on Eva," Brett said. "How about seeing if you can fix him a date?"

"Everybody gets a crush on Eva," Stephanie replied. "It might not be that easy, though. When she isn't studying, she's always got something or other going on with the Constitutional people. I'm not sure that I see any more of her than you do. Maybe you should think about joining them, Mel."

"I think he already is," Brett said.

Since he had some free time that afternoon, Mel decided to walk over to the social sciences department to ask about the chances of enrolling in one of Brodstein's classes. On the way, he tried to visualize what a Constitutional amendment along the lines that Brodstein had described would mean. If *all* forms of trade or transfer of property were to be free of legal restriction, did it mean that things like drug smuggling would become legal? In fact, surely the very term *smuggling* would lose its meaning. What about prostitution? Mel didn't care one way or the other about that himself, but the conservative right would never buy it. And how about the question of sensitive exports to the Soviets? Then a further thought occurred to him: If this new movement meant what it said about nobody being forced to pay for anything, then presumably the whole concept of coercive taxation would become illegal. Then what? Perhaps Brett had been a lot quicker than Mel had realized when he'd stated bluntly that it plain, flat, couldn't work.

When he arrived at the office, he found to his surprise that Eva was working at one of the desks behind the reception counter. She looked fresh and trim in a loose white dress with a simple floral design in pink and purple. "Well, hello," she said, getting up and coming over to the counter. "What brings you into alien territory?"

"I didn't expect to find you here, either."

"I'm just helping out. They're missing a secretary in the office." Her voiced dropped to a whisper. "Strictly against regulations. Don't mention it to the union."

"Okay."

"So, what can we do for you?"

"I'm interested in enrolling if I can—in one of Paul Brodstein's classes. What's the situation?"

"Seriously?"

"Seriously. I got to thinking about some of the things you people were talking about the other night. I'd like to hear more about it."

"Well, let's see what we've got." Eva hoisted a large binder off a shelf and opened it on the counter to reveal timetables, charts, and class lists. She stooped over, chewing the end of a pen thoughtfully while she studied one of the pages, then flipped over to another. Mel watched, hypnotized by the way that her dress outlined the curves of her back and bottom, and hung away slightly from her body in front. "It may take a while," Eva murmured without looking up. "I'm not too used to this system."

"That's okay," Mel said. He would have been happy to wait all day.

"You wouldn't believe it," Eva went on absently. "There was a new secretary due to start here today. They were depending on her."

"What happened?"

"Well, she's a single mother, on welfare. But she wanted to get off it. So she shopped around for a job and eventually got an offer from this department through an agency—with a raise guaranteed after six months if she did okay. Her mother had agreed to take care of the baby for her, she was all set . . . and then she doesn't show up."

"How come?"

"It turned out that her welfare counselor told her not to take it. They added up the nickels and dimes and figured that with her gas mileage and everything, she'd be better off staying with her benefits." Eva turned her head to glance at him over her shoulder. "Can you imagine it? Never mind that she'd had the initiative, or about what it would have done for her self-respect and better prospects in the future. See what happens when these people hand out advice like that: it becomes a trap. They're *creating* dependents. But it makes permanent jobs for themselves." She shook her head and looked down at the timetables again. "Ah, here might be something . . . one of Paul's . . ."

Mel liked listening to her. He wanted to keep her talking. "So what would you do with the programs?" he asked her.

"Get rid of them," she replied simply, without looking up.

Mel waited a few seconds before stating what he knew was the obvious. "I know what you're saying, but is it really practical? A lot of people depend on them. What about all the unemployed, for instance?"

"Could it be the government's own policies that created the unemployment in the first place?" she said. "Labor is a commodity that's bought and sold like any other. If you see a warehouse full of unsold goods, it's because they've been priced off the market. The way to shift them is obvious." She looked hard at Mel for a moment, then nodded to concede his point. "I know what you're thinking, but it wouldn't have to be done overnight. . . . And look at it this way. If someone takes my money at gunpoint, we don't hesitate to condemn it as wrong. Where's the difference if somebody else takes it and hands it to him?"

"Yes, but maybe he needs it more," Mel said.

Eva stared at him in a unspoken invitation to consider the remark. "He *needs* it more?" she repeated. "But who's supposed to decide that? Should a stranger have the right to grant someone else a better claim to what I've earned than I have? If you accept that principle, why not apply it to other areas, too? So can the state take my kidney and give it to someone else if a committee decides that for him to live rather than me would be more in the public good? Or once the socialists have achieved equality of income based on need, why not equality of sex? That means the everyone's wife, or girlfriend, or husband, or boyfriend will be taken away for a couple of months of the year and made available to those who have a *need*." Mel was smiling and shaking his head helplessly. "Amusing, yes, but it shows it's the principle that's wrong," Eva said. "I'm not against caring, but charity by force and with other people's money isn't charity at all. It just generates resentments on both sides."

"That's a subject for ethics and education," Mel said.

"Then that's where it should be tackled. Ethics is only meaningful when it relates to a voluntary, individual act."

"That could take a while."

"I don't doubt it. But what is there worthwhile that was done in a hurry? We've tried the quick fixes, and we've seen where they end up."

Mel looked at her curiously across the counter as a thought struck him. "But doesn't that make you people just as bad as all the others with blueprints for a better world?"

Eva shook her head. "Not really, because we don't want to impose anything. We just want to let people live how they want. Once people are free to be better people, the better world will take care of itself."

"Who'd figure it all out, though?" Mel asked. "You wouldn't want computer people trying to do it. I was just talking to Brett about that over lunch."

"Oh God, no," Eva agreed. "Can you imagine being a statistical unit in an algorithm? What are the individual rights of a statistical unit? Do you know?"

"That was my point to Brett," Mel said. "So, who'd play the biggest part in terms of actually making it happen?"

Eva looked intrigued. "I've never thought about that before. I'm not sure if there is anyone in particular. . . ." She chewed on her pen again and went off into a long silence while she considered the question. It was nice to feel that he was listened to, Mel thought as he waited. Finally she said, "Yes, maybe there is."

"Tell me," he invited.

"Lawyers," Eva replied.

CHAPTER 11

Robert Winthram had always struck Mel as the personification of the firm itself, with its polished woodwork and brass fittings, leather-upholstered furniture, and general atmosphere of genteel dignity that belonged to another time.

Originally from England, Winthram was one of the two senior partners of Evron and Winthram, which dated back over a hundred years. Exactly how he came to be part owner of a law firm in Boston was obscure. He had been there for as long as anyone else in the office could remember, apparently having acquired the interests of an uncle in the course of a complicated sequence of family deaths and divorces that had taken place back in the seventies. At that time already a successful solicitor in London, he had left one law business and gone through school all over again in the U.S. to learn American practice in order to manage his own.

William Evron, the other senior partner, was a black from New York, originally, to use his own words, "from the wrong side of every track." How he and Winthram had come together as business partners was anybody's guess. Evron claimed that he owed his success, first in education and later in law, entirely to his father's insistence on self-reliance and a scrupulous avoidance of aid programs, which, he maintained, stifled initiative. Nowadays he applied himself mainly to taking on the cases of other casualties of the system, whose lives had been devastated in the name of helping them.

The firm's style of staid reserve and old-fashioned dependability was an expression of the composite personality of its two partners. It was not the kind of law firm that would attract young, ambitious high-fliers from Harvard and Yale in search of prestigious accounts and seven-figure fees. Instead, its clients tended to be the ultimate victims of all the injustices—the little people trying to make a living and be left alone, caught between the oppressive officialdom of Big Government on the one hand, and the protected privileges of Big Business and Big Labor on the other. Unimpressed by the glamorous and the fashionable, and dedicating itself to what was right according to principles that predated group rights and majority tyranny, the firm, like the two men, would probably never figure prominently in the front-page news, nor especially wish to; but it took pride in having earned what it received, and in its list of appreciative—if not always entirely satisfied—clients.

Mel sometimes wondered if it had been an unconscious searching for such values that had led him there from Chapel Hill. Certainly it hadn't been any lust for riches and fame. But trust and respect are valuable things to hold as well as to command, and he had stayed. And it was that same trust and the certainty that confidence would be respected which finally caused him to bring Stephanie to the offices behind Tremont Street, a short distance from Boston Common, on the afternoon after her arrival from Denver.

* * *

"My God, what a dreadful ordeal for you!" Winthram exclaimed when Stephanie had finished. "And then traveling to Boston. . . . You must be on the verge of nervous collapse. Have you been able to sleep at all with this nightmare?"

Stephanie nodded in the visitor's chair, on the far side of an expanse of mahogany desk. She was still tired, but more in command of herself than the evening before. "I did last night. By the time I got to Mel's I was so exhausted that nothing could have kept me awake."

"I'd imagine you'd have slept through World War III," Evron said from where he had been listening with his back to the window, which looked down from the front of the building over the street. He was a large, broad-shouldered man with thick, curly hair, a pencil-line mustache, and a quick smile. He had been in court that morning and was dressed strikingly in a black three-piece suit with a fine pinstripe, crisp white shirt showing an inch of cuffs, and a silver tie—an outfit which he laughingly said made him look like a penguin. Mel looked on from a deep, wingback armchair below shelves of box files and statute books.

Winthram regarded Stephanie in silence for a while. His expression was a mixture of concern and restraint—a worried father trying to keep from fussing and making things worse. Urbane, impeccable in speech and manners, and tending toward portliness in his sixties, Winthram was surely one of the last true English gentlemen. He had a pinkish complexion, an immense brow, and a smooth head bounded by a crescent of hair that varied from silver above the ears to dark gray with scattered flecks of black above the collar. His cheeks and chin were somewhat saggy, giving his face an expressive quality that was enhanced by a mobile mouth which emphasized his precise articulation when he spoke. His dress, too, was always faultless, and on this particular day he was wearing a buttonhole carnation—no doubt a silk imitation at this time of year, but providing a warming touch of color and relief nonetheless from the bleakness outside.

Winthram had a partiality for flowers. On one occasion, Mel remembered, in the middle of a meeting with some lawyers from another firm to present a deposition, he had remarked casually that there was something very strange about a race that would decorate its home and its person with the sexual organs of other species and consider them things of beauty, yet find displays of its own obscene. But this tendency of Winthram's to directness also had the effect of demolishing the inhibitions of others, which made him approachable. Mel wondered if it was something that Winthram had cultivated deliberately, rather than merely the endearing eccentricity that it had first appeared to be.

"How certain can we be that this unfortunate young man's . . . that Brett's accident was, in fact, no accident?" Winthram asked after he had gone over the salient points in his mind.

"It just doesn't add up," Stephanie replied. She was resigned to having to go through it all again. "He'd worked at the tracking station at Pillar Point for several months while we were in California. He knew that road—he drove it twice a day when we were living in Daly City. And . . . well, Brett knew how to drive."

"He didn't have a drinking problem?" Evron threw in.

"No."

"Um." The same thought had evidently crossed Winthram's mind.

"And it happened two days after he got called back there," Stephanie completed. "What else can I say? It was all just too much of a coincidence."

"And then there was Eva, which there's no question was murder," Mel pointed out. "Nobody could believe that it wasn't connected."

Winthram nodded absently and shifted his gaze back to Stephanie. "You've no idea who this call was from, I suppose?" he said.

"No. Brett wouldn't say."

"Hmm." Winthram sucked in his lower lip thoughtfully and continued staring at her, at the same time drumming his fingertips lightly on the edge of the desk. "And what makes us suspect that he was involved with the Soviets?" he asked finally.

Mel answered, enumerating the points on his fingers as he spoke. "One, at university he developed a phobia about ultra-right extremists being in charge of the country, and concluded that the biggest threat to stability would be us getting too far ahead in the arms race. Two, acting in a way that appears to be out of character, he went into the defense industry and wound up working on a battle-management software team at Livermore. Three, at the same time he was behaving strangely and secretively, meeting with people he wouldn't talk about, and from what we've just found out, he was connected somehow with the WPI, a known Soviet propaganda front."

"I've also heard of instances where it's been used as a cover for direct espionage, too," Evron said.

Mel nodded. "Which strengthens the case. And finally, from what we can gather, when he eventually tried to get out, he was pestered in Denver, then called back to California on some pretext, and two days later he was dead." Mel spread his open hands. "As far as I can see, it's open and shut."

Evron leaned back against one side of the window and folded his arms. "Except that whoever killed Eva still thinks it was Stephanie. So does the rest of the world. That means she can't just go back there and pick up her life again. They'll find out, and they won't miss next time." In her chair, Stephanie nodded in silence and exhaled shakily.

Winthram listened, all the time watching Mel with unblinking china blue eyes. He came back in from a totally unexpected direction. "Did you sleep with Eva at one time?"

"What? . . ." This was Winthram's technique with his clients—not to intimidate or lay them bare, but to break down barriers. He couldn't represent anyone effectively while secrecy persisted. "Yes," Mel replied when he had recovered from his surprise—even after a year of knowing Winthram. There was no need for any exchange of looks with Stephanie, who already knew.

"She is the one you mention sometimes, isn't she?" Winthram said. "The one you had all the difficulties over—the reason you moved away from Florida."

"Yes," Mel said.

So now all the cards were on the table. Everyone knew where everyone else fitted in, and they could all get on with business. Winthram got up from his chair and moved across the office to stand near Evron by the window. The weather outside was a replay of yesterday's, with the night's snow having stopped and the sun trying to break through at a few bright patches in the cloud canopy overhead.

"Well, I can see no alternative but to take the whole thing to the authorities," Winthram said over his shoulder as he stared out. "I appreciate your predicament, my dear, but they do have the means and experience to keep you out of sight. You'll have to trust them to take care of you." Evron nodded his agreement, and in the wingback chair, Mel looked at Stephanie in a way that said he had come to the same conclusion. That seemed to be it. There really wasn't an alternative.

Stephanie didn't appear to be particularly gratified by their unanimity, however. She bit her lip for a second as if trying to judge if this was the right moment to bring up something she had been holding back, and then said, quietly, but with a firmness that was suddenly new in her voice, "No. I can't do that."

Mel looked up. Evron frowned. "How come?" he asked, while Winthram turned from the window and merely raised his chin a fraction, allowing the gesture to ask the question for him.

"There's something else," Stephanie told them. "You've heard of Hermann Oberwald?"

"You mean the scientist?" Winthram said. Dr. Hermann Oberwald was a nationally known figure—a leading adviser to the government on energy, defense, and related matters.

"Yes," Stephanie confirmed.

"What about him?" Evron asked.

"He came down to Pensacola as a guest speaker at a Chamber of Commerce dinner. . . ." Stephanie glanced at Mel. "It was in the year after you moved to Carolina."

"Uh-huh," Mel acknowledged. "So?"

"Brett met him. Oberwald visited the university the next day and had lunch with the Socratics—the political group that Brett was involved with. Brett came home feeling very flattered and excited, which was unusual for him—he wasn't usually the kind of person to be bowled over by celebrities. Oberwald must have made quite an impression on him. In fact, it was after that meeting that Brett began to change and started talking about going to work in the defense sector."

"You mean he stayed in contact with Oberwald afterward?" Winthram said.

"I'm not certain . . . it wouldn't have had to be directly. But the company that Brett eventually went to in California— Spirac, in Santa Clara—was practically a DOD subsidiary run by Oberwald. And I know for a fact that Oberwald was instrumental in getting Brett transferred from there to Livermore later, where the really secret stuff goes on." Stephanie looked uncertainly from one to the other of the faces watching her. "See what that means? I think that Oberwald is part of it. I think that he recruited Brett."

Winthram's brow knotted incredulously. "But that would mean he was in collusion with the Soviets, too," he protested. "A man of his stature and reputation? Surely it's not possible."

"I don't know what's possible or what isn't," Stephanie said. "But one thing I do know is that it means I don't trust *any* authority." She shook her head emphatically. "Who knows who else might be involved? It would only take one person in a network like that to find out that I'm still around . . ."

"She's got a point," Evron said, looking at Winthram. "If your neck was on the line, would you risk it?"

Winthram sighed, turned away, and stared out of the window again.

There was a pause. "So, what do we do?" Stephanie asked at last. Nobody answered at once. The silence dragged on. Finally, Winthram wheeled back to face them again.

"Well, although I understand and agree with your concern, we can't approach anyone, even in confidence, with mere allegations and speculations of the kind you have outlined," he said to Stephanie. "There simply isn't anything even remotely approaching a case. All that would achieve, as you have already pointed out, is that alarm bells would be triggered, and if what you say is true, somewhere in the system the wrong people would be alerted. We don't want that." He turned his head toward Evron. "Wouldn't you agree, William?"

Evron nodded. "What we need right now is more facts."

"Something far more substantive in the way of hard facts," Winthram repeated.

"What are you asking me to do?" Stephanie asked.

"You? Nothing, my dear," Winthram said. "You are officially dead. My advice for your own safety is to remain that way." He looked across at Mel. "Since Stephanie must remain invisible, that only leaves you, Melvin. I think we've established your commitment to the case, aside from the question of immediate personal friendship. What do you say? It's going to have to be up to you. How do you feel about becoming a detective for a while?"

Mel ran a hand bemusedly across his brow. Twenty-four hours previously he had been simply a junior associate at a small law firm, minding his own business and doing a job. . . . And now? Religious fanatics planning the end of the world; a Soviet espionage operation involving strategic defense secrets and a national adviser; two murders already. . . . What in God's name was he getting into? All he'd ever anticipated from life was probably getting married one day, starting a family, and all the things that came with a steady job and a house in the suburbs.

But what kind of a choice was there?

"Of course," he replied. "Naturally I'll help in any way I can." Stephanie nodded a quick smile of thanks.

"Splendid," Winthram said, rubbing his hands together and nodding approval. "Take my word, it'll do your career a world of good, my boy. Very well, there's no reason why we shouldn't begin work right away."

CHAPTER 12

In July 1977, General Hacka Hodi, head of Israel's intelligence agency, Mossad, called upon Prime Minister Menachem Begin. With him he brought a file containing detailed information, obtained by deep-cover agents infiltrated by Mossad into the PLO, of an operational plan drawn up on the orders of Libya's Colonel Muammar al-Qaddafi to use Palestinian hit men to assassinate President Sadat of Egypt. Although the Israelis had no reason to be especially concerned what happened to Sadat—he had sent his armies to war against Israel in the Yom Kippur War of 1973—Hofi proposed doing what Israel had usually done before under similar circumstances, which was to pass the information to the American CIA. They, if they so chose, would then pass it to Egypt as a piece of American intelligence. Begin, however, disagreed, and decided instead to demonstrate that Israel was willing to let bygones be bygones by delivering the file to Sadat directly, with compliments of the Israeli government. Accordingly, within twenty-four hours Hofi was on his way to Rabat, in Morocco, for a secret appointment with the head of the Egyptian General Intelligence Directorate, Kamal Ali. The information turned out to be accurate, and the conspiracy was foiled. This affair played no small part in the events that led up to the remarkable scene enacted over a year later, in September 1978, when Begin and Sadat embraced before TV cameras

to celebrate before an incredulous world the successful conclusion of the Camp David summit.

With its growing population, developing economy, and solid
military capability, Egypt was the nucleus of the postwar Arab
world. To hasten its development, Sadat's predecessor, Gamal
Nasser, had accepted aid from both the Soviet Union and from
the U.S. and World Bank, endeavoring to play one side off
against the other without becoming too tied to either. He was
unable to maintain a neutral balance, however, and by the
time of his death in 1970 Egypt had become a virtual Soviet
client state economically and militarily, which influenced the
entire region accordingly. Sadat's first mission on taking office
was to restore the balance, and in 1971 he purged his regime
of its pro-Soviet elements, following up on this a year later
with the expulsion from the country of fourteen thousand
Soviet technicians and advisers on the grounds that Egypt had
not received the modern weapons that it needed—a requirement that was later fulfilled by the West.

The Camp David accords signed subsequently therefore
represented not only a diplomatic triumph for the cause of
stability, but a decisive shift westward of the entire Middle
East power balance. Not only was the Soviet Union deprived
of its main bases in the area and forced to turn instead to Syria
and Iraq, which with their smaller cultural and economic
weight added up to a far inferior substitute, but the Soviet-
backed Palestinian revolutionary movement suffered a greater
disaster, perhaps, than the maulings it received in the civil war
in Jordan in 1971, and again in Lebanon in 1975. For in a
closed codicil to the Camp David agreement, the Israeli and
Egyptian premiers pledged that Mossad and GID, the two
most efficient intelligence services in the region, would hence-
forth share information, depriving the Palestinians at a stroke
of the support of the nation which, under Nasser, had armed,
trained, and consolidated them.

And now there was a grave risk that all of that might be lost.

Henry Newell, leader of the Constitutional party and now
president-elect of the United States, sat in a room in the
Senate Offices Building across Constitution Avenue from the
Capitol in Washington, D.C., reading again a copy of a report
that the State Department had sent him a few weeks earlier
from the ambassador in Cairo. It now seemed certain that
Mehemet Kabuzak, currently the Egyptian foreign minister,
would become the next prime minister, probably within six

months. Kabuzak's attitude toward the West had been cooling appreciably over the past five years as a consequence of some questionable policy decisions by the U.S., and he was even more dubious of the Constitutional party's stated intention of cutting back ruthlessly on free-handout-style foreign aid, and eventually abolishing it. If the Constitutionals won the American election, he had declared on several occasions, he would take Egypt—and by implication the Middle East center of gravity with it—back to an alignment with the Soviets. Arab politicians were notorious for bombast and bluff, it was true, but according to the report that had been passed to Newell, there were strong indications that Kabuzak was serious.

Newell's whole campaign to an electorate grown cynical from years of duplicity and broken promises had been based on telling it straight. The single most important reason for the popular appeal that had brought his party from nowhere in a few years and swept it to the top of the polls had been the public's realization that the party's concerns went beyond looking good on prime-time TV, and it really did mean what it said. And that meant there could be no question of disillusioning the public now and allowing his to become another more-of-the-same-after-all-the-promises administration by reversing his stated position. Yet, to allow Kabuzak to go through with his threat as one of Newell's first achievements after taking office would hardly be the best way of inspiring confidence for the future.

Newell believed that most misunderstandings are caused by failures of communication. Accordingly, his first reaction—although he would have no official powers until after his inauguration in January—had been to suggest an informal meeting with the Egyptians to explore the implications in greater depth. The State Department had raised no objection, and the Egyptians had accepted. Accordingly, it had been agreed that Newell's vice-president-to-be, Theo McCormick, would fly to Cairo with a small party early in January to prepare the ground. Newell himself would follow up later with an official visit in his capacity as president.

The secure phone programmed to Newell's personal number rang. He picked it up. "Newell here."

"Warren, returning your call." It was Warren Landis, Newell's head of party intelligence matters.

"God, did you only just get the message?"

"Right now I'm in my car, risking a ticket on the Beltway. Even dedicated lieutenants take a break sometimes, Henry."

"Okay. Look, about Theo's visit to the Middle East in January . . ."

"Yes?"

"We've got a reply from Jerusalem, and they've confirmed that the fourteenth is acceptable." That was a matter of protocol. To avoid offending anyone, McCormick's party would also pay a courtesy visit to the Israeli capital before returning to the States. "We need to firm up the dates. Have you talked to Kirkelmayer yet about standing down?"

"Yes, and it's okay. He says he's due for a vacation anyway after the election hysteria. We've found a nice place to hide him away."

"Good." Newell smiled for a second, then his expression became serious again. "So what about the girl? Have we found her yet?"

"Not yet. We're trying everywhere. From the messages in the network box, it appears that the other side is having the same problem."

Newell frowned. "I thought she was supposed to be reliable. And this is important. . . . Look, get Ron Bassen's people onto it, will you? I want top priority on this."

"Okay. I'll talk to him as soon as I check in. I should get there in about twenty minutes."

"Fine. And come straight on over to the Senate when you've done that, would you, Warren? I've got some other things here that we need to go through."

"Will do."

Newel replaced the phone and settled back to read the next item. It was a quote by a religious leader in Louisiana who had interpreted a story in the Book of Numbers, telling how a donkey saw an angel and was able to speak to relay a message to its master, as a biblical injunction against the Constitutional party. Newell sighed and shook his head. To whom or what, he wondered, did an agnostic president pray for patience when the top got lonely? He held no religious convictions himself. In a paraphrasing of Voltaire, he had concluded that if there really were a God, it wouldn't have been necessary for men to invent such an absurd one.

CHAPTER 13

Professor Paul Brodstein turned his hands palms upward in appeal to the packed tiers of seats rising to the back of the lecture theater. "When an industry starts pleading to government for special favors to protect it from competition, it signs its own death warrant," he said. "And it's society as a whole—you and me—that pays in the long run. Probably the most devastating blow that government can inflict is to impose tariffs or quotas on imports, supposedly as an aid to domestic producers. The first person to suffer is the general consumer. The reason why is obvious. Let's imagine, for example, that Bongobongoland can ship T-shirts here and sell them profitably for five dollars, but American T-shirt makers need to charge eight dollars. So, in response to protectionist lobbying, a three-dollar tariff is imposed. But all that's really happened is that everyone in the country who buys a T-shirt gets just that, when they could have had a T-shirt *plus* three dollars left in their pocket to spend on whatever they chose. Now add to that the fifteen dollars they could have saved on a pair of Indonesian shoes, two hundred dollars on a Japanese computer, over a thousand dollars on a French automobile, and so on for all the other items you could list. . . . Now multiply that total by a hundred million consumers, and you can see that billions of dollars are drained out of the economy as additional government revenues, which could otherwise have been spent on goods and services that would have stimulated the creation of jobs. Every one of those evaporated dollars represents somebody's hard-earned wealth that isn't being exchanged for anything of value—in other words, wasted investment in time, labor, capital, and other resources. And then the public is hit a second time with taxes to compensate for the unemployment that the government's own policies have caused."

Brodstein paused and let his gaze run over the rows of faces to invite comment. A big-chested girl near the front chewed on the end of her pen dubiously while she thought this over, then looked up. "But what about the people in the factory back home, who can't make a living at five bucks a shirt? They're all out of jobs, aren't they? Aren't we supposed to care about them?" A few assenting nods from around the room endorsed the question.

"Yes, we're supposed to care about them," Brodstein replied. "But I would argue that in the long run they, just like everybody else, will be better off if the market is left to itself. But tariff laws give an illusion of protection in the shorter term, and that's what gets you votes."

"Would you explain how they end up better off in the long run if they're out of a job?" a black youth in a red sweatshirt asked from the other side.

Brodstein walked across to where he was sitting. "They won't end up out of a job, but they might end up not making T-shirts," he said. "And that might be for the best, anyway. If the industry was that marginal that it needed to plead for protection in the first place, it was probably declining and only able to pay marginal wages. The people will relocate into the other industries that are expanding because of those billions of extra dollars we've left in people's pockets to spend. And since expanding industries are competing for labor, they'll pay better than marginal industries, like the one that the ex–T-shirt-makers moved from. That's why I say that in the long run they'll be better off." Brodstein stepped back to take in the whole room again. "And another thing. . . . The T-shirt maker in Bongobongoland is now earning dollar exchange, which enables him to buy our products, which means we don't have to hit the taxpayer a third time through subsidies for American exporters. And on top of that, since Bongobongoland is earning its own keep, we avoid hitting him a fourth time with foreign aid."

"Are you saying that a country like ours shouldn't provide aid to the lesser-developed ones?" someone queried.

"I'm saying that if that's what you want to do, the most effective way to do it is to let them trade and compete equally across open borders. It may shrink some profits and paychecks, but it would cut everyone's taxes, too. And it puts things on the basis I've been advocating, which is free individual choice." He spread his hands wide again. "When lawmakers start interfering in economics, everyone else loses.

The best way to make sure that crime doesn't pay would be to let government run it."

Laughter came from a few places. Then a Cuban girl at the back raised a hand, checked her notes, and began, "You said earlier, Professor, that increases in real wealth can *only* come from improved productivity. Now, in the case of labor laws that . . ."

Near the center, halfway from the front, Mel clipped more sheets of paper into his ring binder. Eva was sitting a short distance to his right and a few rows father forward, her hair trailing down over a sheer, off-white blouse that buttoned down the back and showed her bra strap, becoming virtually transparent where it touched her body. With it she had clinging green slacks stretched tight and hugging her hips as she leaned forward, arms folded on the desk in front of her, to follow what was being said. For some reason, he would have expected it to be Stephanie that wore bras and Eva that didn't, but it was the other way around. He wasn't sure what the significance of that was, if there was any.

As he watched her, he began undressing her in his mind. It would be slowly, gently, he decided, with nothing rushed that might disrupt the exquisiteness of the moment—although in his fantasy, of course, there was no need for haste to allay uncertainty, because she was delightfully eager. . . . He pictured his hands exploring the contours of her back through the blouse, enjoying the firmness and warmth before opening the buttons one by one to expose the smooth skin and release its odor. And then, the catch unhooking to let the straps fall free, his fingers stealing softly around below her arms to slide inside the loosened cups. . . . He felt himself growing erect and distinctly uncomfortable beneath the desk at the thought of it.

"If better technology is bringing the free-market price of food down to the point where fewer farmers can make a living, then the best thing is for the less efficient producers to get out," Brodstein was saying at the front. "The worst thing you can do is try and prop prices up with guaranteed government purchases. All that does is attract more producers into the business because of the guaranteed profits, which creates surpluses. And the surpluses are made worse by the reduced demand that results from the artificially high prices. Eventually you get a massive price collapse—the exact opposite of what you set out to achieve. That brings further demands for the government to do something, which leads to the kinds of absurdities we've been seeing, with farmers being paid not to produce, and crops and livestock actually being destroyed. . . ."

With an effort of will, Mel returned his attention to his notes. Sex was like money, he told himself. Everybody thought there was more of it around than there really was, and that everyone else was getting a bigger share.

All the same, he made a point of noticing from a distance that after class she headed for the cafeteria on the ground floor of the building, accompanied by a chubby, fluffy-haired girl who had been asking questions about how pro-union laws protected privileged classes of labor. He had been intending to stop by the cafeteria himself, which would enable him to get through the rest of the day without more than a snack. However, to avoid looking as if he were following her around—as if anyone else would have noticed or cared—and to prove to himself that he wasn't, he walked past the cafeteria entrance and out onto the campus, deciding to stop at a Perkins pancake restaurant on the way home instead. But halfway across the lawn, he remembered that it would be two days until Brodstein's next class. Suddenly it seemed a long time.

He circled the lawn in a vaguely unresolved state of mind and found himself going back into the economics building again. In the self-service area at the cafeteria entrance he selected chicken, beef, and cheese with a bun and garnishings to make a sandwich, added an apple, a soda, some cutlery, and a napkin to the tray, and carried it over to the line at the register. Moving nonchalantly, he scanned the tables ahead furiously. Eva and the chubby girl were sitting at a table near the windows to one side. Mel passed through the cash desk and began heading uncertainly in more or less that direction, frantically trying to think of an opener to join them. For some reason, a simple "Hi, can I join you?" didn't occur to him. But Eva had already spotted him and waved. He veered toward their table.

"Have a seat," Eva said. Mel sat down, feeling quite pleased with his initiative. "Mel, do you know Sadie? This is Mel. He's Brett's roommate."

"Brett? You mean your sister's boyfriend?"

"Right."

"Hi," Sadie said to Mel.

"Hi."

"You just joined us a week or two ago, didn't you?" Sadie said. She had alert, attractive brown eyes, and a pretty face that would have been better still if she lost a few pounds.

"I decided to extend myself from computer science," Mel said. "A broader outlook on life."

"Great," Sadie said.

"So, how do you like Paul's class?" Eva asked him.

The translucency of her blouse was even more tantalizing from the front than from the back. "It's . . . interesting." Mel looked away hurriedly and busied himself with fixing his sandwich.

Sadie had a tuna salad on her tray, and Eva, just a glass of iced tea. "Have we recruited Mel as a Constitutional yet?" Sadie asked as she peeled the foil off a pat of butter for her roll.

"We're working on it," Eva replied, smiling.

"Are you one too?" Mel asked.

"Isn't everybody?" Sadie said. "They will be by 2000, anyway."

"Brett's not so sure about that," Mel said. "He thinks you've got no chance. But he's more worried about government putting religion back in the schools than legislating economics."

"Make the whole school system private," Eva said. "Get the government out of it. Let parents send their kids to get whatever education they choose. The market can decide what's wanted."

"You mean everyone has to pay fees?" Mel said.

"Why not? They do anyway, through taxes. But this way they'd have more say in how it gets spent."

"Wouldn't that penalize kids from poorer families?"

"We don't want kids from poor families to starve either, but that doesn't mean the government has to run the supermarkets," Eva pointed out.

It was a thought. Mel considered it as he took a bite of his sandwich.

"Where are you from, Mel?" Sadie asked him.

"Right here, Pensacola. My folks are across in Warrington. How about you?"

"I'm from California, the same part as Eva."

"San Francisco?"

"San Jose—south. Ever get there?"

"Once or twice. I wouldn't claim to know it. You like California?"

"It's not what it used to be. Everybody works for the state, lives off the state, or runs the state."

"Our father used to say that there are three Marxist states in the Western hemisphere," Eva said. "Cuba, Nicaragua, and California."

Mel grinned. "What does he do?"

"He's in aerospace—a systems engineer."

"Is that where Stephanie got her notion to go into physics?"

"Probably."

"So how about you? What got you interested in politics and this whole business?"

Eva sipped her iced tea. "Oh, lots of different things. But part of it was him too. He gets so mad sometimes at the shambles that became of the space program. He thinks that Apollo, back in the sixties, was a bigger disaster for this country than the Vietnam war."

Mel looked astonished. "But it was a success, wasn't it?"

"That's the whole point," Eva said. "Some of the worst mistakes in history have resulted from trying to apply methods that work fine in one field to another where they don't. Even when it becomes obvious that they're making things worse and not better, people refuse to abandon them, precisely *because* they were so successful before."

"Explain," Mel invited.

"After Sputnik and the Gagarin flight, Kennedy redirected all the national resources onto a moon shot. And in less than ten years, we'd done it. A dazzling success. And then people started to think, surely if centralized control and massive federal spending could do that, then centralized control and massive federal spending could do anything. All our social problems could be solved the same way."

"Okay. . . ."

"So, we got the Johnson Great Society programs, and we've been making things worse ever since. But they won't give up. After all, we did get to the moon. How can you argue with success? At least Vietnam was a failure and we learned something from it. Apollo was a wonderful technical achievement, sure, and I'm not trying to knock it, but it came twenty or thirty years too soon. Malinvestments eventually liquidate themselves as depressions. And that's what we've been having in the space programs—a depression caused by the resources invested in the wrong things back in the sixties."

Mel had propped his chin in a hand and was watching her across the table. He was thinking that, without a doubt, intelligence was the world's most potent aphrodisiac. "Okay," he agreed, not taking his eyes off her.

"Does that make sense?" she asked.

"A lot."

"Eva, I've always wondered, where do you get all this information from?" Sadie asked, sounding perplexed.

"Everywhere," Eva said. "It's keeping track of it all that's the problem. My place is getting to look like a print shop that got hit by a library wagon. . . . Oh, and that reminds me, I still want to see that library-organizer program that you told me about."

"I'll get a copy," Sadie promised.

"What's this?" Mel asked them.

"It's a program Sadie has that I wanted to play with," Eva said. "I'm trying to hook up my own local reference system off the net."

"Are you managing okay?"

"With a lot of fooling around . . . but I think I'm getting there."

The opportunity was too good to miss. "Well, that's my field," Mel said. "Maybe I could stop by and have a look at it for you sometime? I've got a few hacker's routines that might help."

Eva regarded him for a second or two with eyes that held just the right mixture of mischievousness and curiosity— twinkling, but not enough to be mocking, and for long enough to be more than indifferent. "Sure, why not?" she said.

"I'll provide the know-how. You get the pizza," Mel offered.

"You've got a deal."

"How about tonight?" Mel wasn't about to quit while he was on a roll.

"I can't," Eva said. "I'm tied up for a few evenings. Can we make it next week? Wednesday would be good."

"Sure, Wednesday it is." Mel couldn't believe his good fortune. Sadie winked at him slyly.

Back in his car, he sang out loud all the way to the intersection of Fairfield and Palafox, where, in his exuberance, he failed to see the red light. The truck coming across the intersection almost failed to see him.

"Officer, have you ever been in love?" he asked, grinning like an imbecile at the highway patrolman who, as luck would have it, had been parked across the street, drinking coffee at the time.

"Buddy, either you're drunk, or you're on dope, or you're an asshole," the policeman said, unimpressed, as he wrote out the ticket. "Which do you want it to be?"

CHAPTER 14

The countryside around the village of Uspenskoye, to the east of Moscow, was a serene area of regal old pines, birch groves, winding rivers, and open fields, reserved for *dachas*— luxurious country homes—allotted to members of the classless society's privileged elite. General Leonid Goryanin of the KGB stood looking out through a window at a landscape which after the snowstorm of the previous day had taken on a fairy-tale appearance, with snow clinging to the trees like frosting on a cake, picked out in the moonlight of a now cloudless night. Behind him, the Soviet Minister of Defense, Marshal Georgi Androliev, who was also the First Deputy Secretary of the Party, spoke over a brandy glass from a recliner to one side of the room's open pine-log fire.

"You know, Leonid, I don't mind saying it—there's something exciting about what's happening in America right now. Don't you think so? Come on, admit it. It has a new, fresh air . . . a clean feel about it. I think these people are the first honest thing that's happened in the world since 1945. They've discovered that old-fashioned thing that we're so used to laughing at these days that most people forget it was ever taken seriously: Principle."

Goryanin turned away from the window and smiled tolerantly. The dinner before the rest of the company left had been fine, with a lot of joking and old anecdotes. Androliev was getting on in years, and his tongue was running a little loosely after the generous flow of drink. "You mean all this about freedom and dignity, and realizing everyone's full potential?"

"But isn't that exactly what Marx was calling for? He was interested in the economic system only as a means of creating the conditions for individual emancipation. That's something that everyone forgets. The ironic thing, when you really take the trouble to look at it, is that our Revolution and the American Revolution were both fought for virtually the same ideals." There was a pause as Androliev gazed into the flames. Then he added distantly, "We were both betrayed . . . by the same forces. And now we've joined them."

Goryanin frowned and moved back toward the center of the room. "Betrayed? By whom?"

Androliev made a meaningless gesture in the air with his free hand. "Oh, I don't know. . . . Circumstances, maybe." Goryanin wasn't sure if the older man was just rambling because of the drink, or backing off from something that he shouldn't have mentioned to someone of Goryanin's lower rank. Either way, Androliev went on, "I heard an American joke the other day, that they tell about us. It goes, 'How many remaining true-believers in Marxism, east of Poland, does it take to change a light bulb?' Do you know what the answer was?"

"What?"

"'Both of them'. . . . And it's true, isn't it? You know how much all the slogans are worth, as well as I do. But we play the game of pretending, and in the process we forget that we manufacture our own form of logic, which the rest of the world doesn't share. Only three percent of our farming land is privately owned, and not a tractor or an ounce of fertilizer. Yet that three percent feeds most of the country. If those owners were given another half percent—just another half of a percent, mark you—we wouldn't have a problem producing food. But instead we choose to waste four hundred tons of gold each year buying it abroad. Now try and explain that to me in any language that both you and I know is common sense. . . . We have to build walls and fences to keep our own people in . . . can't let them see any example of another way of life that might be possible. . . . It can't go on, Leonid. We have to change or disintegrate. I think this is an opportunity. We must seize it somehow."

Goryanin set his own glass down and glanced at his watch. "Anyway, it's time I was getting back. I've already stayed

longer than I meant to. The evening was very enjoyable, thank
you." He lowered his voice pointedly. "And this isn't a wise
way to be talking, you know, even for someone in your
position . . . and of all people, to someone like me. Who
knows who I might be reporting this too, first thing tomorrow
morning?"

"Nobody, as you very well know," Androliev said, rising.
"Because KGB though you might be, you are also a dear
nephew. But you are right. . . . I babble too much." He
pressed a button by the fireplace. "My driver will take you
back, of course. Are you going back into the city?"

"Yes, my apartment on Kutozovski Prospekt." Goryanin had
his own *dacha*, too, a smaller one, with smaller grounds
around it—his rank didn't merit treatment comparable to the
defense minister's.

The door opened, and a servant appeared. "Bring the
general's coat and hat," Androliev instructed. "And have the
chauffeur bring a car around to the front door to take him back
into the city."

Later, reclining comfortably in the back seat of the minister's handmade Zil limousine as it rolled along the snow-
cleared highway into town, Goryanin thought over the things
that Androliev had said. He hoped that his uncle wasn't
attracting attention from other, less forgiving directions—he
was genuinely fond of him. Had Goryanin worked for any of
several other directorates within the KGB, the situation would
have presented a real problem of conflicting loyalties, and he
didn't like to think too much about which side might have won.
But as things were, his area of responsibility lay purely with
technical matters and the protection of secrets relating to
military equipment. Worrying about who might or might not
be reliable to whom at the top, along with all the messy
business which that entailed, wasn't his problem. And he was
perfectly happy, he decided as he looked out at the Moscow
suburbs, stark and austere in the patches of light from the
streetlamps, to let things remain that way.

CHAPTER 15

Mel wasn't exactly sure what he hoped to learn or achieve as he drove out of the Denver-Boulder airport, bound for the General Plasma Dynamics corporation. But Hermann Oberwald was a national adviser on energy matters, and GPD was a research corporation involved in the energy field. Stephanie had confirmed that from the little she knew about the political side of GPD's affairs, some of the corporation's executives had dealt with Oberwald on occasion, and his name had appeared on several documents that she'd seen. It didn't add up to a lot to go on. But the situation hadn't exactly offered much in any direction when he and the others analyzed it over and over back at the offices of E and W, and they had to start somewhere. Mel was simply interested in any information that might provide a beginning to unraveling more of Oberwald's activities and connections. There could be nothing approaching a plan of action beyond that at this stage.

His other reason for choosing to begin with GPD, of course, was that Stephanie's working there gave him a legitimate "in." In his call to Edward Gilman, the corporation's president, he had said merely that he represented the law firm of Evron and Winthram, and that he needed certain information concerning the affairs of the late Stephanie Carne. As Mel had hoped, Gilman had agreed to see him without delay. Mel had no idea at this point of whether or not he would reveal the truth about Stephanie, although she had left no doubt that she considered Gilman to be trustworthy. It all depended on how the interview went. The partners had left it to his discretion.

Mel had also called Stephanie's family from Boston to express his condolences at the news of her death, which he said he'd received from a friend. He had learned that the body was being flown back to California, and that the funeral would take place there in three days time. The girls' father had asked Mel if he knew of Eva's whereabouts, since they had been trying to locate her ever since the tragedy, but without success. Mel could only say that he hadn't been in touch with Eva for a long time now, which at least was the truth. He had assured them that he himself would be there.

That gave him today to fly to Denver to find out whatever he could at GPD, leaving Stephanie to get some rest in his apartment in Boston. Then, two days later, he would have the strange experience of going to California with her to attend her funeral—she had insisted that she wanted to be there. Mel wasn't too sure how they were going to handle that part of it. But he dismissed the thought from his mind as he identified the shape of GPD's main reactor building a quarter mile or so off the highway, and moved a lane rightwards to take the next exit ramp.

One day at a time . . .

Ed Gilman listened stonily as his older cousin, Kenneth, spoke from the telescreen in Gilman's office. Kenneth, who lived in upstate New York, was an investment banker from the more aristocratic side of the family. Gilman's notion to rid himself of the strings that came with government financial support went back a lot further than the recent meeting with Roth and the deputation from the Industrial Liaison Commission. Kenneth's call was in response to a question that Gilman had put to him some time ago on the possibility of a private loan to pay back what GPD had been granted and to cover its further liabilities. A group was prepared to put up the required funds, it turned out, but the terms were far from Gilman's liking. In fact, they completely defeated the object of the whole exercise.

"Only on the condition that the entire fission-fusion hybrid project is scrapped," Kenneth repeated. "I'm sorry, Edward, but they were unanimous and quite firm—and if you want my opinion, I fully agree with them. It was ill-conceived from the start, it has major technical and safety problems, and it's highly doubtful if it could ever pay its way economically. I did try to advise you against it ten years ago, if you remember, but to no avail. Now I'm afraid the bird has come home to roost." Kenneth was a big man, with saggy jowls and a droopy-eyed face that gave him something of a bloodhound look. His conveying of regrets, as Gilman well knew, was purely a matter of form. Behind his expressionless countenance he was probably delighted. He had never disguised his disdain for what he regarded at his cousin's "mechanic's" tendencies.

"But that's ridiculous," Gilman protested. "This whole corporation was founded specifically to develop the hybrid. What else do you suppose we'd have left to do here if we drop it? It's what GPD *is!*"

"It's in the energy business, which as we all know is crucial these days," Kenneth replied. "The suggestion is that its resources be redirected into sounder, more proven technological areas, such as direct solar generation and wind turbines."

"*Windmills!*" Gilman exploded. "God man, we're just entering the twenty-first century and you want to put us back in the fifteenth! And the whole solar thing is a fraud. The government has been trying to make it efficient for years by decreeing that it will be, regardless of what the laws of physics and economics say. But it can't work. Have you any idea what—"

"Such approaches would earn significant tax concessions, as well as generous direct subsidies, which would put you in a far more viable financial position than you can boast of at present," Kenneth retorted coolly.

"It's government money that I'm trying to get away from," Gilman protested. "We can't afford to take their money. It's ruining us."

"Then I don't think you're really in a bargaining situation," Kenneth replied.

Gilman slumped back in his chair and shook his head tiredly. "Look, how did we get back to this myth that the fission-fusion hybrid isn't viable? We've been running tests and analyses for over two years. The basic physics derives from work done at Princeton, Livermore, Sandia Labs, Oak Ridge, MIT, Culham in England, and the Osaka laser institute for decades before that. It'll work. It's safe. It's the future. We've shown you all the reports. We've given you the figures. What else do you want?"

"We have other reports from sources of our own—highly authoritative sources, I might add—that are less optimistic," Kenneth said. "Enthusiasm is commendable, but it does run the risk of allowing subjectivity to cloud one's judgment."

"What sources?"

"That is confidential. But as I said, they are highly authoritative, and my associates have accepted their view as being the more objective and impartial—a decision with which I concur."

Gilman was shaking his head. "No, I wouldn't do it. It's totally out of the question. We'll keep looking. I'd rather see us sell what we've got for scrap than turn it over to making windmills."

"That's a matter for you and your colleagues to decide. I'll not take this as final. Perhaps we'll leave it with you awhile to think over."

"Don't hold your breath."

"Well, we'll see. Good day."

Gilman stared mutely, and the screen blanked out. A moment later Ruth's voice came from the intercom. "Mr. Shears from Evron and Winthram in Boston is here. I've brought him up. He's out here with me now."

"Lord, is it that time already? Very well, Ruth, show him in, would you?" Gilman closed the folder of financial figures lying on his desk and set it to one side. Then he got up, crossed the office, and opened the door. The young man who had been in Ruth's office rose from his chair and approached, carrying a briefcase. Ruth introduced them and they shook hands. Gilman ushered him into his own office, closed the door behind them, and showed him the visitor's chair. Then he resumed his own seat behind the desk. "Well, Mr. Shears, what can I do for you?"

Mel opened his case and set it on his knee. "Thank you for fitting me in at such short notice. I'll try to keep it as brief as I can." Gilman nodded and waited. Mel had hoped for a more animated response. There was no option but to press on. "As I said when I called, it's to do with the late Ms. Stephanie Carne. There are a few details concerning her affairs that I hope you might be able to help us with."

"Yes, if I can. What do you wish to know?" Gilman replied. One of the advantages of being with a law firm was that motives and credentials were so rarely questioned.

"A sad thing to have happen to one of your employees, Mr. Gilman," Mel said, making a pretence of sorting through papers behind the lid of his briefcase.

"More than that, Mr. Shears. To me it was a personal tragedy. I was very concerned for her. She had tremendous promise as a scientist." Gilman shook his head sadly. "You know, I was talking to her that very evening—only a few hours before it happened, I suppose. I really thought she was over the worst of it. The news came as a terrible shock. The people that she worked with haven't gotten over it yet. They all felt for her when Brett was killed. . . . I take it you knew about that?"

"Oh, yes."

"She was very popular."

"You knew Brett Vorland, Mr. Gilman?"

"I met him once or twice, at company social events—barbecues, things like that. He moved here from . . . California, I think it was, sometime around early summer."

"Now, let me see . . ." Mel opened a notepad, took a pen from his inside pocket, and looked down at the list of questions he had prepared. They didn't mean anything. It was just to get Gilman talking. "Stephanie was with the firm how long?"

"Oh, a year or so as far as I remember. The personnel people can get the exact date for you before you leave."

"Fine. And her exact job title?"

"Research physicist, grade three."

"What kind of work did that entail?"

"She helped design and develop measurement equipment that we use on the prototype reactor that's under construction here. . . . I assume you're aware of the nature of our main program?"

"Er, sufficiently so, I think. And, ah, tell me, Mr. Gilman, during the year she worked here, was there ever any reason for dissatisfaction with her performance? . . . Or maybe I should say, any reason to suspect anything irregular in her actions?"

Gilman looked surprised. "No. None. . . . I'm not sure exactly what you mean by 'irregular.'"

"Does any of your work here involve classified information?" Mel asked.

"Classified? You mean in the military sense? Secret stuff?"

"Yes."

"Well, some of the more advanced physics does overlap with certain areas of defense work, especially in the space defense sector, yes. . . . But only one or two of our senior scientists have any involvement in that. Basically we're in the commercial energy business. We don't do military research."

"So Stephanie wouldn't have been connected with the overlap area that you mentioned?"

"No. As a junior staff member, she didn't have the clearances." Gilman stared dubiously across the desk for a second or two. "Mr. Shears, could I ask what the purpose of all this is?"

Seeing an opportunity, Mel ignored the question. "The senior scientists who do get involved in the more advanced physics, do they deal from time to time with Dr. Oberwald, the national defense adviser?"

"What does that have to do with Stephanie Carne?"

He was too far in to back off now. The only choice was to go for it. "My particular interest concerns Stephanie's friend, Brett Vorland," Mel said. "I am aware that Dr. Oberwald has visited this establishment on occasions, and that he does have technical connections with some of your work. Now, what I'd very much like to know is if you have any knowledge of dealings between Dr. Oberwald and Brett Vorland." Mel adopted the greatest look of sincerity he could manage. "Believe me, it is important."

He wasn't sure just what reaction he expected, but it certainly wasn't the one he got. Gilman had started to stiffen even before Mel finished speaking. Then, without warning, he reached out to flip a switch on his desk intercom, and without taking his eye off Mel, instructed brusquely, "Ruth, get the number of Evron and Winthram in Boston, would you? Call them and find out if they have a Mr. Shears on their staff, and if he's supposed to be here today. Let me know right away." He released the switch before she could reply. "I don't know who you are or where you're from," he told Mel icily. "Now tell me what's going on. I warn you, if I'm not satisfied, I'll have the police here before you can get off the premises. Now?. . . "

For a few seconds Mel was too taken aback to respond. He had no idea what he'd said to provoke the reaction, but it was clear that he was on to something. There would be only one way to find out more now. He drew a long breath, closed the lid of the briefcase, and placed his hands palms down on top of it in a gesture of candor.

"My name is Shears, and I am from Evron and Winthram," he said. "But I'm also a very close, old friend of Stephanie's. And yes, you're right—I'm not dealing with her affairs following her suicide. You see, Mr. Gilman, Stephanie isn't dead."

Gilman stared hard for a long time, his eyes flickering in a silent interrogation over every inch of Mel's face. Eventually he had read all he wanted to. "Go on," he said, remaining expressionless.

"It was her sister, and she didn't kill herself. She was murdered. They were always being mistaken for each other. I knew both of them, and Brett, for many years. We were all at university together. Brett was working on the space-based defense program in California. To cut a long story short, we believe he was mixed up with an espionage operation to pass information to the Soviets. We suspect that he was killed by them when he tried to opt out, and that has a precaution in case she knew more than she should have, they decided to eliminate Stephanie too . . . except they got her sister by mistake."

There was silence for a while as Gilman took in what Mel had said. He sat back in his chair, and the look in his eyes changed as the full awfulness of the situation sank in. He looked back at Mel, horrified. "My God!" he breathed. Mel waited for a moment longer. "Then she could still be in great danger," Gilman said.

"Exactly."

"Where is she?"

"She's in a safe place, and as well as can be expected."

"In Boston?"

"Yes."

The intercom buzzed. Gilman touched a switch and said mechanically, "Yes?"

"I've called Evron and Winthram, Mr. Gilman. Mr. Shears is employed by them, and yes, he was scheduled to be here today. Everything seems to be in order."

"Yes . . . er, thank you, Ruth."

"Will there be anything else?"

"No. It's all right." Gilman still seemed numbed. He sat for a while longer, slowly absorbing the implications. Mel waited, staring at the desktop. At last Gilman said, "So exactly what aspect are you pursuing? I know you can't be a part of any official investigation into Brett."

Mel frowned. "You do? How?"

"Because if you were, you'd know about the rest of what has been going on. You see, the FBI were here yesterday, asking the same questions. They weren't very forthcoming with details, but I got the impression that his previous employers have uncovered something about him that made them suspicious, and called in the authorities."

"You mean Livermore Labs? Or Spirac, where he worked before that?"

"I don't know. They didn't say. There wasn't really anything I could help them with."

Now it was Mel's turn to stare numbly. Deep in his own mind he had tried to convince himself that Brett wouldn't really have gone over to a hostile power, that the WPI documents had nothing to do with anything important, and that everything else would turn out to have an ordinary explanation. But if the FBI was involved, alerted independently by the people that Brett had actually worked for, that seemed to clinch it. He emitted the long, heavy sigh of someone who at last had no choice but to accept the inevitable.

"You didn't really believe it," Gilman said, again reading the signs.

"I guess not."

Gilman studied Mel's face and frowned momentarily to himself as if uncertain of having missed something. "What I don't get is, why are *you* hiding her, and why aren't you talking to the proper authorities? Why get involved like this? Why not let them handle it?" He thought for a moment longer over the things Mel had said earlier. "And you still haven't told me how Oberwald figures in all this."

There could be no evading the issue now. "He's the reason we don't want anyone to know that Stephanie is still alive," Mel said. "We have reason to believe that the person who recruited Brett in the first place . . . was Dr. Oberwald." He allowed a moment for that to sink in. "Can you see where that puts Stephanie?"

Had the statement come earlier, Gilman's reaction might have been different, but by this time he had heard too much to be completely shocked by anything. He draped his arms limply on the sides of his chair, and stared distantly at the far wall. "Je-sus!" he muttered finally, more to himself than to Mel.

"A mess," Mel agreed.

Gilman refocused inside the room. "Do you have any plans for lunch, Mr. Shears?"

"No. I was just planning on going back to my hotel later this afternoon. I'll be going back to Boston in the morning."

"Let me take you to a good place that I use a lot. They have private dining rooms where we can talk. I can't promise anything for sure, you understand, but I'd like to help you if I can. First, however, I want to hear the whole story."

Over lunch, Mel related the story of Brett and Stephanie, Eva's visit to Denver, and his own involvement from years gone by. Gilman listened intently, needing to ask only a few, infrequent questions, which reinforced the impression that Mel had already formed of a man with an agile mind, and the deep, analytical ability that marks a thinker. Gilman reaffirmed his willingness to help, which for the present could mean little beyond that he would reexamine GPD's dealings with Oberwald and let Mel know if he came across anything unusual or suspicious. Mel said he would be grateful.

Then the conversation turned to the project under development at GPD. Stephanie had told him it was a fission-fusion hybrid and tried to describe it, but Mel still wasn't really clear what that meant. "You can think of it as a halfway step between fission and pure fusion," Gilman said. "Basically you use the neutron flux from a low-grade fusion process to breed high-grade fuel for fission reactors from fertile elements such as uranium 238 or thorium 232. Then, you use that to produce power instead of from fusion directly. The advantage of doing it that way is the amplification factor that you get from neutron multiplication in the fertile material, while the fast fusion neutrons are being slowed down and absorbed—which can be twenty, thirty times, or even more, theoretically. What it means is you can relax the performance criteria significantly from what you'd need for pure fusion to be economic."

"Are you saying pure fusion isn't practical, then?" Mel asked.

"Not at all. The physics is well understood now, but there are still some formidable engineering hurdles. What I'm saying is, we could be on-line commercially with this a lot sooner."

As his enthusiasm warmed, Gilman went on to talk about how, one day, controlled hundred-million-degree plasmas would provide limitless energy and revolutionary ways of producing materials of every kind. Every square mile of deep ocean contained enough deuterium—fusion fuel—to deliver as much energy as all the oil under Saudi Arabia. "The whole universe consists of energy and matter," he said, making a wide, sweeping motion over the table with his arm. "And every advance in human knowledge makes more of it accessible to us. Resources become cheaper and *more* abundant with time, not less. All this doomsday nonsense we've been hearing for years in the biggest fallacy of the age. Look at how the prices of just about every commodity you can name have come down in real terms over the last two hundred years—despite all the insane economic policies to prevent it."

Mel smiled. "I take it you're a Constitutional, then?"

"God, how could anyone not be?" Gilman took the salt shaker and poured a little onto the side of his plate. "By Einstein's equation, mass is energy, yes? Well at the rate of energy equals mass times the speed of light squared, those grains—or any matter, come to that—at today's energy prices, are worth about ten million dollars per thousandth of an ounce. The only difference between a shovelful of dirt and unlimited resources is knowledge." Mel stared at the salt, fascinated. He'd never thought about it that way before. Gilman sat back in his chair. "And we're sitting on a ball of it eight thousand miles across. Convert that into dollars, divide them out on a per-person basis, and then tell me that the human race is poor." He swept his arm out exuberantly again. "And that doesn't even take account of what's out there beyond the planet."

"You've no doubts that we'll get out there, then?"

Gilman looked astonished. "Of course not. That's what it's there for."

It was uplifting to hear such vision and enthusiasm for a change. All the same, Mel had heard too many reservations expressed to let himself be carried away. "A lot of people wouldn't agree, though," he said. "They say they've heard it all before, and technology has failed to deliver. All they see are risks and pollution."

"I know, and they're wrong," Gilman said. "It's worked so well that they don't see it any more. They've forgotten how people used to live. When a culture loses its confidence that it can comprehend and solve its problems, that's when it goes into decline. Negative thinking and defeatism are the only kind of pollution we have to worry about."

Mel arrived back at his hotel in the middle of the afternoon. He had a drink at the bar and watched the news on TV, which was still dominated by prognosticators of every kind speculating on likely developments following the election. It was like a roulette game with every number covered. Since every prediction conceivable was being made, one of them at least was bound to get it right. So, another expert would be acclaimed and a new guru found to follow—for a while, until the next one. The stock market worked the same way. Computerized superstition.

Afterward, he went up to his room, where he wrote down all his facts, guesses, and questions concerning Brett and Oberwald. Then he sat staring at his notes for a long time, trying to reconstruct the probable sequence of events. As he sipped his third cup of black coffee from the room's do-it-yourself stock, the chilling realization dawned of how the pieces fitted into place.

Sometime in the comparatively recent past, somebody connected with Brett's work, either at Spirac or Livermore, had stumbled on something amiss, which had led to the FBI's becoming involved to investigate a possible espionage connection. From what Gilman had said, it didn't seem that the FBI had so far uncovered anything implicating Oberwald, too; however, that could have changed by the time they amassed sufficient evidence to confront Brett directly. But before they had been able to take the investigation to that point, Brett had had an accident. And just for good measure, in case she knew too much about Brett's recruitment and who was behind it, they had tried to eliminate Stephanie, too. Brett's accident and the attempt to kill Stephanie hadn't been simply to protect the investment when Brett tried to get out. It had been to prevent the exposure of Oberwald's collaboration with the Soviets. Mel blanched at the realization of the enormity of what they had taken on. It would have been a formidable enough task for a national intelligence agency. But there could be no backing out now. He and his colleagues would have to pursue it as best they could.

The place to begin, as Mel saw it, was where it had begun with Brett himself: Oberwald's initial recruitment of him. He didn't think that something like that would have begun only after Brett and Stephanie's move to California. It was more likely that the organization which Oberwald represented had been aware of Brett's potential usefulness ever since his days at university. If so, what would have singled Brett out to them? Mel wondered. He doubted if it could have been simply Brett's potential for doing classified work later, for the same could have been said for any other gifted programmer, too. Probably it had more to do with things like motivations and ideological convictions—things that would incline him to be cooperative. With people of Oberwald's caliber involved, injecting him into a suitable area of the defense program for the investment to pay off would be something that could be engineered later. . . . And that was where it all suddenly started to make more sense. For Brett's almost manic fear of national policy being dictated by the ultraright had been hardly a secret around the campus; and such incidents as throwing Rudshaw down the library stairs would mark him as a person who didn't shrink from drastic action when he thought the occasion warranted it. Thus, the ingredients were there for him to have been spotted early on as not only having the right talents, but also as possessing a lever that would make him potentially manipulable.

Who, then, had done the spotting? It seemed improbable that Oberwald had just happened to meet and talk with Brett by chance when Oberwald visited Pensacola—the occasion that Stephanie had described, when Brett came home feeling flattered and excited. The encounter had to have been set up, which implied that somebody who had been around at that time was an information conduit (though not necessarily to Oberwald in person). It could have been a member of the Socratic society, where Brett liked to go and argue, who had hosted Oberwald to lunch on the day after his address to the Chamber of Commerce; or somebody in the computer department; or one of the antifundamentalists that Brett had mixed with. Or it could have been somebody else entirely. But whatever the answer, the time and place to begin looking was not here, but among the events that had taken place four years previously at the University of West Florida, in the year after Mel had moved to North Carolina.

He could be doing more with the rest of the day than sitting here in a hotel, he decided. And the whole of tomorrow was available. He checked his watch, then called Continental Airlines. There was a late flight leaving in a little over an hour and arriving at midnight, which would just give him time to make a few phone calls to set up a schedule for tomorrow and make it to the airport. He booked a ticket, spent the next thirty minutes finalizing his arrangements, and then called Stephanie at his flat in Boston to see how she was doing and let her know his change of plans. Then he called the hotel desk to summon him a cab, packed his things, and settled his bill on the way out. An hour later, he was gazing down at the receding view of Denver from a window seat of an aging Boeing 757 bound for Pensacola.

CHAPTER 16

Eva lived on her own near the center of the city on Palafox Avenue, the main north-south thoroughfare. Her apartment consisted of a suite of rooms above a coffee-shop restaurant called The Viennese, which had a small dance floor and bar in the basement. She had her own outside door, under an archway at the top of a flight of stairs at the rear. Another door next to it opened through to a flight of inside stairs leading down to the restaurant. Although, when Mel first met her, Stephanie had talked about moving in with her sister, nothing seemed any closer to happening in that direction, and Mel had formed the impression that Eva was gently but firmly steering Stephanie off the idea. When Eva showed him into the place, he began to see why.

He had come to think of Eva as a very "feminine" kind of female, who dressed tastefully and matched colors that were vivacious without being showy, and who never failed to keep herself tidy and personable. He had half expected her to have created what he considered a "feminine" habitat, probably with lots of plants and wickerwork, glassware and china, and soft, silky things draped over fluffy furniture. But what he found was more a mixture of office, mail room, studio, and library, with vague suggestions of a place that somebody might actually live in barely managing to make themselves noticeable here and there.

There were two rooms facing down over the street, in addition to a bedroom and a bathroom. The smaller of the front rooms had a skylight and was dedicated to Eva's work. It contained a drawing board that hinged down into a worktable, a copying machine, a corner with a table and sink that seemed fitted out as a photography lab, and two four-drawer file cabinets. The larger room fared a little better in that it did have a long couch by one wall—albeit stacked with books and papers except for space for one person to sit—a comfortable looking leather recliner, and a low wooden coffee table with a computer on one end, surrounded by manuals. There was a kitchen area at one end. But most of what was visible—piled on tables and displayed on the walls—was connected with the two passions that dominated Eva's life—her political work: posters, pamphlets, bulging files, labeled wads of newspaper clippings; and her studies: books on history, books on philosophy, books on political theory, books on economics, heaps of references and notes.

But then Mel began warming to it all as he looked around. It was as uniquely *her* as everything else she did. He had walked, he realized, inside Eva's head as near as it was possible to do. Here she would be alone when she chose, with her thoughts, her mood, her mind, and her work. There was no place for a chattering younger sister.

They had stopped for the pizza on the way. Eva put it in the oven to reheat, filled a pot of water for coffee, and then cleared away some space around the terminal. Mel took the things he had brought with him out of his bag, and settled down to begin work. Eva brought the pizza and coffee over on a tray, moved the box of brochures off the footrest of the recliner, and sat down. She watched as he worked in silence, using the keyboard deftly, pausing to examine a response or check a section in one of the manuals, then tapping in another string of code.

"I like watching people who know what they're doing," she said after a while.

"It's my subject. It'd be kind of embarrassing if I didn't," Mel replied. In fact the system was almost identical to one he'd looked at a few months previously. This was going to be a piece of cake. "What does Dave Fenner do?" he asked, trying to sound more nonchalant than he felt. Dave had gone back to Washington a couple of days after Mel's first visit to the Brodsteins' with Brett and Stephanie, but that hadn't prevented Mel from wondering how things stood.

"He's a purchasing consultant," Eva said.

"What does that involve, out of curiosity?"

"I don't really know."

"Oh. . . ." He was never going to find out if he didn't go for it now, he told himself. "So, how is it with you and him? I mean . . ." Despite himself, his mind gummed up and left him hanging.

To one side of him, Eva smiled and got him off the hook. "I'm my own person," she said. "Nobody owns me."

"Yes, that's how I think people ought to be, too. . . ." Anxious not to make it sound as important to him as it was, he searched for another subject to move the conversation along. "You remember what you were saying when we were in the cafeteria with Sadie last week—about Apollo and Big-Government social programs, and people trying to apply methods that work in one area to other areas where they don't?"

"What about it?" Eva asked.

"I've been thinking about it. It was really a case of history repeating itself wasn't it?"

Eva looked intrigued. "How do you mean?"

Mel spoke as he continued working at the keyboard. "The Renaissance that ended the Dark Ages in Europe. In what seemed like no time, the new method of science brought understanding of subjects that had been dominated by superstition and ignorance for a thousand years."

"Religious tyranny couldn't stand against the printing press," Eva agreed. "So?"

"A lot of people thought that the human race had found the solution to all its problems. It was like you said with Big-Government spending: poverty, oppression, injustice, inequality—all mankind's social problems—would be solved by the same method that had proved so successful elsewhere. If science could unify astronomy with gravity, and explain things like heat, matter, motion, and all that kind of stuff, then science could accomplish anything. What we needed was the scientifically planned society."

"Oh, but it was with the best of intentions," Eva said, with just the right touch of irony in her voice. "We must all be prepared to sacrifice ourselves for the greater common good."

Her tone was mildly mocking, not at him, he realized, but because she agreed with him all the way. Mel had never before had the feeling of being able to *communicate* with anyone so instantly. "But that's exactly what destroys everyone's freedom," he said. "Because people who have a choice will never all agree with any one person's idea of what's best for them, and the only way you'll ever get them to go along is by force. The institutions of a free society become obstacles to the plan and get swept aside to be replaced by coercion. And once you've made that start, the end of the line is the secret police, the Gestapo, the Gulag, and the concentration camp. Science may be great for explaining the physical universe and building machines that work, but it's not the way to try and run a society—you end up turning that into a machine, too. Yet people keep on trying because it works so well in its own field. As you said about Apollo, it's difficult to argue with success." He glanced at Eva. "Isn't that right?"

"Yes . . ." she said. There was a fascinated light in her eyes as she watched him. "It's *so* right. . . . You think more than most people do."

Mel shrugged, enjoying the compliment. "I try." He nodded at the screen. "Anyhow, I figure we may have cracked it. Let's give it a try." He entered a command. At once an instruction menu appeared on the screen. "There," he pronounced. "You're into the system executive. You can follow its directory from there. All you have to do now is define your own linking structure." He sat back and looked at Eva challengingly.

"Great," she said. "You're a genius."

Mel sent her a look of exaggerated surprise and innocence. "What did you expect?"

"You never know. . . ." Eva spoke softly, with a curious edge to her voice, her eyes regarding him unwaveringly. Then, before he knew what to make of it, she unfolded herself from the recliner and went over to the cooking area. She had on a light blue dress that buttoned down the front and clung to her figure as she moved. She had kicked off her shoes, and the sight of her bare, tanned legs going up into the skirt of the dress excited him. "How about another coffee?" she said over her shoulder.

"Sure, why not?" Even though she was only a few feet away, he missed the closeness that he'd been conscious of for the last hour. He looked around and saw the plates and mugs from earlier still on the coffee table. "Here, I'll bring these." He stacked everything else on the Styrofoam container that the pizza had come in, and walked around the counter close up behind her. The question had been building up inside him all evening, and now his chest was thumping suddenly with the realization that one way or another he would have to resolve it in the next few seconds. Eva turned, still with that same befuddling mixture in her eyes of interest and curiosity. They were only inches apart, close to each other to a point that couldn't be ignored. Move or back off; this was the moment. Her eyes were scanning his face impishly, reading him,

challenging him to dare it. And at the same time there was a
sparkle in them, a hope that he would. For another fraction of
a second he agonized.

And then Eva moved her face forward and brushed her lips
lightly on his. It was hardly a kiss, but it carried just the
amount of reassurance he needed. "Society's a bitch, isn't it?"
she whispered. "It gives men such a hard time."

Then he kissed her, just a peck, but with no mistake about
it. She did the same back, and smiled. His slid his arms under
hers and hugged the body he'd fantasized and dreamed about,
then kissed her chin, her cheeks, her forehead, her eyebrows,
her nose. And then their mouths found each other again,
lingeringly this time, tongues feeling tongues and teeth. She
tasted fresh and clean. She was breathing heavily, her breasts
heaving against his chest. He slid his hands down her back and
over her rear, pulling the middles of their bodies together, and
felt her thrusting back at him wantonly. Then Eva pushed him
away slightly and slipped through between him and the
counter. For one panicking moment he thought she was
stopping it there before things went further. But without
saying a word she took his hand and led him into the bedroom,
which opened off the back of the large lounge. He closed the
door behind him, and when she turned to face him, he saw
that she had already unbuttoned her dress. He watched,
fascinated as she peeled the dress off her shoulders and let it
fall onto a chair. Then, slowly, keeping her eyes on his face,
she reached behind and took off her bra, slid the rest of her
underwear down her legs and stepped out. She was as perfect
as he had imagined, he saw as she straightened up.

"Wow!" he murmured approvingly, but still not quite believing it.

"Pleased? You said you wanted to seduce me."

"What? . . . But I never said anything . . ."

Eva moved forward, silenced him with a kiss, and began
undoing his shirt. "Mel, you've been saying it ever since that
first night at the Brodsteins'. And you've been seducing me
with your mind all evening."

And the bedroom, he noticed for the first time, was
different. It was soft and warm and . . . *feminine*.

Exactly the way it should have been. . . .

CHAPTER 17

After renting a car at Pensacola airport, Mel made a detour on his way to the hotel, which took him along Palafox again. He couldn't pretend that it was a sudden impulse. He had made the decision quite deliberately during the flight from Denver, with a mixture of nostalgic anticipation and curiosity to discover his own reaction. When he came to the block where she had lived, he eased over to the inside lane and slowed to a crawl—it was after midnight and the traffic was sparse. The Viennese restaurant was still there, lit up and doing business, with the usual mix of late-night coffee drinkers and arguing intellectuals huddled around the tables behind the plants in the front window. Prominently displayed in the door and visible in the light from a lamp across the street was a poster showing the Constitutional tortoise. Written underneath in large letters, presumably added since the election, were the words, GO WINNER. NOW THE 28TH!

And the apartment above was still there, too, just as it had been. Mel drew in to the curb and sat for a while staring up at the windows, his mind engulfed with memories, some happy, some tender, some painful. There were pleated orange drapes across the window of the large lounge, lit from behind by a lamp that gave a warm and inviting look to the whole place. He was glad that it still seemed to be well kept and taken care of. The thought crossed his mind of going into the restaurant for coffee, but he decided against it. He had just passed by out of a sense that it seemed proper to do so—as a gesture of respect to something that once had been; it hadn't been to drown himself in a flood of emotion. And besides, he didn't want to meet any familiar faces from the past. Somehow that would have been an intrusion into the privacy of a moment that belonged only to him and to a memory.

He looked up again one last time, and noticed the flowers along the bottom of the window, to his mind looking forlorn in front of the orange drapes. . . . Flowers for Eva. A lump formed in his throat. He swallowed, brushed the corner of his eye, put the car into drive, and pulled out into the traffic lane to head for his hotel.

His first call from Denver the previous day had been an attempt to solicit Paul Brodstein's help in approaching the university. But the call had been redirected to the number of a friend of the Brodsteins, who informed Mel that they were away on one of their travels again, this time to the Middle East—he believed, to Lebanon. So, Mel had contacted the university directly, using his ploy of representing a Boston law firm again, and talked to the deputy registrar, a Mrs. Betty Crouch. He explained that he was working on a case involving patent rights for a certain type of computer software. There were claims that part of the design work had been the subject of student projects at the university several years ago, which placed it in the public domain, and Mel was anxious to contact some of the people who had been involved at that time. The information could be subpoenaed, of course, but it would be so much more convenient if he could obtain it informally. His story had been accepted without question, and the visit went without any hitches. He was even assigned a clerk to help him make copies of the records that he needed.

From there he went to the Pensacola Chamber of Commerce, which had offices in an attractive Spanish-style villa near the waterfront, this time as an old friend and former student of Professor Paul Brodstein, whom he knew was well known to the Chamber through his work with the Constitutional party. He was doing some research on the guest speakers that the university had hosted over the years, he said, and in cases where the invitations had been handled jointly with the Chamber, he was anxious to make sure that the Chamber got appropriate credit and mention where due. The image of local education and local business working together would be good PR for both. Again, everything went smoothly, and he left feeling more than satisfied with his morning's work. There were times, he reflected, when all the hours he'd spent researching facts as a lawyer had its advantages.

On his way across town to return to his hotel, he passed Obee's. He was dismayed to see that the place was closed down, with weeds growing on the forecourt, the workshop doors padlocked, and the office windows boarded. Mel pulled off the highway and into Mac's, the convenience store next door.

"Hey, I remember you from a few years back. Well, say, talk 'bout a face from the past. . . . Mel, that was it!"

"Hi, Mac. How are things?"

"Oh, cain't grumble, y' know. Well, you can if you want to, but it won't do you a helluva lotta good, hee, hee. . . . How's 'bout yourself? Where'd you finally end up?"

"In Boston. I'm with a law firm now."

"Oh—made out okay, eh? Well, that's good, that's good. Ever'thing's much the same around here as it ever was. Cain't say as I'll live to see it much different, either."

"What happened to Obee's?"

"Oh, yes, exceptin' that, 'o course. Yep, that was a real shame, a real bad shame."

"What happened?"

"Well, the government was always givin' Sam a hard time, what with regulations and taxes and the like, and he got to complainin' and talkin' to the papers, and I guess he musta got hi'self wrote down somewhere as a marked man. One day he came back to the shop and found some inspector woman from the Occupational Safety or whatever they call 'em had been right in there while he was out and listed over twenty infringements that she said she'd found, and she left a paper tellin' him it was a two-hundred-dollar fine right there, no messin'."

"You're kidding!"

"Right as I'm standin' here. Well, he went to court and fought 'em—cost him upward of two thousand dollars. 'Said, 'How can I be guilty when I ain't had no trial?' And he won, too, 'cause it turned out that she didn't have more 'n a month 'o learnin' in some kinda class they run, and he'd been in the business all his life. . . . But it took the heart out o' him, y'know. Didn't wanna carry on no more. He said people shouldn't be havin' to fight their own government on top of ever'thin' else. That wasn't the way it was supposed to be. So he quit and moved down south someplace. I ain't too sure what he's doin' these days."

"Gee, that's too bad. I'm sorry to hear it."

"What ever happened to that other guy, the one you used to live with—big feller with the beard. D'you and him still stick together?"

"I've . . . been out of touch with him for a while."

"Oh? Well, he'll be doin' okay, I reckon. Remember me to him next time you see him."

"Sure. Look, it was good seeing you again, Mac. But I have to go."

"Nice of you to stop by. You take care, now, young feller."

Mel had a light lunch in the hotel coffee shop and then went upstairs to his room to spend the rest of the afternoon going through the information he had obtained while the details were still fresh in his mind. The records he'd taken from the university would, for the most part, no doubt, lead only to dead ends and trails petering away amid the vagaries of four years. The former members of the Socratic society, Brett's fellow postgraduates in computer science, and the others that Brett had associated with, were now scattered among dozens of geographic locations and occupations, some at home and some overseas; some—typically the ones who were faring more successfully—had remained visible and kept in touch with the university's alumni organization, while others had vanished without a trace. And without a doubt, practically everything the records showed them as doing now would turn out to be just what it seemed and far removed from Soviet espionage. But the whole haystack would have to be checked for the single needle that might be in there somewhere. Thoroughness and monotony went together in this kind of business.

Then he turned to the material from the Chamber of Commerce. The formal letter inviting Oberwald down to Pensacola as an after-dinner speaker had been sent by a Bernard Lehnard, who was the Chamber of Commerce secretary at the time. Mel set the sheets aside. He would have expected the official invitation to have been sent by the secretary, whoever initiated the process.

Next he turned to copies of correspondence that had been exchanged between the Chamber and the university's student union body during 1996, relating to visits and speaking engagements by public figures. Mel scanned over the next few pages quickly and put them aside. President of a local canning company . . . commander from the Naval Point air base across the bay . . . assistant secretary of state—Mel raised his eyebrows; somebody had been aiming high back then. . . . Then, when he turned to the next sheet, the name Hermann Oberwald caught his eye straight away. He separated the sheet out. There was more pertaining to it farther down the pile. The person who seemed to be handling it at the university's end at that time had been a Joan Flassner. She signed herself 'Coordinator of Current Affairs Liaison,' whatever that meant.

Mel stared at the name, then turned his head and frowned at the collection of sheets that he'd set to one side, relating to Oberwald's visit. There had been something about the tone of one of them that stuck in his mind as odd. He picked up the pile and shuffled through it until he found the letter, and read it again. It was one of the ones from Joan Flassner to the Chamber of Commerce, and began: "*Dear Mr. Lehnard, we are delighted to learn of Dr. Oberwald's acceptance of your invitation . . .*" Mel's eyebrows knitted as he read the opening once more. That was it. It didn't have the ring to it that it should have had if Flassner had simply heard of an intended visit by Oberwald and was writing to inquire about the possibility of including the university in his schedule as well—which was the way Mel had assumed it had happened. Rather, from the way the letter was worded, it sounded as if she had been aware already that the Chamber had invited him, *before* he'd accepted. And the rest of the text, too, he saw as he read on, supported the same conjecture.

Mel stared at the letter and rubbed his chin reflectively. Did it mean that somebody at the university had initiated the whole thing, not the Chamber at all? He rummaged down a few more sheets and picked out another letter that he'd noted, this time from Lehnard to Flassner, dated three days after Oberwald's visit. In the second paragraph he found: ". . . *we applaud your initiative and hope that this successful event will pave the way toward more cooperation between the City's student population and its business community.*" He read it again. "*Your* initiative"—the university's initiative. That seemed to clinch it. But like Lehnard at the Chamber of Commerce, Flassner would have been simply the club secretary doing the work. It was unlikely to have been she who originated the proposal to invite Oberwald. But she would have known who did, Mel thought to himself.

He laid the sheets out along the room's bureau-top and stared at them for a long time, then got up and paced over to the window to stand contemplating the Pensacola suburbs while he pondered on what to do next. At length, he came back and sat down at the bureau again, picked up the phone, and punched in the number of university's administration department.

"Registrar's office."

"Betty Crouch, please."

"One moment." Music started playing in his ear. Mel groaned beneath his breath. Surely universities weren't doing this now, too? He wondered how long it would be before the Samaritans started.

Then, cheerfully, "Hello. Betty Crouch speaking."

"Oh, hello, Mrs. Crouch. This is Melvin Shears again. We met this morning."

"Ah, yes. The young lawyer from Boston. What can we do for you?"

"Er, I've been going through some of the information you were kind enough to let me have. It's fine, thank you, but there is just one small thing I need in addition."

"I'd hate to think of you going all that way back without it. What is it?"

"A couple of the people I need to contact were members of the political debating group there—the Socratic society."

"Yes."

"The secretary of the Socratics four years ago was a person called Joan Flassner. It would help very much if I could talk to her. Do you happen to know how she can be contacted?"

"Is she still with the university, do you know, Mr. Shears?"

"I'm afraid I don't."

"Well, let me see what the computer says. Even if she's left, she might have stayed in touch." In the background at the other end, Mel could hear the clicking of a keyboard being operated. Then, "We don't have a number for her, but she is on our mailing list. The address we have is in Tallahassee. . . ."

The address turned out to be an old one when Mel called Information, but he was able to get the numbers of four Flassners listed in the Tallahassee area. He hit lucky on the third.

"Hello?"

"Hi. Is this Joan Flassner?"

"Yes."

"The Joan Flassner who was with the University of West Florida at Pensacola around four years ago?"

"Yes, I was. Who's this?"

"My name is George Bradey. Do you have a moment now?"

"It depends what you're selling."

"I'm not selling anything. I just need some information."

"What kind of information?"

"I'm writing a section of the history, and I wanted to ask you—"

"What history?"

"Oh, you mean the secretary hasn't contacted you yet and told you?"

"Secretary of what?"

"The UWF Socratic society. You were the society's secretary when you were here four years ago, right?"

"That's right. I was."

Mel went on to explain that he was writing a history of the society, sensing Flassner loosening up more as he talked. Finally he said, "I noticed that you had Dr. Herman Oberwald as a guest back then."

There was a pause. "Did we? . . . I don't really remember."

"It was back in 1996."

"Oh, maybe."

"It seemed a pretty prestigious name, compared to most of the others I've listed—you know, presidents of local canning companies, guys from the Navy base, and that kind of thing. I was hoping for some more background on how you got ahold of him."

"Oh yes, I remember now. He didn't actually come down to Pensacola to visit us. He came down to talk at the city Chamber of Commerce annual dinner. We just got him for lunch the next day, before he went back."

"I see. Joan, can you tell me how you found out about him from the Chamber of Commerce?" Mel tensed as he waited. This was the crucial part. The records didn't support the version that Flassner remembered.

The silence dragged. Then Flassner spoke again, sounding less certain of herself now. "Wait . . . I don't think I did find out from them . . . No, that was it. It was somebody at the university who came up with the idea. He thought he could get Oberwald down here, through some connections he had. It sounded like a good idea. I think it was us who suggested it to the C.o.C. They sent him the invitation, though."

"That sounds interesting—just the kind of material we'd like to develop. Can you tell me whose idea it was?"

"I'm thinking. . . . It was a tall guy with a ginger mustache, from the Business School. Unusual name, started with a Q. . . . Quinn? No, Quintz, that was it. Sheldon Quintz."

"I'd like to talk to him. Do you happen to know how I could get in touch?"

"Sorry. He could be anywhere."

"Not to worry. I'll see what we can dig up in the records here. Thanks a lot for being so helpful. Can I call you again if there are any more questions?"

"Sure. It was nice talking to you. . . . What did you say your—"

"Thanks again. 'Bye now." Mel hung up.

Mel exhaled a long breath and looked at the notes he had been making. So, Sheldon Quintz had suggested inviting Oberwald to Pensacola. And Quintz had indicated that he had the right contacts to get the invitation accepted. Could that have been the way of getting Oberwald and Brett together, after Quintz had spotted Brett as fitting a profile that he'd been told to watch for? It made him a possible candidate all right. And it had been arranged in such a way that the direct link from Quintz was obscured.

There was nothing further Mel could do that day. He called Winthram to pass on as much as he had learned, and then turned his attention to the one other duty that he had left to do before leaving. He tidied his papers away and locked them in his briefcase, then showered and changed into some fresh clothes after a day of subtropical humidity. At six-thirty he left, heading for Beach Haven by the Bayou Grande on the west side of town, across the water from the Naval Air Station. Pensacola was his home town, and he hadn't seen his family for a long time.

CHAPTER 18

"It'll be a disaster, you wait and see," Mel's father, Stan, said over the dinner table. "They were talking about it last night on TV. It's going to mean going back to a completely uncontrolled, unregulated, dog-eat-dog existence—runaway development everywhere, pollution, destruction of resources, exploitation of the common man. That's who's behind it—the big corporations."

"They have to be kept in line by somebody," John, Mel's younger brother by three years chimed in. Mel had never had a lot of time for him. He drifted in and out of jobs, got bored with them, and in between collected from the state. "That's what government's for. Take it away and you'd have anarchy."

"I don't know why you let yourself be duped into believing all that stuff," their father grumbled. "You used to have more sense."

Mel sawed off another piece of steak. The trouble was that Stan was an employee of the Department of the Interior, and he took any criticism of government as a personal attack. It was even worse when the criticism came from a member of the family, since that constituted a betrayal of his values and beliefs which, as head of the household, he had a right to expect would be shared by everyone else, too. Mel always tried to stay off politics because they inevitably ended up arguing, but it always happened, anyway.

"That's just what they say to scare people," Mel said. "They're playing on the stereotypes in people's heads. Look, free-market capitalism and big-business politics are not the same thing. They couldn't be more different, but people confuse them all the time. Big corporations don't *want* a free market, whatever else their PR people pretend. It disciplines them, and it benefits the public. They want political protection—economic privilege enforced by law. That's what we're against. The silly part about all this is that you and I are really on the same side."

His father shook his head in a way which said that couldn't be true, and he'd find a reason why when he'd thought about it. "I still say you can't just let them run wild to do anything they want," John insisted again. "They'd destroy everything for profits. I mean, what do they care about you and me? You have to have regulation."

"I'm not saying that you shouldn't regulate *anything*," Mel answered. "If regulations genuinely protect people, such as in setting safety standards, say, then that's fine—as long as it applies equally to everybody and every company, without discrimination. In fact that's a good example of what government should be doing. But the kind of thing I'm talking about would be phony environmental regulations, for instance, that are sold to the public as protection from some nonexistent risk, but whose real effect is to keep out the smaller companies with new ideas that might undercut prices. In other words they raise the costs of getting into the business—like a license. The big companies can afford the costs of complying, but the little guys can't put up the ante to get into the game. So the Constitutional position is simply that if a lawyer can show a court that the real effect of a regulation or piece of lobbying is to protect somebody's economic privilege, which always means that the rest of us end up paying for it, then it's struck off the books."

The other two chewed their food silently, each hearing only what had been in his mind to begin with. Mel wondered why he bothered trying to explain anything. Their mother, Delia, looked up as the lull continued. "Anyway, we're glad you were able to stop by, Mel. It's been a long time. What did you say you were in Pensacola for?"

"Oh, some research to do with a case I'm working on."

"I never thought you'd end up a lawyer. You seemed so settled in computers at one time."

"I heard a new lawyer joke the other day," John said, sniggering.

"We don't want to hear it," Delia told him.

"Now that the Constitutionals have done it, there are going to be some big changes," Mel said. "That's where a lot of the important work will be."

"What about the poor people? What about the ones who need help, the unemployed?" Stan demanded suddenly. "They say they're gonna stop all the payments, cut out the taxes, everything. . . . What happens to the people who can't function? You just going to let 'em starve, or what?"

"Dear, do we have to go into all that again?" Delia said.

"He doesn't have an answer."

Mel put down his fork. "Look, nobody's against compassion or caring for people who need it. But why does it have to follow that the only way to achieve it is through government coercion? I'm not against your goals. I'm just saying that your method isn't the right way to achieve them."

"Look at the size of the problem!" Stan exclaimed. "You're talking about millions of people out there. Who else is big enough to handle it?"

"But that's my whole point," Mel said. Most of the dependents on the rolls are caught in a trap that the system created.

I mean, how many of them really couldn't take care of themselves if they had the opportunity and the incentive?" He couldn't resist a glance in John's direction. "Most unemployment is created by bad legislation, either through pricing labor out of the market or restricting business, which is the natural employer of people. If you shrink the problem to the real, residual needs that are left, private charity could easily cover it. There was an explosion of schools, universities, hospitals, orphanages, parks, theaters, in the last century, all built with private money. People can be amazingly generous when *they* decide where their money will go, and who really deserves help and who's on the take."

"It still sounds to me as if you're trying to get rid of government altogether," Stan pronounced. "As John said, it adds up to anarchy."

"Not at all," Mel answered. "It has plenty to do in its proper role: defense, law enforcement, running the courts, and the minimum of legislation beyond that protects everyone's rights. Essentially it's a passive function."

"The little guy would get crushed," Stan declared.

"He would *not*. It's the little guy who'd benefit. Almost all unnecessary law exists to keep him in his place. Government doesn't create a dollar of wealth. It can only hand out what it takes, and ultimately it's the little guy who it gets taken from, every time."

"I think it's just more work for the lawyers," John said.

Their mother collected the plates together across the table. "Well, I don't know. It seems there are people around who are going to need some kind of help. There's a retired couple along the street who send over a third of their income to the TV ministries. They think it'll guarantee them a place in heaven."

"There's nothing you can do about a self-imposed stupidity tax," Mel said.

"Did you ever see any more of that girl you used to know—one of the two sisters?" Delia asked. "Eva, wasn't it?"

"They were still seeing each other after he switched to law school," Stan said.

"Were they? I don't remember."

"I haven't seen her for a while now," Mel said.

"And you haven't taken up with anybody new since?" his mother asked. Mel detected a trace of disappointment in her voice.

He grinned apologetically. "Not really. It's just been a lot of work and staying alive."

"I think she's dropping a hint that she wants grandchildren to visit," Stan murmured with a wink, evidently deciding to forget further differences—for the moment.

"You know the score," John said, looking at Mel. "Little painted people-box, someplace. Boredomsville, nine to five. All safe and secure and nice. . . ."

"I don't see what's so wrong with that," Delia said.

Mel sat back in his chair and thought about the things that had been happening in his life in the past few days. "Yes," he said, nodding distantly. "I suppose so, eventually. Life does seem to be heading in that direction."

The next morning he left Pensacola on a westbound flight to San Francisco. Stephanie would travel directly from Boston and meet him there. The next couple of days, he reflected, would perhaps be the toughest time for her of all.

CHAPTER 19

". . . into thy hands we commend the spirit of thy servant, Stephanie." The minister raised his eyes to glance at the black-clad mourners seated beneath the awning set up at the graveside to shade off the California sun. "Rise, please. Oh Lord, to whom . . ."

In the third row, behind the seats reserved for immediate family, Mel felt a lumpiness growing in his throat as the attendants began lowering the coffin with its covering of flowers. His feelings were intensified all the more by the inner knowledge that of all those present, he alone at that moment was thinking of Eva. It seemed a cold, unjust way for a life to end. He looked along the lines in front of him—solemn uncles, tearful aunts, cousins, the younger brother, Andrew, Eva's mother shaking visibly, and the father steadying her arm; all of those who had been closest . . . and they didn't even know. So he tried in his mind to compensate for all of them, remembering the person she had been: the intense student, talking eloquently outside on the deck of the Brodsteins' house against a background of ocean beach and blue sky, or craning forward over her desk at lectures; the fair-haired, long-legged shapeliness that had turned heads on campus lawns and city sidewalks; the thinker, to whom ideas were the greatest stimulant, with a maturity beyond her years, and who could accept anything with forbearance except culpable ignorance and the spectacle of an able mind going to waste. He thought about the apartment that had been the expression of her, and the first time he had gone there . . . about a spirit so consumed with the ideals of freedom and individualism that her life had become a personification of them.

There had been times when he thought of her as callous, in his hurt and rage, long ago now, when he had tried to possess what couldn't be possessed. And in the end he had left, either to forget or to come to terms with it. And in the time that had passed since, he thought he had grown to understand better what she had been. He had hoped to be able to tell her that one day. Now, he never would.

When the ceremony was over, he joined the other friends in offering final sympathies to the family.

"You do your best, you spend years of your life . . . and it ends like this. You never know, do you?" Her father blinked and dabbed hastily at his face with a handkerchief. Then he recovered his composure. "Anyhow, Mel, it was good of you to come. It's been a while. What are you up to these days?"

"Law—a small firm up in Boston."

"So, you gave up computers, eh? Oh, well . . . How's it going? Making out okay?"

"Sure. I'm okay."

"It was such a pity that Eva wasn't here," her mother said. "Have you seen her at all lately? You seemed very close once."

"No, I haven't seen her for a long time," Mel said.

"We've gotten used to being without Eva. She was so distant, wrapped up in her own way of life. This is like losing both of them."

"Are you coming along to the house?" their father asked. "Some of us will be getting together there. . . ."

Mel stared past the group and into the distance, at the gateway into the cemetery, flanked by banks of rhododendron and laurel. The figure who had been watching from outside was still there. She was wearing a long coat and hat, and held her collar high about her face despite the weather. As Mel looked, she turned and walked away.

"Thanks," he said. "But I have to be getting along."

"It was good of you to come," her father said again.

"The least I could do," Mel replied.

After a few more minutes of exchanging words with some of the others there that he had met before, he walked over to his car, parked with the others in a line nearby, pulled forward a short distance to turn at an intersection with another of the gravel roads crossing the cemetery, and drove out by the gate through which the cortege had entered.

He picked up Stephanie a quarter mile farther along the road. She was calm, but not talkative. He glanced at her from time to time as they drove, and at one time laid a hand on her arm reassuringly. She returned a quick smile that said she was okay. In his concern, he failed to notice the black Buick that had been parked a short distance from the cemetery gates, which was now following them.

They drove westward out of the San Mateo area, taking the Route 92 bridge across the Crystal Springs Reservoir—actually a flooded section of the San Andreas fault—and over the Coast Range to Half Moon Bay. There, they turned north on Highway 1, a scenic coastal road that hugged the cliffs in a spectacular succession of roller-coaster bends, dips, climbs, and curves, all the way from Santa Barbara, two hundred miles to the south. With the Pacific Ocean stretching away to the left, they passed small beaches and rocky coves, alternating with tiny fishing villages turned into resort attractions. Inland from the road the land rose to the ridges of the Coast Range, rounded and green at the top, with scattered clusters of houses on the lower slopes. There was a small airfield, and beyond it the radar dishes and communications antennae of the Pillar Point tracking station, where Brett had worked for a while. Stephanie grew tight-lipped and tense, and Mel drove on in moody silence, wondering why people insisted on inflicting things like this on themselves.

Farther on, the houses petered out, giving way to bleak hills of grass and exposed rock, and the road began winding and climbing. There was little traffic. Mel caught occasional glimpses of a black car a short distance behind, but paid little attention to it. The road became a twisting ledge scratched high along a series of precipitous drops, where whole mountainsides had slid away to form immense sweeps of bare rock plummeting sheer to the water. Between them, the road cut through the rocky spines that had been left jutting out into the sea. This was where Stephanie had wanted to come. Ahead of them, Mel spotted a turnout cut into the crumbly rock on the side of the road away from the edge. He pulled into it, stopped the car, and switched off the engine. He said nothing, but sat looking out through the windshield.

Stephanie got out and walked across the road to a shallow mound of rubble fringing the far side, above the drop. She climbed the mound, moved cautiously a couple of paces forward to the edge, and stood staring down. She had taken off her hat in the car, and her hair and coat flapped around her in the wind, causing her to draw her collar close about her face. Mel watched from the driver's seat of the car, giving her a few minutes to be alone with her own thoughts. Then he climbed out and went across to join her.

The wall of rock curved outward and away on both sides of them to form an immense bite. Far below, the sea crashed into it in angry surges of white foam streaked with green, boiling around rocks and debris fallen from above, before withdrawing sullenly and consolidating for the next onslaught. A few feet beneath them, the outlet of a metal drain conduit from beneath the roadway protruded from the face to empty into a gully that fell almost vertically for several hundred feet to the water's edge. And as Mel stood next to Stephanie, staring down at the scene, his mind went back once more over the years to happier times and another face that would come into his life no more. . . .

What a day this was turning out to be.

From the inquiries that Stephanie had made, Mel knew that Devil's Slide had a reputation as a black spot for accidents. A rescue team from the local sheriff's department had gone down on ropes to conduct the initial investigation and examination of the wreck. After that, a helicopter and boat search by the Coast Guard had failed to locate the body, which again was not uncommon—the victims were frequently thrown clear of the vehicle in Devil's Slide accidents and carried out to sea. The final report, filed by the California Highway Patrol, had classified it as a straightforward accident, with no suggestion of foul play.

"I don't believe it," Stephanie said finally, raising her voice above the wind. She continued staring down as she spoke, not taking her eyes off the waves breaking and swirling around the rocks below. "I've driven this road a hundred times with Brett. He wasn't a drunk or a Sunday tourist. He'd never have just gone off like that. I *know* he wouldn't have."

"It sure doesn't seem like the kind of—" Stephanie had turned her face as Mel started speaking, but she shifted her gaze as something beyond him caught her attention. Her eyes widened in sudden alarm.

"Mel!"

He turned abruptly. The Buick that had followed them from the cemetery was parked on the shoulder, partly visible around the last bend. Two men were coming toward them, one slightly ahead, heftily built and wearing a navy blazer, the other in a tan suit. Moving purposefully, the man in the blazer reached out toward Stephanie. Mel heard her scream in terror. Panicked by the thought of the drop only feet behind him, he succumbed to pure, animal, survival reflexes and was only half-aware of himself scooping a rock the size of a football up off the ground and heaving it at the other assailant's head.

"Jesus! . . ." The man in the tan suit raised his arms to ward off the rock. Mel hurled himself away from the edge and tore at the arm of the one grappling with Stephanie. The man held her with one arm and tried to push Mel off with the other. The three of them swayed, locked together, Stephanie still screaming and clawing with her nails, and for an instant it seemed that they would all pitch over into the abyss together. Then the man in the tan suit grabbed both Mel and the other's jackets and yanked them back down off the mound fringing the edge. He tripped as Mel fell onto him, and then Mel tumbled over too, but at the same time managed to grab the legs of the one who was holding Stephanie.

"Goddamit! . . ." the one in the blazer snarled, trying to beat Mel's arms away with his free hand.

Then Stephanie broke away. "The car!" Mel yelled at her desperately. "The keys are inside!" But the other man, the one in the tan suit, was already on his feet again and blocked her, seizing both her wrists in his hands. She kicked out and tried to shake herself free, but he was too strong. Then the one in the blazer regained his balance, and Mel felt himself hauled to his feet, spun around, and his arm clamped and a wrist locked across his throat in a hold that left him unable to move.

The man in the tan suit had moved his grip to Stephanie's arms and was shaking her . . . but more imploringly than roughly. "Eva! What the hell do you think you're doing? What's the matter with you? Don't you recognize us?"

"Not here," the other said from behind Mel's ear. "Anyone could come by. Get 'em in the car, for chrissakes."

Mel was propelled irresistibly across to the Buick, feeling as if his arm was on the verge of snapping at every step, and bundled into the backseat. The man in the blazer piled in alongside releasing Mel's arm, but keeping a cautioning grip on his shoulder—unnecessary, since now that Mel's adrenalin surge had run down, he was past trying any further heroics. The other man steered Stephanie over to their own car, and keeping a hold on her arm with one hand, took the keys from the ignition and locked it up before bringing her back to the Buick. He heaved her into the passenger seat, slammed the door, and walked quickly around to climb in the driver's side. "Back to the hotel?" he said, glancing back as they pulled away.

"Where else?" the man next to Mel replied.

The other thing that had subdued Mel was a feeling, now that he had calmed down a little, that the actions of these two men had not really been motivated by hostility. His first instinctive assumption had been that they were Soviets, but now he wasn't sure. For if they were, then from the few words he heard, the KGB was doing its recruiting a long way from home these days. And the man in the tan suit had called Stephanie "Eva."

CHAPTER 20

The Constitutional party's headquarters was situated on K Street in Washington, D.C., between Vermont Avenue and the greenery of Franklin Square. In a room on the fifth floor, Ronald Bassen, executive chief of the party's security apparatus, stood looking at a wallscreen that was showing George Slade, one of his operatives, speaking from California.

Bassen, a solidly built, dour-faced man with a fleshy complexion, droopy eyelids, and straight black hair combed flat, was a one-time policeman, turned private security agent, now filling out a little and getting jowly above the collar. Prior to his current retainer with the Constitutionals, he had worked as a private bodyguard, contracting to protect notables and public figures, from business executives and visiting political exiles to religious gurus and pop singers, against threats to their lives and safety, real and imagined. His way of making a living had bred the hard-headed kind of attitude that the best way for people to learn fast and develop a sense of responsibility was to experience the consequences of their own decisions and mistakes. Though previously politically indifferent, he had been drawn to the Constitutionals by a growing conviction that a large share of the problems that he saw every day were the products of misguided idealists bent on creating a society that was achieving exactly the opposite. That was okay by him if they were spending their own money. But that wasn't good enough for them; they were taking his. The Constitutional philosophy of denying anyone's right to spend someone else's money had suited his frame of disgruntlement admirably. He had provided his services to the party voluntarily to begin with, then professionally on a regular basis, and he now contracted exclusively to them full-time.

It had been a hectic year for everyone connected with the organization, and not least its security people. The surprise result of the New Hampshire primary in February— traditionally an early barometer of public mood and an indicator of the leading issues of the day—had signaled the nation's terminal weariness with more-of-the-same formulas that never delivered, and finally revealed the new Constitutional platform as the first thing to have truly excited people in years. Reacting belatedly to what they should have been alert to long before, the two traditional parties had then come up with a mixed bag of token concessions of their own, hastily cobbled together after the Constitutional model. But the people, recognizing an insult to their collective intelligence for once, rejected the imitation and registered their contempt and derision in the even greater Constitutional victories at the primary elections in Alabama, Florida, Georgia, Alaska, Illinois, and New York, held from March through July. Now that the final verdict was in, there would be the backlash of all the defeated and frustrated passions that had built up through the campaign. The Constitutional victory had particularly incensed the extremist factions of both political polar regions, and with all kinds of crazies on the loose from rabid Bible freaks avenging Jesus to demented Trotskyites out to save the Revolution, there was more than enough going on to keep Bassen and his people busy and worried. And now, on top of everything else, all he'd needed was to learn that they'd screwed up out on the West Coast.

"What else could we do?" Slade asked from the screen. He was calling from a suite in the San Francisco airport hotel where he and Larry Molineaux had checked in after arriving from Washington, following Newell's priority directive to find Eva. "We brought them both back here. They're in the next room with Larry. We need directions on how to play it from here."

Bassen passed a hand agitatedly across his brow. He had paced away from the screen and turned to look back at it from the window. "How are they acting?" he asked.

"Pretty calm, as a matter of fact. No screaming fits or threats to call the cops—yet, anyway. But the guy's starting to get demanding, and he seems to know what he's talking about."

"And they won't say who they are?"

"Why should they? He wants to know who we thought they were first, and who we are. What am I supposed to say? We've got an open-and-shut case here of assault, abduction, forcible detention . . ."

"You're telling *me*, George?"

At that moment the door opened and a slimly built man came in, wearing the pants and vest of a gray, glen-check suit, the vest unbuttoned, and shirt cuffs rolled back. It was Warren Landis, who ran the organization's intelligence arm. With his large brow and head balding prematurely in his late thirties, heavy-rimmed glasses, trimmed beard, and polka-dot bow tie, he fitted Bassen's image of the archetypal intellectual, always methodical, analytical, and impossible to panic because he never quite seemed to make the final connection with the real world in which people could get hurt. Landis folded his arms and rested his butt against the edge of a desk, facing the screen. "So what's this about getting the wrong girl?" He glanced at Bassen, then looked back at the image of Slade. "How could you? I thought that you and Larry both knew her personally."

"It's either that or she's got total amnesia," Slade said from the screen.

Landis's brow creased into furrows. "But wasn't she at the

sister's funeral? I thought someone said her old boyfriend picked her up. It doesn't make sense."

"She wasn't actually *at* the funeral," Bassen said.

"She watched it from outside the gate," Slade explained.

"Her own sister's?" Landis looked mystified. "This is getting stranger." He looked at Bassen. "Just to be sure I'm in the picture, run the whole thing by me again, would you, Ron? In brief."

Bassen moved a couple of paces back from the window. "It's been a week now since Eva took off. First, it's simply not like her to disappear for that long without letting anyone know, and with it being election time and this Kirkelmayer situation just coming to the boil, it's even stranger." He shrugged. "Maybe it had something to do with her sister committing suicide in Denver. . . . But anyhow, we'd drawn blanks everywhere else, and there was a chance that she'd show up for the funeral. So, we had George and Larry stake out the cemetery . . . ." Bassen waved a hand at the screen.. "You take it from there, George." He turned away to face the window.

Slade continued. "Naturally, we expect her to be out there with everyone else if she does show up, so that's where we look. But she's not there. There's a woman at the gate, all wrapped up and in a hat, but she just looks like somebody passing by who stopped to watch, so we don't pay any attention. However, we do recognize an old boyfriend of Eva's, Shears. Since there doesn't seem to be anything else going, we decide to tail him when he drives out, on the off-chance that he might give us some kind of lead. But a little way down the road, he picks up the woman who was outside the gate. They drive out to the ocean and stop to look at the view. Why? Who knows? But when the woman gets out of the car she's taken her hat off and let out her hair. It's Eva."

"You thought," Landis interjected.

Slade shook his head. "No, we were sure, Warren. She's right here in the next room with Larry and Shears at this moment, and we're still sure of it."

"Okay. So what happened then?"

George shrugged. "We get out and go over to talk to them, but as soon as they see us, they go crazy. She's yelling as if we're about to mug 'em or something, he grabs me when I try to stop her going over the edge. Everyone's yelling. So we bundled them in the car and brought them back here."

Landis shook his head reproachfully. "You mean you used

force? That's bad. I suppose you know that Shears is a lawyer?"

"Shit, that's all we needed," Bassen muttered over his shoulder from the window.

George's voice rose in protest and his hands flashed in front of his face on the screen. "We were on the edge of a mile-high drop straight into the ocean, for chrissakes! They guy was heaving half-ton rocks at Larry's head, and she was about to pull us all over the edge! Anyone could have come along. It wasn't exactly the time for a conference."

"Okay, okay. So what kind of a mood are they in now? Is there still trouble?"

"George says they're taking it pretty calmly, considering, which is something, I guess," Bassen answered, turning back from the window.

"They're not saying much, but I think they thought we were somebody else," Slade said.

"Hum." Landis stroked his chin. "Who did they think you were? Any idea?"

Slade shook his head. "They won't say anything until they've got a better idea who we are."

"And we don't want to admit that and invite a public circus over it," Bassen said. He came back to stand next to Landis in front of the screen. "I say we just wrap it up. Give 'em a grand each with apologies and no explanations, say it was all a big mistake, and get the hell out. What else is there to do?"

"I agree," Slade said simply.

Landis, however, was stroking the sides of his face thoughtfully with the fingers and thumb of his cupped hand and gazing through the wall at a point somewhere near Saint Louis. Bassen's uneasiness increased as he sensed the intelligence analyst's instincts rising in response to a challenge. "There's only one possibility it can . . ." Landis began. But then he seemed to change his mind. He uncrossed his legs and crossed them the other way around, without changing his leaning posture against the desk, and tried it from another angle. "This sister who killed herself and was buried this morning—did you know they were look-alikes? I read through the file before I came in."

"So that would—" Bassen started to say, then frowned. "No, that doesn't explain anything, does it?"

But Landis nodded, reading the part that Bassen had left unsaid. "It would if it was *Eva* who was buried this morning," he said soberly.

Bassen stared at him. "Eva? Dead?" A dazed look had come over his face. There was a pause while he struggled to absorb it. "What are you saying?" On the screen, Slade was craning forward incredulously, as if unsure that he had heard it right.

"It would start to make sense if the one you've got there in the hotel is the other one, Stephanie," Landis said. He reflected for a moment longer, then added, "And it might have something to do with why she didn't go into the cemetery. It was supposed to be *her* funeral."

Bassen's rugged, fleshy face contorted as he puzzled over the possible implications. "But . . . that would mean that her own family didn't know what was going on, either. How could that be? This is getting crazy."

"But this guy Shears knows what's going on, maybe . . . if he picked her up outside," Landis suggested. "See what I mean?"

"Sure, that's all very interesting, but what are we supposed to do right now?" Slade said. "We're liable for a criminal lawsuit already. I'm not about to tell them that Larry and I are official agents of the Constitutional party."

"Obviously we need to know what's going on," Landis said. "If we let them go now, we could lose the whole thing. My suggestion is that you take them out for the best dinner you can find and exercise some diplomacy. If we could find out what their attitude toward the Constitutionals is, it would help a lot. Try and get them talking about the election."

"But how long do you think we can keep them?" Bassen asked. "And what for? What, exactly, are you trying to achieve?"

Landis looked at him with a distant, thoughtful expression. "Look at it this way, Ron," he said. "It involves one of our people, who might be dead. If she is, then the whole business with Kirkelmayer will have to be scrapped. That's something that Henry Newell is very concerned about. Now, he's over there on the West Coast in Seattle at the moment. See my point? He might need to get involved in this personally. I don't want to let them vanish again before I've had a chance to talk to him."

Mel's first reaction to the two men's sudden appearance had been that they were from the KGB or otherwise connected with the Soviets, and that having failed to get rid of Stephanie the first time, they had somehow discovered their error, picked up her trail, and were seizing the opportunity that had presented itself at Devil's Slide to finish the job. He was now satisfied that such was not the case.

The question remained, What organization, then, were they from? It was obviously one that Eva had had some connection with; also, it employed people who did furtive things like watch people covertly, tail cars, and decline to reveal who they were. The first thing to suggest itself was that it had to be CIA, a branch of military intelligence, or some other national-security outfit. One convoluted possibility that crossed his mind was that if Eva had gotten herself mixed up in that kind of business, then maybe her death hadn't been a case of mistaken identity after all. Was it conceivable that the KGB, or whoever the opposition was, had *deliberately* rigged her assassination to look like a faked suicide that had been botched by a nonexistent someone else who was supposed to have some reason for killing Stephanie, as a means of covering their own tracks? He found himself getting a headache from trying to untangle the logic of the double-double deceptions which that would imply. Could things become that devious in the world that he was being drawn into?

However, the best way to find out more, he had decided, would be to say nothing. For it was clear that George and Larry—as they had been calling each other since the drive back from Devil's Slide to the Embassy Hotel—although now acting amiably enough, didn't have the authority to reveal even who they were, let alone what was happening. And if Mel and Stephanie were just as firm in not revealing anything to them—he had said that his name was John, and she had followed suit by giving hers as Mary—eventually they would have to bring in somebody higher up to break the deadlock. And from the amount of time George had spent on the phone in the next room, it seemed that was exactly what was happening. So, Mel was more than willing to wait it out in the hope of learning something. That was one of the reasons why they had come to California, after all.

If movies were anything to go by, this was a very strange kind of abduction, Mel reflected as he sat at a table on the veranda outside the suite, sipping a gin and tonic and watching the jets coming gracefully down on their approach runs from the south over San Francisco Bay. George and Larry had brought them back up to the suite after standing them an afternoon lunch in the hotel's buffet restaurant, evidently endeavoring to make life agreeable—and coax out any further information that they cared to divulge—until answers came back. It had also become clear to George and Larry that they in turn had their own motivations for not objecting to staying around, and an unspoken mutual understanding had established itself, along with a far more relaxed atmosphere.

"San Francisco Bay Blues," George's voice said from behind. Mel looked around as George came out onto the veranda and leaned with his elbows on the rail. Stephanie was inside with Larry, watching a movie on the TV. "Ever hear that song, John?"

"Can't honestly say I have."

"Old Jesse Fuller number—old-time blues singer. Black. Played a twelve-string guitar. Lived across the water there in Oakland."

"I wouldn't have thought that was your kind of music."

"Oh, I went through a phase of it way back, when I was a kid. Even had a guitar myself. Straight, six-string round-hole. Electric didn't go with the style. It seems a long time ago now."

George hadn't removed his jacket, Mel noticed, even though it was a warm day. "Out of curiosity, George, are you carrying a gun?" Mel asked.

"Sure. It's all licensed and legal—part of the trade."

"What's the 'trade'?"

"Come on, John. We've been through that."

"Can I see it?"

"Why?"

Mel shrugged. "As I said, just curious."

George pulled across one of the chairs on the far side of the table at which Mel was sitting, sat down on it, and produced an automatic from an underarm holster. Without getting too close, he held it out for Mel to see. "Know anything about guns?" he asked.

Mel shook his head. "Not a thing. I've never even fired one."

"Best to stick to proven, dependable designs," George said. "This is a point three-two *ACP* Walther *PP*, double action. It's concealable, reasonably accurate as handguns go, with a four-inch barrel, and reliable."

"That's a fairly light caliber, isn't it?"

"I use copper-jacketed lead rounds, which give you a fair wallop and stopping power at close range. You don't want the lethality of heavier calibers and all the legal complications that can get you into. If you have to use it, you'd rather have the guy live to confess and account for himself."

"A point," Mel agreed. "I'd never thought of it that way." It also said to him that he was dealing with an organization that had respect for the law and concern for staying on the right side of it. That was reassuring, anyway.

"That's why most of the European police forces prefer lighter rounds, too," George said.

"So, are you in the people-protecting business?"

George returned the gun to its holster and sighed in a what-the-hell kind of way. "You could say that's part of it."

"Karate and stunt-man driving too?"

George snorted. "You can forget that kind of stuff. Ninety-nine percent of the time, all you're concerned with is getting your principal from one place to another alive and in one piece, despite the efforts of the idiots behind the wheel you get anywhere anytime—drunks, housewives spaced out on Valium, pissed-off rednecks, students loose in daddy's Porsche, you name it. . . ."

"And there are more lunatics out there right now," Mel remarked. "The election's had them pouring out of the woodwork."

"Do you work in politics, then?"

"Come on, George. We've been through all that."

"Hm." George looked away and watched a Pan Am wide-body and a Japanese Airlines SST coming in almost neck and neck toward the airport's parallel main runways. "What do you think of the Constitutionals, then?" he asked, sounding casual.

Mel couldn't see any reason not to be frank. The situation was the reverse of that which applied at cocktail parties, where jobs and personal affairs were the stock of conversation, and politics was taboo. "Oh, I'm a tortoise," he answered.

"What about all the things they're saying?" George waved toward the doorway from the suite, through which they could hear the sound of the movie that Stephanie and Larry were watching inside. His gesture meant the TV, the media, and public-opinion-molding machinery in general. "Won't the little people go to the wall?"

Mel shook his head. "Not if the taxes go as well. Let the economy grow and create jobs, and you won't need the handouts."

"Wouldn't we lose all our friends overseas if they wrapped up the foreign-aid programs?"

"What friends? You get about the same respect from running international welfare schemes as we got from domestic ones. It isn't appreciated as a favor. It gets to be demanded as a right. If you want real friends, all you have to do is let them trade on equal terms, and keep their self-respect."

"But if there's no restrictions on free trade, wouldn't that mean drugs would be legal?"

George seemed to be interested in sounding out Mel's position generally, for some reason. Mel was curious, too. George was a lot better informed on such things than somebody conforming to Mel's picture of a gun-toting strong-arm man ought to have been. "What of it?" Mel replied.

"Wouldn't you be guaranteeing a crime epidemic?"

"I'm not sure you would. Why?"

"To pay for all the habits."

"If the price came down, there'd be less to pay for. Besides, if that's really your objection, why not ban pretty women, fast cars, and exotic lifestyles while you're at it? Banks get robbed to pay for those, too."

"What about all those demented crazies you'd have?"

"Most drugs don't work that way. The stereotypes of conventional wisdom don't have much to do with reality. It all gets blown out of proportion for political reasons: scare the public, and then get elected for touting a program to deal with the problem. Back in the seventies, Rockefeller got the governorship of New York state largely on claims of drug-related crime that were exaggerated by factors of hundreds. You can still find those figures repeated in sources that are quoted as authoritative today. Nixon tried to create a personal police force for himself on the pretext of the drug menace. No . . . I think there are other problems to worry about that are a lot more serious."

"You don't think it matters if people's brains get scrambled?"

"It matters, but the point is it's their brains. They own them, I don't. It's not for me to tell them how they should use them."

George stared at him for a few seconds longer, then nodded abruptly and looked away. Mel got the feeling that the questions had been more than just curiosity. "That's interesting." George said. "I'll talk to you later." With that, he disappeared back into the suite.

Mel resumed contemplating the scenery, trying to make

something out of the conversation. A goon-for-hire with political awareness? No. Whatever else he might be, George was no goon. So, they were dealing with an organization that got involved in covert activities, and which employed not only professionals, but smart professionals. And it seemed to have a strong interest in the Constitutional party. That sounded like Eva, all right.

"More and more intriguing," Mel murmured to himself.

He spent a few minutes finishing his drink, than set the glass down on the table, stood up, and followed inside after George. The movie was still showing in the lounge, but Stephanie was alone. "Hi," she said as he came in.

"Where are the others?" Mel asked her.

"Through there." Stephanie nodded at the door to the outer room of the suite. "I think they're having a conference. What were you and George talking about out there? He seemed very earnest all of a sudden?"

"Politics, believe it or not."

"Did you find out anything interesting?"

"Maybe. I think that Eva might have been working for the outfit they're from. They lost track of her, and they thought you were her. Now they want us for something."

"What makes you say that?"

"Why else are we here? Why the lunch and the treatment? We don't know who they are ar anything about them. If it was all just a mistake that they wanted to forget, they'd have taken off long ago."

Stephanie raised her eyebrows and shook her head quickly a couple of times as if to clear it. "Any idea what?"

"No," Mel said. He looked across at the room's datanet extension terminal by the bed. The "busy" light was on, indicating that George and Larry were making another call from the main terminal in the outer room. "But I don't think it'll be very much longer before we find out."

The outcome was that George offered them rooms of their own at the Embassy, courtesy of the "firm," for them to stay overnight. He explained that "somebody from the top" would come to San Francisco to talk to them in person. However, he was in the middle of a pressing schedule and couldn't get there until morning.

"What if we don't want to stay?" Mel asked.

"Then, naturally you can go. We're not the police." George seemed anxious to keep the record clean. "But it would be in your interests to hear him out," he said. "Think of it as a business proposition."

They agreed to stay. Mel then pointed out that they had rooms of their own already booked at the Crowne Plaza, another in the complex of airport hotels, just a few blocks away. That was where their things and their clothes were. How would George and Larry feel about their going back there and coming back to the Embassy for breakfast? That would be fine. The atmosphere had changed a lot in the course of the afternoon.

George and Larry drove them back to Devil's Slide to collect their car, and they returned with the two vehicles to the hotel. Mel and Stephanie went to their own hotel to freshen up and change, and later all four of them went into San Francisco for dinner. By the end of the evening they were getting along like old friends. Now, however, the only subject that George and Larry refused steadfastly to discuss at all—was politics.

CHAPTER 21

Two hundred and fifty miles above the Earth's surface, the XDS–6 orbital defense platform swept southward on its precessing circumpolar orbit, which on this pass would carry it down over the western Pacific. It was the fourth in a series of military satellites to be equipped with full-scale experimental beam weapons to test the ballistic-missile space defense concept first promulgated in the early 1980s in what began as the Strategic Defense Initiative. The tests of microwave and laser devices operating over various frequency ranges that had been conducted with the three previous satellites had proved encouraging. (The first had been designated XDS–2, mainly to cause hostile intelligence agencies such as the KGB to lose some sleep fretting over the secrets of the hitherto unsuspected XDS–1. XDS–5 had been skipped for the same reason.) Now, XDS–6, in addition to carrying a scaled-up version of the laser system carried by XDS–3, also mounted a high-power, narrow-beam projector capable of pinpointing and destroying conventional aircraft in flight. Confidential CIA reports indicated that the Soviets had constructed at least two such systems in orbit within the previous eighteen months, and a third was believed to be imminent.

As the satellite came within range of a tracking station on Wake Island,' a team of military technicians and contractors' engineers prepared to commence the series of firing trials that had been scheduled to take place on that pass, code-named "Mustard." Voices called from around the control room as console indicators flashed and things started happening on readout screens.

"Ranging is good. Correct slew for point-five degrees negative."

"Point-five negative, Roger."

"Sampling on groups five through nineteen. All muxes are synched. Do we have computers?"

"Computers are running."

"How are we on the uplink?"

"Steady on twenty-oh-two-five."

"Echo Nancy on-line and holding."

"Attitude correction effected. We've commenced response testing, Phase One."

"How's it looking?" the voice of the general supervising the tests inquired over the link to Ops Command in Hawaii.

"It's looking good. Ground check on pilot laser reads clear."

"Keep us posted."

"Wilco."

The satellite communicated with ground control via a very tight beam, which was one among a variety of measures taken to render it unresponsive to, and therefore insensitive to interference from, any other signals originating from outside a narrow radius. Its target-tracking radar, however, necessarily scanned a far wider area. As the first of the unmanned target aircraft being used in the trials entered the designated firing zone, a burst of electromagnetic energy was beamed at it from an unimposing, battered-looking fishing boat of Singapore registration, which just happened to be in the vicinity at the time. The reflections from the aircraft's skin bounced off in all directions and some found their way to the sensitive detectors aboard the XDS–6 satellite. The radiation was not at one of the satellite's command-channel frequencies, which were secured by hardware protection devices and software encryption, but at the frequency of its targeting radar. Normally, information coming in through those circuits would be treated as pure data, incapable of affecting the operation of the programs in the system's on-board computers. In this instance, however, a routine that shouldn't have been there responded to the pattern carried by the reflected signal, and fired the craft's hydrazine thrusters to redirect its antennae in the wrong direction.

"Hey, what's going on? We're losing it."

"The beam's gone. We've lost it! We've lost the beam!"

SYS3 ABORT SYS5 ABORT SYS16 ABORT

AUTO OVERIDE EXECUTED—OUT OF LIMITS. REVERTED TO MANUAL

GROUP CHECK NEGATIVE

"Negative function on transponders. They're dead."

"Secondary loop has cut out. That's it. Nothing. Zilch. Now what?"

"What's happened?" the general's voice demanded from Ops Command.

"I'm not sure, sir. We've lost tracking. The beam seems to have shifted completely off, or it's shut down."

"What, on all bands? Standby too? It can't have. You're sure it's still up there?"

"Guam and Hawaii still have it on radar."

"Give me another check on . . ."

Mustard was hurriedly rescheduled to be tried again on the satellite's next pass. By the time XDS–6 came around again, contact had been reestablished. This time the trials went without a hitch. Nobody had any explanation to offer for the freak occurrence. All that could be done was to order a thorough analysis of all the data collected during the incident.

Dr. Hermann Oberwald turned away from the diagram that he had drawn on the wallboard in the study and faced the two men who had been listening to his explanation.

Of Austrian descent from parents who had fled from Europe during the thirties because of his mother's Jewish ancestry, he was a big man in his fifties, with thick black hair, parted conventionally and clipped unfashionably short at the back and above the ears, hollow cheeks, dark eyes, and broad shoulders that would have cut a better figure had it not been for his tendency to a slight stoop. He had studied nuclear physics at MIT and Princeton, worked at Los Alamos, Oak Ridge, and the Argonne Laboratories, and before assuming his current

Washington-based position of defense and energy adviser, had spent several years in Europe liaising with other member NATO nations on nuclear policies and technology.

He had a strongly conservative public image and toured the university lecture circuit extensively, receiving standing ovations on some campuses, while being burned in effigy on another. When accused of helping bring about global nuclear destruction by his contribution to nurturing the bomb, he replied simply, "What destruction? The world is still out there, if you look." His position, simply stated, was that having come from a background in which he had seen more war firsthand than most Americans, he detested war. The object of bigger and nastier bombs was precisely to put any thought of it out of the mind of a would-be aggressor. It worked, and that was what mattered.

This was not to deny that politically the world was in a mess, which in Oberwald's view was hardly surprising, given the feeble intellects that had ended up running most of it. He attributed this primarily to misguided notions of democracy that allowed the opinions of two morons to outweigh one mind of any worth. What had been happening in the West was the inevitable outcome of allowing the children of the family an equal say in running the household. There was a natural ordering of any social structure which was futile to try and idealize against. And the modern, industrial, technological world would be far better off under the benign direction of people able to plan rationally, who comprehended the organizational relationships and functional dynamics of complex systems—scientists like himself, for example.

"In summary, the demonstration proves that we can now override the fire-command system and deactivate the Western space-defense satellites at will," Jordan Vandelmayne said from a leather armchair by the window.

"Precisely as was intended," Oberwald confirmed.

The third man present in the room, sitting with one knee crossed over the other on an upright chair from where he had been listening, was squat and heavily built, with a balding head and wispy mustache. His name was Wilson Clines, and he was also a financier, closely connected to the Vandelmayne-Myer group. "Very well, so the satellites can be neutralized," he said. "What happens then?"

"That's the point at which the Soviet end of the operation

comes in," Oberwald replied. "Have you ever heard of an SA–37?"

Clines shook his head. "No."

"It's a supersonic air-to-ground cruise missile, with ideal performance characteristics for what has been proposed."

Cline's eyes widened. "Missile? Good God, what are you trying to do—start a war?"

"It won't come to that," Vandelmayne assured him. "But you know as well as I do what's at stake. We were promised that the Constitutionals would be wiped out at the ballot box, and they weren't. Now it's time to claim on our insurance. It won't do any good going just for the heads—it'll grow ten more for every one you lop off, like a Hydra. We have to destroy the whole organism. And there's one place at which, very soon, all of them who matter will be together at the same time. . . ."

CHAPTER 22

Mel and Stephanie arrived back at the Embassy Hotel the first thing next morning as agreed. George answered the phone when Mel called the suite from the lobby, and told them to come on up. They found two waiters from the hotel staff there, preparing a table for breakfast to be served in private. Larry had gone to the airport to collect whomever was coming to talk to them. Assuming that if George wanted them to know who it was he would have told them, they suppressed their curiosity and confined themselves to small talk until a call from downstairs announced that Larry and his party had arrived.

The half dozen or so aides who entered the suite first when George opened the door a couple of minutes later made no particular impression, apart from looking like what could have been clean-cut executives from any corporation or government department. But the figure who followed after them brought Mel and Stephanie to their feet in astonishment. With his broad frame, craggy but easy-natured features, and thick head of silver hair—early for his years—that had become the kind of nationwide symbol that political cartoonists love, he would have been recognized by anyone who hadn't been marooned on a desert island for the last year. Mel had seen him only once before, from a distance, when he had come to speak in Boston.

"Good morning," he said, in his familiar voice, firm and a shade gravelly, which enhanced the no-nonsense image that so many found inspiring. "Thank you both for staying to hear us. I'm sorry for the misunderstanding yesterday, but I think you'll find that what we have to say is sufficiently interesting to make up for it."

It was Henry Newell, president-elect of the United States, the next occupant of the Oval Office.

Newell was one of those men who possessed what is described as a "presence"—that intangible quality that sets apart "naturals": entrepreneurs of business, captains of ships, generals of armies, and leaders of popular movements. It was that kind of quality which is at work whenever a freely interacting group of people, whether it be the occupants of a barrack room, the staff of an office, the guests at a cocktail party, or a bunch of guys out on the town, spontaneously acknowledge one individual as the final decision maker, arbiter, and collective conscience for all. Some just have it and others haven't, and nobody really knows what it is, though everyone recognizes it.

In Newell's case, certainly, it had nothing to do with brute-force assertiveness; rather—and more appropriate to a democratic setting—it was an ability to elicit the willing acceptance of all concerned. Indeed, one of the first things to strike Mel in his first opportunity to observe at close hand the man who had been figuring so prominently in the public eye, was Newell's disarming soft-spokenness. He didn't belabor his listeners, so much as persuade them. His manner credited them with a capacity of their own to reason, to choose, to agree or disagree, and they responded. His style was akin to that of the skillful orator who, instead of thundering out the concluding words as he reaches his crescendo, drops his voice suddenly, compelling a moment of focused attention at the crucial point, lest it be missed. Mel felt as if he had gone back two centuries in time. It was like being privy to the thoughts of one of the minds that had founded the nation.

Since the mistake had been theirs, Newell and his people accepted the onus of opening after they all sat down to eat. Much of the talking here was by Warren Landis, a vigorous,

bearded, and bespectacled man with a high brow and balding
dome, who had apparently flown overnight from Washington
to attend. Mel thought that his face seemed vaguely familiar,
possibly from the background groups seen with Newell during
coverage of the election and the campaign that had preceded
it. Mel was astounded to learn that Landis knew of him and his
past relationship with Eva, and that the two agents staking out
the cemetery had recognized him as a possible lead back to
her. Following the confusion at Devil's Slide, Landis had also
deduced that the girl found dead in Denver—whom they also
knew about—was not Stephanie, but Eva. This, Mel and
Stephanie were able to confirm.

Mel and Stephanie, in their turn, met frankness with
frankness. They explained about Brett's Soviet connection, the
suspicious circumstances of his death, and their conclusion
that Eva had been killed in mistake for Stephanie. Newell
expressed sympathy for Stephanie's loss and understood her
present consternation. He was confused, however, about her
reasons for having acted in the way she had.

"And you haven't been in touch with your company at all
since you left Denver?" he asked from one end of the table,
laden with breakfast plates and dishes. The others were still
seated where they had eaten, apart from two men that Mel
assumed were security guards, one of whom had positioned
himself in an armchair between the table and the door, and the
other at a side table by the window.

"No," Stephanie answered.

"What are your intentions?"

"I'm not really sure," Stephanie replied. "Officially I'm
dead. If there are people out there who went to those lengths,
they probably wouldn't hesitate to try again. So we figured it
would be best for me to stay dead for the time being . . .
until we come up with some ideas of what to do."

"I would have thought that the obvious thing would be to go
to the authorities," Newell said. "Why haven't you done that?"

Stephanie and Mel glanced at each other guardedly in the
same automatic reaction. But then each read the same on the
other's face: If it wasn't safe to be straight with the next
president of the country, then everything was as good as over,
anyway. Mel looked back at Newell and took a long breath.
"We're not sure which authorities we can trust. If what we
suspect is correct, it was a prominent public figure, with close

government connections, who was responsible for recruiting Brett."

Newell pursed his lips for a moment. "Who?" he asked.

There could be no backing down now that they had gone this far. Mel raised his eyebrows at Stephanie and then looked back at Newell. "Dr. Hermann Oberwald," he said.

There were some shufflings and exchangings of looks among the others at the table. Mel tried to read whether the information had come as a surprise to them, but their expressions were impenetrable. Newell cast an eye around to invite comment. "Can you substantiate this?" Landis asked Mel.

"It's a complicated story," Mel warned. "It could take a while."

"Perhaps you could go through it with them in detail later, Warren," Newell suggested.

"Yes, I'd like to," Landis said, sounding intrigued. "I'd like to very much."

One of the aides refilled everyone's coffee cups. Then Stephanie said, "We've told you as much as we can about what we think happened to my sister, and why. They mistook her for me. You mistook me for her. What we don't know is why you were looking for her."

There was a short silence. "We appreciate that it could be none of our business," Mel said. "But then if that were the case, we'd hardly all be sitting here right now."

Newell stared at them for what began to seem like a long time. When at last he spoke, he seemed for a while to have gone off on a completely new tangent. "This nation is about to enter the twenty-first century filled with optimism and expectations of changes for the better. And there's nothing wrong with that. We intend that those expectations will—perhaps after some reversals and disappointments, and a few lessons of the kind that can only be learned by mistakes—be met. But the issues that concern most people are relatively superficial. Of course the majority of people like the idea of lower taxes, increased opportunity, and less official meddling in their lives. Those things follow from the principles that we built our platform upon; in themselves, however, they are not the essence of our goals, but consequences of them. They form the icing that any democratic cake has to have to be accepted—the things we had to stress to gain the necessary popular appeal." He held up a hand as if anticipating an objection. "Yes, we will keep our promises. But they on their own do not represent what the Constitutional movement is really all about.

"The conventional left-right political spectrum that people think in terms of is, in most meaningful senses, a myth. After all, if virtually every facet of the individual's life is controlled by government; if he can make his living only with the permission of others, and keep only so much of what he has made as they allow him; if he can be compelled to work for causes that don't concern him; and if his private life and even his thoughts are subject to somebody else's approval—then what does it matter to him if you call the system communism or fascism, Stalinism or Hitlerism, or Caesarism, Pharaohism, Maoism, or anything else you like? As far as the individual is concerned, the differences are rather academic. The only spectrum, that really means anything, I would submit, is one that extends from 'Total Government' at one end to 'No Government' at the other—in other words, complete anarchy, which is the only system that kills more human beings than totalitarianism does.'

Newell paused and looked questioningly from Mel to Stephanie. He evidently wanted this to be a two-way exchange. "And you would place the Constitutional party where, on that spectrum?" Mel responded. He already knew the answer, but it would be interesting to hear it from Newell himself.

"Toward the No Government side of center, but well short of the extreme. In other words, a constitutional system with limited powers, those powers being essentially passive and concerned with the defense of the individual's rights against those who would deny them by force. But you know all that already, of course. I also happen to be informed of your activities on behalf of our party, Mr. Shears." Mel nodded.

"So how does this connect with my sister's death, and involve Mel and myself?" Stephanie asked from beside him.

"My point is that whatever label it attaches to itself in the popular mind, our opposition is political extremism," Newell replied. "And regardless of the cause or slogans that it masquerades behind, the aim of extremism is invariably to deliver to a few the power, one way or another, to loot the pockets of the population at large. It achieves it by controlling society's economic assets. The Left seizes them outright in the name of the collective good; the Right awards itself monopoly privileges to eliminate competition. Although they may be rivals in squabbling over the spoils, the relationship is like that of parasites competing in the body of the same host. The real enemy of both of them is the same: the free and independent individual, who can't be compelled to serve anyone."

"In other words, the Constitutional position is the enemy of both of them," Mel said.

"Quite. We are a common threat to all such interests. We may have won an election, but we still have enemies that command enormous power, who can be expected to subordinate their superficial differences to the common objective of seeking our destruction by all of the not inconsiderable means at their disposal. There's an old Arab proverb that says, 'My enemy's enemy is my friend.'"

Mel frowned as he tried to see where this was leading. "What are you saying?" he asked. "That what the public sees is a facade? Behind it there's some kind of collusion?"

"Oh, I wouldn't say it's as cut and dried as that," Newell answered. "But one thing we can be sure of is that the prospect of the legislation we intend carrying through will unleash ferocious passions. There are people who would go to any lengths to stop it. Therefore, you will appreciate that it is vital not only to our interests, but to our very survival, to try to know who these people are, and their plans."

"You mean that political parties are like military organizations," Mel said. "They have secrets to protect, and enemies whose capabilities and intentions it would be foolish not to try and find out about."

"Exactly," Newell said. "And it should come as no surprise, therefore, to learn that we have our own intelligence-gathering machinery as well." He indicated Landis with a nod. "In fact, Warren runs it."

"So, do you know who these people are?" Mel asked.

"Some," Newell said. "But the picture is far from complete. I don't think it would be appropriate to be too specific at this particular juncture."

Warren Landis interjected, "We lump them together as the 'Opposition.' Just think of all the interests that stand to lose if the twenty-eighth amendment goes through."

Stephanie was staring at Newell with a strange look of sudden revelation in her eyes. "That's what Eva was doing, isn't it?" she said slowly. "She was with your intelligence operation." Newell nodded affirmatively.

"In fact, she worked for me," Landis informed them.

"But there was more than just that," Newell said. "You see, Eva had infiltrated a part of the Opposition—in fact it's in no small part due to her that we know as much about them as we do."

"I'm not sure I know what you mean by 'infiltrated,'" Stephanie said. "Do you mean she was a kind of a spy?"

"Yes," Newell said candidly. "Sordid, I know, but a regrettable necessity these days. But what made her so valuable was that *they* thought it was themselves who had infiltrated us—that Eva had turned, and was working for them, inside the most secure part of our organization."

"You mean that she was a double agent," Stephanie said.

"As far as they were concerned," Newell agreed. "But in reality she was a triple. Can you see what a priceless asset she represented to us?"

"Irreplaceable," Mel said mechanically.

Stephanie thought for a moment, hesitated, then said, "That possibility must have crossed their minds too."

"Of course," Newell agreed. "We expected them to come up with some form of loyalty test for her." He looked toward Landis to elaborate.

Landis obliged. "In the middle of January, the future vice president, Theo McCormick, will be visiting Egypt and Israel for preliminary talks on envisaged changes in U. S. foreign-aid policy. A man called Josef Kirkelmayer, from our Washington headquarters, was originally scheduled to go with McCormick's party as the on-the-spot public-relations man."

"You mean he's not going now?" Mel said

"No," Landis replied. "Eva was given . . ."

"By the Opposition?"

"Yes . . . some documents which expose Kirkelmayer as having leaked confidential party information to our opponents before the election. The idea was to make us think that she'd obtained them in the process of working for us. The documents had been faked, of course, but the question was, would we act on them?" Landis shrugged. "Well, it has been announced publicly that Kirkelmayer has been dropped from McCormick's team, the official reason being ill health. But we also fed it into the grapevine, in a way we knew would get back, that there was a big internal row going on over it, which hadn't been publicized."

Mel looked a shade skeptical. "But isn't that what you'd

expect anyone to do if they weren't taken in but wanted to keep up the deception?"

"True," Landis conceded. "But it was their game play. They were calling the shots. Anyhow, it gets more interesting. You see, Eva automatically became Kirkelmayer's replacement."

"And the Opposition knew that would be the case?" Mel checked.

"Oh yes. They were very anxious to be sure of it before they came up with the scheme to remove Kirkelmayer. In other words, they had some reason for wanting to get Eva sent to the Middle East in his place." He glanced at Newell to resume from there.

Newell acknowledged with a nod. "All we have won so far is the popular vote, which adds up simply to an indicator of the public mood—no more. As far as anything concrete is concerned, until after the inauguration next January, it changes nothing. The Opposition has no intention of sitting back and accepting the situation as it stands. We have reason to believe that they're planning something serious—something aimed at damaging or discrediting us, or even toppling us completely, perhaps—before the inauguration takes place. Exactly what, we don't know. But our indications are that it will happen during McCormick's Middle East visit, and that Eva was to have played a crucial role in it."

Mel recalled George's comment about the purpose of all this being a business proposition. It had to be something that they considered vital if Newell had seen fit to interrupt a demanding schedule in order to be here. He nodded. "Yes, I can see you have a problem."

Newell placed his hands palms down on the table and stared directly first at Mel, then at Stephanie. "We both have a problem," he said. "If your suspicions of Soviet espionage and the involvement of people in high positions are correct, then your predicament is an impossible one. I applaud your initiative, but it's not something you could have handled on your own. I think you already knew that. But now that will become a matter to be taken care of by the appropriate agencies at a national level." Mel and Stephanie exchanged quick glances that contained their first glimmer of real hope since the whole thing began. Newell lifted a hand from the table in a brief gesture of resignation and went on. "However, that will have to wait until after I take office. And in any case, it won't bring Eva back." He paused. "But *we* also have a problem, a far more pressing one, which cannot wait. And we think you can help us. What I want to propose, therefore, is that we hold off temporarily on Brett Vorland's activities, Dr. Oberwald, and what happened to Eva, and concentrate for the moment on finding out what the Opposition is planning to do in January. Then, assuming we're successful, we go all-out to crack this other business."

Stephanie frowned and looked at a loss. "Yes, I can see what you're saying, but what do you want us to do?" Newell hesitated for an instant, as if considering how to phrase something delicate.

Landis looked pointedly at Mel. "You said a little while ago, Mr. Shears, that Eva was 'irreplaceable.'" His voice held a curious, pointed quality. He waited, watching Mel's face. Then Mel's jaw dropped as he saw at last what the entire conversation had been leading to.

Newell nodded and directed his words to Stephanie. "But then, not quite irreplaceable, maybe. You and your sister have been mistaken for each other twice already." Stephanie started to say something, but Newell raised a hand. "I know. Make no mistake about what we're asking. There's danger involved. But try and think of what it means to us, to the country, and what it meant to Eva. There isn't time to come up with any alternative approach. As you said yourself a few minutes ago, for the time being, officially you don't exist. And that could be convenient. You see, what we want you to do is become Eva. We want you to take your sister's place."

CHAPTER 23

Mel propped himself on an elbow and ran his other hand through Eva's hair spread loosely over her back as she lay face down, naked, on the bed. "Mmmm," she murmured contentedly. He grinned and ran his fingertips lightly along her spine and the crease of her behind, and down the back of a thigh to her knee. She twitched and giggled.

"That tickle?"

"Mmmm . . . Hey, you stopped."

"Why are backs of knees sexy?"

"Why is anything sexy? It's all because of evolution."

Mel leaned over and touched his tongue along her shoulders. "You smell nice, Know that?"

"Most of sex is smell." Eva rubbed the side of her face against the pillow, keeping her eyes closed. "I've never understood why people turn it into something to feel awkward about and spray stuff on to camouflage it. I mean, it's nice. We're programmed that way."

"I thought we were visual animals," Mel said. "Isn't sixty percent of the cortex supposed to be involved with processing visual data?"

"I don't care. It may be true, but smell goes back further. It's closer to the emotions. Have you ever noticed that smells trigger memories much better than anything else? Even old nostalgic tunes."

"Oh, some people get hung up about it, I guess."

"Some people get hung up being alive at all." Eva rolled over onto her back, still with her eyes closed. "Smell me all over."

"You don't have any inhibitions about anything, do you?" Mel said.

"Life's too short. People talk about Chinese foot binding. What about Western mind binding?"

Mel kissed down her throat, between her breasts, and around a nipple. "You'll start me off. Then we'll have to do it all over again."

Eva opened one eye impishly. "Want to?"

"You like sex a lot, don't you?"

"Sure. It's great. Want to?"

Mel held her one-eyed stare for a second or two, then conceded defeat with a sigh and settled his face against her shoulder. "Hell, there's a limit. Let's just cuddle up for a while."

"I like that a lot, too." She pulled up the sheet, slipped inside his arm, and snuggled close.

"That's another thing that I like about you," Mel said.

"What?"

"That kind of . . . animal quality. You don't get shocked by things. It makes most other girls seem kind of antiseptic."

"Not like you."

"Well, guys are more, well, 'earthy,' I guess . . ."

"Oh."

"If you know what I mean."

"Sure."

"I'm not being sexist or anything. It's just—"

"That's okay. I understand."

"You see, you're broad-minded. I feel free and easy talking to you. It's different. I feel I can talk to you the way I can with other guys."

"I'm glad." She stroked his chest with a fingertip. Mel squeezed her body with the arm around her back. "Have you ever heard of a sootikin?" she asked lightly.

"What's that?"

"I read about them in an English social commentary from centuries ago. It was a mouse-shaped accumulation that formed in the vaginal cleft through not washing for weeks, or even months. They had to sweep them up after church service, because poorer-class women didn't use underwear, and—"

"Christ, that's gross!" Mel sat up abruptly. "What are you trying to do, put me off for life?"

Eva laughed. "I thought guys were supposed to be earthy."

"You made it up."

"Not at all. But if you're really not in the mood . . ." She pulled the sheet aside, swung her legs over the edge of the bed, and sat up.

"Getting up?"

"Time's getting on. . . . And I need to take a shower."

"I'll put some coffee on while you're in there."

"That would be nice. Are you going back to your place after?"

"I guess so."

"If Stephanie's there, tell her that Sadie will drop off the books she wanted."

"She probably will be. Brett said something about them going over to Mobile later today." Mel stretched out an arm and ran a finger down Eva's back. It was a perfect back, lean and evenly tanned, with the muscles moving hynotically as she rolled her head and circled her shoulders to loosen up. "Are you sure we can't get together again later today?" he said. "Maybe have lunch, go out somewhere tonight?"

"I can't. I'm tied up for today. You've got things to do, too."

Mel sighed. "I know, I know."

Eva stood up, slipped on a lilac flannelette robe, and

disappeared out through the door. Moments later the sound came of the shower being turned on in the bathroom.

Mel lay back and stared contentedly for a while up at the ceiling. Then he let his gaze wander around the room, taking in the shorts and top that Eva had worn the previous evening, draped over the chair by the vanity, and his jeans and T-shirt, piled on top of the laundry basket. There were her clothes in the partly-open closet: dresses, from white with pale blue trim and a simple floral pattern—the kind a girl might wear at a casual Sunday brunch—to richly textured, ankle-length evening gowns; skirts of various colors, straight, pleated, one of denim, one of chequer; slacks, pants, some beach shirts; shoes, from worn canvas sneakers to suede boots and high heels in patent leather. Across the room, her makeup things scattered on top of the vanity: lipstick, tweezers, comb, eyebrow pencil; hair slides, a box of Q-tips. *Her* things. Personal things that she handled and which were close to her—not like gifts to be hung on the wall at a distance or shoved away in the back of a drawer. Lying here in her bed looking at them gave him a warm, secure feeling of belonging to the world they were part of. *Her* world. Him a part of it. He liked the feeling.

On the nightstand by the bed, two glasses, one still half-filled with fruit juice, the phone, with a scribbling pad, wind-up clock—Eva said that clocks ought to be clockwork, because that's what the word means. The shelf below, as with every expanse of horizontal space that she owned, crammed with books and papers. Mel rolled over to the edge of the bed and scanned the titles idly. Popper, *The Open Society and Its Enemies*; Hazlitt, *Economics in One Lesson*; Heller, *Catch-22* . . . Mark Twain, Oscar Wilde. A postcard, being used as a bookmark, had fallen partly out of a volume that had been pushed in the wrong way round with its open side outward, and was on the point of dropping to the floor. Mel reached out and lifted the card clear to reinsert it properly, holding the place with a fingertip. As he did so, he paused curiously to look at it. It was from Washington, D.C., and showed the Lincoln Memorial. The message on it, written in firm italic executed with a broad-nibbed pen in black ink read:

Eva,
   Arr. 14th as promised, Delta Flt 56, lands Pensacola 5:16 P.M. If you're not at the gate, see you for dinner,

Lenox Inn—say 7:30? Bring toothbrush. Don't bother with nightie! Interesting news on the slot with the firm that we talked about. Will tell you all about it over wine and candles. I think we've an offer you can't refuse. Looking forward to seeing some sun and surf again, not to mention more of you,

Affectionately, as always,

Dave F.

A numb feeling came over Mel as he stared at it. Today, Saturday, was the fourteenth of the month. The card was postmarked nine days previously. No wonder she was tied up for the rest of the day. A sickening tightness took hold of his throat and stomach. He was only peripherally aware of himself throwing the bedsheet aside, crossing the room to the door, and entering the bathroom.

Too overcome with hurt and bewilderment to speak, he pulled the shower curtain aside and thrust the offending card into Eva's face. For an instant the sight of her naked body make him want to strike out, but he fought back the impulse. She saw what he was holding and closed her eyes momentarily with a resigned sigh. It wasn't so much an expression of remorse, but more an acknowledgment that she had made a mistake.

"What the fuck is this?" Mel demanded, finding his voice. "I mean, what is it, huh? What the hell's going on? . . ." He stood fuming, as if he were about to explode. Eva turned off the shower, stepped out, and put on her robe. But as he turned to confront her again, she evaded the encounter and walked past him and back through to the bedroom. Mel pursued her furiously, more enraged by her silence than if she had screamed or thrown something at him. He bore into the room and slammed the door shut behind him with a kick. "It's him, isn't it? It's Dave Fenner. You're seeing him today, right? That's why you're tied up."

"Why don't you put some clothes on?"

"Isn't it?" Mel demanded.

"Yes, it is. What of it?" Eva's voice was calm—firm, but not icy.

"What of it? What the hell is that supposed to mean? Don't you think that it might just happen to be a little bit of my goddam business?"

"Why?"

Mel stared at her disbelievingly. "Why? Why do you think, for chrissakes? When my girl gets cards from other guys fixing up—"

"*Mel.*" The sudden sharpness of her tone stopped him short. "I've told you before not to get any wrong ideas. I like you a lot and I like your company, but I've never said anything about cutting myself off from the rest of humanity or agreeing to become anyone's property. If you've jumped to some other conclusions, I'm sorry, but I never gave you any reason for making those kinds of assumptions."

Mel shook his head and looked at her incredulously as he took his things off the laundry basket and began pulling them on. "You bet I'm putting some clothes on. You bet I'm getting out of here just as fast as I can. . . . You don't understand, do you? I really went for you. It could have been just us, know what I mean? Something special. So, what's the matter with you? Aren't I good enough? What are you, man crazy or something? Is that the problem?"

Eva sat in the basket chair by the window. "I think it's you who doesn't understand, Mel. Yes, I think a lot of you."

"Yeah, right . . . It sure shows." He pushed a foot into his jeans.

"This may come as a surprise in your present state of mind, but no, I don't go to bed with every man I like. But if I choose to, then it's my business. I own my body, my mind, and my life. If you're looking for someone to build a mutual prison with out of obligations and guilt, someone you can own and enslave yourself to in return, then that's fine, but you're talking to the wrong person."

"What do you take me for? Do you think I'm some kind of performing pet dog that you can stand in line . . . who'll come running with his tail wagging when you snap your fingers next time?" Mel sat on the edge of the bed and pulled on his shoes. "No way, lady! I do have a little piece of something called 'pride,' which you've obviously never heard of." He stood up and fought his way into his T-shirt. "So when he goes back this time, don't bother calling. And don't hold your breath waiting for me to call you. The sun might have gone out by then."

"It's a pity you feel that way. . . ." Eva refused to be provoked, which made it all the more infuriating. "You're right. I should have told you about Dave. I almost did a couple of times . . . but I didn't because I got the feeling something like this would happen."

"Does he know about me?" Mel demanded, making it sound like a challenge.

"Yes."

Mel hadn't expected that. His confusion increased. "Oh, really? So how come you can talk about things like that to him but not to me? He's older, is that it? What am I supposed to be, then, just a kid who wouldn't be able to handle it?"

"You are making that rather obvious." Eva covered her eyes with a hand and went on before Mel had a chance to react. "We've known each other for some time. You may not understand this, Mel, but he'd rather think of me being free to have some warmth and affection and somebody to be close to in my life when *I* need it. He likes to think *I'm* happy. I'm not something he owns, that has an obligation to make him happy. Doesn't that sound more like loving somebody than what you're talking about?"

"Well, enjoy. I never was much into sainthood," Mel said as he moved toward the door. "And have a nice day." He went into the main lounge to retrieve the bag he had put down the night before, then crossed to the front door. As he opened it, he turned to survey the scene of book-laden shelves, tables, and chairs, boxes overflowing with papers, and clutter around the computer, which he had no doubt he was seeing for the last time. He closed the door with a satisfying bang, and descended the stairs to the yard at the rear of The Viennese, where he had parked his car.

CHAPTER 24

In his office in the KGB's headquarters building in Lubyanka on Dzherzhinsky square, a few blocks from the Kremlin, Oleg Kordorosky, deputy chairman of the KGB, tossed the report down on the desk in front of him. "This is a disgrace to your directorate. I want them found, and I want the people responsible identified and apprehended by whatever means are necessary. One thing I'm certain of is that heads will roll over this—theirs or yours. Do I make myself clear, General?"

Goryanin sat stiffly in the upright wooden chair opposite. A heavy artillery unit in Hungary that had been issued with nuclear-explosive shells—kept locked in concrete vaults and under guard at all times during nonemergency conditions— had been unable to account for two of them when a routine inspection was carried out in September. As head of the Second Chief Directorate, which concerned itself, among other things, with the security of classified information on advanced Soviet weaponry, Goryanin knew that finding out what had happened was part of his job—although the implication that the loss somehow represented a personal failure on his part was hardly called for, since the responsibility for equipment supplied to the operational military command was not his. "Colonel Chelenko is conducting an expert analysis of other incidents that might be related, to see if any pattern emerges," he said. "There were some SA–37s shipped for dismantling earlier in the year—"

"I don't want expert analyses, I want results. Put Chelenko on it full-time and see that he gets whatever additional assistance he needs."

Goryanin nodded.

"That will be all for now. I expect to see some positive results by the end of next week."

Kordorosky had a pale, blotchy face with thin red hair and colorless eyes, devoid of expression, that gave him an inhuman, bloodless appearance that Goryanin always found chilling. His progress upward through the ranks of the KGB had shown him to be admirably endowed with the traditional qualifications of ruthlessness, the capacity for intrigue, and treachery, and it was no secret that his sole drive now was to oust the incumbent chairman and take over the organization. Goryanin, by contrast, was an intellectual, originally from an engineering background, who had been drawn into the KGB through its growing need for technical expertise to keep up with a changing, modern world. Kordorosky eyed him with a predator's innate suspicion of ability sensed as a potential threat, yet recognized at the same time as indispensable. It was the kind of insecurity that sought constantly to control.

As Goryanin rose to leave, Kordorosky said, "You may be Defense Minister Androliev's nephew, but that won't count for anything when I'm in command here. I go only by performance. . . ." He paused for a second, then added in a curious voice, "And besides, he and his soft-line generals might not be around for very much longer." He made it sound almost as if he wanted Goryanin to pass the tip-off to his uncle. To induce the aging marshal to do the sensible thing and stand down now, perhaps? To save others the inconvenience and risk of complications by having to do it forcibly? . . .

Goryanin's concern grew as he made his way downstairs to the directorate's offices two floors below, and fitted the implications into perspective along with the other things that rumor, experience, and instinct told him were going on.

The strongest and most rigid geometric figure is the triangle. From the Eiffel tower to the framework of any railroad bridge, engineering uses triangles universally to produce structures of strength and stability. And the same is true of political structures. Political systems based on division of power and the interplay of three balancing forces have been the most stable and enduring throughout history.

Ever since the Soviet Union's inception, outsiders had been looking at the problems confronting it and predicting its imminent collapse. But it had survived four years of struggle against the Russian Army; it survived the mutiny of the Baltic Fleet, which had helped bring about the Revolution; it survived the mass exodus of its intelligentsia, the opposition of the peasants, the Civil War, the slaughter of millions during the period of forced collectivization, and endless bloody purges. It had also withstood diplomatic isolation and political blockade, the enslavement of millions of its own citizens, and the decimation of its officer corps, followed immediately by an unexpected onslaught by 190 of Hitler's divisions—and emerged from it all to achieve military parity with the United States. So it didn't do to be too hasty about burying the Soviet regime.

The political system of the USSR was based on a triangle of forces. The three corners of the triangle were the Party, the Army, and the KGB. Each of these possessed enormous power, but power which could be exceeded by the combined strength of the other two. Of the three, the Party had the fewest resources for self-defense in an open conflict. But to counter this weakness, it had the lever at its disposal of authorizing the appointment of all officials—every general of the Army and every colonel of the KGB could be posted, promoted, and demoted only with the approval of the Party's

Central Committee. This right was supported by both of the Party's rivals; for if that privilege were to pass to either of them, then the other would be in mortal danger, and both of them knew it.

The system thus functioned as a tripod that would stand, provided that none of its legs tried to extend itself too far. Whenever this began to happen, the other two immediately intervened to chop off the excess. There were many examples of the process in action, even in comparatively recent history.

When Stalin died in 1953, observers concluded that Beria, the feared head of the predecessor organization to the KGB, would take command. He possessed files on every senior party official and general that would have enabled him to put any one of them before a firing squad. But it was this very power which destroyed him. The Party and the Army, understanding their joint predicament, executed the chief executioner and eliminated the heads of his security apparatus. But this released one of the two leashes around the Army's neck. Marshal Zhukov, the legendary commander of World War II fame, began acquiring extraordinary powers at home and abroad, and demanded the removal of all political commissars from the Army's units—to shake off the leash remaining. The Party and the newly formed KGB promptly closed ranks, Zhukov was dismissed, and the military machine drastically pruned. This extended the Party leg of the tripod to an alarming degree, and in response the impossible happened when the two mortal enemies, the Army and the KGB, united to bring down the Party's head, Khrushchev, who fell almost without a sound. And in the era that followed, the regime had survived Czechoslovakia, Vietnam, repeated Middle East crises, Poland, and Afghanistan. The secret of Brezhnev's survival lay in his skill at maintaining the triangular balance, restraining any two of its sides from combining against the third.

But now there were ominous shiftings of loyalties and all kinds of dealings going on behind the scenes. The feelings that Goryanin's uncle had expressed after the dinner at the *dacha*—that what was happening in America represented an opportunity to escape from the tramline that had been trapping everyone on a course for disaster, and should be seized eagerly—was typical of how many of the military high command felt. They understood the awesome destructiveness of modern weapons and were under no illusions as to what an all-out conflict with the West would mean. Furthermore, they had the least to fear from a radical restructuring of the regime, or even its complete demise as a recognizable political entity. For the Party and the KGB leadership knew full well that if Communism should collapse, they would in all probability be shot by their own countrymen. But that wouldn't happen to the Army.

Hence the Party and the upper echelons of the KGB had much to be concerned about in the prospect of seeing the American economy unfettered, which would lead to expansion of industrial and scientific innovation on a scale that no regimented system could match. This would translate into unchallengeable military and economic superiority, putting a permanent end to any hopes of eventual world revolution. In the view of many that Goryanin had talked to personally, a war sooner than later—before the disadvantages became tangible—would be the preferable alternative. And if Kordorosky's remark meant that Androliev and his supporters were being quietly moved aside to make way for a new cadre of top military who would go along with the harder line, then it was already as good as official policy.

CHAPTER 25

The valley lay broad and shallow between rounded, sunbaked hills, an arid desolation of sand, boulders, stunted acacias, and thorn bushes, which except for the camp, had remained essentially unchanged in appearance for a thousand years.

The camp consisted of several rows of barrack huts painted lime green, along with workshops, storerooms, a transportation depot, and communal facilities, standing inside a fifteen-foot-high double chain-link fence topped by barbed wire. An inner compound contained a two-story headquarters building, officers quarters, and an armory.

The sounds of shouted orders and the irregular coughing of a truck engine trying to start came in through the barred window. From farther away, the intermittent chattering of a machine gun firing on the flats beyond the end of the ridge that ran behind the camp. Short bursts of three or four seconds. Probably the squad that had marched out at daybreak, practicing at the range that was somewhere in that direction.

Brett Vorland sat pen in hand at the wooden table by the wall of the quarters in which he was being confined, an open mathematical textbook propped before him, and a large notepad lying open, its pages covered with symbols and equations. For a prisoner, from the things he'd heard and read, his treatment could have been a lot worse. The quarters consisted of two rooms, clean and airy, if somewhat simply furnished— although it did contain a TV—and he had been liberally supplied with books, magazines, and occasional chess and cards partners from among the guards and recruits. He had begun teaching English to some of them in return for odd favors. Security was about as rigorous as it needed to be in view of his conspicuous appearance, the remoteness of the location, and the harshness of the surroundings. Exactly why he had been brought here had never been made clear. He guessed that with his specialized knowledge of American defensive systems, he was a bargaining chip in some kind of game being played thousands of miles away.

With ample time to reflect on the things that had happened in recent years, he felt a lot older now. Older, and belatedly wiser. The realization of his own gullibility still caused him to wince inwardly when he allowed himself to think about it too much. It was his paranoia—there was no kinder word for it— that the influence of the far right would plunge the world into all-out war upon the ungodly that had set him up. That was what had made him easily persuadable that the leaderships of both sides were insane, and that the certain recipe for catastrophe was to leave global destructive power in the hands of either of them. He could hear some of Oberwald's words now. "We represent an unaligned association of concerned and influential people, who have no allegiance to any particular flag, creed, system, or ideology. We are an organization that transcends nationalism, which is committed to reason, sanity, and the creation of a better future for the entire human race. We believe that can be achieved, but not while the concentrations of destructive power that exist today remain in present hands. This is where we believe that you can help us, Mr. Vorland. As you know, I occupy a position that is not without some influence in the machinery that decides the strategic policy of the United States. . . ."

It had been exactly what a million young people with high ideals and no experience of the world were waiting to hear. And Brett had fallen for it. Now he was being held captive in a remote part of Syria, a client state of the Soviets, which meant that Oberwald had been a front for them all along. The chilling thought was, how many more like Oberwald might there be, working in the nation's most trusted top circles? Brett had pondered for weeks on why, but a consistent motive had eluded him. Why would those who had apparently gained the most from a system, and who would apparently stand to lose the most, be among the most ardent working for its destruction?

Keys rattling in the lock made him look up. The door opened, and Hamashad, one of the guards, came in, carrying a tray with Brett's evening meal: greasy soup, a meat-and-vegetable concoction in a spicy sauce with rice, dark bread, strong tea, and some fruit. Hamashad was a little on the chubby side for Brett's conception of a Palestinian guerrilla, with deep olive skin, large brown eyes, and a clipped mustache. He was wearing combat fatigues with a British-style webbing belt and sidearm, and on his head a red-and-white kaffiyeh. There was nothing of the crazed fanatic in his manner, and he had always treated Brett considerately—maybe on orders.

"Lamb with curry," Hamashad said. "Very good. You see, we good hotel, yes? Take good care."

"Okay," Brett said knowingly. "I'll give you a star. What's the deal? What do you want?"

Hamashad grinned. "No movie tonight. Guys very sad. Movie box, it bust. You see if fix? Can do okay?" Being able to fix the barracks VCR and other odds and ends was something else that Brett had gained a reputation for. When none of the orthodox Muslim officers were about, the favorite fare was X-rated stuff smuggled in from Europe.

"What's the chance of a couple of Budweisers?"

"Bud-veisser? What is that?"

"American beer. Find me a cool beer and I'll think about it. Can do okay?"

"No beer here. Very strict." At the same time Hamashad pointed at the ceiling, winked, and nodded his head.

Brett understood: the room was bugged. "Okay," he said with a sigh. "Get an okay from the chief and I'll come across with you after supper."

Hamashad came back an hour later with another guard, whom he sent away with Brett's empty tray. Then Hamashad led Brett out of the headquarters building, and they began crossing the inner compound toward the cluster of buildings containing the canteen, transportation depot, and repair shops. "Maybe can do Russian beer," Hamashad said in a low voice. "Is not allowed, but who knows? Might find. Is okay, maybe?"

"Sure. I'll risk it."

As they moved out of earshot of anyone, Hamashad glanced at Brett and murmured in suddenly fluent English, "Act normally and do nothing to betray surprise. We have very little time, and you must trust me. I know that you are an American. I can arrange communication with the Western authorities."

"Who are you working for?"

"For now, that does not matter."

Brett obeyed and continued staring at the ground ahead as they walked. It had been so sudden and unexpected that for a few seconds his mind refused to function. The most obvious possibility was that it could be a trap to extract information from him. But on the other hand, Brett possessed vital information on what had transpired between himself and Oberwald, which it was crucial to send back into the right hands. Some risk would be unavoidable. He thought furiously for a few seconds, then said, "First I need proof. How can I be sure that you are in communication with the West?"

"You tell me. What would convince you?"

"I'd have to think about it."

"Well, don't take too long. . . . Enough now, we are getting close." They were approaching the workshops, where some other Palestinians were talking in a group outside the door. Hamashad grinned and raised his voice. "Is inside. Picture all in lines and pieces. You fix good, yes?"

They led him inside to where the VCR and monitor were already up on one of the benches. Brett plugged it in, ran a few checks, and took off the cover. As he had suspected, it just needed a thorough cleaning job; but he stretched it out and spent some time poking and prodding around inside to make it look good, and to give himself time to think. The problem was deciding who the right people would be to risk trying to communicate to. "The West" was too vague a term to be safe, for there was the risk that Oberwald might not be alone in working for the other side. Who was there, then, he asked himself—some group or organization—that he would feel completely confident in dealing with?

For his services, Brett was allowed to stay and watch the movie, which turned out to be a stock Russian World War II saga that had the American and German high commands in league as the bad guys, and the Russians, who were the real objects of the conspiracy, struggling valiantly to defeat the Nazi world threat single-handedly despite the treachery and double-dealings of both of them. Afterward, Hamashad conducted him back across the compound to his quarters.

"Yes, there is one thing that would convince me," Brett said. "I want to talk to somebody high up in the U.S. Constitutional party. Nobody else, understand? I'll only deal with the Constitutionals."

"And what would prove to you that we were indeed talking to them?" Hamashad asked.

"That's something I'll leave you to figure out." Brett answered.

CHAPTER 26

The Pinewood Hills Lakeshore Conference Resort was situated a little over an hour's drive inland from Washington, D.C., amid forested terrain in the mountains of West Virginia, a few miles south of the Potomac River valley. It was managed and operated by a combination of interests that made its actual ownership obscure, and unlike the typical business conference center, it didn't go to any great lengths to advertise its existence or keep its bookings schedule healthily filled. Also, it was never available when an organization inquired about renting its facilities exclusively. Whatever the season of year or the duration requested, a part of the place, at least, had inevitably been reserved by somebody else already. Thus, every group that did use the resort found strange faces there and other groups involved in other functions that they didn't know about. That seemed natural enough, and nobody thought more of it. In fact, Pinewood Hills was jointly owned by a group of supporters of the Constitutional party, who made it available around the year for meetings, briefings, training sessions, and the like. It also functioned as a permanent base for activities of the kind which the party preferred to conduct discreetly, away from public scrutiny—such as its security and intelligence-gathering operations. Not that there was anything illegal involved; but the kind of people who worked in such fields were accustomed to keeping a low profile as a matter of professional prudence, and unnecessary visibility of any kind made them reflexively nervous.

It was Friday afternoon, November 24. Mel sat at one of several paper-strewn tables positioned in a horseshoe before a screen, for the moment blank, in an annex room set apart from the main cluster of buildings. He still wasn't sure why he had been rushed down here. Stephanie had agreed to the request that Newell had made in San Francisco, and since it didn't involve Mel personally, he had flown back to Boston to tell Robert Winthram and Bill Evron the story, intending then to get on with his job. But a couple of days later he had received an urgent call from Warren Landis, asking him to get down as quickly as possible and rejoin them in Washington.

The room had lots of polished woodwork, a stone fireplace, and windows the entire length of one wall, looking out at boats moored around a jetty, and beyond, the lake with tree-covered slopes rising from the far side. A sign outside the door read, nebulously, J AND B ASSOCIATES. PRIVATE. George Slade was sitting next to Mel, closest to the door. Facing them from the opposite side of the horseshoe was Warren Landis, head of the party's intelligence operations, with his large brow and prematurely balding head, heavy spectacles, open vest, and loosened tie; on one side of him, heavily built, dark-haired, with droopy lids, Ronald Bassen, the security chief; and on the other, a swarthy-skinned girl who was operating a computer terminal connected to the data base at Party HQ in Washington. Stephanie sat at the head, facing the screen, her face strained from the concentration she had been sustaining since the session began early that morning, with just a short break at noon for coffee and sandwiches.

"Okay, let's review the basics one more time, from the top," Bassen said. "What's your name?"

"Eva Carne," Stephanie replied.

"Your date of birth?"

"October twenty-six, nineteen seventy-three."

"Social security number?"

"Five six one, five eight, one four five three."

"Where do you live?"

"Four thirty-seven Pacific Heights condominiums. On Ocean Park Boulevard, Santa Monica."

"What kind of location is that?"

"On the cliffs, overlooking Santa Monica Beach."

"How long have you lived there?"

"A little under a year. I moved there in February."

"On what date?"

"I don't remember without checking."

Bassen nodded. "That's fine. Most people wouldn't." He looked at a map that was lying folded among the papers in front of him. "How would I get there from, say : . . the Ventura Freeway?"

Stephanie hesitated and licked her lips. "Take the San Diego Freeway over Mulholland Pass and through Westwood. Then the Santa Monica Freeway east, toward the beach. Exit at Fourth Street, make a right, and carry on to Wilshire. At Wilshire, make a left and go four blocks to the boulevard."

"Good. What would I see in front of me as I was driving along Wilshire?"

"Er . . ." Stephanie brought a hand up to her brow. "Sorry." ·

"I'd see the Pacific Pallisades hills." Bassen turned his head. "Do we have a picture, please?"

The operator tapped at the computer terminal, and the screen came to life to show an excerpt from a movie record that two of Bassen's operatives from the party's Los Angeles office had taken while driving around the area the previous day. Stephanie studied the view, noting street names and salient landmarks. Finally she nodded. "Okay." The screen blanked out again.

"Don't worry," Bassen said. "From now on, you're going to *be* Eva. We'll move you into her apartment when it's time for her to reappear, and by January you'll be able to drive it blindfolded. Now . . ." He looked down at his papers and resumed. "What's your job?"

"Full-time public-relations officer with the Constitutional party, specializing in foreign affairs."

"Where are you based?"

"The West Coast regional office: Suite 1256, Wallman Tower."

"Where's that located?"

"Downtown Los Angeles, on the east side of the Pasadena Freeway."

"Your boss there?"

"John Wadlow, the regional coordinator."

Bassen nodded, satisfied. "Okay. What we'll do is let you work there for a spell and take Eva's shifts until you know all the people there by sight, what offices they're in, what time they take their coffee . . . Warren?" He turned his head as Landis raised a hand.

"I've got a better idea," Landis said. "Suppose we prime her with all the information on the LA office—mugshots, floor plan, and so on and so on . . . I wonder if we could pass her off as Eva." He turned toward Stephanie. "See the point? It would make a good test . . . to see if you can fool the people there, who actually worked with Eva."

George Slade thought for a moment and then nodded. "I like it. If the act isn't good enough, it would be a damn sight better to find out that way than the first time she tries it for real." At the end table between them, Stephanie swallowed visibly.

Bassen looked at her curiously. "Think you could handle it?"

She nodded. "I'll give it a try. As George says, if I can't, I'd rather find out now."

"How long would it take you to put together a package of material?" Bassen asked Landis.

Landis bunched his lips. "Let's see, pictures of the people and the interior layout, review of procedures . . . We'd need somebody there to be in on it—to fill us in on the things Eva had in progress and that kind of stuff."

"Well, let's make that John Wadlow," Bassen said. "He runs the office. It wouldn't be a good idea to screw him around by keeping him in the dark, anyhow."

Landis nodded. "Fine. In that case we could have a package, complete with visuals, by . . . oh, say, lunchtime Tuesday."

Bassen shuffled the papers he had been referring to into a pile and closed them in a folder. "It's coming together. Time for a break, guys. How about a walk outside to get some lake air and stretch our legs, eh?" He stood up. Slade rose and went to the door. Mel pushed his chair back and stretched, while Landis completed some notes. Stephanie moved toward the door behind Slade. "Oh, Stephanie," Bassen called after her. She turned automatically to look back. Bassen shook his head. "You don't respond to that name any more. You're Eva. Twenty-four hours a day, you have to think like Eva."

Stephanie nodded with a sigh of self-rebuke. "I'll get it right," she promised.

In her unofficial role, which had involved penetrating the Opposition, Eva had worked for Warren Landis. She had been thorough in her reporting back, and he was able to furnish a reasonably accurate account of her dealings with them.

The screen showed a still picture of some people emerging from the entrance of a building. A big man in a three-piece suit appeared to be the center of the group, but the circle superposed on the picture singled out the head and shoulders of another man, off to one side, dapperly dressed in a bottle-green blazer, wide necktie, and flared pants. The camera had caught him with his head tossed back in a laugh and arm half raised exuberantly as he said something to the woman next to him. It suggested somebody who was flying high and on his way up in life. Mel was aware that such fleetingly captured images could be misleading— PR firms and the media employed people to spend days scanning through hundreds of hours of footage for just the right shot of some-body they wished to promote or destroy—but the impression remained, nevertheless.

The view changed to a blow-up of the the circled face. The man was perhaps in his late thirties, with a high forehead, fair hair spreading flamboyantly at the back to his shoulders, and spectacles with round, metal-rimmed lenses that gave his eyes a singularly intense look—vaguely reminiscent of the staple comic-book mad scientist of his younger days, Mel thought. He had a wisp of a mustache, which hadn't been discernible in the wider-field shot.

"Louis Seybelman, California-based political activist, and campaign organizer," Landis announced from his seat opposite Mel. The meeting had reconvened, and Landis had taken over from Bassen. This part was for Mel's benefit. Stephanie had been through it all before Mel's sudden summons to Washing-ton. Landis went on, "You might already know him from the political scene, although he tends to stay more of a background figure. He is well connected and was a big factor in our not doing better than we did on the West Coast in the elections.

His style is to pull strings from behind the throne. He was instrumental in the engineering of such pieces of legislation as the Occupational Security Act and the Inflation Control Act, which a lot of people still believe help their economic security. . . . Well they might for some people, I guess, but only by stopping a lot of other people from making a living. He poses as a champion of the people against rapacious capitalism: protect the environment, conserve the resources, save the exploited natives, and all that kind of stuff. Styled a left-liberal, but in reality it's fascism in a different suit: seizing the economy through state control, and promoting public fears as the justification."

"Save the commercials, Warren," Bassen murmured beside him. "The election's over now. We won."

Landis grinned. "Seybelman started out as a sociology and political science major at Cornell. Nobody's sure what got him into the 'America stinks' department. His family was prosperous and secure, father a dentist, mother in marketing, no big problems that we know of. Maybe it was the rich-kid-in-a-world-where-people-still-starve-guilt-trip syndrome. He showed early talent as an organizer, and in his campus days we see him instrumental in various student protest movements. . . ." A series of pictures followed as Landis spoke: Seybelman posing with a group of students; Seybelman and a girlfriend standing in front of a car; Seybelman speaking at a rostrum. "Too late for Vietnam, but antinuclear power, anti-agricultural chemicals, anti–South Africa, and that whole bag of beans.

"But all that was running out of steam by the end of the eighties, and he moved on to antibomb and the peace movement, becoming involved in the opposition to revitalizing the space program, because of the military implications with regard to space-based defenses. Seybelman moved west in 1995 with his new wife, physician-turned-activist Gertrude Weinkompf—evidently with access to plenty of funding to make life comfortable for them—and he's been a rising star ever since." The final shots showed the Seybelmans' half-million-dollar home in the San Fernando valley, and the Seybelmans in evening dress and ballroom gown, sharing a joke with the state governor.

Mel turned his eyes away from the screen when Landis stopped speaking. "Do I assume that Seybelman's organization was what Eva had infiltrated?"

"Yes," Landis replied. "She had one last meeting with Seybelman, which we don't have the details of. It seems he was going to fix her up to meet someone else, but we don't know who."

"Let's make sure I've got this straight," Mel said. "Eva was still employed officially at the Constitutional LA office, and Seybelman knew it, but he thought that she had turned and was really working for him."

"Yes."

Mel frowned. "How did she convince him? I mean, what was her motivation supposed to be?"

Stephanie answered. "I used to believe the Constitutional ideology. You could say I was almost a fanatic about it at one time. I gave it total commitment for years. And what did I get? I'm still practically an office clerk. It isn't what I expected. In contrast, this new circle that I'm getting to know offers money, glamour, exciting people—the kinds of things that life is all about. I'm through with being a dedicated servant of the cause."

"In other words, ego and frustrated ambition," Landis said.

"It happens," Bassen threw in.

Mel nodded and looked back at Stephanie. "Okay. So how did you become part of that circle? What got you in there in the first place?"

Stephanie didn't answer but looked toward Landis in an unconscious appeal for him to take it. Landis said, "The political group that Seybelman belongs to in California has a guy called Arnold Hoffenach, who runs security, hires the bodyguards, and takes care of things like that. He's pretty well cut out for the job, and good at it, too: former SEAL, then stunt man, two years of agency work, martial arts expert—but smart, and with enough polish to look right in a tuxedo."

The operator found the reference, and a picture appeared on the screen of a broad-shouldered, yet lean and athletically built man, dressed in a conventional suit and carrying a briefcase, crossing what looked like a hotel lobby. He had light hair, cut short in a casual, shaggy style that enhanced his rugged good looks—the kind of material that made movie stars.

"Seen here carrying the money," Landis commented. "But Hoffenach is also the dominant breed: a man's man, who scores well with the ladies. And one of Arnold's notable conquests this year, which put a real feather in his cap as far as the guys upstairs who decide his pay raises are concerned, was a certain lady he fished right out of the middle of the enemy camp . . . who just happened to be staying in the same hotel and playing in the same casino, lonely, bored, and available, when he took a short vacation in Vegas with a couple of his pals last February." Although his tone was still bordering on flippant, the look in Landis's eyes hardened behind his spectacles as he held Mel's gaze. At last they were down to business.

Mel nodded his head slowly. Now it all made sense. Eva would have done it. She wouldn't have hesitated to insinuate herself in that way, if that was what it took. . . . But Stephanie? That was a different matter. Now he understood the confusion he'd seen in the look she'd flashed Landis a few seconds earlier, and why their plan had run into trouble. That was why they had rushed him down from Boston.

Bassen had been watching Mel's face and read him correctly. "That's right," he said. "She can't go back in to pick up that script. No fault of hers, but with the best will in the world, she couldn't handle it. So we need to invent some new happenings of the last two weeks to keep Hoffenach away from her. And that, Mel, is where you can help us out."

CHAPTER 27

". . . no solution to the problem at all. The biological hazards are completely unknown, and all I can say is that the whole, ill-conceived project represents an irresponsible misuse of resources and a reckless gamble with the health and safety of the public. Thank you." Marcus Chissek, a bald-headed man with a white beard and thick-rimmed spectacles, professor of current affairs from the Colorado State University, sat back in his chair and inclined his head to acknowledge the applause from the audience. The three men and two women seated with him at the green-felt-covered table on the stage beneath the arc lamps that had been set up for the TV cameras nodded to show their agreement. At the other table, facing the audience from the opposite side of the stage, Ed Gilman scanned over the notes he had been taking and turned to a pile of reports and reference data that he had brought with him.

Alongside him were two scientists from GPD and a health physicist from Pennsylvania whom he had persuaded to fly out to join them. The utilities had declined to send a spokesman, stating that it was not their policy to get involved in controversial topics; the various people that he had contacted in the academic world, while expressing sympathy, had elected to stay out, too, apparently fearing for their career prospects and unwilling to attract professional disapproval. The days had apparently gone when the unfettered search for the truth—and nothing else—dictated the mores of science.

Another storm had blown up in the Denver area over safety-related aspects of GPD's fission-fusion project, and as usual a garbled version had found its way into the media. As a rule, Gilman tried to avoid personal publicity. He wasn't in show business, he said. Ample information was available for that part of the populace who had minds of their own and were willing to take the trouble to find out, while the rest were beyond reach, anyway. On this occasion, however, with a camera team sent from one of the major networks, he had agreed to meet the critics at a public debate in the hope of putting the record straight once and for all before the nation.

"Well, this is quite a long, and if I may say so, rather confused list of allegations to have to straighten out," Gilman began. "However, taking the question of radioactive waste, which is the one that seems to produce the most misunderstanding—"

The production manager who had come with the camera team interrupted from one side below the stage. "Before you go on, since we are on a tight time schedule, could we get in a few summary lines?" Gilman stopped, momentarily taken aback. There had been no mention of time pressure all the while that Chissek and his crew had been waffling on. Before Gilman could respond, the production manager addressed the man sitting to Gilman's right. "Dr. Murray, regarding the claims made about radiation emissions."

"Something that very much needs clearing up," Murray agreed. "First, we should cover some basics that were apparently not understood. It's simply a fact of life that—"

"Specifically with regard to the GPD project, can you say for certain that no radiation will ever be released into the local environment?"

"No, and I wouldn't attempt to. In fact there *will* be releases. But—"

"Can you prove that even a low dose is completely safe?"

"Nobody can *prove* that. It's the kind of thing that can never be proved, purely on a philosophic basis. You can only draw conclusions from what you observe. But what we can say is that no ill effect of any kind has ever been observed—"

"Dr. Bailey, is a serious accident absolutely impossible?"

"Well, no. . . ."

"In other words, one could happen?"

"Yes, the probability is not zero. But neither is—"

"Thank you." Bailey looked at Gilman and shook his head in helpless bewilderment. One of the cameras rolled in on its dolly to catch it in close-up. "And one from Mr. Gilman, please. Mr. Gilman, it's true, is it not, that the federal government has decided to withdraw funding support of the project?"

"Yes it is."

"And is it true that the private investors you've approached have received negative appraisals from independent technical authorities on the grounds of economic and practical unfeasibility?"

Gilman colored visibly. That information was confidential. Not even *he* knew who had authored that report. Suddenly his patience with the whole atmosphere of cross-examination evaporated. "Look, would you please let me answer in my own way? I had started to talk about the eternal what-do-you-do-with-the-waste? thing, which was brought up earlier. Now this issue is a fraud that's been going on for years and it's about time we got some facts straight. Nuclear processes give thousands of times the energy yield of any kind of conventional combustion. That's why they require thousands of times less fuel. And for the same reason, despite what people are told, they produce thousands of times less waste. And what you do with that is put it through reactors and process it into new fuel, which is what Europe does, what Japan does, what the Soviets do. You see, spent fuel and waste are entirely different things, but the public is never told that. Ninety-five percent of what comes out of reactors can go straight back in, and what's left at the end of a year's operation of a big plant if you do that will fit under your kitchen table."

He waited, but nobody asked. Finally Murray, beside him, prompted, "But we're not doing it?"

"We were!" Gilman replied. "We had a whole plant ready to go to do just that, back in the seventies—over in South Carolina. The government never let it start up. It's still there. They were worried about terrorists making bombs, which is nonsense—there's a dozen ways I could show you right now that are easier, cheaper, and safer than fooling with power-plant waste. So the utilities have had to treat one hundred percent of what comes out of reactors as if it were high-level waste, to store it in ways that were never intended, and that's what gets all the publicity. It's a totally unnecessary problem, created by politics. . . ." He broke off as the arc lamps went out and the room seemed suddenly dark. As his eyes re-adjusted, he saw that the cameras were being dismounted and the lights taken down. Below the stage, the production manager had lost interest in him and was giving directions to a technician who was picking up a microphone cable. Some of the audience were leaving. "What's going on?" Gilman called down from the table. "We're not finished."

"That's okay, you carry on," the production manager told him. "We've got all we need for the tape. It's no good on the air when you get into long explanations. You lose people, and they switch off. They just want to hear it in one line."

Gilman stared down at the notes that he'd taken days to prepare—all to be reduced to a series of defensive one-liners spliced into the footage on an editor's whim. That was what the world would see, and anything he had to say from here on would be just to a small-town meeting. Somehow his heart had gone out of it now.

CHAPTER 28

Eva had worked officially as a public-relations specialist at the Constitutionals' West Coast office, which had been a cover for her real job with the party's intelligence arm. Louis Seybelman and his people, however, believed—so it was hoped—

that she had changed loyalties to become a double agent working for them. The fact was that she had not, which put her in the notoriously perilous position of being a triple. The Opposition could hardly be expected to be blind to such a possibility, and it was not a time to aggravate their suspicions by prolonging her disappearance more than was absolutely necessary.

To protect the supposed secrecy of her connection with Seybelman, she had been given a procedure for maintaining contact covertly. Using the pseudonym Annabel, she would deposit messages for him at a certain address in one of the public data networks, while ones for her would appear in the same place, signed "Simon." The system thus functioned as a two-way electronic drop box, in which either party could leave information which the other could access remotely, with neither the source nor the destination being traceable. Eva's last message to Seybelman had been a precoded phrase advising that, as anticipated, she had received confirmation that she would be substituting for Josef Kirkelmayer in the party accompanying McCormick to the Middle East. Since then, five messages of progressively increasing urgency had accumulated from "Simon," requesting Annabel to get in touch. The first thing Warren Landis had done after Stephanie's agreement to cooperate was to buy more time by depositing a reply from Annabel, saying that she had personal complications that would keep her out of circulation until after the end of the month.

The plan was that Stephanie, as Eva, would resume contact in the first week of December, rehearsed in a story that would accord with actual events as far as was practicable: A sister in Denver had committed suicide while depressed, following her boyfriend's untimely death—as checking would verify—and in the course of attending the funeral in California, she had met up with a former lover from university days. It turned out that their feelings for each other were still very much alive, and the relationship was blossoming again. This, of course, was where Mel came into the picture, the intention being to keep Arnold Hoffenach at a distance. There was little time and a lot to get through. They remained out of sight at the Pinewood Hills resort, working to assimilate their roles.

Leaden clouds were piling up over the ridge across the lake, and rain had been sputtering intermittently all day. After taking a late-afternoon walk to stretch their legs and get some air after a morning of reading and memorizing, Mel and Stephanie approached the resort buildings along a path that meandered among birch and pine trees near the water's edge. There were only two days left now until the end of November. Stephanie, wearing a red ski jacket and white woollen hat, seemed at ease for the first time since her arrival in Boston. The stay here was doing a lot to help her get over the trauma of Brett and Eva, and her confidence seemed to be growing as she absorbed more of the personality whose part she would be taking. Perhaps that had been the intention.

"Entrepreneurs are one of the most valuable assets that our society possesses," she said. "People who can recognize an opportunity, who know how to set up a business, and who are willing to take the risks. They create the jobs that provide income and security for everyone else. You'd think they'd be appreciated, wouldn't you? But instead, we treat them as criminals to be punished. Nature rewards achievement and ability, and punishes nonachievement. We try to create a system that does precisely the opposite, by levying a progressively more savage tax on success, and rewarding inability with cash prizes. So, of course that system is falling apart. It was judged by the promises it preached, instead of by the results it produced."

Mel kicked a stone off the path as they walked. "Did you ever think of you and your sister as complementary sides of the same person?" he asked curiously.

"In what kind of way?"

"Oh, in being pro-people . . . but in different ways. You talk about their individual rights, their freedom. Stephanie used to see technology as the means to realizing those ideals. As long as it's impossible to create enough wealth for everyone to be well off, the defense of privilege by force is inevitable."

"Sure. The only real way for people to be better off is by increasing their productivity—the value of the work they do. And that's what technology does. Everything else turns out to be an illusion in the longer term. You can manipulate numbers and cook the books to look as if you're making more dollars, but the currency will devalue and each dollar won't buy as much. You can't take out more than you put in."

Mel turned his head to stare at her. She was looking out at the lake at that instant and didn't notice. It was uncanny. She *was* turning into Eva—talking like Eva, and now starting to think like Eva. They played this game all the time now. At first they had felt self-conscious and slightly foolish; now it came more easily and naturally. That was the idea.

"You're saying that capitalism is defensible, then?" Mel said. All afternoon he had been talking her through the things that he and Eva had talked about, prompting her until she could respond as Eva would have.

She nodded lightly. "Genuine free-enterprise capitalism, based on voluntary exchange. It's not only defensible. It's morally superior to anything else you can name."

"How can you justify some people living on interest from investments and doing nothing, while others have to work?" Mel challenged.

"Well, if I've built a building that I don't have a use for right now, but which you could run your business in, would there be anything wrong with me renting it out to you?"

"Of course not."

"So if using my building enables you to make profits for yourself, I should be entitled to a share of the proceeds."

"I guess you'd have to be. If not, why would you let me use the building?"

"Right. Now suppose I've developed a machine that will enable you to produce ten times the output from that business. You'd hardly expect me to hand it over free, without any benefit to myself, would you?"

"Nope."

Stephanie tossed out a hand briefly. "And now suppose I provide the capital for you to buy the machine. Is there any difference? Interest is the rate that spare capital is rented out at. If it's fair for you to pay me a share of the profits you make through using my building and my machine, then it's just as fair to have to pay a share of what you make through using my money. If I hadn't lent it to you, I could have used it to make something for myself."

"What about ordinary wage earners, who don't own any capital? How do you let them get in on the act?"

"By allowing them to keep what they make, for a start. Get rid of the union mentality that keeps them there. Let everyone be self-employed. How many strikes would you get then? People shouldn't be bought and sold along with the company like feudal serfs tied to the land."

Mel nodded that he was satisfied. "Okay, you've convinced me."

They emerged from the trees and crossed a strip of lawn to reenter the resort through the outside pool area. As they came to the empty sun lounges and tables with furled shades, they slowed their pace, both, seemingly, wanting to put off the moment of going back in after the peace and solitude outside. Mel halted and lifted a foot up onto one of the chairs, propping an elbow on his knee.

"When did it finish between us?" he asked, staring out across the lake.

"I'd have said when you went off to Chapel Hill to become a lawyer. I moved out to LA not long afterward."

"Haven't we seen each other since?"

"You came out to the West Coast a few times."

"When was the last time?"

"Last fall. We drove out through Death Valley and went to Nevada."

"You were writing for a living then," Mel said. The statement wasn't quite accurate—a try at catching her out.

"That was over a year earlier, before I went to work full-time with the Constitutionals. And it was more of an editorial job."

"Oh, that's right. With that magazine, what was it called? . . ."

"*The Free Rationalist*. They had offices on Figueroa, opposite the Meath Tower."

"We stayed at Las Vegas. There were those two guys losing hundreds of thousands, and they thought it was hilarious. You figured they were laundering drug money through the casino."

"We had fun," she agreed. "But it wasn't the same."

The sound of a chain saw came distantly from somewhere in the forest. Mel leaned forward to pick up a piece of twig from the tabletop and toyed with it absently. "Do you know why I went to Chapel Hill?" he asked.

Stephanie shrugged. "To get away for a while, think it out. . . . You wanted to own me, and I wouldn't be owned. You had a problem dealing with that."

"But you didn't let it be just for a while. You moved away to LA."

"At the time, I thought I was doing you a favor . . . doing us both a favor."

Mel turned his head toward her. "And the irony is that now, after all this time, I think I finally understand what you were trying to say. I could love you all the more now for what you are, but I can't because you're . . ." He stopped and licked his lips, unable to form the word, and the twig snapped in his fingers. He threw the pieces down, realizing that he had been getting out of line.

"You know," Stephanie said, "one thing I never did understand was why law? What made you switch to that?"

Mel grinned thankfully and accepted the out that she was giving him. "There were several things. You had something to do with it."

"Did I? You'd better remind me."

"It was a short time after we met, back at UWF. I stopped by Economics when I was thinking of enrolling in one of Brodstein's classes. You were helping out in the office because a secretary hadn't shown up."

"Was she the one who'd gotten a job offer, but her counselor told her not to take it?"

"Something like that."

"So, where do lawyers come into it?"

"I'd been talking to Brett about who'd play the biggest part in making a free society happen. We didn't think it would be computer people. I asked you what you thought, and you said lawyers."

Stephanie laughed. It was a haunting echo of the way Eva used to laugh. "And just because of one word you went off and changed careers?"

Mel smiled back. At that time, he couldn't take being laughed at by Eva. Now he could laugh along too. "That was six years ago. A lot of other things happened too. But maybe it was a part of it. Who knows what goes on in our subconsciouses?" Around them an evening breeze was coming up, blowing leaves onto the tarpaulin stretched over the pool for winter. Mel took his foot down off the chair. "Anyhow, it's starting to get chilly. Let's go in."

As they approached the entrance to the rear lounge, the door opened and Larry appeared. "Ah, you're still out here," he said. "We saw you coming from the office. Ron wants to see you there right away."

"It sounds like trouble," Mel said as they followed him in.

"I'll let Warren and Ron explain it."

They went up some stairs to a group of secluded rooms at the back of the main building. Inside one of them, Landis was sitting at the desk, reading something in a file, while on the far side, Bassen stared moodily out of the window at the trees that Stephanie and Mel had emerged from. He turned as they entered. Landis looked up. George Slade was in an adjoining room through a half-open door, talking on the phone.

"Wadlow's being a prick out on the West Coast," Bassen said without preamble.

"What's happened?" Mel asked.

"He's being obstructive about putting Stephanie in there as Eva."

Stephanie took off her hat and unzipped her ski jacket. "What doesn't he like about it?"

Bassen waved a hand vaguely. "It's an image and turf thing. Basically he's worried that some of his people might think they should have known about it, and they'll feel jerked around if we don't tell them. He wants so many of them in on it that the whole thing would cease making any sense. What he's trying to do is cover his ass from all angles. But if office politics is coming into it, it's not going to work, anyway."

"Couldn't Newell just tell him to do it?" Mel asked. "He is the boss, isn't he?"

"He could, but it wouldn't be Henry's style."

"I think the atmosphere is all too wrong to try it now, anyway, even if Wadlow changes his mind," Landis said from the desk. Bassen nodded.

Mel looked from one to the other. "You're not saying we'll have to send her in cold?"

Landis looked at Bassen and shook his head. Mel got the feeling that they had discussed this between themselves already. "We can't Ron. Not without some kind of test in friendly territory. She needs to know she can do it. We all do."

Bassen turned back to the window and nodded with a sigh. "I agree, I agree. But where else is there?" They talked for a while, but nobody could come up with an immediate alternative.

It was an hour later, while they were still debating the issue over a cold-cuts snack brought in from the restaurant, that Mel at last saw the obvious. "There are two people who knew both Stephanie and Eva from our university days," he said. "In fact it was them and Eva who got me involved with the Constitutionals in the first place." He looked around at the circle of faces. "We go back to Florida. Let's try Stephanie out—and me, for that matter—with the Brodsteins. We'll go visit Paul and Martha Brodstein."

CHAPTER 29

Earlier in the year, a terrorist group claiming to be the militant arm of an Iraqi political sect had kidnapped the eight-year-old grandson of a wealthy Iranian while the boy was on vacation with his family in Italy. The Iranian was, in fact, an agent of the Israeli intelligence service, Mossad, who had been installed in the country many years previously under a carefully prepared cover identity. Since then, he had been accepted socially into Iran's highest political and military circles, which had enabled him to send a flow of valuable information back to the Israelis.

The kidnappers demanded the release of a number of prisoners being held in Israeli custody, and when the Israelis stood firm, sent the severed end of a finger through the mail as an inducement, along with the grisly warning that the pieces would get larger. Mercifully, however, Mossad in the meantime had pinpointed the hideout near the harbor at Palermo, in Sicily, where the boy was being held. Fearing hesitation and delay on the part of the local authorities, which would have made tragedy inevitable, the Israelis decided to take matters into their own hands and sent in one of their antiterrorist units. The commandos landed silently at night from rubber boats, located and stormed the house, wiping out all six of the captors who were there at the time, and brought the boy out safely.

But the Israelis were not satisfied. The six kidnappers killed at Palermo had been small fry, and further investigations, along with tip-offs from various unlikely sources that were united only in their disgust at this new turn that old grievances had taken, revealed that the mastermind responsible was one Wadal Zuvi, of indeterminate origins, who had long been suspected of being behind a long list of outrages. Zuvi, however, did his masterminding from a safe haven far removed from the action: his luxury villa at West Palm Beach, a little to the north of Miami. And Zuvi took no chances. The house was heavily protected by alarms and security devices, and filled at all times with armed bodyguards, who also surrounded Zuvi wherever he went.

The results of the early American primary elections and other indicators of public mood at that time were beginning to point to a Constitutional victory in November, and with the changes in the international scene that this was likely to bring, the Israeli government had been loathe to risk anything that might sour relationships. Any thought of a covert Mossad operation on American soil, the Israeli prime minister therefore decreed sternly to his intelligence committee, was out of the question. Accordingly, a discreet approach was made to the Americans through channels used when official communication was precluded, and shortly afterward in Washington, the word was quietly passed down to an unlisted office in the Pentagon underworld.

A week later, a water-company truck appeared at the end of the street where Zuvi's villa was situated. In the course of the next few days, a hole appeared in the ground, some lengths of new pipe were stacked beside it, and Zuvi's house guards paid it no further attention. But the two men in white coveralls down the hole were less interested in water pipes than in the local telephone feeder cable, which, since it was an exclusive residential area, ran underground. Soon, Zuvi's telephone started giving intermittent trouble. When one of the bodyguards called the phone company's number to report the fault, the voice that answered expressed apologies and promised that somebody would be there that afternoon. A man bearing phone-company credentials duly appeared, traced wiring around the house, performed tests, and replaced something in the phone in Zuvi's private office. He said that everything should be fine now, and went away again. The water company's work farther along the street finished on the same day, too.

The next morning, a caller asked to speak to Zuvi. "Who wants him?" the bodyguard who took the call demanded.

"I'm afraid that's confidential."

"What's it about?"

"I wouldn't dare tell you."

"I'll transfer you to his office."

There was a pause. Then, a belligerent voice answered, "Yeah?"

"Hello. Are you Wadal Zuvi?"

"Yes I am. What of it? Who are you?"

Zuvi lived long enough to tell the doctors that he heard a high-pitched whine just before the bomb exploded.

The agent who had placed the device and transmitted the acoustic signal over the line to detonate it returned to Washington a few days later. Around the office and in its files he was referred to by the nom de guerre of Marco Polo, while his code name in the field was Obsidian. Had he been working covertly in another country, he would also have had a third name—the official cover by which he went openly about in his day-to-day affairs. In fact, when off duty, he went by the easiest name of all to maintain, which came easily and naturally: his own. It was Dave Fenner.

The Colonel—that was the only name that Fenner had ever known him by—stared distastefully down at the file on his desk. He was a lean, hollow-faced man with protruding eyes and a droopy, ragged mustache. Fenner had always pictured him as looking more at home in a uniform of the Civil War period, of either side, instead of a tweed jacket, check shirt, and knitted tie. "Nasty business. It can't go any lower than snatching children and dragging them into it. . . . Well, at least let's be thankful that it's the last time he'll try anything like it. Good mission, Polo."

Which, from the Colonel, was the ultimate in dizzying heights of praise that one could reasonably expect to hear. "My pleasure," Fenner said. And meant it.

The Colonel closed the file, pushed it aside, and reached for another underneath it, which he had been studying. "The communication that our friends in Florida brought back from Lebanon contained something that looks as if it could be in your area, too." He was referring to the Brodsteins. Having known Dave for years, they occasionally functioned as couriers for him on their trips abroad, particularly in situations where one end or the other wished the connection to remain unofficial. "It's from Mossad again. I'm beginning to think we should transfer you to them permanently. Let them pick up the paycheck."

"What do they want this time?" Fenner asked. "And why the roundabout approach?"

"I don't know exactly. But it seems that one of their infiltrators who's been operating inside PALP has stumbled on something unusual."

Which meant that it had something to do with Syria. The

People's Army for the Liberation of Palestine was one of the dozens of splinter groups that the guerrilla movements, such as PFLP and Fatah, of twenty years earlier had spawned in their ceaseless squabbles and internal rivalries. It had its roots in the Saiqa movement, and obtained its backing primarily from the Syrian Baath Party, which meant it was Soviet-driven.

The Colonel went on. "The main thing he's been assigned to is getting some inside information on an airplane hijack that they're thought to be planning."

Fenner looked askance. "Hijacks aren't our line. That's what the Delta Force guys are supposed to be for at Fort Bragg."

"That's not the side of it that interests us. In addition, their agent has also made contact with a mysterious person that they refer to as Mustapha, who's being held by PALP. Mustapha claims to have urgent information concerning our—the American—space defense system, that he wants to send back to us." The Colonel glanced over the top of the document at Fenner for a reaction.

Fenner shrugged. "Why can't Mossad's agent relay it out?"'

"It's not so simple. Apparently Mustapha doesn't trust anyone. In fact he doesn't even trust our own people—most of them, anyhow. According to the message we've got, the only organization he'll deal with is the Constitutional party." The Colonel looked across the desk. "Weird, but there it is."

"Okay . . ." Fenner was nodding as he saw where he was starting to fit into the picture.

The Colonel went on. "You have a reliable contact inside the Constitutional party organization, whom you've known for years."

"Mayfly," Fenner said, which was the department's code name for Eva.

"Yes. . . . Now, in January, the future vice president will be visiting Egypt and Israel for political talks. It has also reached my ear that Mayfly will be going too, as a member of his party. Since you know Mayfly and Mayfly is close to the party leadership, it ought to be possible to use her as a channel to Mustapha, via Mossad. That's what I want you to organize. How long has it been since you were in touch with her?"

"Quite a while. The last time I talked to her, she was wrapped up in election stuff."

"Well, arrange a meeting with her to make sure she can do it, et cetera. Then, I want you to get over to Jerusalem and do

the groundwork with the Mossad people to have a specific plan worked out by the time Mayfly arrives. I've already cleared it with the chief there. You know the drill. Any questions?"

"I'll get to it right away."

"Well, what are you still sitting there for, Polo?"

"I'm on my way, right now."

CHAPTER 30

Brett's voice came through the doorway from the kitchen. "That's right, Marty, you've got it. I don't feel like a bayou barbecue tonight. . . . Because I have other plans. . . . No it won't, it'll be a circus. You know as well as I do that it's always a circus. . . . No we won't. First, the logistics will get screwed up. Harry and Jeff will fight over Marge. Charlie and Lisa will get Sylvie all upset. It'll be the usual stuff, and I've already seen it. . . ." At the far end of the lounge, Mel sat staring morosely out through the picture window at Pensacola Bay and paying little attention. Two dark-painted navy jets were climbing and turning after taking off from Chevalier Field at the Naval Air Station to the west. Behind him, Brett's voice continued, "Well, if you have to know, I thought I'd go over to Steph's. . . . What do you mean, and what? Play records or something and talk, that's what. People can still have a good time without needing swarms of noisy assholes around them all the time. . . . Sure I've changed. It's called getting older. . . . Yep, 'fraid so, Marty. . . . Some other time, maybe, eh? Sure, and you. So you and the guys have a good time, okay? . . . Yeah. . . . Yeah. . . . See ya."

Brett appeared in the doorway, wearing a thigh-length flannelette beach robe over white shorts. Mel showed no reaction. He had been like this ever since they got up, and for most of yesterday. Brett stood, hands on hips, regarding him for a few seconds, then said, "You look like a suicide commercial. Hey, come on, brighten up. Who knows, the war might happen today. We might all be nuked by supper time."

Mel returned a scowl. "That might be an improvement.

Life's too much of a hassle, anyhow. It's like sex: all things considered, the time would probably be better spent doing something else."

Brett came into the room and stood by the large walnut dining table, where the ignition sequencer from his car was lying partially dismantled in a shoe box. "What's been bugging you for the last couple of days?"

"Oh, it doesn't matter." Mel looked away over the bay again.

"It's gotta be trouble with Eva, right? I've got all day if you wanna talk."

"Not really. . . . Don't worry about it. It's just a down, that's all."

"Marty called. He says the gang are having a barbecue out at the bayou tonight. Why not go along?"

"I might enjoy it, and I'm not in the mood."

"Jesus H., you've really got it bad, Mel! Okay, how about coming over to Steph's with me? Better than moping around on your own. We all know each other. Maybe it'd help to unload."

"You go ahead. I'd rather be on my own, anyhow."

"Watcha gonna do, stay here?"

"I dunno." Mel carried on looking out of the window. "Maybe I'll go into town and get a drink someplace. See who's around . . ."

Brett waited for a moment, then went back into the kitchen. He finished putting the dishes in the washer that he had been stacking when Marty called, and then moved back to the doorway. Mel was still in the same position and took no notice. Brett watched him for a while and then went through into his own room, closing the door behind him. He sat down on the edge of his bed, picked up the phone extension, and called Stephanie's number.

"Hello?"

"It's Brett," he said, keeping his voice low. "Look, about me coming over tonight. This is a bit sudden, and I'm sorry, but do you think you could find something different to do?"

"You mean you can't make it?"

"That's right. Something's come up."

"You're not coming through very loud, Brett."

"I don't wanna speak up, because Mel's in the next room and it's about him. See, he's been acting kinda weird, and I figure it's to do with him and Eva. So I thought maybe I'd take him

out on the town for a beer or two, you know . . . talk it out.
Try and cheer him up. I think it'd do him good."

"Well, it's disappointing, but I guess it'd be best if he's really
that bad. It should be a good night to get him out of it, too.
Finals are over. There'll be a lot of people out celebrating."

"Exactly. That's what I thought, too. So, you don't mind,
eh?"

"Of course not. You have fun, and take care of Mel, okay?"

"I knew you wouldn't. So I'll give you a call tomorrow,
then?"

"Of course. Let me know how it goes."

"Right, and ah . . . I guess it would be best not to mention
it to Eva if you talk to her."

"You know I wouldn't. She takes care of herself."

"Okay, and thanks a lot. I appreciate it."

"Take care."

"You too. Bye."

He waited until Marty called again, as he knew Marty
would. Marty was one of those born organizers of people, who
worried and fussed and always called everyone at least three
times. "No, I don't think Mel wants to come either, Marty," he
said, taking the call in his room. "We're already going out
tonight. It's already fixed. . . . No, we don't have one of
those we can loan you. . . . Because I'm in the middle of
fixing it. Try Donna. I think she's got one. . . . If they
borrowed it, try them. . . . Well, it's all I can suggest. . . . Okay, Marty. Have a good one. . . . Sure. So
long."

He hung the phone up and went into the lounge. Mel had
moved to the table and was playing solitaire. "Say, what do you
know," he said. "That was Steph. Something's come up and
she's wiped out tonight. I guess I'm gonna be at loose ends.
How would you like some company over that beer you were
talking about?"

Mel looked up. He hesitated for a moment and then said,
just a trifle grudgingly, "Sure, why not?"

"Maybe shoot some pool. Feel lucky today?"

"When did I ever need luck to whip your ass?"

"Ah, now we're hearing it! When somebody comes along
who can whip my ass at a pool table, I'll write and tell you
about it, okay?"

"You won't need to. I reckon I'll already be there."

"Oh, is that so? Okay, ten bucks says you're a dead man. First five games."

Mel grinned his first real grin all day. "You've got it. Ten bucks."

Trader Jon's Pub and Oyster Bar was situated just in the respectable fringe, a couple of blocks from the waterfront area around the bottom end of Palafox. It was a popular lunchtime spot for journalists and businesspeople during the week, and a favorite downtown haunt for the younger set in the evenings. On Saturday nights it was always packed and noisy, and by ten o'clock Mel and Brett, a considerable number of Coors and Budweisers the worse for wear, were sitting at a corner booth out of the line of fire from the band's formidable battery of speakers, which were blaring a medley of thumpy, beat-heavy college hits from the sixties. The dance floor on the far side of the room was crowded, the tables and booths around them filled with groups and couples, and the area along by the bar thick with singles, mainly males reconnoitering the territory.

Mel gestured appealingly over his glass. "It's just not a way I'm used to thinking, Brett. Does it make sense? I mean, you and Steph don't have that kind of complication. You get along just the way I always thought steady people do, don't you? You've got one person and you stick with it, right? Or do I belong to some other century or something?"

He raised his glass and took a swig. His head was swimming, and a part of him knew that his mouth had been running away with itself in a way that he'd normally have cared more about than he particularly did right now. But that was what alcohol was for. It gave people a socially acceptable excuse for saying all things they'd been wanting to, and a ready-made reason for claiming afterward that they hadn't really meant it or didn't remember. The custom also obliged everyone else to say it was okay, even when they knew damn well you had meant it and you did remember.

Brett, listening with an arm draped along the back of the booth, stroked his beard with a knuckle while he thought how to answer. "Well, I guess that's just the way Eva is. I know how you feel. But it's not because she thinks less of you. You can't really judge her by the regular rules. She lives by her own rules. This may sound kinda strange, but the fact that she goes for you at all makes you pretty exceptional . . . er, in her way of thinking . . . if you know what I mean."

"Oh, come on. What do you take me for?"

"No, really. If she thought you were just some regular schmucko-nerd, she'd never have bothered. She's got better things to do. You ought to try and see it as a compliment."

Mel's eyes widened indignantly. "Compliment! This dildo can breeze into town and screw my woman whenever he feels like it, and you say I should feel it's a compliment? I feel like a spare toy. What kind of compliment is that supposed to be?"

"Okay, then why stick around?" Brett challenged, matching Mel's tone. "Just tell her to go fuck herself."

Mel sighed and drained the rest of his drink. "Shit, you know why. . . . She's different."

"There you are, then. You can't have it both ways."

"Intelligent is the word, I guess. It's her mind. She's free, in a way I can't really understand. . . . Do you know, I've got a suspicion that deep down I might be envious that she can be that way . . . but I don't want to admit it to myself."

Brett nodded seriously, in a way that said he did know. "You called her your woman a second ago. Maybe that's your problem. She never accepted being anybody's woman. Wouldn't Dave have as much right to bitch about that dildo down in Pensacola who screws *his* woman while *he's* out of town? What's the difference? In fact, he was there first."

"I don't know if I can handle it."

"Then there you are. That's the difference." Brett waved a hand vaguely near his shoulder. "It's the way she is, and the way she'll always be."

Mel stared at his empty glass and shook his head. "Fuck it, no, Brett. That's not it. I think I could handle that. What bugs me is the feeling of being put on the line like some kind of rat in a lab test. Why should I *have to* handle it? See, it's not just her freedom that I envy. I envy the power she has . . . the power to make me play by her rules. Why should I have to?"

"You don't. You could opt out."

"But I already said I don't want to."

"Then what are you asking me to say?" Brett indicated Mel's glass with a finger. "You're already ruined for tomorrow, anyway. Want another?" Mel nodded mechanically. Brett sat back, looked around until he caught the eye of the waitress who was serving drinks at a nearby table, and signaled with a hand. She nodded that she'd seen him. Brett hunched forward and rested his elbows on the table. "Maybe you're mad because she won't jump into the trap that you want to catch her in," he suggested.

"What trap?"

"Come on. You know what I mean. Why should *she* have to play by *your* rules, either? Just because some people who think they're nice Christians, and that everyone else ought to be like them, say she should? If you think about it that way, it isn't her who's trying to hang rules on anybody at all. It's you. Maybe you're in a trap, and she's giving you a chance to jump out. Try thinking about it that way, maybe."

Mel leaned back and peered at Brett oddly for a few seconds. "You know, I get the distinct impression that this isn't especially news to you," he said. "You already knew Eva was this way, didn't you?"

Brett pursed his lips, then nodded. "Steph's her sister, after all. We talk about things. . . . I mean, hell, what do you expect?"

"She told you about the way Eva is?"

"She . . . sorta mentioned it once or twice, I guess, yup. . . . Warned me that you might have problems."

"You shithead! And you never said anything to me. What kind of a pal are you supposed to be?"

"Aw, come on. There are things that are best to keep to yourself if you're smart. You know that. And anyhow, I was straight about it. You asked me, and I told you. It wouldn't have done any good to say anything before."

The waitress came over to the booth to take their order. The name badge on her skimpy, frilly-skirted costume said that she was Muriel. "Can I get you another, guys?" she asked.

Brett was just about to answer, when three figures that had been threading their way between the tables from the bar arrived noisily at the booth. They were Chuck, Harry, and Scottie, all from the campus, obviously out on the town for a night and making the most of it.

"Hey, waddya know, it's Mel and Brett! Want some more company?" Chuck slid into the booth beside Brett without waiting for an answer.

"Perfect timing," Harry said, squeezing in next to Chuck. "You can get us one, too, Muriel. Mine's a Bud."

"Miller Lite, and your phone number," Chuck said.

Muriel turned her eyes briefly upward. "Oh boy, all I needed was these three. The beer, I can get. You couldn't afford the rest."

"Get a load of this!" Chuck exploded, howling with laughter. "Say, how about negotiating?"

"I'll give you my heart. Anything else, you have to fight for."

Scottie sat down next to Mel. "Make mine a Beck's dark, please."

"And the same for us, I guess," Brett added.

"Got it." She turned away to head for the bar.

"Hey, Muriel," Chuck called after her as she moved away. She stopped and looked back. "What's the difference between a cocktail waitress and a proctologist?"

"I couldn't begin to imagine."

"A proctologist only has to deal with one asshole at a time. Ha ha ha!"

"Gimme a break." Muriel moved away, shaking her head.

"I thought you guys would be out at the barbecue," Brett said.

Chuck shrugged. "Ah, we decided to give it a miss."

"Have you two eaten yet?" Harry asked. "We were thinking of going on over to McGuire's later."

"I'd rather go Chinese," Scottie said.

"Why did the pervert cross the road?" Chuck asked.

"Go on," Scottie said.

"Because he'd gotten stuck in the chicken!"

Mel caught Brett's eye for an instant and covered his brow with a hand. He didn't need this just now. Brett shrugged, but there was nothing he could do. There would be no way of getting rid of them now without being a lot more unfriendly than the situation warranted.

Mel turned to Scottie. "Before you get too comfortable, I need to go to the can."

"What? Oh, sure." Scottie got up again to let Mel out. Mel stood up a little too quickly, and his head went dizzy. He swayed and bumped against Scottie. "Hey, steady on there, Mel," Scottie said. "You two must be making a night of it, eh?"

"Sorry about that," Mel mumbled.

"This Polack joins the airborne, see . . ." Chuck went on behind him as he lurched away.

Mel felt curiously detached from the surroundings of people and noise. His vision telescoped to just a patch immediately in front of him, through which faces, bodies, legs, and tables passed disconnectedly as he made his way to the edge of the dance floor, and then along to the corridor at the rear where the washrooms were located. The two doors were side by side.

The door to the right carried the sign GENTS, with a hand pointing to the one at the left; the door to the left said LADIES and had a hand pointing to the one at the right. As always, there were a couple of people standing bemusedly outside, trying to figure it out. Knowing the place, Mel went into the left-hand door, just as an embarrassed-looking man emerged from the other. Never a night went by without someone being caught.

He didn't want to go back and have to listen to Chuck and the rest of them, he decided while he was inside. He'd rather be on his own. Suddenly, the thought struck him of calling Eva. Then he wasn't sure if he should while he was like this. But then, maybe it would make her a little guilty to see the state she had driven him to. Would it be a good idea or a bad idea? He would go somewhere quieter to think it over. And anyway, he needed some air.

He was emerging onto the street—parked cars, neon signs, some people about. Since the oncoming traffic was stopped at a red light at the end of the block, he crossed over. Images and impressions flowed by in a blurred procession. Packed coffee shop with booths and faces inside the plate glass window; black couple talking outside the door; smell of steaks. . . . Bumper sticker on a parked van: DON'T TELL ME WHAT KIND OF FUCKIN' DAY TO HAVE. . . . Pizza parlor; lights, loud music inside; more cooking smells. No, not hungry. . . . Pay phone. Call Eva? Stop. Maybe not. Sit down somewhere and think about it first. . . . Corner store, still open: newspapers, magazines, liquor, and groceries. Gray cat asleep in window.

Darker street, narrower, leading toward docks. Dingy bar; shuttered stores; greasy restaurant. . . . And then he became aware of the figures of two women standing by a doorway near a small bar a short distance ahead on the far side, picked out vaguely in the light from a streetlamp. Something compelled him across the street as he came nearer. One was tall, dark-haired and dusky-skinned, with a red leather coat and a skirt showing lots of fishnet-stockinged leg. The other was fairer, in a blouse, tight pants, and high boots. Although he was now in the part of town where the hookers hung out, he didn't make the connection until the taller one smiled, eyeing him seductively, and spoke as he approached. "Hi. Looking for a good time?"

Confusion swamped him suddenly, and he kept walking. By the time any kind of coherence had returned in his head, he was already several paces past them. "How about an even better time with two girls?" her voice suggested after him. But if he'd stopped, he wouldn't have known what to say, so he kept going and rounded the first corner he came to.

But the glimpse he'd seen of the taller one's body in the low-cut top inside her open coat, and the firm lines of her hips had aroused him. As he walked on in his stupor, he found himself fantasizing about following her upstairs to a room, probably less than a block away . . . watching her undress for him . . . and as he turned the next corner, he knew he was going to circle the block to bring him back to the same place. He had never tried it with a hooker before. As with most young men of his age, the subject was one that had filled him with curiosity, purely because of its mystery and illicitness. He'd brought a wad out with him tonight, and he had plenty left. He sensed the decision that his mind had already made somewhere below its ragged level of consciousness, and the anticipation increased his excitement.

Then he thought about Eva again, and in that moment the prospect became not simply a matter of an adventure to satisfy curiosity, but a deliberate gesture of self-assertion and defiance. Minutes ago he'd been considering calling her and . . . and then what? Go scampering back to agree to being one of her pets? "No way!" he muttered aloud to himself. And suddenly he felt a foot taller, and his stride swung into a jaunty swagger. "No way." he repeated. "I don't need your kind of shit, lady!"

But when he came around the last corner and was halfway along the block, he saw that the darker-haired girl was gone, and a man in a light jacket was talking to the one in the pants. Mel walked on by, trying to act nonchalant and natural—as if either of them cared. When he came to the bar a little farther along, he turned on impulse and went inside.

It was smoky and sleazy, and a jukebox was playing a rock-jazz number. There were whites, blacks, Cubans, Hispanics. Several of the heads turned to follow him curiously as he crossed to a vacant stool at the bar. The bartender, tall, lean, unsmiling, with black curly hair and swarthy, pock-marked features, raised his eyebrows inquiringly. "Scotch," Mel told him. "Just on the rocks." He pulled out his billfold and pushed a twenty across the bar. The bartender scooped ice into a glass, topped it up from a bottle of Johnny Walker Black Label, and sent it back with change. Mel raised the glass, then

esitated for a moment and gripped the edge of the bar as the
oom swam sickeningly. For an awful moment he thought he
vas about to lose his balance and crash off the stool in front of
he whole place. But the feeling passed. He took a long breath
o suck oxygen into his lungs, drained an inch of the amber
iquid, and set the glass down. Then he half turned on his seat,
esting an elbow on the bar to show he was at home and
oelonged there, like in the movies. But it was girls he was
ooking for. His eyes roamed unsteadily around the room. An
matched one? An available one? Fat or older or ugly—he
lidn't care now. He was aroused and drunk, and he wanted
ction.

She read easily the signals that he was telegraphing, and
came from somewhere at the back of the room, squeezing
oetween him and the next customer to get to the bar. Mel
ooked at her: tall, dark-skinned, with wavy black hair hanging
to her shoulders, and a low-cut top. For a moment he thought
she was the one he'd passed outside, without her coat, but
when he looked down he saw that she had plain stockings, not
fishnets. Cuban or Central American, he decided.

"Some change for the cigarette machine, Enrico," she said
to the bartender, proffering a bill. The bartender took it and
turned away. Then she turned her head and seemed to notice
Mel for the first time. "Hello. Out all on your own tonight,
eh?"

Mel shrugged and tried to look what he hoped was appropriate. "It happens." Full, thick lips, with dark lipstick. Long
lashes, accentuated with mascara. Firm, well-rounded body,
nipples pressing against the material of her top. He wanted to
bite them, run his hands all over her, and felt himself going hot
and cold at the sudden realization that something was going to
happen. It was like the feeling he'd had at Eva's place that first
night.

"Oh . . . " She turned fully, leaning closer to let him peek
down between her breasts, and lowered her voice. "Looking
for some company, maybe?"

"Sure. Who isn't?" he managed to toss out indifferently.

"How about me? You like it? Think we could have a little
fun?"

"Want to go someplace?"

She pouted reproachfully and touched his chin with a
fingertip. "You men! That's not very romantic. First we must
get to know each other a little. Is okay, yes? If you're a

gentleman, you buy me a drink." Mel frowned uncertainly.
She moved closer, rubbing her hip against the inside of his
thigh. Her perfume was nice, not too heavy. "Come on, what's
a little drink?" she said. Her finger played at the neckline of his
collar. "I'll give you a real good time, I promise."

He grinned then, feeling slightly foolish. "Sure. What'll it
be?"

"That's better. Vodka tonic with a little lime. What's your
name?"

"Mel."

"I am called Juanita." She nudged his arm and indicated a
small table off to one side, with two empty chairs. "We can take
our drinks over there and sit. More cozy."

Mel raised a hand to get the bartender's attention. "Vodka
tonic with a splash of lime for Juanita here, Enrico. And
another Black Label for me." He produced his billfold and
peeled out another of the twenties with a flourish, a man in a
man's world, now. So, even if he did decide tomorrow that
he'd been a prick, what of it?

As Mel opened the billfold, Juanita stole a glance at it, and
while he was paying Enrico, she sent a barely perceptible nod
to two Puerto Ricans who were watching from near the back,
where she had come from. One was long and lankily built, but
with powerful shoulders, sinewy hands, and a craggy face with
a cruel, thin-lipped mouth. The other was stockier, with
neck-length hair, a ragged Pancho Villa mustache, and narrow
sardonic eyes. Mel picked up the glasses, and Juanita steered
him by his arm to the table she had indicated. They talked for
about five minutes, she rubbing his leg with hers and touching
his arm constantly, he trying hard not to show his rising
impatience. By the time they got around to the money side of
it he would have agreed to twice the going rate, and the figure
she named came almost as a pleasant surprise. While this was
going on, the two Puerto Ricans rose and left through the rear
entrance.

Finally Juanita said, "So, we go now, yes?"

"Just lead the way, honey."

She laid a restraining hand on his arm. "There is just one
little problem. Is not good for us to leave here together. The
police give us trouble all the time—they watch this place. Is
snack bar one block from here, called Star. I have to meet you
there in five minutes. Is okay, yes? Then we go to my place,
just a short walk."

Mel frowned, but there was no choice but to go along with it. Besides, he hadn't paid her anything yet. "Where's this place?" he asked.

"You go out rear entrance here, into alley. Go left to far end, then right when you come to street. Star snack bar is along on same side."

Sitting at the bar was a pale, blond-haired man who had been watching them in the mirror since they sat down at the table. Also, he had seen the two Puerto Ricans leave. He knew how the three of them operated, and didn't like it. And there was still a score to be settled with them over the deal on the hot BMW that they'd cut him out of. . . . Besides, this was only a kid. The pale man got up and sauntered out of the bar and down the steps that led to the basement and toilets. He went to the pay phone outside the men's room, lifted the receiver, and tapped in a number. "Police," he murmured quietly, covering the mouthpiece with a hand.

At the table upstairs, Mel got unsteadily to his feet, with Juanita holding an arm to assist. "You go now," she whispered. "I see you at Star in five minutes. We have good time. You see."

"Gotta go downstairs first."

"Is okay. I wait."

On the way down, he passed a pale-faced man coming back up, who ignored him. He relieved himself in the tiny men's room. It smelled of urine, and its floor was awash with overflow from the blocked toilet in its single cubicle. He splashed water on his face and went back upstairs. Juanita, still at the table, winked at him and nodded in the direction of the far end of the room. He nodded back at her, made his way to the rear entrance, and left.

Outside, he found himself in a narrow, poorly lit alley. It led to wider streets at both ends, extending for a greater distance to the left. He headed in that direction, staggering uncontrollably now, and unable to focus on the lights he could see at the far end. They seemed distant, then near all of a sudden, and then far away again. A wall bumped him in the face unexpectedly, grazing his cheek, and he meandered on, wondering vaguely how he'd managed to walk into it. . . . There were two figures ahead of him, in the shadows . . . men . . . big men, just standing there. . . .

Then a shout: "Hey, I think that's him guys." It had come from behind him, back at the far end of the alley. "Yes, it is.

Mel! . . . Mel, it's us." It was Brett's voice. Mel turned and looked back dazedly. They were coming along the alley at a run. Brett and Chuck were in front, Harry and Scottie following. "What in hell are you playing eh? We've been looking for you all over the place." Then they were all around him, taking his arms and babbling. He didn't know what was going on.

Moments later, a police cruiser slid into view across the end of the alley just in front of them. It stopped, and its spotlight came on, directed straight at them. "Oh shit," someone muttered behind him. He also registered vaguely that the two men he'd seen a moment ago had vanished.

Then everything was lights and voices, and the whole world was revolving in confusion. He had a hazy impression of two officers in Pensacola city police uniforms, while other arms held him steady on his feet.

"Are you guys okay here? What's going on?"

"Oh, he's in bad shape, but he's okay. We'll take care of him. He's getting married tomorrow. . . . You know how it is, officer."

"Were you planning on driving tonight? Seems to me you need a cab."

"Oh no, it's okay. We walked. He lives with me. It's only a few blocks."

"Where?"

"Pace Avenue, just off Sonia Street."

"How about you three?"

"We're out at Cordova. We'll get a cab."

"Well, look at him. He's out of it. So there's just you and him?"

"Right."

"Come on, get him in the car. We'll take you there."

"Gee, thanks a lot, officer."

Then hands were propelling Mel toward the police cruiser, and a black-sleeved arm was opening the rear door. Suddenly Mel giggled. "Offisher, do you know . . . what's the difference between a Pens'cola police offisher and a proc—proc . . . tolo-gist?" But the answer seemed so hilariously funny that he was laughing too much to be able to get it out. He was being dumped on a cold leather seat. . . .

And that was the last he remembered until Brett woke him with a mug of hot, black coffee at one-thirty the following afternoon.

CHAPTER 31

It was the last day of November when Mel and Stephanie flew south to Pensacola after arranging to see the Brodsteins. Their story was that they were simply visiting the city again for old time's sake. They had decided not to complicate matters or mar the atmosphere by mentioning anything about Brett or "Stephanie."

Paul Brodstein hadn't changed at all in appearance, and after the election was even more ebullient than Mel remembered. "Well, goddam, we did it!" he laughed, thumping the countertop in the familiar cluttered kitchen, with its view out over the Gulf. "All those years . . . Didn't I tell you we'd make it in 2000? Oh boy, are we gonna see some differences now!" Mel grinned. Anyone would have thought that the election had been yesterday. Brodstein looked at Stephanie. "And you look as if you've lost a couple of years . . . even after all the work you people must have put in. It's no wonder we haven't seen you for so long." He looked across at Martha, who was preparing some cheese snacks to go with the coffee. "How long has it been since we saw Eva?"

"It must be getting on for a year," Martha answered without looking up. Compared to Paul's, her manner had been cooler, Mel had noticed. She hadn't sounded as enthralled over the election, which seemed strange, considering her seeming involvement with Paul's work at one time. But then he recalled that she had seemed to be withdrawing, even during the two years he had remained in Pensacola after the evening he had first come to this house. People, like things, changed, he supposed.

"Well, it's good to see that you two are still together," Paul said. "The last time Eva was here, she said she hadn't seen you for ages. Isn't that right, Eva?"

Stephanie smiled. "Oh, we've had our ups and downs like anyone else, I guess."

194

"Another drink?" Paul suggested.

"Sure," Mel said.

Paul took their glasses and turned to the counter that he had used for mixing the cocktails. "You know who I wish was here right now," he said over his shoulder. "That tall guy with the beard that you used to live with, the one who was always saying it'd never happen—Brett, that was it . . . just to see his face now. Is he still with that sister of yours, Eva? The last thing I heard, they were going to . . . Where was it, Martha?"

"California," Martha replied.

They had expected something like this, and Stephanie was ready for it. "They moved to Denver," she said evenly. "Steph went to work for a nuclear research company there."

"Wasn't Brett going to work for the defense industry out there?" Martha asked. It was the first real curiosity she'd shown.

"He quit that," Mel said. "I guess it just wasn't his line after all."

"How long are you and Eva going to be in Pensacola?" Paul inquired.

"Only until tomorrow," Mel said "It was just an impulse trip to see old places . . . you know how it is. I have to get back, though."

Paul turned back and handed them their drinks. He stirred his own and looked at Mel. "A lawyer in the end, eh? I'd never have guessed it. It just shows how life can be full of surprises."

"Actually I was here a couple of weeks ago, researching a case," Mel said. "I tried to call you then, but you were out of town on one of your trips. The guy who took the call said Lebanon or some place, wasn't it?"

Paul nodded. "We must have got back just afterward. So was that what gave you the idea of bringing Eva back for a visit?"

"Yes, exactly," Mel said.

"Well, we're glad you remembered us."

"Of course. How could we not? . . . So, how was Lebanon?"

"Good," Paul said. "Oh, which reminds me. We picked up a new curiosity. Come and look at this."

He put down his drink and filled another glass with plain water. Then he handed an empty one to Mel and led the way out of the kitchen and through the eternal confusion of books and papers that the Brodsteins somehow managed to live

among, to an alcove on the far side of the lounge. Standing on
a shelf in the alcove was an oriental-looking two-handled vase
made of brass, on a circular base. Paul picked it up, turned to
face the others, and in full view of them, emptied the glass of
water into it. "Care for a drink?" he asked Mel.

Mel looked confused. "What is this?"

"Hold up your glass," Paul instructed. Mel did so. Grinning,
Paul tipped the vase over it, and red liquid the color of
burgundy wine poured out. "Neat?" he said.

"Astounding!" Stephanie exclaimed.

"Try it," Paul invited. Mel did. It was burgundy wine. He
sipped approvingly and passed the glass to Stephanie to try.

Paul turned the vase around and showed them two small
vents near the base of one of the handles. "The trick is knowing
which air holes to cover with your finger," he said, grinning.
"There are compartments inside. Changing water into wine
was one of the favorite wonders worked around the eastern
Mediterranean in ancient times. Heron of Alexandria in his
Pneumatics, and Philo of Byzantium described fifteen kinds of
apparatus for performing the trick. Does it sound familiar?"

Stephanie raised the glass. "Well then, to the future," she
said.

Just then the sound of a car drawing to a halt came from
outside. "We've got visitors," Mel remarked.

"It's probably Dave Fenner coming back," Martha said.

The smile froze on Stephanie's face. Mel turned slowly.
"Dave Fenner?" he repeated.

Paul put a hand to his forehead. "There was so much to talk
about after all this time that I clean forgot he was here." He
motioned toward Stephanie. "He called a couple of days ago,
asking if we'd seen anything of you, Eva. Apparently he'd been
trying to get in touch with you over something urgent. It so
happened that Mel had called only the day before to say you
were coming to Pensacola. When I told Dave that, he decided
to take a break and come down here as well. He arrived in
town yesterday."

Martha was watching Stephanie with a strange look on her
face. Mel got the feeling that she hadn't forgotten about Dave's
being there at all.

Footsteps sounded on the wooden steps up to the front deck
outside. A few moment later the door opened and Dave
Fenner came briskly into the house. "So, they've arrived
already. It's been a long time."

"Hello, Dave," Mel said mechanically.

Dave slipped an arm around Stephanie's waist and kissed her lightly on the cheek. Then he sensed her confusion, drew away again, and looked at her oddly. "Didn't they tell you I was here?"

"I clean forgot," Paul confessed. "It was only hearing your car that reminded me."

"See what you get with absent-minded professors," Dave said, laughing. "In that case, surprise, surprise." He turned toward Mel and extended a hand. "Good to see you again, buddy."

Mel felt a surge of relief inside as he took the hand and shook it. As long as thing didn't get too personal, Stephanie had passed the ultimate test. "You too," he replied.

"Did you and Eva decide to take a nostalgia trip or something?"

"Exactly."

They went back into the kitchen, and Paul made Dave a drink. There was more talk about the election, Dave asked about Brett and Stephanie, and Mel told his earlier story again. Finally Dave asked, "What plans do we have for eating tonight?"

"We hadn't talked about it," Paul said. "I guess we could go out someplace. Would everybody like that?"

"To be honest, I've had too much eating out lately. I was hoping we'd stay in," Stephanie said.

"Suits me, too," Mel agreed.

Paul nodded. "That's fine. I could cook up some steaks."

"Why don't Mel and I go get a couple of pizzas?" Dave suggested. "I just picked up a few packs of beer and some wine. They're in the trunk. It'd go great with the evening."

"I'll go for that," Mel said. The others agreed.

"We'd better get the booze into the refrigerator first," Dave said. "Want to come down and give a hand, Eva?"

"Sure." Stephanie got up.

"I'll toss up a salad while you're gone," Martha said.

Dave went back down to his car, followed by Stephanie and Mel. He opened the trunk and took out a couple of twelve-packs, which he placed in Mel's outstretched arms. Stephanie stood aside as Mel went past her to the stairs. Dave lifted out a liter flask of Chianti. She took it. "Wait, there's another one somewhere," he said as she started to turn away. "Now, where was it? . . . Thought I put it under here." Mel reached the

top of the stairs and disappeared out of sight across the deck.
"Remember Redman, Eva?" Dave asked casually as he rummaged in the trunk. "Who did he work for?"

Stephanie hesitated for just a split second, then answered
lightly, "That was a while ago, now. I'm not sure I remember."

"Oh, it doesn't matter. . . . Ah, here it is: one Chablis."
He lifted the flask out, and Stephanie hooked a finger of her
free hand through the ring at the neck.

Mel reappeared at the top of the stairs and came down.
"We'll see you guys later, then," Stephanie said, turning to go
back up. "Have fun.".

Dave indicated the front of the car to Mel with a nod of his
head. "Jump in."

Stephanie went up to the house, and Mel let himself in the
passenger side of the car. It was a Chevrolet, rented, from the
document folder lying in the tray between the front seats, and
smelled clean and new. Dave slammed the trunk lid, came
around the other side, got in, and started the motor. "It's been
a while, Mel," he said, looking over his shoulder as he backed
up. "So, how are things going?"

"Oh, pretty good. Yourself?"

"Can't complain."

"Still purchasing consultant in D.C.?"

"Uh-huh." They came to a sandy road fringed by sea oats and
turned west toward Sikes bridge, which would take them
across to Gulf Breeze.

"What does that involve, exactly?" Mel asked. "It's been six
years now, and I've always wondered."

"Oh, a little bit of this, a little bit of that. What about you?
Did you make it in law?"

"Yep. I moved north. I'm with an outfit in Boston now. A
small firm."

Mel sat back and enjoyed the warm, lazy sensation of
driving by the sea in Florida again. They lapsed into silence.
Dave's eyes were moving constantly, scanning the mirror and
the road ahead. They came to an isolated stretch of road, and
he slowed the car and pulled over to wave on another car that
had been behind them, the only other sign of life. As it passed,
he checked the mirror again, and then, without warning,
wrenched the wheel over to steer into a narrow trail leading
down between the sand dunes. "What the—" Mel exclaimed,
startled, as Dave braked to a halt and switched off the engine.

Suddenly Dave's joviality had left him, and the eyes confronting Mel from the other side of the car were hard and humorless. "Okay, talk," he snapped.

"What? I don't—"

"I want to know what the hell's going on, and I'm not in a mood to play games. I've been trying to get in touch with Eva all week. I called the place in Denver where Stephanie worked, and they told me she killed herself three weeks ago. I didn't mention it to Paul and Martha until I got to hear what Eva had to say. . . ." Dave gave a slight nod back over his shoulder to indicate the direction they had come from, and shook his head. "But she isn't Eva."

CHAPTER 32

Stars were coming out as the sky darkened. The water beneath the Sikes Bridge shone in the light of an early-evening moon. Dave drove in silence, eyes fixed on the roadway flowing through the headlamp glow ahead, mouth tight, preoccupied in thought. Mel sat dejectedly beside him, waiting for whatever outcome Dave was about to pronounce. It was the same feeling of inferiority when Dave was around that had made sharing Eva intolerable, but which Mel had been powerless to change. He'd thought that times were different now, that he was different after the years. But nothing had changed.

When it was obvious that the attempt at deceit had failed and there could be no question of trying to bluff further, he had abandoned himself instead to total honesty and told the whole story. He had told of Brett's suspected manipulation by a Soviet-managed espionage ring that involved prominent people, and his "accident" when he tried to break away; how Eva had been murdered in mistake for Stephanie, and the death rigged to look like suicide; about the incident at Devil's Slide, when the two Constitutional agents had mistaken Stephanie for Eva; how Eva had worked for Newell's organization and learned of a plan to compromise it somehow, before the inauguration; and finally, of the plan for Stephanie to impersonate Eva in order to find out more, and the idea of using the Brodsteins in a dummy run to test it out. "And it was a good thing we did, too," Mel had concluded in a tired voice after they had been talking for almost an hour. "Obviously there's a lot we don't know. It this had been the real thing . . ."

"If it had been the real thing, you'd have gotten her killed," Dave had completed. It hadn't been for any dramatic effect. Mel had the impression that he'd meant just that.

They came off the bridge and followed the road for three quarters of a mile to Northcliffe, where there was a small mall consisting of some stores, a steak house, a pizza parlor and bar, and a gas station. Dave pulled into the parking lot outside the pizza parlor and switched off the motor. He made no move to leave the car. "Now I'll tell you a few things," he said, breaking his silence at last. "They don't go any further than you, and when we get a chance to talk to her alone, Stephanie. Is that understood?"

"What about the Constitutional people that we're working with?"

Dave shook his head. "For the time being, no."

"Okay," Mel said.

"I don't think it'll come as any big surprise if I tell you that what I do doesn't have a lot to do with purchasing or consulting." Mel had already pretty much figured that out. He said nothing and waited. Dave went on. "All I will say is that I'm with a department of the government."

"I take it it's not important which one," Mel said.

Dave nodded. "That's all you need to know." He rested his arms on the wheel and started straight ahead at the neon signs in the bar window. "Eva and I had a professional relationship, besides being just friends. She and I worked together unofficially." He paused to allow Mel a moment to digest that. "It was the kind of trust that grows over years. I was a source to Eva about things that were going on in parts of government. And her work with the Constitutionals enabled her to supply information that helped me. It was a two-way thing."

"So you already knew she was working for Newell?"

"Oh, sure."

Mel frowned as he tried to visualize the chain in his mind. Warren Landis worked for Newell, and Eva had worked for Landis. But Landis, no doubt, also had his own contacts and informants in official circles, and somewhere in the tree of subordinates reporting to one of them was Dave. And Dave's personal relationship with Eva had led to their helping each other informally. However, in view of the uncertain environment that prevailed, it was understandable that Eva should have kept details of those dealings to herself, and it made sense that Landis and the rest of Newell's people had known nothing about it. In this light it was all the more curious that Dave should be revealing as much as he was.

"You didn't think it was Eva back at the house, from the first moment you walked in, did you?" Mel said.

"No."

"What gave her away? I mean, that's something we have to know about."

"Nothing that Seybelman or any of those would have spotted." Dave paused for a moment. "I'd been trying to contact Eva for over a week. That doesn't sound like a long time, but we had ways of getting in touch when we needed to. I knew something was wrong. I ended up trying the long shots, and one was to call the Brodsteins."

Mel nodded. "Paul told us about that. So?"

"Eva wouldn't have gone there. After she got in deep over in California, she quit contact with most of her old circles of friends and what-have-you. You don't want to leave audit trails all over the country of where you go and who you talk to. Paul and Martha were part of the old scene. So were you. She wouldn't have shown up in the middle of it all again. When we had business to discuss, either I went to LA, or we met somewhere between."

It sounded almost right, but something didn't quite add up, Mel thought. Or, more precisely, there was something that hadn't been said. Why would Eva not want to leave trails pointing back to the Brodsteins?

"Were Paul and Martha working with you too, somehow?" Mel asked when he pinpointed what was nagging him.

Dave conceded the point with a nod. "The Opposition extends a long way past the borders of the U.S.A. Keeping tabs on it can involve contacts overseas that you don't always want the world to know about."

"So that's why they're always traveling?" Mel said.

"Not exactly. They travel because their jobs take them places and because they like it. But it does make them a good cover for carrying out other errands on the side."

Mel thought about their recent visit to Lebanon. "Did you

know that Eva was supposed to go to the Middle East in January with McCormick?" he asked.

"Yes."

"So, what about the trip that the Brodsteins have just come back from? Was that just a coincidence, or what?"

There was a short silence, as if Dave were weighing things one last time in his mind before committing himself irreversibly. Finally he said, "No. That wasn't a coincidence. The reason I was looking for Eva was to brief her about a job that we want her to do for us while she's out there. Paul brought back details of a contact in Tel Aviv."

"But how could he?" Mel queried. "I thought you said the Brodsteins weren't in touch with Eva."

"They didn't know Eva had anything to do with it. It was a contact for me to make, to set things up."

"You mean you'll be going out there too?"

"That's right."

Which gave Eva three jobs to handle on the trip: her official PR duties with McCormick's party; the scheme that Seybelman wanted to use her in; and now this, whatever it was, for Dave. "She was in for a busy time," Mel commented dryly.

"Well, you knew Eva."

Mel waited, but Dave volunteered nothing further. Now Mel saw the situation clearly. "You're going to have to tell us the whole thing, Dave," he said in a quiet voice. "Because you need Stephanie out there to do your job, just as much as we do. That's what this conversation is all about, isn't it? It's the only reason you'd have for telling me all this." Dave drummed his fingertips on the rim of the steering wheel and looked about uncomfortably as his professional instincts rebelled against disclosing anything further. Mel waited, but the silence persisted. Finally he asked, "Why Eva? Why do you have to have someone from McCormick's party to do this job? You must have enough people of your own, especially in an area like that."

"We've been instructed specifically that it has to be somebody connected with the new administration."

"Why?"

"We don't know. But I will tell you that it involves one of the Palestinian groups connected with international terrorism. And some of the covert backers of that group have financial connections to certain interests over here, in the U.S.—

interests, that seem to be centered on the conservative Right. Does that strike you as odd?"

Mel frowned. "But I thought those people were supposed to be backed by the Soviets."

"Exactly. A strange coincidence of interests, you'd think . . ."

"The same as discovering that somebody like Oberwald is running a spy operation for them," Mel commented distantly. "It's strange all right."

Dave let him mull over it for a few seconds. Then he added in a curious voice, "Until you remember that the far Right is against Constitutionalism because it promotes individualism and secular values. And the Soviets aren't exactly wild about the political changes we expect to see over here, either." He looked across the car, as if inviting Mel to complete the rest for himself.

Mel wrinkled his brow as he assembled the facts into order in his head. "A lot of people—here, and abroad—won't like what will happen if the twenty-eighth amendment goes through," he began. Dave nodded. Mel continued, "From California we learn of something that's being planned to happen before the inauguration, but we don't know what. And now you're telling me that another side of the Opposition has links to a Middle East terrorist group controlled by the Soviets."

"You're getting there," Dave said, nodding.

Mel brought a hand up to his mouth and thought it through. "The Soviets are in collusion with the factions that are aligning against the Newell administration—foreign, at home, some inside the government, even. . . ." His eyes widened. "Christ!" he whispered as the implication dawned. "The Soviets could be orchestrating the whole thing."

Dave nodded. "Right. And think of some of the people it might involve. Oberwald was something I didn't know about."

Mel nodded dizzily. "Everything fits . . . almost," he murmured. He could see tantalizing fragments of the pattern. It was like a multiple-peaked iceberg with just the tips showing. They all connected together somehow, just below the surface, but exactly how was obscured.

Dave opened the door and stuck a leg out. "Anyhow, that's more than I should have told you," he said. "Come on. Let's go in and have a drink. Then we'll get those pizzas."

CHAPTER 33

There was an airstrip of some kind behind the ridge at the back of the camp. Brett had heard the sounds of engines several times, echoing distantly and distorted by the surrounding hills. He had thought idly that maybe it could provide the basis for a way of getting out. . . . But there was nothing more to build the idea upon, and it had never gone further than that.

It was the first day of December. A year ago he would have never dreamed that he'd be spending it like this, at an unheard-of spot somewhere in Syria. He had followed world reactions to the American election on the news and wanted to be back there now to share the excitement. During recent years he had been too wrapped up in his work to devote a lot of thought to the political developments that had been unfolding, but since coming here he'd had more time to think than at any time previously in his life. Lying on his bed, staring across the room with his hands clasped behind his head, he could think of a lot of people he'd known who might have benefited from being kidnapped for a couple of months.

There were a number of socialist intellectuals in the camp—political officers to indoctrinate the troops, he supposed—who had sought him out to open his eyes to the errors of his ways, or perhaps to hone their own rhetorical skills. They had struck Brett as sincere, convinced that the road to improving the world lay with "scientific" direction and rational planning. The same methods that produced machines which functioned flawlessly, with no redundant parts and everything serving a purpose, would yield a society with similar attributes. Cooperation would replace competition, and everything would be waste-free and efficient.

Which was great, Brett had told them, for people who wanted to be pieces of a machine—and who were these guys to be telling him, from the U.S. of A., how to run a more efficient production economy, anyway?

He'd told them they were full of shit. For a start, it was a fallacy that private enterprise prevented cooperation. The people involved in turning raw material from all over the world into, say, an automobile—miners, rubber growers, oil drillers, metal smelters, machinists, chemists, shipbuilders, truckers, packers, accountants, salesmen, storemen, clerks, to name just a few—managed to cooperate very effectively. It was something he remembered hearing Mel talk about years ago, but he hadn't given it a lot of thought at the time.

Second, eliminating the competition of a free market wouldn't eliminate competition. For the command system erected in its place would create new positions of power—to allocate, license, grant approvals, issue permits, vote their own pay raises and other peoples' taxes—whose favors would be competed for every bit as fiercely—but with a greater guarantee of graft and corruption.

They had asked why he didn't think that the solution to wars was a single-government world order. "How do you vote with your feet when there's nowhere else to go?" he'd answered.

Shortly after that, he was branded as "subversive" by somebody higher up, and no more debating had been permitted. So he must have been brainwashing the brainwashers a little too effectively, he reflected with satisfaction.

He got up and walked across to the bookshelf, but at that moment the sound came of keys in the door. Hamashad entered. "Is time for use some exercise," he said. "Will be soccer game outside. You play, yes? Come now."

Brett shrugged. "Sure, why not?" They began crossing the compound.

"First, I have some bad news, I'm afraid," Hamashad muttered. "The girl that you asked me to get a message to in the U.S., Stephanie Carne."

Brett's chest tightened. "Yes?"

"She's dead."

Despite the importance of keeping up normal appearances, Brett stopped in his tracks and closed his eye. "How? . . . How did it happen?"

"You were reported as killed. Your car was found at the bottom of a cliff by the sea. She committed suicide three weeks later. . . . I'm sorry."

Brett exhaled a long, shaky breath. If Hamashad had no means of contacting the U.S., and therefore couldn't relay anything back about Stephanie, this would be exactly the kind of lie to be expected. "Hamashad," Brett whispered. "If it's true, and if I find out that you're really one of the people who brought me here, I swear I'll kill you."

They started walking again. There was little time. "You claim that you are an expert on Western missile defenses," Hamashad said.

"I've told you as much as I'm prepared to at this stage," Brett answered.

"Why were you brought here?"

"You're asking me?"

"You don't know?"

"No."

Hamashad glanced quickly around. Two other guards were approaching, but they were still some distance away. "Has anything been said to you about the presence of missiles here?" he asked.

"Here? . . . You mean at this camp?"

"Somewhere in the vicinity."

"This isn't an original method of interrogation," Brett said.

"You must trust me."

"Why should I?"

"This is important."

Brett shook his head. "That isn't good enough. . . . And in any case, I don't know anything." He paused. "You were going to come up with some way of proving that you are dealing with the West. That could make a difference."

"Yes, I know."

"Any ideas yet?"

Hamashad shook his head. "Not yet. . . . But we are working on it."

CHAPTER 34

Lieutenant Colonel Sergei Chelenko stood with his hands clasped behind his back, staring at the thick, downy snowflakes falling past the window of his office on the fifth floor of the KGB headquarters. He had a deep-lined, pinkish, face, darkening to purple at his ears and a rather bulbous nose, but his eyes were keen, and the look in them on this white December morning was a perplexed one.

Since General Goryanin's assignment of him full-time to the mystery of the two missing nuclear shells in Hungary, a dismal picture had emerged of the security record for the past year. Pilfering and unexplained disappearances of everything from housepaints and cans of beans to television sets and automobile engines had been accepted as a part of life for as long as anyone could remember—much the same as anywhere else, he supposed. But it wasn't supposed to happen with military equipment.

The list of items lost or inadequately accounted for was appalling—and it had probably been doctored to hide as many sins as was humanly possible before it reached him. Yes, there would no doubt be the ritual demotions and removals from office, but invariably only of second-ranking scapegoats. Too much buying off and mutual covering up went on at the top for the real culprits ever to be incriminated. But that was hardly a new problem, and Chelenko could live with it.

What alarmed him more was what some of the items buried in that list could add up to when somebody who knew what to look for—such as the weapons-systems specialists that he had brought in on Goryanin's orders to evaluate the damage—sifted them out and revealed the possible connection between them.

After a round of disarmament talks with the Americans, it had been agreed to destroy two hundred of the Soviet SA–37 long-range, supersonic, air-to-ground missiles—they were reliable but getting old, and the nuclear material in the warheads would be better used reprocessed into fresh explosives for newer models. Accordingly, early in the year, the airframes, stripped of warheads and security-sensitive components, but with the electrical and hydraulic flight-control systems intact, had been shipped under the supervision of an international inspection team by a procession of trucks from a servicing depot in East Germany to a railway yard, and from there by train to a plant near Lvov for final dismantling. But somewhere along the seven-hundred-kilometer route, two of the missile carcasses had disappeared. Or had the number dispatched been miscounted somehow? Nobody knew.

In April, an inventory check at a testing ground near Tashkent had failed to locate a version of the type of motor used in the SA–37, and another had been written off as destroyed at air base six weeks later. A complete flight-control computer had been reported missing from a military engineering college in Odessa sometime in May, and careful scrutiny of the list of missing electronics components had revealed enough from a dozen different places to build another.

And worst of all, the specialists had confirmed that shells of the type unaccounted for in Hungary could be modified to fit an SA–37, and would give it approximately the punch of a tenth of a Hiroshima bomb.

If all of those pieces found their way to the same place, it meant that whoever possessed them could put together two weapons capable of taking out with precision a couple of city blocks from several hundred kilometers away.

Who would want something like that? He had begun by considering a number of possible candidates, none of them reassuring. But as the range narrowed, it was becoming clear that the chains of clues that his analysts were beginning to link together out of the flood of reports, information summaries, message intercepts, hints, allegations, rumors, and tip-offs, that poured into the KGB headquarters daily from its various sources throughout the Soviet Union and beyond, all pointed in one direction.

It concerned a particular guerrilla camp in the remote eastern regions of Syria, which the Israelis had been quietly developing an interest in, also. Chelenko's group had given the place the code name Glinka.

The door opened, and Goryanin entered. Chelenko turned from the window. "How are we doing, Sergei?" Goryanin asked, crossing the room to inspect the summary board fixed to the wall, covered with a web of names, dates, questions, and comments, written in various colored inks.

Chelenko moved over to stand beside him. "Well, although it's described as one of the PALP training bases, it operates autonomously from the regular PALP command structure. In fact no one seems to know anything about it."

"What do the Syrian authorities have to say?"

"To put it mildly, they're being less than forthcoming. It's almost as if they're under orders from the top to forget that it exists."

"Hmm . . . Odd."

"And now we have this latest snippet," Chelenko said. He pointed at an area on the board that related to an American couple who had visited the Middle East a few weeks previously, both of them university professors. While in Lebanon, they had met one of the Israeli intelligence people involved with Glinka, who passed them confidential information to take back to someone in the U.S. The new Constitutional party came into it too, somehow, but in what way was obscure. But the connection had been sufficient for Goryanin to arrange for the couple to be put under surveillance in the U.S., after their return. Chelenko went on, "Three days ago, they were visited at their home in Florida by a man called Fenner from Washington, who we think works for U.S. military intelligence, and a girl that he's been associated with for years, who—and could this really be just a coincidence, do you think, Leonid?—just happens to be a full-time employee of the Constitutional party."

"Ah! . . ."

"And not only that. She will also shortly be traveling to the Middle East, on the vice president's visit to Egypt and Israel."

Goryanin, intrigued, nodded his head slowly. "Yes, this is getting very interesting indeed."

"There was also another man there, too, who we've got nothing on," Chelenko said. "I got DS6 over there to check him out, all the same. It turned out he's a lawyer from Boston. It seems he arrived with the girl—probably just her current boyfriend."

"I'd like an eye kept on him, anyway," Goryanin said. "Kordorosky is throwing a fit upstairs again."

"Yes, I've already arranged it," Chelenko said.

"Good. . . . You know, I don't mind telling you, Sergei, if that man does take over here, I'm heading for Kamchatka or anywhere else at the far end of Siberia, as far away from Moscow here as possible." Goryanin continued staring at the board for a few seconds, then snorted to himself as an afterthought occurred to him. "In fact, if things go that way, I mightn't have much of a choice in the matter."

CHAPTER 35

It was something that happened every three years or so. Some group or other—more often than not, one that included a lot of insecure wives who felt it was the state's job to keep their menfolk respectably in line for them if they weren't able to— would call for the city to "clean up its act." The media would pick up the story, and the City Fathers would dig up an ordinance to enforce to demonstrate their sense of responsibility as custodians of public morality. Then, within a few months it would be quietly forgotten, things would return to normal, and three years later the cycle would repeat. This time they had banned nude or topless dancing in places that sold alcohol.

Brett stamped around at the far end of the lounge by the picture window, fuming. "Hell, I don't especially wanna sit anywhere watching tits and asses all night, but the point is it's none of their goddam *business*! You know, Mel, I'm beginning to think there might be something to this Constitutional thing that everyone keeps talking about, after all."

"Come over to Paul and Martha's again sometime," Mel suggested. He was sitting at the large walnut table by the shelves, with an open folder and a heap of papers for a class assignment strewn in front of him.

Randal Crewe, a skinny student with heavy, horn-rimmed spectacles and a long, hollow face with a pointed chin, looked across from where he was lounging on the couch. "Are they the Brodsteins?" He had stopped by ostensibly to return a propane torch that Marty had borrowed, but really to hear firsthand the story of how Mel had been driven home by the police two nights before.

"Yes," Mel said.

"That might not be such a bad idea." Brett stared out at the bay and continued grumbling, half to himself. "It's the same mentalities that used to put people on racks or set fire to 'em

210

for saying their prayers wrong. They'd still do it today, too, if the Constitution didn't keep that kind of stuff out of government. But they're trying to change it. They run half the country already and own the other half, and they're insane. What do you do? Another ten years of this, and we'll have the Inquisition back."

"I saw a picture of a head crusher that the Inquisition used to use," Randal said. He licked his lips with relish. His eyes gleamed behind their thick lenses. "It had a bar that your chin went on, an iron skullcap over your head, and a big screw to force it down, like on the old printing presses."

"Have you any idea how crazy some of those people are?" Brett asked, turning to look at Mel. Randal irritated Brett, who usually responded by acting as if he were not there. "I mean, have you ever listened to some of the things they believe? They actually *want* a nuclear war with the Soviets!"

Mel looked skeptical. "Okay, I agree that maybe the best way to prevent a war is to be ready to fight one, but how could anyone actually *want* one?"

"That's what I'm telling you. They're insane."

"First, your teeth were crushed into their sockets," Randal said, speaking in the way he had of stressing the sibilants. "Then they broke and splintered the jawbones. Your eyes were forced out of their sockets as the pressure increased, and your brains squirted out in jets when your skull cracked."

"Randal, give us a break." Mel said. Then, to Brett again, "How could anyone actually want one?"

"That's religious compassion and tolerance for you," Randal said.

"They've got it right there in the Bible that human history is gonna end with the battle of Armageddon in a last, great, apocalyptic war," Brett said to Mel. "And that's when Christ is gonna come back. And they've convinced themselves—and this is the really scary part, Mel—that the conditions that were prophesied for it to happen are all here, right now. They think that Russia is Magog, and Libya and the rest of 'em were all in the Bible, and that it will all start when they attack Israel. . . . They'll even tell you the exact place where the last battle will be."

"You mean they're saying a nuclear war with the Soviets is prophesied in the Bible?"

"Like I said, they *want* it to happen. Because the sooner it happens, the sooner they'll have their Second Coming. And the thought doesn't worry them at all, because they don't think they'll even be there: Christ is gonna lift 'em all up into the sky and away from it all. And there are people who think like that running the country. That's why they're not all that bothered about running the national debt into trillions, what they do to the economy, or why we don't have a space program anymore."

"You're kidding," Mel breathed incredulously.

"None of it's gonna last long enough to matter. All that counts is building up the military to win the war for Christ when it happens. That's what they think God is telling them."

"Do you know what being broken on the wheel was?" Randal asked.

Just then the front-door buzzer sounded. "I'll get it," Brett said, moving away from the window. "Are you expecting anyone?"

"Not that I know of," Mel said from the table. "Maybe it's evangelists come to save your soul. They've heard about you, Brett. The word's out."

Brett snorted and walked through to the hallway. A few seconds later Mel recognized Chuck's voice. He sounded excited. "Hey, Brett, have you heard?"

"Heard what?"

"About Alfonso's."

"Over on Barrancas?"

"Yes."

"What about it?"

"You know about the crackdown they've been having on the stripper bars lately?" Chuck came into the lounge with Brett. Harry was behind them. "Hi guys," Chuck said to Mel and Randal.

"We were just talking about it," Brett said. "They're taking over the world."

Chuck laughed. "But you haven't heard yet what Alfonso's place has done. The law says you can't have strippers where you sell alcohol, right? Well, they've done it the other way around from what they were supposed to. They've kept the strippers and stopped selling booze. So now you don't have to be overage to go in there any more. It's full of high-school kids with cokes right now, all having a great time!"

Brett gaped. "You mean they're watching the strippers?"

Chuck nodded delightedly. "It's a sellout—packed house. The cops are outside, but they can't do anything because it's legal. The City's having a panic session to redraft the law. It's a scream!"

Brett threw back his head and guffawed at the ceiling. "I don't believe it! That has to be the best thing in years. Hey, I gotta see this. Are you two heading that way?"

"That's why we stopped by," Harry said. "Marty called us about it. Everyone's on their way there."

"Especially since Rudshaw and his pals are there, too, making a fuss outside and waving Bibles," Chuck said. "We figured you wouldn't want to be left out."

"Let's go," Brett said. "Coming, Mel?"

"It sounds fun, but I have to finish this," Mel replied.

"You're sure?"

"Yes, really."

"If you say so." Brett looked at Chuck "Okay for a ride? I'm still waiting on Obee's for a part for my transmission."

"No problem," Chuck said. Harry had already led the way out again.

"Can I come along, too?" Randal asked, getting up. He seemed disappointed at having been cheated out of his chance to shine.

"Sure," Chuck told him. Which meant they'd get all the gruesome details on the way over.

"See you later, then, Mel," Brett called back as they followed Chuck out.

"Have fun."

The door closed, and quietness descended. Mel heard Chuck's car start up and pull away outside, then returned his attention to his work. The problem was to construct a schematic design at the logic-gate-and-register level of a multiplexer to handle sixteen communication lines, then write a machine-code routine to drive it, with programmable parameters and options. He worked for the best part of an hour. As the time passed on, his eyes drifted with increasing frequency toward the phone, and his pauses became longer. He'd hoped that she might call him during the last couple of days. By this morning he'd been ready to consider climbing down a notch and calling her, but had put it off with Brett around. Now he felt restless and unsure of what he wanted to do. Finally he shook his head determinedly. "Like hell I will," he said aloud; and with that he turned a fresh page and resumed writing. She was the one who was messing him around. Why should he be the one to go running? . . .

Because he wasn't doing anything tonight . . . No, that wasn't it. Because he wanted to tell her straight to her face—nothing to get excited about, just cool and direct—that he wasn't going to play that kind of game. Then the record would be straight, and he'd be able to walk away with no misunderstandings and his self-esteem intact. He tossed the pen down, stood up, paced over to the window, then back again, and stood staring down at this notes. "Aw, what the hell?" he muttered.

Ri-i-i-i-ng. Ri-i-i-i-ng. Ri-i-i-i-ng. Hell, don't let her be out. He'd never get this thing finished until he knew what was going on. *Ri-i-i-i-ng. Ri-i-i-i-ng. Ri—* "Hello?"

"Eva?"

"This is Eva."

"Er . . . hi. This is Mel."

"Well, it's good to hear from you. How have you been?"

She sounded warm, friendly, genuinely pleased to hear him. Despite his determination to stay cool, he couldn't help reciprocating. "Oh, not bad, I guess."

"I heard that you and Brett had your own escort home on Saturday."

"Oh, that. . . . As a matter of fact, it was mostly my fault." He heard Eva giggle over the phone—in a fond kind of way, not a mocking way. It brightened him up. "Who told you?"

"The grapevine's amazing. Where were you?"

"Down at Trader's most of the time. Then in some back-street place farther downtown," Mel said vaguely. "I don't remember."

"Why don't you come on over and tell me about it? Are you busy?"

Act cool, he reminded himself. "Well, I do have an assign-ment that's got to be finished. . . ."

"Oh well, it was just a thought."

". . . but it probably wouldn't take more than the after-noon," he added hastily. "I could be there by, say, seven."

"That'd be great. It would give me time to get a few things done, too."

"I wanted to talk to you about something, anyway."

"Fine. About seven, then?"

"See you."

"Oh, and Mel."

"What?"

From the tone of her voice, he could almost see her biting her lip impishly. "It's your turn to get the pizza."

He was glad that he had called her. It gave him a feeling of having faced up to things squarely, in a manly kind of way, instead of putting them off with some lame excuse to himself in his mind. . . . And besides, he liked being here, at her place. It wouldn't do any harm to leave the hard-line part that he'd come about until just a little later, he decided.

He sat sprawled along the couch, from which he had moved some boxes of books to make room. Eva was in the leather recliner by the coffee table with the computer terminal, still laughing uncontrollably at the story he had related about Alfonso's. Although she could be so serious at times, she could let herself go with abandon when the mood took her. As if to compensate for its excesses, her personality seemed to go to extremes in all directions. "See what I mean. Look at you now," Mel said. "I've never met anybody who was such a mixture of opposites."

"Well, statisticians will tell you that it's a healthy way to be," Eva said.

"How come?"

"Manic-depressives average out at about normal." She skimmed a tear off her cheek with a knuckle. "And the cops were there, and so were Rudshaw's Bible freaks? . . ."

"That's what Chuck and Harry said."

"Oh, it's just too funny. . . . I love it when holier-than-thous fall flat on their faces like that."

"Brett was raging about them all morning. He says they think the Bible is telling them to fight the ungodly."

"You mean Armageddon and the Second Coming, and so on?"

"You know about all that?"

"I've read some of the things they believe. It's terrifying. You can see why the Constitution separates church and state." Now the serious Eva was coming back.

"I thought it was just to let everyone follow whatever religion they choose . . . or none at all if they want," Mel said.

Eva shook her head. "It does achieve that, but more as a side effect of something that goes deeper. It expressly rejects religious doctrine as a basis for regulating public affairs. In other words, science and reason provide a more effective means of discovering reality and deciding on permissible behavior than notions of divine revelation. Steam engines and electronics work; magic and miracles don't. Appealing to facts and logic is a better way of deciding a person's guilt than tying him up and throwing him in the river to see if he drowns. Life under the Supreme Court is better than under the Inquisition. Ask Randal."

As Mel sat back to ponder on the implications, Eva picked up a paper from the litter scattered on the coffee table in front of her and began scanning over it idly, letting him think. Finally Mel said, "That's dynamite. What you just said means that all the claims about the country being founded on God and the Bible are garbage."

"Exactly," Eva agreed, without looking up.

"The Constitution expressly mandates a secular state."

She rested the paper on her knee and looked at him over the top. "Sure. If religion really *were* a superior road to truth, there'd be no reason *not* to use it as the basis for all aspects of life, public and private. But the Constitution rejects it. That's what the far Right won't accept, and they're trying to get their hands on government. They want to go back to the way things used to be when the meek and merciful could squash your head if you disagreed with them. That's why they're so against the Constitutional movement. The two established parties pay lip service to the Constitution, but they've been around too long to have that freedom of choice—they're both sold out to entrenched interests. They belong to the last century and can't change. They can't respond to the way popular thinking is going. That's why we'll win in 2000."

"I've got a feeling you'll end up recruiting me yet," Mel said.

"Great. And if we do, become a lawyer. That's where all the excitement will be after it happens."

"What's that you're reading?" Mel asked, sitting up and nodding at the paper on Eva's lap.

She replied matter-of-factly. "A paper on defense that Dave Fenner left, about how appeasement doesn't work. You only end up being taken advantage of."

Mel stiffened involuntarily at the mention of Dave's name. He got up and strode over to the window, where he stood for a moment, looking down at the evening traffic on Palafox. This was the time to say his piece, leave, and be done with it . . . if that was what he wanted to do. The problem was that now he wasn't so sure anymore that he did. He turned back to face the room. Eva was watching, but at least she wasn't insulting his intelligence by pretending not to know what was on his mind. "Who is Dave?" he asked finally.

"An old friend. I told you that before."

Mel made a face and gestured in the air, searching for a continuation. "I mean, what is he—to you?"

"A very close old friend."

"Isn't he a bit old for you?" Mel managed finally, in a gruff voice.

"At thirty-two? I don't think so. Some people tell me I'm too old for my age anyway. But even if he were, what of it?"

She was wearing slacks of a thin, pink material that clung revealingly to her legs. Her breasts swelled deliciously against her blouse. Mel's hormones were in a hopeless conflict with his feelings. He knew what he wanted to say, but somehow he couldn't turn it into words and spit them out. An urge flashed through him to pick something up and throw it, simply to vent the frustration of not knowing how to communicate, but he fought it back. Finally he said, "Look, this may sound kind of old-fashioned and quaint to you, but I had hoped that . . . that . . . Oh, forget it." He shook his head and sighed hopelessly.

"Mel," Eva said. Her voice was quiet, but firm. "We went through this when you were here before. I own my own person—body and mind. I don't want to be possessed. If I meet somebody one day who makes me feel differently, well, then maybe that'll change. But right now that isn't true with you, and it isn't true with Dave either. We can be friends. We can have fun. But that's all I've ever offered. I can't be more honest than that."

"And how many more are there?" Mel asked on impulse— and immediately wished he hadn't.

"If there are any, it isn't your business."

Mel pulled a face, spread his hands, started to say something, stopped, and turned away again. Then he turned back. "Okay, it's your right, I guess, but . . . I mean, hell, what am I supposed to feel like? Doesn't that matter? I feel like I'm some kind of pet on a leash."

"Why? Nobody's saying you aren't free to live your own life."

"I feel you're putting me inside a cage . . . making me be the way that suits you."

"But Mel, isn't it you that's wanting to put me in one?"

She was right, a part of him knew, but he couldn't accept it. He was cornered. "I don't know," he mumbled. Then the image of himself walking out straight, tall, and uncapitulating came again as the salve to his smarting pride. "I don't think there's a lot of point in talking about this," he said. "I thought it could have been nice with us, but I guess that's not good enough for you, eh? Okay, well, if that's the way you want it. . . . I think it would be best if I just went on my way." He waited.

She said, "I'm sorry you feel that way."

"Hmmm." Mel straightened himself up haughtily. "Then, I guess that's it. See you around, then."

"Take care, Mel."

He walked to the door, striving not to move awkwardly, and let himself out. At the bottom of the stairs behind the restaurant below, he paused, staring across the rear yard at his parked car. He could still see the pink slacks clinging to her body. A faint trace of the perfume she had been wearing lingered in his nostrils. He hesitated uncertainly.

Once, at a lecture a year or two back, he remembered seeing an illustration of the age of the Earth, in which all of geological time since the world's formation was expressed in terms of one year. On that scale, although multicelled life had been around since October, the emergence of consciousness with the appearance of modern man hadn't taken place until six minutes before midnight on December 31, and the last two thousand years of history were all compressed into the last sixteen seconds.

How could the feeble stirrings of a thin veneer of will and intellect overlaid so recently upon the human psyche hope to prevail against the power of biological programming that went back hundreds of millions of years? he asked himself. Obviously they couldn't. It was a no-contest. It was futile to pit oneself against Nature. It had to be unhealthy, too. That was the kind of thing that people gave themselves high blood pressure and ulcers fighting against.

"Shit," he muttered resignedly.

He walked into the building and punched her number into the pay phone at the back of the restaurant. "Hello," her voice answered.

"Do you want beer or wine with the pizza?"

She laughed—warmly and without hesitation. "I'll leave it to you."

CHAPTER 36

Stephanie had continued using Eva's car, and left it at Denver airport on the day she flew to Boston. After returning to Washington from Florida, she and Mel spent two days going over the lessons that had been learned from the experiment and completing their final preparations. During this time, two of Bassen's agents collected the car from Denver and drove it to Los Angeles. It was thus waiting at LA International Airport for Stephanie to collect when she arrived with Mel to assume her role as Eva.

With Stephanie at the wheel, they headed north on 405 toward Santa Monica, and twenty minutes later left the freeway and followed the route to Ocean Park Boulevard as naturally as if she had been driving it every day for months. Mel had never been this way before. Eva had moved to her most recent address only during the last year, which was after his visits to her in California.

Pacific Heights was an irregular arrangement of a half dozen or so condominium blocks, dark finished in wood shingle and rough pine. They stood shaded by palms and secluded from the roadway and from each other by stands of buddleia and trellis-trained bougainvillea along a stretch of lawns between the boulevard and cliffs overlooking the beach. Stephanie stopped the car at the bank of mailboxes by the gate and opened the one marked 24, CARNE to reveal it crammed with a month's deliveries. Although they had been preparing themselves for this moment, she was tight-lipped as she passed the bundle to Mel. She closed the mailbox without saying anything, and drove on along a curving driveway into the complex.

Mel turned through the pile of envelopes. There were lots of junk solicitations and come-ons. . . . A couple of bills, some magazines, subscription renewal; bank statement; what looked like some of the newsletters on politics and current affairs that Eva had always subscribed to. . . . Business mail, much of it in Constitutional envelopes. A few personal letters. . . . Invitation to a party. Postcard from Sydney, Australia, signed "Shirley." Card advising of a registered package being held at the post office. Something caught in his chest as he ruffled through the assortment. Just a month ago, everyday items in a normal life. Now that life was gone. All that was left to express a personality that had taken twenty-seven years to shape was a collection of return addresses and titles. He sighed and pushed them together again.

The front door to number twenty-four was at one end of the building, across a small tiled porch atop a short flight of wooden steps leading up from a brick-gravel path. In the center of the block, a pair of aluminum up-and-over garage doors faced out over a parking area shared with the unit next door. Stephanie parked in front of Eva's garage, climbed out, and went back to open the trunk. Mel came around the other side and hoisted out their two suitcases; she took the bag of groceries they had picked up at a convenience store just off the freeway. He had ostensibly come to stay for a week, which supported the story of Eva's having run into an old boyfriend and taken up with him again. It was also to give her a source of moral support through the days ahead, as well as an ever-present link to George and Larry, who had installed themselves in an apartment less than two blocks away to be on hand if needed, with several backup agents to relieve them in shifts through a twenty-four-hour watch. Just before they left Washington, Landis had deposited a message for Simon in the data-network drop box, saying that Annabel would be back by tomorrow. Explaining away her absence was going to be the first tough part.

Entering the home, being inside the personal space and among the effects of a person who has died recently, is always a sobering experience. There seems something irreverent in disturbing the last tangible evidence of someone who no longer exists, and who never again will. Stephanie opened the door and went in first. A few paces into the entrance hallway she paused uncertainly. Mel waited inside the door behind her, saying nothing. Ahead was a short passage with several doors, all closed. A kitchen opened off to one side, and beyond it, approached through an arched entrance from the hall, he could see one end of what looked like a lounge. Stephanie drew a deep breath to gather her resolve, and then walked on into the kitchen to put the grocery bag down. Mel closed the front door with his heel and carried the suitcases into the lounge. He stood there for a while, fighting down a tight feeling that formed in his throat as he looked around.

The surroundings were definitely Eva, but they told of an Eva changed from the one who had lived above a downtown restaurant in Florida. The student had gone; the woman had emerged. Inevitably, the place was filled with books and papers, but the shelves were more orderly, the furniture more stylish and free of clutter to serve its intended purpose, and there were pictures, draperies, and ornaments that acknowledged needs other than the purely functional. It was something that Mel had never before managed to associate with Eva's turbulent, mercurial lifestyle: a home.

The place had been closed up for too long. Mel crossed the room and opened a window. Facing the window was a desk with a computer and communications terminal. Its message light was flashing, indicating calls received. That could wait for the time being. He went to the end of the room and checked the two doors there. One was a closet containing assorted boxes, more books and magazines, and domestic bric-a-brac; the other led to a reading room, with an armchair and a comfortable-looking couch, liquor cabinet, stereo system, and French window opening out onto a leafy veranda. Back in the main lounge, another door at the same end as the arch opened directly to the kitchen.

He went out through the arch and back into the passage. The first door was a hall closet with shelves and hanging space. The next was a linen closet, aired by the water heater, with a laundry room and small workroom adjacent. Past that was the bathroom, and beyond it a small bedroom that Eva had used as an office: messier than the rest of the place, with a littered desk and papers piled on a table to one side—a remnant of the old Eva. The door at the end of the passage led to the garage, and the single door in the opposite side, to the main bedroom, which had its own private bathroom. That would work out fine: Stephanie could have the bedroom, and he would use the couch in the reading room off the main lounge. He carried their suitcases through accordingly.

He didn't realize how much he had been struggling to keep his own feelings under control until he came back into the kitchen to rejoin Stephanie. It was the first time he'd seen her close to breaking down since the evening he had met her at Logan. She was sitting on one of the stools at the breakfast bar, the groceries still beside her untouched, staring unseeingly in front of her and crying silently. That was when he found the lump in his own throat that he couldn't swallow. He moved forward and laid a hand on her shoulder. She clutched at it and buried her face against his chest. "I'm . . . not sure if I can do this," she whispered.

He held her close, saying nothing. There was nothing he could say. He couldn't have said it if there were. For by then, he could feel tears on his own cheeks, too.

It was going to be even tougher than he'd thought.

Stephanie checked the refrigerator and stowed the groceries, and Mel went back out to put the car away in the garage. When he came back, he brought a toolbox and a leather carrying case containing an electrical impedance-measurement bridge, which one of Bassen's specialists had instructed him in the use of before they left Washington. These, he took through to the lounge to use later. First, while Stephanie was putting on some coffee, he settled down at the desk with a pen and notepad to play through the phone messages.

It was like listening to a potted history of the last four weeks. Early on, there was a pathetic series of messages from California, corresponding to the time immediately following Stephanie's arrival in Boston. "Eva? This is your mother," the frail voice said. "Where are you? Please call. We have some terrible news about Stephanie." Mel quietly erased them.

Most of the rest were personal, giving first names only and conveying little that meant anything. There was a series from Landis, and later Ronald Bassen, trying to locate Eva, and more recently another string from Dave Fenner. And then, just as Stephanie came through the kitchen with the coffee, he found one from a week previously that had immediate significance. The voice was highish in pitch for a man's, with a nasal twang. It sounded tense. "This is Simon. Look, I don't know what's going on, but we haven't heard from you and we need to talk. If you're there, get in touch immediately. This is urgent. I don't have to remind you that we have very little time."

Mel pursed his lips and played it through a second time. "That's Seybelman," he said. They had listened to enough public speeches and other recordings of his voice. Some of them had sounded like private conversations. Bassen hadn't said how those had been obtained.

"He broke their security rule and called here direct," Stephanie said. "Things must be getting desperate."

Two days later Seybelman had called again, this time more tersely. "This is Simon. If you're there, call at once. Most urgent."

And finally there were a couple of messages from Landis asking Eva to call him when she got back from Washington. They had expected to find those.

After listing the calls, Mel used the terminal to interrogate the drop-box address in the network. There was one new message that they hadn't seen before, which had come in late the previous night, after the last message had been lodged for Simon from Washington. It read:

> *Annabel,*
> *Rec yours of 12/4—at last! Where in hell have you been? Imperative that we talk immediately. Disregard instruction to call. Meet Breadman at Apple, Wednesday. Usual time & pickup.*
>
> > *Simon*

So, Stephanie already had an appointment. They knew from the information that Eva had given Landis that "Breadman" was Arnold Hoffenach, the ex-SEAL security boss that Eva had used as her first entry point to the organization. But they had no idea where "Apple" was, or what time was "usual."

"Oh boy." Mel stared at the screen and sank back in the chair, exhaling a sigh. "We're in trouble already."

Stephanie drew across a folder of notes from Pinewood Hills that Mel had open by his elbow and checked the entries of known code names, but as she had as good as known already, there was nothing. "So now what do we do?"

Mel stared at the desk. "Let me think about it. In the meantime, the sooner we get on with checking the line, the sooner we'll be able to use the phone."

Since paranoia was his profession, Ronald Bassen had assumed that Seybelman would accept Eva's defection story about as unquestioningly as Bassen himself would if the situation had been the other way around. That meant that whom she communicated with and what was said would be matters of extreme interest. It was unlikely that anyone would have risked a break-in to bug the apartment internally—since Eva lived alone, there would have been little to overhear. Bassen had assumed, however, that her phone line would have been tapped. The electrical test bridge that Mel had brought was to try and find out.

Mel set the case containing the bridge up on the desk and opened the lid to reveal a panel with a dial meter, miniature display screen, numeric keypad, and various terminals and knobs. Inside the lid was a compartment containing an assortment of connecting leads and probes. Mel took a screwdriver from the toolbox he had brought in with him and ran a lead to the connecting jack by the window, where the line from the communications unit connected with the feeder from outside. Then he came back to the desk and used the bridge to make some reference measurements of the line's impedance. "Okay, make a call," he said to Stephanie.

A couple of the recorded messages were from Eva's dentist, reminding her of an appointment nine days previously. Stephanie picked up the phone and punched in the number.

"Dr. Kellman's office, Sandy speaking. Can I help you?"

"Hi, Sandy. This is Eva Carne. I had an appointment over a week ago on Monday the twenty-seventh." Beside her, Mel was busy repeating the impedance measurements and checking the line current.

"Eva! We were wondering what happened to you. I tried calling a couple of times."

"Yes, I know. I got the messages."

"Where in the world were you?"

"I had to go away suddenly, and I clean forgot about it. I'm sorry."

"Okay. Well, now that you're back, would you like me to put you down for another time?" Mel signaled that he had gotten the readings he needed. He pointed at the phone and nodded his head slowly and distinctly two times.

"Look, it's all a bit up in the air at the moment, Sandy," Stephanie said. "Can I get back to you when things have calmed down a bit?"

"Well, you know how it is. Don't leave it too long. That could get expensive."

"I won't."

"Talk to you later, then."

The last thing they wanted was anyone checking Stephanie against Eva's dental records.

Stephanie replaced the phone and looked at Mel inquiringly.

"Bingo." He blinked and shook his head disbelievingly at what he was saying. "It's being tapped." These things only happened in movies. They didn't have any place in the real world of his own life.

The fact that the tap was detectable through impedance measurements indicated that it was of a simple type, probably a series-connected transmitter drawing its power from the line itself. It would be located somewhere along the local subscriber loop, which consisted of the drop wire to the building, the distribution cable to a pole anywhere within two or three blocks, and the branch feeder that would connect somewhere to the area's main feeder cable. A physical search by one of the experts stationed in the apartment nearby would soon have uncovered it, but that wasn't the purpose of the exercise. The object was not to neutralize the tap, which would have given the game away, but to know for sure that it was there. Because now that they knew, they could use it to their own advantage.

Stephanie called Warren Landis on his direct line in Washington. "Hello, Warren," she said when he answered. "This is Eva. I got your messages. I'm home in LA now."

"Hi, Eva. How was the flight?"

The official story had been put out that because she would now be going to the Middle East with McCormick's party in place of Kirkelmayer, Eva had been reassigned to reporting directly to Landis in Washington. It also avoided having to involve Stephanie with John Wadlow, who had caused the difficulties at the LA office. Stephanie and Landis talked routine business matters in this vein for a few minutes, set some tentative target dates for the month ahead, and Landis hung up. The opening words that Stephanie had used in her call were to a prearranged code, and had confirmed to him that her line was being tapped.

The next task was to begin going through every drawer, box, and scrap of paper in the place for any additional clue that might help recreate the Eva who had existed four weeks before. One of the first things they scoured was Eva's notebooks and telephone pad for a key to interpreting the message that Seybelman had left, but they found nothing.

Later that evening, Dave Fenner called, also by prearrangement. Before leaving Florida, the three of them had debated whether to tell the Constitutional people about the informal working relationship that Dave had had with Eva, and the task he'd wanted her to help him with in Israel—which Stephanie would now carry out instead. Dave had been strongly against saying anything, his argument being that it would serve the cause of realism better to keep Stephanie's situation as close as possible to what Eva's had been. Mel suspected it was more Dave's instinctive reluctance to reveal anything to anybody that they didn't absolutely have to know, but in the end they had agreed to do it his way.

Dave, of course, had also assumed that the line would be tapped. One of the reasons for his call was to corroborate for the eavesdroppers' benefit the story that Stephanie would be telling later.

"Eva, hi. This is Dave," he said when Stephanie answered. "It's been a while. I tried calling a few times, but all I've been getting is your machine. So, how are things?"

"Dave. Oh." Stephanie injected an appropriate note of confusion into her voice. "I've been away for a month. In fact I only got back earlier today." Again, her choice of words confirmed that the call was being monitored.

"Really? Where did you go? Did you just decide to take a sudden vacation? You should have told me. I might have managed a few days off."

"It was my sister . . ."

"Stephanie from way back? How—" Dave's voice changed abruptly, as if he had just registered the tone of her voice. "What's happened? Is she okay?"

"She's dead. . . . A month ago."

"Oh my God! How?"

"She . . . she killed herself. Brett—you remember Brett?"

"Of course."

"He was killed in an accident—"

"Jesus Christ! I—"

"It seems that Steph took it real badly, and . . ."

"Look, do you want me to come out there? I could get a plane tonight."

"No, Dave." Stephanie's voice was firm. "I'm fine. As a matter of fact I ran into Mel again, and—"

"You mean Mel Shears?"

"Yes."

"I thought he was in Massachusetts. Didn't he become a lawyer or something?"

"He showed up in California, for Stephanie's funeral. And we just . . . well, you know how it is sometimes . . ."

"You mean you might be getting together again?"

"I guess so. He's here with me right now."

"There was a pause. "I see. Well, look, I'm glad you've got somebody there at a time like this, but . . . I mean, are you sure it's for real? It's not just a reaction to the stress or something?"

"I'm not sure. . . . I don't think so. I mean, yes, I think it's real. Dave, let me work this out in my own time, please? I'm okay, honestly. And Mel is being a real help."

"You're sure, now?"

"Yes, really."

"Then, I wish the best for you. You know that, anyhow."

"I know. And thanks. I do appreciate it."

"If I can help at all, you just let me know."

"I will."

"Get plenty to eat. Stay looking nice."

"You're terrific. . . . And Dave, stay in touch, okay?"

Stephanie hung up the phone and looked questioningly across at Mel, who had been listening on an extension set. He nodded. "You did good. It sure would have convinced me."

Which left only the problem of making the rendezvous that Seybelman had indicated for the next day.

"It's no good," Mel said when they had talked it over for the umpteenth time. "There's no way we're going to find out where or when it is, and you can hardly call him and ask. You'll just have to try and get him to change the whole thing."

"*I'm* supposed to tell Seybelman what to do? Aren't we getting a bit out of our depth here?"

"Dave's call will help. Use that."

"You think I should just brazen it out."

"Yes. I think that's got the best chance."

"Why?"

"Because it's what Eva would have done."

They used the terminal to browse through the public directory of local services and places of interest, and found a large shopping mall, located a little over ten miles north at Reseda, which seemed suitable for their purpose. After driving north past Beverly Hills to Reseda, they found the mall and spent some time touring it to familiarize themselves with the layout. Then they drove to a steak restaurant nearby and had dinner while they waited for eleven o'clock, by which time, they figured, details of Stephanie's earlier conversation with Dave should have reached Seybelman. While Mel ordered desserts, Stephanie called Seybelman's private number from a pay phone in a booth near the door.

"Annabel," she said quietly when the familiar high-pitched, nasal voice answered.

Seybelman didn't sound pleased. "I distinctly told you *not* to call," he hissed. "Didn't you read the drop?"

"Yes, but things have changed. Look—"

"You're not calling from home, I take it." That was funny— *him* cautioning that the line might not be secure.

"Of course not. Listen, I don't want to go into detail now, but I've had a lot of personal problems. Sorry to have messed you around, but there were reasons."

"Reasons! We're into December already, and you take it into your head to disappear for a month. It's not like you at all. Not at all. I always took you as being more professional."

"I left several messages telling you that I'd be out of circulation until the beginning of the month," Stephanie countered, raising her voice a fraction. "It was the best I could do."

There was a sharp intake of breath at the other end. "Very well. Now, what do you want that can't wait until tomorrow?"

"Something has happened on a personal level that would complicate the arrangement. I don't want any contact through Breadman any more. It isn't anything he's done. As I said, it's personal."

Seybelman responded too promptly for this to have been a complete surprise. It suggested that, as they had hoped, he already knew about Mel. "If you insist . . . although I can't imagine why." Now Seybelman was playing deception games—trying not to sound as if he already knew. "I'll arrange for somebody else to pick you up."

They had anticipated that. "No," she said firmly. "I'm not happy about using Apple. I have a suspicion that it mightn't be secure. I want to set up a new pickup, to be sure it's clean." She went on before he could respond. "How about the Spanish Hat Mall at Reseda? Could you send somebody there?"

"I suppose so, if that's what you want . . ."

"The eastern parking lot is on Balboa. I'll be on the top level, that's Level E, by the exit ramp. How would that be?"

"Wait a minute," Seybelman mumbled. "Let me make a

note. Spanish Hat Mall, eastern parking lot, Level E exit ramp." Stephanie had to fight to stop her sigh of relief from being audible. "Usual time?" Seybelman asked.

"How about noon?"

"That is the usual time."

"Yes, that's what I mean," she said hastily.

"Very well. We can talk more tomorrow. The designation for this pickup will be 'Pineapple.' Have you got that?"

"Pineapple," she repeated. "I've got it."

Mel was waiting with two hot fudge sundaes when Stephanie rejoined him at the table. He looked up at her as she sat down. "How'd it go?" His expression became concerned as he saw that she was shaking. "Are you okay?"

Stephanie nodded and pulled her coat closer around her shoulders as if she were feeling cold. "It went okay. Tomorrow at the mall, noon."

CHAPTER 37

So, Stephanie at last met Louis Seybelman. He was far from amused—with some justification—at her prolonged disappearance and failure to respond to his attempts at communication. She had already formed an impression of him as somebody who alternated between extremes of mood, radiating exaltation when things went his way, and switching rapidly to pique at being victimized by fate when they didn't.

As arranged, she had driven to the Spanish Hat Mall and parked her car near the place that she had indicated. Precisely at noon, she had got out and walked to the exit ramp, and within seconds a Nissan that had been hovering a short distance back drew up alongside her. She had then been driven a couple of miles east to another parking lot, where Seybelman was waiting in the back of a Cadillac. Now they were cruising at slow-lane speed along 101 in the direction of Glendale and Pasadena.

Seybelman waved a hand irritably in the air as he spoke. He was wearing an open-neck, pale orange shirt with a lightweight navy jacket, and his mane of shoulder-length blond hair tossed behind his neck. The two men in front of the glass partition stared at the road ahead impassively. "So, who is he, this person that you've brought back with you? At a time like this, with barely a month left before you go to Egypt. I mean, it's utterly beyond my comprehension, it really is. I had classed you as professional, but I'm beginning to wonder. How *could* you go and allow personal matters to intrude at a time like this? I mean, who *is* he?"

"We've been through this. He's somebody that I've known since I was at university." Stephanie suppressed her impulse to blurt apologies, and forced her voice to carry the note of rising exasperation that Eva's would have if she were being pressed pointlessly when there was nothing left to say. "I ran into him at the funeral. My sister killed herself, okay? That isn't exactly something that happens every day."

Seybelman's manner mollified for a moment. "Yes . . . and I was sorry to hear about that." Then he became peevish again. "But all the same you could have informed us. I know that you have, shall we say, strong feelings concerning your personal affairs. . . . But a whole month, with no idea of when you were going to appear again. It's quite intolerable."

"That's not true. I told you I'd be back by the beginning of December. I delivered the package on Kirkelmayer, and he's been taken off the job. I was involved in that up to my neck for half of November. And yes, I have a personal life. Don't you? If it isn't going to fit with working for you, then we'd better forget the whole thing, because it's not going to go away." She sat back, turned her head away, and watched the scenery flowing by off the freeway. After a few seconds she added in a less strident tone, "Besides, he could be useful. He's a lawyer who gets involved in a lot of Constitutional litigation."

"You didn't tell me that."

"You've hardly given me much of a chance to."

Seybelman's mouth worked irascibly for a few seconds, but when he next spoke, his voice took on a note of grudging restraint. "So, it's definite that Kirkelmayer is out, is it? And you will be going in his place?"

Stephanie nodded without turning her face from the window. "It was confirmed just before I left Washington. We're leaving on January ninth for Egypt, arriving in Israel on the fourteenth, and back home by the eighteenth for the inauguration." There was a short silence. She could sense Seybelman watching her.

"So, how do you feel about what we discussed?" he asked at last.

Something dropped in the pit of Stephanie's stomach. She had been dreading something like this. "Which do you mean specifically?" was all she could answer.

"What kind of a question is that?" Seybelman asked.

Stephanie turned to face him. "It's been a month, and a lot of things have been happening in my life."

Seybelman looked at her strangely. "Possibly to the point of deranging you completely, I'm beginning to suspect. I take it that you do recall the purpose of this meeting?"

Stephanie could feel her palms sweating upon her knees. The seconds of silence dragged agonizingly. There was no response she could make. She stared numbly at the backs of the two heads in front, struggling desperately to recall any clue to what Eva was supposed to have decided. But nothing would come. Her mental processes had seized up.

"Do I take it that the answer is yes or no?" Seybelman demanded, sounding impatient.

Stephanie licked her lips. It was a fifty-fifty chance. What else could she do? "Yes," she said, realizing with surprise of how dry her mouth had become suddenly.

Seybelman was looking at her dubiously. "I must say, you sounded more sure of yourself a month ago. If you've had second thoughts or something, for God's sake say so now. We can't risk—"

"No," Stephanie said, endeavoring to retrieve her position by sounding decisive. "Nothing like that. I think I'm a bit spaced after traveling, that's all. I need to catch up on some sleep."

"Hmph," Seybelman made no attempt to hide his disapproval.

"There was a month's worth of mail and calls to catch up on," Stephanie said, sounding strained.

"Very well, very well. So you'll do it? There's no question?"

At last. That could only refer to the job that Eva had been preparing for in the Middle East. Stephanie felt herself being carried toward shallower waters. She nodded affirmatively. Was she supposed to talk knowledgeably now about what that job was to entail? . . . No, she wasn't in any danger there.

The indications were that even Eva hadn't known what it was about.

Then the pieces came together in a way she felt should have been obvious sooner. From the information that Eva had passed to Landis, Seybelman had hinted that she would be introduced to someone, or some others, later. What Seybelman must have agreed with Eva was simply that this would be arranged after it was known for sure that she would be replacing Kirkelmayer. She played her hunch accordingly.

"Of course I'll do it. I wouldn't be here otherwise. So when do I get to find out what it's all about?"

Seybelman's smile told her that the gamble had paid off. "That sounds more like you," he said. "You've talked a number of times about your disillusionment after so many years of dedication to your present associates. Well, just to show that I do listen, I'm arranging a small social gathering of certain individuals who share, shall we say, a certain congruence of interest in the outcome of the operation, which I would like you to attend—probably within the next week. From some of your past remarks, I take it you are not averse to such occasions." She looked at him questioningly, as Eva would have done—Stephanie was finding it exhausting, having to do the thinking of two people. Seybelman went on before she could say anything. "Don't worry. You can take my word that everyone involved will have the highest credentials. Totally reliable and utterly discreet. But I want you to see for yourself the kind of club that you'll be earning yourself a place in. I think you'll be suitably impressed. So, I take it you're agreeable, then?"

"Sure."

"And this boyfriend that you have at the place, this . . . lawyer? I assume he won't pose any difficulties?"

"No. He'll only be around for a few days, anyway."

"Even better. Very well, I will make the necessary arrangements. You will receive details via the drop. Do you have any other questions for now?"

"No. I guess that's about it."

"Good." Seybelman tapped on the partition. The man in the passenger seat in front turned and opened it a fraction. "Back to Reseda," Seybelman said. And then to Stephanie, "We'll drop you off at the Spanish Hat." She nodded. The man in front closed the partition. "And now," Seybelman said, settling back in his seat, "tell me as much as you can at this stage of what your duties with McCormick will be . . ."

Earlier that year, Stephanie recalled, there had been an incident at General Plasma Dynamics in which about fifty gallons—enough to fill a trash barrel—of cooling water from a low-power experimental reactor connected with the fission-fusion hybrid program had spilled over the floor of the building and had to be cleaned up. The water had been mildly radioactive, with an activity level of sixty to seventy picocuries per liter, which put it at around half that measured in typical four-percent-alcohol beer, or a twenty-fifth the level found in the waters of the spa at Bath in England, which have brought relief to sufferers from rheumatism and similar afflictions since Roman times. Nevertheless, headlines such as "NUKE LEAK CONTAMINATES RESEARCH PLANT" proceeded to appear in the local papers, and accounts based on the accompanying stories soon made national press and TV.

To allay the ensuing spate of fears and hysteria in the area over leukemia, cancer, sterility, and genetic mutations, the city had imposed an emergency injunction that prohibited further operation pending an official inquiry and public hearing, and a new batch of restrictive regulations had descended from Washington that made even less sense than the original curfuffle. The whole episode had achieved nothing except the waste of a lot of people's time and a considerable amount of public and private money, and additions to GPD's already formidable list of woes and tribulations. Also, of course, it had added to the public's misperceptions of technological risks; and the general belief that "thousands could be affected by what happened in Denver" had become an ineradicable part of the popular mytholoy.

From her training as a physicist and her subsequent experience, Stephanie had been too familiar with the routine contrast that existed in such instances between what the public was being told the scientists were saying, and what they were really saying, to be especially surprised. She had learned to accept it all with weary resignation, knowing that the laws of physics couldn't be deceived, though people might, and that in the end, as had been its habit throughout history, truth would assert itself and endure after the superstitions had been long forgotten.

But at the same time, she was acutely aware that the daily

diet of misinformation was too systematic to be due simply to ignorance and inaccuracy. When the views of less than one percent of the scientific community commanded ninety-nine percent of the coverage that an issue received, and this happened not once, but repeatedly and predictably, something was going on that was far removed from any simple misreporting attributable to lack of expertise or the pressures of deadlines. In short, the sources that the public relied on for facts were being used, instead, to maninpulate ideological images and opinions. And from some of the material that Stephanie had been studing during the previous two weeks at Pinewood Hills and in Washington, she knew that an active figure in the web of influences that orchestrated the misdirection of the information media was Louis Seybelman. As she drove back from Reseda to Santa Monica after the meeting, she went over in her mind what she had managed to fathom of his motives and the aims that lay behind them.

It was not technology, in itself, that constituted the great evil. The real target of the kind of antagonisms which Seybelman's exemplified was the Western democratic process. Capitalism provided the economic foundation that supported it, industry was the engine that drove capitalism, and technology made industry possible. And the crusade didn't end with technology, but became an attack on the sciences that were the origins of technology, and ultimately upon the faculty of reason itself, of which science was the formal expression. In earlier years, Stephanie had considered herself apolitical, devoting all of her time and energy to her scientific studies. But now, perhaps as a result of two weeks of concentrated effort at having to think like Eva, she found herself seeing the situation through Eva's eyes and recognizing many of the things that she remembered Eva trying to convey.

For what the Seybelmans of the world hated with such ferocity at the root of it all, she realized, was not capitalism or democracy, but freedom. The freedom of ordinary, unaspiring individuals to live their lives as they chose, following their own whims and preferences, independently, self-sufficiently, without the license, approval, regulation, or permission of anyone. The ultimate, unforgivable sin that would-be social engineers like Seybelman could never tolerate was a world that didn't *need* them. And a free world would be such a world. For what did they have to offer that anyone with the freedom to choose would ever want, expressed either with a dollar spent freely in the marketplace or a vote cast freely at the ballot box?

Nothing.

In a world where innovators, producers, creators, entertainers—anyone with knowledge or ability that others judged to be of value—could make millions, every nickel of it given willingly by customers who had earned it, they could never compete. And so they directed their suppressed envy at the institutions responsible for the existence of a world in which others could. Incapable of earning the recognition they craved, unable to persuade, they would compel society to take notice of them by resorting to force. With the powers to pass laws and the rights they could confer upon themselves to bestow favor and privilege, they would *make* people need them.

Such goals were never admitted openly, but hid behind moral pretensions. Deception and coercion were thus inseparable from such systems by their nature. Every form of tyranny and totalitarianism that the world had known had begun the same way.

Now, for the first time, Stephanie felt the revulsion that she had sensed from Eva but never really understood. Eva had often said that the biggest single fault of true free-enterprise capitalism was its consistent failure to defend itself against enemies who used lies and violence as a matter of policy, and then claimed the moral high ground. The people who practiced it were too busy doing something useful and getting on with their own lives to have any interest in controlling other people's. After talking to Seybelman, she now thought she knew exactly what Eva had meant.

CHAPTER 38

By the time Stephanie got back to Pacific Heights, her tension was finally releasing itself. She found her hand shaking as she let herself in. Mel had heard the key in the door and was coming out of the room that Eva had used as an office. "How'd it go?" he asked.

Stephanie leaned against the side of the kitchen doorway and tossed her purse down on the hall table. "Well, I'm still alive. I need some caffeine—preferably intravenous."

"You see, I'm a long-range mind reader, too." Mel moved past her into the kitchen and indicated the coffee pot, perked and ready on the counter.

"You're a saint." Stephanie went through into the lounge and sat down.

Mel poured out two cups, put them on a tray with a couple of sandwiches that he'd prepared, and joined her a minute later. "Was it rough?" he asked as he sat down.

"At times."

"What happened?"

Stephanie sipped from her cup, put it back down, and rested her head on the back of the chair. "He doesn't like you here—says it makes me unprofessional."

"Too bad."

"Uh-huh. But he got friendlier when he found I'd delivered the package to scuttle Kirkelmayer and was definitely going in his place."

"You think you passed off okay?"

"There was a time when I thought it was all about to blow up . . ." she exhaled a long breath at the recollection, "but we got through it. But yes, I think it went okay." She sat forward and picked up her sandwich.

Mel waited expectantly, but she began to eat. "So," he said finally, "did you find out anything about what they want you to do there?"

Stephanie shook her head. "Seybelman has decided it's time for me to meet some of the faces farther up the totem pole. My guess is that that'll be when I get to know what it's all about."

"Hmm . . . because you passed your brownie test?"

"Presumably."

Mel scratched an eyebrow. "I'm surprised they're willing to show themselves at this point. It seems needlessly risky." He glanced across at Stephanie. "Eva would have picked up on that. I hope—"

"I know, and I made the same comment. It's to make sure I'll be suitably impressed—which fits with the line Eva gave for changing sides. I never realized how well she'd played it."

"To get names, you mean?"

"Exactly."

"So, you don't know who you're likely to be meeting."

"Not yet."

There was a strange, mischievous light in Mel's eyes, Stephanie saw as she resumed eating, the look of somebody who had been successfully keeping a secret. "Would you like to?" he asked her.

"What are you talking about?" Stephanie asked.

In reply, Mel got up, walked out of the room, and Stephanie could hear him go back into Eva's office. He came back a few moments later carrying some sheets of handwritten notes and a wad of papers bound into a blue folder. He lifted the top sheet of notes and glanced down at it. "How about a man called Wilson Clines? Ever hear of him? Not many people have. He keeps out of the public eye. Ostentatious displays aren't considered to be in good taste these days—or very prudent, come to that. His family is known to be worth at least twenty million—and that doesn't say anything about the reserves they've scattered away among various trusts or dispersed in other ways to avoid concentrations that would be too conspicuous. Most of it comes from international financing and the capitalization of Third World development projects at ruinous interest rates underwritten by U.S. and various European governments—he has a cousin who's married into the Vandelmayne-Myer international banking group." Stephanie, looking astounded, opened her mouth to say something, but Mel continued. "Behind the scenes, he's also one of the country's archconservatives. His pet obsession is getting the Bible back into the schools. He's on public record as being in favor of making adultery punishable by law. How's that for a throwback to the Dark Ages? Interesting?"

Stephanie took the sheet of paper from Mel's hand. "This is Eva's writing. Where did you find it?"

Mel ignored the question and read from the next of the sheets he was holding. "Jeffrey Matterson, intellectual—it says here." His voice took on a ringing tone as he exuberated, "Originally a humble professor of social studies, but now elevated to the ranks of the better-than-the-likes-of-us, and heading up his own bloatocracy in Washington. Chauffeured limousine, automatic cost-of-living-linked raises, and full-salary retirement, all out of your pocket and mine. He's best known for the plan he's been pushing for years to set up a full-blown, Department of Economic Planning. He also wants to nationalize the ten biggest insurance companies and soak them to stave off the social security mess."

Mel abandoned his affectation of a variety-show compere and carried on in his normal voice as he sat down. "I found a dossier that Eva had been putting together but presumably hadn't passed on to Landis yet."

"Let me see those." Stephanie held out her hand. Mel passed her the rest of the notes but kept the blue folder. She looked down and turned the sheets slowly, one by one as he carried on speaking.

"It seems that she was in the process of finding out quite a bit about who pulls the strings," Mel said. He gazed at her soberly. "I don't think either of us realized how good at this business she was."

He watched in silence as Stephanie scanned quickly down the next page, flipped it over, and read on. A puzzled frown formed on her face. She looked up. "Does anything strike you as strange about these people?" she asked.

Mel seemed to have been waiting for her to notice something. "How do you mean?" he asked curiously.

"First we had an ultraright banker who wants to institute a new feudal order. Then a rabid socialist trying to set up an American Gosplan." She inclined her head briefly at the papers on her lap. "This one here is in the public eye because of his anticommunist, antidrug crusade, but half his money came from arms deals that were funded by drug money. But the next page talks about a woman who'd be thrown out of the Young Trotskyites for being too far over on the left." She looked up.

"Go on. What?"

Stephanie gestured at the notes again and shook her head. "It's just a weird mix of bedfellows. Everything from about as far right as you can go to about as far left. And yet from what Eva is saying, they're all connected in the same network. It just seems . . . incongruous. It doesn't seem to make sense. I mean, these people are supposed to be enemies aren't they?"

Mel nodded. "I agree. But doesn't it bring to mind what Henry Newell said when we met him in San Francisco? He said that the conventional left-right spectrum that people think of doesn't really mean anything. Both ends are out to screw the middle. One end does it by confiscatory taxes and seizing control of the economy, the other by outlawing competition. But both depend on a command system as the basis for society, as opposed to individual freedom and choice. So both are natural enemies of the Constitutional party." He nodded toward the papers in Stephanie's hand. "And that's what we're seeing here: an alliance of what appears to be opposites at first sight, but which are really mirror images of the same thing."

Stephanie looked down again and nodded distantly. "Yes. . . . And that's what Eva was on the verge of uncovering, wasn't it? . . ."

"Have you looked at the last couple of pages yet?" Mel asked.

"What? No." Stephanie turned to them, and at once became absorbed.

"I thought you'd find that interesting," Mel said after letting her read in silence for a short while. "The energy business is represented, too. You don't need any introduction to the five names at the top there. They own Texas, Colorado, and Alaska. Ever since the early seventies, their companies have been quietly buying up mineral and surface mining rights from federal and state governments—in some cases for as little as one dollar an acre—in areas designated the Powder River Basin and Fort Union formation, which covers two hundred fifty thousand square miles from North Dakota to New Mexico. That area holds the richest deposits of coal ever discovered. The strip-mining rights alone are worth thirty billion tons—more coal than the U.S. has used since it began mining it in the eighteenth century. How's that for collusion at the public expense?" Mel smiled humorlessly. "And purely by coincidence, of course, those same sources turn out to have virtually bankrolled the antinuclear movement. Oh, I know they own that too. . . . But if you were holding both cards, which would you want to play first?"

Stephanie turned over the last page, and a moment later gasped audibly. There was a list of figures and references, and halfway down, scrawled in ink in Eva's handwriting and circled for emphasis:

Sabotage of advanced energy technologies to maximize returns on existing investments? Or ploy to steer Third World over to outmoded methods, then go nuclear and pull out rug? (Who wants ten more Japans on planet?) Possible connection with problem at GPD, Denver? Talk to Steph for background.

There was no date on it.

"Do you think . . ." Stephanie's voice trailed off as if she'd had second thoughts on what she was about to say.

But Mel had already wondered the same thing. "When we talked that first night at my place, you said that Eva had some other reason for calling, apart from just social, but she never got to tell you what. " He nodded at the sheet that Stephanie was holding. "I think this could be it."

Stephanie nodded. "I think you're probably right. . . ." She frowned. "But what did Eva mean by a possible GPD connection?"

Mel produced the blue folder he'd been keeping back. Stephanie leaned forward to peer at it. The title read: PROPOSED FISSION-FUSION PROGRAM OF GENERAL PLASMA DYNAMICS INC.— TECHNICAL AND ECONOMIC APPRAISAL. She stared and read it again in astonishment. The document was a hefty affair of at least two hundred pages. "My God!" she whispered. "Where on earth did she get that from?"

"Who'll ever know? But look inside at the credits page. Tell me if there's anyone there that you recognize."

Stephanie took the folder and opened it. From the preamble, it had evidently been prepared at the request of a consortium of investment banks and other prospective financial backers. A list of contributors appeared a few pages farther in. Figured prominently among them as "Chief Scientific Advisor" was "Dr. Hermann M. Oberwald, National Advisory Commission on Advanced Energy Systems."

"Interesting, isn't it?" Mel said. "The network of mirrors connects. We started out with Oberwald over on the right, and his connection with a Soviet spy ring. Then we put that aside for a while and came here to help Henry Newell follow up a different line that had nothing to do with that, but involved the liberal left. But here they are, as you said, all in bed together. Let's make sure that it all gets back to Landis this time, before anything else happens."

CHAPTER 39

Brett threw the newspaper down on the breakfast bar in disgust and buttered himself another piece of toast. "Goddam Gestapo!" he growled.

"What?" Mel asked as he pushed aside the bacon sizzling in the pan on the stove and cracked a second egg into the space.

"Guy comes back from overseas someplace and finds the IRS have grabbed his house, and his wife and kid have had to move in with the people across the street—all over a lousy seventeen hundred bucks! I mean, what's it all coming to? Gas chambers next for defaulters?"

"How old's the paper?"

Brett glanced at the date. "What's today?"

"The sixteenth."

"Ten days."

"Brett, when are you going to finish fixing the TV? Then maybe we'll be able to get some up-to-date news"

"The scan output driver blew up. I just need to get a new part. It's a simple job."

"You've been saying that for two weeks."

Brett smeared marmalade on his toast and gulped from a mug of coffee. "Wasn't Eva saying something the other day about getting rid of taxes altogether?"

"Eventually, maybe."

"It couldn't work."

"Maybe it seems that way right now because of the attitude that people are conditioned to. I mean, who likes having what they've earned taken away at gunpoint? But it doesn't mean you can't have it as an ideal to work closer to."

Brett snorted. "Who the hell's gonna give it if they don't have to?"

Mel scooped the bacon out to drain and slid some mushrooms off a plate into the space in the pan. "Well, there was a time when English and Americans were famous for paying their taxes on time, and in full. If people believe that what they're being asked for is reasonable and that everyone else is paying their share too, they'll go along with it. They don't *want* to be carried."

"You're gonna get some free riders all the same," Brett insisted. "What do you do about them? Just accept it?"

"There have to be other ways of getting people to pay for what they want," Mel said. "Ways that don't involve coercion. You'd have to experiment and see what worked."

"There'd still be problems."

"Hell, are you saying that what we've got doesn't have problems? The amendment they're proposing doesn't pretend to have all the answers. It just sets out the basic principle that any acceptable system should measure up to. Figuring out the specifics is going to be what it's all about for the next fifty years."

Just then the sound came of the front door being opened. A moment later Stephanie appeared with some bags of shopping. "You couldn't have timed it better," Mel said. "I just put yours under the grill."

"Wonderful." Stephanie used a cloth to take the plate from the grill, and sat down at the table by the window.

Mel looked at her purse, which she had put down with the bags. "Are you still carrying that thing around? Hey Brett, you've been promising Steph a new one ever since we met her."

"I'll get around to it."

"*I'll* get you a new one," Mel told her.

"You've been saying that for nearly two years, too," she said.

"Well, we're going to the beach today," Brett said to Mel. "Since Eva's out of town, why don't you come along? It's about time you took a break and got some sun, anyhow."

Mel thought about it as he munched his breakfast. "Sure, why not?" he agreed.

On the way to the beach, Stephanie had to drop something off for a girl in her class, whom she arranged to meet in The Viennese. Mel and Brett decided to go inside with her for coffee while they were there. As they got out of Mel's car in the area at the rear of the restaurant, he noticed to his surprise that Eva's silver Subaru was there, parked in its usual slot. He looked up the outside stairway and saw that the light was on in the hall window next to her door.

Inside, at the table, he remained quiet and preoccupied while the other three chatted, glancing furtively toward the far end of the room and growing more agitated as the minutes went by. In the end he stood up suddenly. "I'll be back in a minute. Get me a refill if the guy comes by."

He went to the back, walked past the restrooms, and carried on out the rear of the building. There he hesitated, uncertain now. But he had to know what was going on. He climbed the stairs to Eva's door and stared at it woodenly. One part of his mind was in a quandary, unable to initiate any action, yet at the same time equally incapable of allowing him to return downstairs without seeing the thing through. A vague, absurd, fleeting picture of himself standing there all night flashed through his brain, and then in the moment that he had been distracted he realized that another part of him had seized control of his hand and made it press the doorbell. Something akin to panic gripped him then, and in the same instant a desperate hope materialized out of nowhere that perhaps she had simply gone away and left the light on. He had given it long enough. Leave now, he told himself. . . . And then he heard the latch turning in the door.

Eva's eyes widened in surprise. She didn't look pleased. "Mel! What are you doing here?"

He started to grin awkwardly, then quashed it in the same instant. "I saw your car, so I figured I'd stop by. I guess you changed your plans, eh?"

She made no move to invite him in. He moved forward, more insistently. She stood firmly in the doorway. It was the first time that Mel had ever seen anger showing openly on her face. "Mel, if I wanted company, I'd have called. *You* could have called. Look, I don't like people creeping around and spying on me. Haven't you ever heard of respecting a person's privacy?"

"I was *not* creeping around. I was downstairs with Steph and Brett. I told you, I saw the car." Now his tension was beginning to show. The situation was turning into a confrontation.

"So, I park my car outside my own place. Is that okay?"

"You're not supposed to be here, remember?" Despite himself, Mel heard his voice rising. "You told me you were going out of town."

"Who the hell do you think you are to come here cross-examining me on my own doorstep? So I changed my mind. I don't have to talk to you like this, Mel. Go away."

"Not until we get one thing—"

"What's going on?" a man's voice asked from inside. He moved into view from the door of the large lounge. It was Dave Fenner. Eva sighed and stood aside.

Something dropped in Mel's stomach. "I should have guessed," he grated.

Dave was looking at him calmly, without any suggestion of owing explanations. As always the alpha-male, secure and impregnable. "You should know that Eva lives her own life, Mel." His tone was matter-of-fact, not needing to make any exhibition of dominance. "There wasn't any need for this. You're just bringing a lot of grief on yourself. Sorry, but this is the real world. It's not about to change for you."

Since he couldn't counter, Mel ignored him and was looking accusingly at Eva. "You—"

She nodded wearily and closed her eyes. "Yes, Mel, I lied. And I'm sorry about that, because I shouldn't have. I knew it was the wrong thing to do as soon as I said it, but . . . Okay. It was a mistake. We all make them."

"What kind of—"

Eva saw the attack coming and retaliated immediately. "Because I know how you react, Mel. I've told you, I'm me. But you've never accepted it. You keep insisting on wanting me to be someone else. But that person doesn't exist. She's a fantasy that you've manufactured in your own head. Can't you get that straight?"

"What the hell's happening up there?" It was Brett's voice, from halfway up the stairs. Stephanie was a short distance below. Mel turned away feeling crushed, looking for a hole to vanish into.

"Look, I didn't start this," Eva said. "I wanted a weekend to myself and he can't accept that. Would you take him home, please?" Dave moved into full view behind her.

"It's time to go, buddy," Brett told Mel. His voice was low, but firm. "This isn't going to do any good."

Avoiding Eva's eyes, Mel allowed himself to be steered back to the stairs. He felt numb now, as some kind of anesthetizing self-defense mechanism intervened. But he'd known, even before they went into the restaurant. Why couldn't he either accept it or get out of it? He didn't know.

CHAPTER 40

In 1857 a shrewd Irishman purchased Malibu, a picturesque strip of coastal bays and beaches twenty-five miles north of Los Angeles—at that time a sprawling rancho—for ten cents an acre. About thirty years later, a Yankee from Massachusetts first saw the possibility of an "American Riviera" developing there, and his widow later leased property to the actress Anna Q. Nilsson in 1927. In time, a host of other stars, as well as many of the more socially conscious well-to-do by whatever means, built homes there. The Malibu strip became famous—and infamous—as a focus of wealth, ostentation, and influence.

The sun was setting in a blaze of crimson and orange that seemed to have ignited the entire Pacific when the car that Seybelman had sent to collect Stephanie arrived at the house. She had no idea who owned the place since without advance information on where she would be brought, there had been no opportunity for checking. The gates were opened remotely in response to a password radioed from the car by one of the two escorts sent to fetch her. Through the gates, they drove between palm-shaded lawns fringed by floral beds and rose trees to the front of the house, which stood on a landscaped mound, partly screened by a canopy of shrubbery and vines. It was a low-built, long affair, with a tennis court and bowling green on the landward side, screened from the lawns by hedges. The driveway ended in a forecourt in front of a glass-fronted vestibule. Several other automobiles were parked along one side, all gleaming and expensive.

The entrance hall, with its marbled floor and miniature waterfall chattering over a rockery, brought to mind more the lobby of a Hyatt hotel than the front of a private residence. Seybelman was waiting for her there, with a shorter, slimly built, dark-haired man whom she recognized from her briefings as Philip Challin, the California congressman. A maid came forward to take her coat, while a majordomo in tie and maroon jacket watched from the side. It was the full treatment.

Seybelman showed his teeth in a crocodilian parody of a smile and offered his hand. Stephanie took it, at the same time glancing quickly at the surroundings again in an effort to look suitably awed. "Delighted to see you again so soon, Eva," Seybelman said. "Oh, don't look so lost. Remember, you're almost one of the family now, eh, heh-heh."

"You're looking as pretty as ever," Challin said in his turn.

"Hello again." Stephanie knew that Eva had met Challin, but not how she had addressed him. Her impulse was to add something flippant, but that wouldn't have been Eva's style.

Then she saw the tall, well-built, figure in a dark suit, watching unobtrusively from a short distance farther back, but positioned—Stephanie would never have noticed before she'd gotten to know people like Ronald Bassen—to keep an eye on the front door and to be ready to block the way through into the rest of the house if need be. Yellow hair, hollow cheeks, solidly carved features, body poised loosely, yet alert to move at an instant's notice, missing nothing.

Hoffenach's eyes came back to the group in the foyer and held hers directly. Although Stephanie had anticipated and tried to rehearse herself for this moment, she found she had no idea how to react. Hoffenach solved the problem for her by nodding almost imperceptibly and allowing the corners of his mouth to twitch momentarily upward in recognition. Stephanie hesitated, then sent a smile back. She didn't try to conceal it from Seybelman or Challin, who obviously knew about Eva's association with Hoffenach. That was in line, too, Stephanie reasoned. Affecting sudden pretensions of social airs and graces wouldn't have been Eva's style either.

Seybelman took her arm and steered her on into the house. Challin, who had caught Stephanie's gesture, stopped for a moment to murmur in Hoffenach's ear. "Remember, orders. An old boyfriend of hers has shown up from the past. We don't need any more complications in her life right now. She's off-limits, okay?"

Hoffenach nodded and looked mildly pained. "The job always comes first with me. You know that."

"I know you, too, Arnold. Don't forget, that's all."

Stephanie was a physicist, not a connoisseur of arts and craftsmanship. But she didn't have to be to sense, as they moved on through elegantly carpeted and furnished rooms, adorned with paintings, sculptures, and china, that she had passed into a different world. This was the world of those who could shape the lives of millions on a whim, by the stroke of a pen; where nations could be bought or sold; where an idea that could revolutionize civilization would live or die, or a decision made if an Edward Gilman was to be destroyed. She abhorred all of it. She wanted nothing more at that moment than to escape. But at the same time she had never felt closer to Eva, and more determined to see through to its end the task that she had accepted.

The house was considerably larger than it appeared from the front, being stepped downward toward the side facing the sea. Here, they came to a long lounge with a curving wall of glass that formed a crescent looking down over a terraced pool, which was separated from the ocean only by a rocky scarp and a strip of private beach. The inside wall of the lounge consisted of library shelves and had an open fire as its centerpiece. There were two large tables in the center of the floor, one each side of the fireplace. Four men were sitting in a loose semicircle formed by a couch and several armchairs facing the fire. They stood up as Stephanie entered with Challin, who had caught up after talking to Hoffenach, on one side, and Seybelman on the other.

"Gentlemen, I'd like you to meet Eva," Challin said. "Eva, these are a few of your new friends."

"What can I get you to drink?" Seybelman asked.

"A vodka tonic with a touch of lime?"

"Phil?"

"Make mine a Manhattan." Challin said. Seybelman moved away to a bar in the corner below the steps down to the lounge, via which they had entered.

Stephanie recognized two of the faces. One was from the notes of Eva's that Mel had found: Wilson Clines, the Bible-thumping financier who wanted to put the fear of God back in the schools, and everyone else back in their own proper beds. He was a squat, paunchy man with a balding head, ragged mustache, and the outward appearance of a genial, fatherly uncle. The other was from a list that Landis had produced from his own files, of known connections to the names that Eva had identified. He was Groveland Maddock, an energy magnate associated with the investment group that had commissioned the GPD report, slack-faced and fragile in appearance, with thinning hair, pale eyes, and folds of skin hanging at his jowls and throat. He was holding a brandy snifter in one hand and a partly smoked cigar in the other. Challin introduced him first as "Howard." Stephanie had hardly expected them to volunteer their real names; it was surprising that they were willing to meet her face-to-face at all. Challin said simply that Howard was "influential in determining energy policy, both here and across a large piece of the world."

Next was a younger man, perhaps in his mid-fifties, lean, tallish, and swarthy-skinned with dark but graying hair and deep, intense, brown eyes. More of Middle Eastern than Hispanic extraction, Stephanie decided. Challin introduced him incongruously as "Pat"—"well connected in the field of international relations. He probably manages the flow of more money than the whole of the oil business put together." Which probably meant, Stephanie guessed, that he was involved in administering the international welfare program that Newell wanted to abolish and replace with free trade.

"Alan" was heftily built and tanned, with close-cropped hair and lined features. Challin described him merely as "very high politically," which could have meant influential within Congress or powerful in some branch of the standing bureaucracy. Stephanie viewed the latter as more threatening. Congressional bills had come to be so vague that their interpretation— in other words, what was to constitute law—was left to a vast army of permanent civil servants who were masters at stalling any measure they didn't approve of until the administration that had tried to implement it was out of office. It meant that most—the estimate was 85 percent—laws were now passed by a new, unelected branch of government, unaccountable to anyone, who were able, in effect, to run the country as they chose. The positions of power thus created made them valuable allies to be sought after, and enhanced their market value, both financially and socially, accordingly.

Finally, Wilson Clines was introduced as "Graham," who "provides the money to make the world go around."

They all sat down. Seybelman returned with the drinks and joined them.

Landis had been curious to find out which of the group that Stephanie was to meet would be in charge. Most likely it would be whoever took the initiative at this point. That turned out to be Clines. He settled back more comfortably, picked up the glass which he had set on the arm of his chair, and regarded her with interest for several seconds. Finally he said, "So, Eva, we understand that you've been a loyal employee of the illustrious new party for a number of years now."

"That's right. Since I left university at the end of 1996—and before then, in fact." There was no point in holding anything back. All the available facts would have been checked already.

"Would you say you were a strong follower of theirs?"

"Completely."

"But now, Philip says, you're agreeable to working against them."

"Yes."

"What changed your mind?"

"I grew up."

"How do you mean?" he asked.

"I still think it's a good ideology. So is communism. So is Christianity. But like them, it won't work. It can't."

Pat, the swarthy one among the four, sat forward and looked interested. "Why can't it work?"

"Under a free market, some people are going to make more money than others. Either because they work harder, are smarter, or simply more lucky—for whatever reason, some will do better. That wealth will buy them access to the lawmaking process, which they'll use to protect their interests. As soon as that happens, a free market has ceased to operate. Therefore, it's self-defeating."

The question had been expected, and Stephanie had deliberately offered an intellectual answer—as would Eva. The whole thing was a game being played for form's sake, anyway. She could hardly admit what was supposed to be the real reason, which was simply that she was conscious of getting older, felt she was in a rut, and craved to become part of the world of glamor, excitement, and power that her affair with Hoffenach had revealed a glimpse of. But Seybelman would already have told the others that.

"Did they pay you well?" Howard asked.

Stephanie looked around her. "Not such that I'd ever think about living somewhere like this."

Howard and Clines exchanged brief looks. "Would you like to live somewhere like this?" Clines asked.

"Show me a girl who wouldn't."

"And you'd knowingly operate against the interests of the party you've served for over four years to achieve that?" Alan said. He seemed to be taking the role of devil's advocate, sounding dubious and skeptical.

Stephanie forced a note of indifference into her voice. "It doesn't mean anything to me anymore. I married what I thought was a shining knight when I was still a college kid, and he turned out to be a sham. If that's what it takes, then that's what it takes."

"Is that all there is to it, though, Eva?" Clines asked. "Do you just want to get away, or is there something else? Isn't there just a little bit of a feeling for getting back at them—a need to even the score for what you've lost?"

Although she knew the right answer to give, Stephanie went through the motions of trying to decide whether to admit to her supposedly true feelings. Finally she looked him straight in the face and said, "Yes, there is. But not just a little bit. A lot."

There was a short silence, and then Howard asked her quietly, "How far would you be prepared to go, Eva?"

That was an unexpected question. She grappled with it for a while, looked genuinely perplexed, and then said, "I don't know how to answer that."

"You'd lie and cheat?"

Stephanie shrugged. "I already have. What about Kirkelmayer?"

"Under oath, in court? Perjury?"

"Well, I suppose it would depend what . . . But yes, if I had to."

Howard's voice became very soft. "How about killing somebody?"

Stephanie swallowed involuntarily. She forced herself to remember that this was just a charade. She wouldn't really have to do it. She was here only to find out what they were up to.

But at the same time, if they were sounding her out as suitable material, she didn't want to appear unaffected. Landis had said that people who were identified by the psychologists as being capable of killing too easily, or even of relishing it—and such did exist—never got through the preliminary screening interviews for hard-line intelligence work. The best agents were those who could be trained to kill reluctantly, only as a last resort, and who detested it—the ones who thought more and risked less.

She tried to think herself into the correct frame of mind, then bunched her mouth tightly and gave a brief nod. "If it was absolutely necessary and there was no other way, I think so . . . But how can you know?"

There was a long silence while the others looked at each

other. Howard stubbed the butt of his cigar in an ashtray. To the side, Stephanie was aware of Seybelman emitting a long breath. She waited, but already something undefinable in the air told her that their impressions were favorable.

Then, completely unexpectedly, Wilson Clines laughed loudly, got up, and walked over to the bar. Still chuckling to himself, he refilled his glass, helped himself to a cigarette from the box at one end, and turned back toward the fireplace. "Well," he said as he retraced his steps to his chair, "it's nice to know you're so determined, but we're not asking you to do anything like that." Howard and Pat were smiling too, now, inviting her to share the joke. Clines sat down. "We don't want you to kill anybody. But what we do want to do is cause our friends a certain degree of embarrassment that will contribute to undermining their position politically." He stopped and waited, studying her face for signs of her reaction.

She nodded. "Go on."

"Do you use drugs, Eva?" Howard asked suddenly.

She turned her head sharply. "No, I never have." It was true, too, as they probably knew already. Eva used to describe herself as probably the only person in California who had never smoked a joint. It was something that had simply never interested her, and that was that. Eva had never been a follower of any fashion. She had always been totally her own person.

"What do you think of them?" Howard asked.

Stephanie shrugged. "People's lives and bodies are their own business." Again all Eva, through and through.

"Some people say that if the twenty-eighth amendment goes through, then by the terms of it all drug sales will have to be legal," Howard said. "A lot of people don't like the sound of that. How do *you* feel about it?"

"It's a long and involved argument, but basically I wouldn't mind," Stephanie said. "I think that with what we've got, the cure's worse than the disease."

"Hm, I must say you don't sound as if you've changed your Constitutional views very much," Alan said, sounding dubious.

"I never claimed I had. I said, it's a good ideology. I'm just through with working myself into an early grave for nothing over it."

"But suppose that the *real* reason the Constitutional leaders wanted to legalize the trade turned out to be that they themselves are among the biggest traffickers in it?" Howard continued. "What would you think then?"

The suggestion was so unexpected that Stephanie had to pause to absorb it. Finally she shook her head. "It's too ridiculous. . . . I couldn't buy it."

"But just suppose . . ." Howard persisted.

"I . . . I don't know. I'd have to think about it."

"How do you think the public would feel?" Clines asked.

This time her answer came more readily. "Oh, there's no question. The party would be in trouble."

"Finished politically, do you think?" Clines asked her pointedly.

"Maybe not quite that bad, but they'd certainly have a hard time . . ." Stephanie's voice trailed off as the implication registered. A large proportion of the opium that heroin came from was grown in the Middle East. "This has got something to do with why you wanted me to replace Kirkelmayer, hasn't it?" she said.

Clines nodded curtly and drew on his cigarette. The humor had gone. Now his manner was all business. "You will be traveling as a member of a delegation which formally represents the new administration. The party will naturally be accompanied by a considerable amount of baggage, both official and personal, which will enjoy diplomatic immunity from examination." Clines paused and scratched his chin delicately. "But suppose that just before it left Jerusalem to return to this country, a member of that party were to take advantage of that privilege to attempt the concealment of a large—and in money terms, I mean a *very* large—quantity of such narcotics. . . ." He let it hang there, inviting her to make her own completion.

"That's what you want me to do?" she said.

"More than that," Clines said. "As I said earlier, the object is to implicate the party, not just you. You see, the customs authorities will have received a tip-off. We want you to get caught." Stephanie's jaw dropped. Clines ignored it and went on, "We want you to stand trial, and in court and in full public view, to confess that you were operating under the instructions of and with the full knowledge of the Constitutional leadership; that it was they who stood to profit personally, and with the connivance of senior members of the Israeli government. In fact, if the truth be known, their big aim in maneuvering to get the traffic legalized was to make personal fortunes. Now if that isn't enough to sink them, at least it will put a pretty big torpedo into their midships."

Before Stephanie could reply, Challin spoke for the first time. "Eva, it probably seems odd to you that Graham and his colleagues should have risked meeting you and revealing themselves like this. That was done quite deliberately. You see, we wanted you to have some idea of the kind of influential people who'd be on your side. Even though you would stand trial and might even be convicted, you'd have the right people behind the scenes to make sure of a very light sentence, or even, maybe, to get you off completely. And after that . . ." Challin sat back and waved a hand expansively to take in the room, the whole house, the world, "luxury and whatever you want for life. That's the deal."

"And a hundred thousand dollars up front, in your bank within a week, with no interest on the part of the IRS, guaranteed," Clines said.

"What exactly—" Stephanie began, but Clines waved a hand.

"That's all you need to know for now. You'll be contacted with further details after you arrive in Jerusalem. All we need to know, Eva, and we need to know right now, is: Will you do it?"

CHAPTER 41

Ostensibly because of her place on McCormick's staff, Stephanie, as Eva, had officially been reassigned to report directly to Washington. After her meetings in California, this arrangement also provided a cover for her to return to the capital for an evaluation of the situation so far. Mel returned with her. After spending a day with Landis, he left Stephanie there to continue analyzing the information they had obtained. He himself arranged another visit to Denver, to convey to Ed Gilman the contents of the blue file that Eva had procured.

There was a crowd of maybe two or three hundred people outside the gates of General Plasma Dynamics when the cab that Mel had taken from the airport turned into the end of the road. Some of them were carrying placards saying NO HYBRID BABIES HERE and ANY DOSE IS TOO MUCH DOSE, while a woman standing on a makeshift rostrum was leading some kind of chant. Several Denver City Police Department cruisers were parked in the background, and policemen were stationed at the plant gate and in a loose string around the periphery of the crowd, keeping an eye on things.

"What's happening?" Mel asked the cabbie.

"Aw, it's the radiation from the thing they're building in there. People don't want it around, see. There was a lot in the papers and on TV about how it causes cancer, deformed babies . . . stuff like that."

Mel had heard it all before from Stephanie. Yes, sometimes the plant did emit some radiation. But no adverse effects on humans had ever been detected below a radiation dose of a hundred rem. A person standing on GPD's perimeter fence for a whole year would absorb a maximum of one tenth of one thousandth of one rem. Mel himself had absorbed five times as much that very morning from the more intense cosmic rays at high altitude, just flying from Boston. And everyone experienced thirty times as much in a year from the isotopes occurring naturally in their own body tissues.

"How do you feel about it?" he asked the cabbie.

"Me? Sure, I say get rid of it. They don't know what they're doing with that shit. I had an aunt over on the other side of town die from cancer last year. How do I know it wasn't because of this place? It could be killing thousands of people all around. They wouldn't tell you."

"But people have been dying of cancer all over the world for thousands of years," Mel pointed out. "It has a latency period of thirty years. This place hasn't been running for ten."

"Yeah? So what does that mean? It's just numbers. Whenever they've got something to cover up, they snow you with numbers. I saw it on the TV. Even the president of this place admitted it could blow up the whole town."

The main gates were closed and locked when Mel got out. A plant security guard opened the pedestrian gate at the side for him, while police officers cordoned back the crowd. A murmur went up at the sight of his camel-hair overcoat, general business attire, and leather briefcase. "Look at him," a voice shouted. "There's a fascist!"

"Fascist! Fascist!"

"Go fry your own babies, not ours."

From the midst of them somewhere, a bottle sailed over the gate and smashed on concrete. Somebody cheered.

"Okay, let's move it back," one of the officers called out.

Mel felt a chill at the mindless hatred he could feel being directed at him from complete strangers. People had been killed in situations like this, and with no better reason.

The chanting started up again behind him as he went inside. *"GPD, Don't zap me! . . . GPD, Don't zap me! . . . GPD . . ."*

He eventually found Gilman, wearing oily coveralls and a baseball cap, in a maintenance pit surrounded by pipes and girderwork underneath a piece of machinery in the reactor hall. A chest was open to one side of him, with various tools and instruments laid out around it. He had removed the casing of a piece of machinery, exposing a rotating assembly inside. "Some of the staff were intimidated by what's going on outside and stayed out today," he explained, ducking out and wiping his hands with a piece of rag. "We've got some urgent tests to get through, and this centrifuge needs a new seal." He shrugged. "So I figured what the heck. There isn't a lot else happening today. Anyhow, it's good to keep your hand in." Mel marveled at his coolness. At the same time there was a tiredness in Gilman's eyes that Mel hadn't seen on his earlier visit. The pressures were clearly building up. Mel was struck by the contrast between this picture and the neo-Luddites outside: knowledge versus ignorance; reason versus superstition. The creator; the destroyers.

"What's it all about?" Mel asked, although he pretty well knew.

"The media are going through one of their frenzies. An ass from the state university who calls himself a professor has discovered he can be a celebrity by telling housewives they're going to have two-headed babies."

"I saw the piece they did about it on TV," Mel said. "They didn't exactly give you equal time."

"Oh, God, that was a horror story." Gilman tossed the rag down and hauled himself up out of the pit. "Do you believe the things they tell you?"

"No, but I've talked to Stephanie."

"How is she?"

"Just fine."

"That's good. Come on, let's go upstairs. Could you use a coffee?"

"After flying from Boston? Sure. It sounds great."

They began walking. "And that's not all of it," Gilman said. "We've got union trouble, too."

"Just what you needed. What's their problem?"

"Somehow they found out that we had an offer of private funding if we agreed to forget the hybrid program and went to windmills. I turned it down. They're threatening to shut us down, anyhow, unless we change our minds. Can you imagine it?"

"How would they get hold of information like that?"

"Somebody somewhere leaked it. I don't know. *Cui bono?*"

Several people were in the staff cafeteria, trying to hide their nervousness and talk as if it were just a normal day. Gilman exchanged a few morale-boosting words with them, then he and Mel got two cups of coffee and took them to Gilman's office for privacy.

Gilman's first concern was for Stephanie, and he listened intently while Mel updated him on developments since their last meeting, or at least as much as he felt comfortable divulging. Then they got around to the current situation with GPD and its problems. "Do you think that it's a safety issue pure and simple?" Mel asked. "Or might there be more to it?"

Gilman rubbed his nose. "Well, I've always thought so. People are worried because of what they hear, and you can't really blame them when you look at the garbage they're fed. I've tried to do something about it, but the system's against you. It conditions people to want ever greater sensation, not facts. I don't know how you go about fighting it."

"But could it go deeper than that?" Mel persisted. "Suppose that were just the front, and the real reasons were more political."

"Well, I've heard theories like that, of course . . . but what would be the point? We're being told every day that the country's got energy problems. Why would anyone want to sabotage a solution if they really knew it was workable? What sense would it make?"

"Oh, nothing especially new in the world," Mel said. "Unlimited energy means unlimited prosperity, and that would mean freedom—for everybody. Not everyone would like that. The ones who want to control other people's lives wouldn't like it. The godlike power they crave requires childlike dependence on the part of everyone else."

Gilman eyed him dubiously. "Maybe . . . I don't know. I've never had much time to worry about things like that," he said.

"But you've told me yourself that all the scares about proliferation are really a sham to keep nuclear production technology out of the hands of Third World competitors," Mel replied. "Isn't that the same thing: keep the little guys in their place and preserve privilege where it belongs?"

Gilman raised a half-open hand and seemed about to say something, then changed his mind as the pragmatist in him reasserted itself. "Anyhow, Mel, we're getting a bit speculative and academic. You said you had something serious that concerns the company. Let's get down to that."

But Mel seemed unwilling to leave it quite there. "Would you say that Hermann Oberwald knows the truth about your work here and its ultimate potential?" he asked. "Or does he believe the popular myths too?"

Gilman looked taken aback. "Well, there's no question . . . Of course he knows the real story. He's a national adviser, for heaven's sake. I mean, what kind of a question is that?"

"So if he said differently, he'd be lying?"

"Well, yes, I'd have to say so."

"Why might he want to do that?"

Again Gilman looked perplexed. "Look, what is this, Mel? Quit playing riddle games with me and get to the point, would you, please?"

In answer, Mel withdrew from his briefcase a copy of the blue-bound report that he had found in Eva's apartment in California. "I think when you read this, you'll agree that what I said a moment ago was far from speculative and academic," he said, passing it across. "Multiply what's in there by a factor of thousands to give you what's been going on across the whole country, and then tell me what it adds up to."

CHAPTER 42

The snow from the north had reached Washington, and the city was getting ready for a white Christmas. At the Constitutional party headquarters on K Street, Stephanie had been working with Landis and Bassen since early morning. The large table in the center of the room where she was sitting was buried in a litter of files, papers, styrofoam coffee cups, and the remains of a take-out hamburger lunch, and computer screens on all sides glowed with reports and personal profiles of the people they were interested in.

She had identified the house in Malibu easily from photographs transmitted from the LA office. It belonged not to Wilson Clines, as Stephanie had speculated, but to a man called Bertram Slessor, who owned a publishing group that was largely financed by Clines. This connection was interesting but not especially surprising. Slessor was known to have a high opinion of his own political astuteness, and harbored something of an obsession to go down in history as a shaper of great events. He cultivated friends in high places and maintained many connections abroad. Landis thought that it was conceivably through him that "Pat" had come into the picture.

Pat turned out to be Mahmoud Salayah, an Iranian exile from the revolution in the seventies, now living in Zurich. Finding him in such company had come as a surprise. Salayah held a high-power, low-visibility position in the upper hierarchy of the UN, which explained Challin's remark about his international connections. It also accounted for the vast flows of money that he had been said to direct—not out of the U.S. through its aid programs, as Stephanie had supposed, but at the receiving end. The UN had largely degenerated into an international platform for anti-Western propaganda, with America still graciously footing most of the bill. Salayah, an outspoken anticapitalist, was noted as an advocate of socialism for the masses and vigorously supported the nationalization of

Western-owned assets by developing nations. All of which made his liaison with a banker like Wilson Clines and an energy mogul like Groveland Maddock—"Howard," whom Stephanie had recognized herself when she was at Malibu—intriguing, to say the least.

Stephanie had been nearer the mark with her guess about "Alan." His real name was Duncan Forstner, and he was highly placed in the rarefied levels that decreed the regulatory policies of the Washington bureaucracies—some of which had come close to driving Ed Gilman insane.

That was another of the subjects that she'd had to undergo a crash course on in the process of becoming Eva. The popular belief that state-regulated industries, such as the railroads in the nineteenth century, and later the telephone and electrical utilities, had been brought to heel to protect the populace against exploitation was, for the most part, erroneous. Rather, it had been the owners themselves who had fomented the public outcries for government intervention—to protect *themselves* from competition. For the first step in response to such demands was invariably to appoint an expert committee to investigate and recommend on the legislation to be passed. And where else could the experts who understood an industry be obtained other than from within the industry itself? The inevitable outcome was that the foxes would be left in charge of the hen coop, while the reformers, heady with success, moved on in search of new dragons to conquer.

In this light, Forstner's presence made a lot of sense. Stephanie rubbed her eyes, turned over the sheet she was studying, and called a new reference onto the screen at her elbow. What were the sources? What corroborated them? Could it mean anything else if looked at a different way? Is this the right question? In ways it was more demanding than scientific research, requiring a peculiar twist of mind. The world that science studied could be complex and devious at times; but it never deliberately lied.

Bassen picked up a phone and called somebody in a library somewhere. A clerk came in and handed Landis a file from another group working next door. Stephanie checked an entry in another report. She sat back to ease her cramped shoulders and looked across at Landis. "This has even got a note of somebody's shirt and shoe sizes," she said. "Is it important? I mean, was it really worth somebody's while finding that out, and somebody else's to record it in here?"

Landis looked up and grinned faintly from the far end of the table. "You never know," he said. "It gets to be a habit never to let any scrap go, no matter how trivial it seems." He gulped from a cup of lukewarm coffee. "I'll give you a good example. In the Six-Day War in 1967, the Israelis wiped out the entire Egyptian, Syrian, and Jordanian air forces in the first couple of hours. The main reason was because they knew just about everything about the other side. They knew the names, abilities, popularity, and habits of the army commanders down to platoon level. Even the menus for the meals served in the sergeants' messes."

Stephanie looked puzzled. "What use was that to anyone?"

Landis's grin broadened. "In the following days, the Israelis captured somewhere around three thousand Egyptians. Having that information enabled them to make sure that their enemies were better fed as prisoners than they had been in their own camps. A little bit of subtle propaganda, you see."

Bassen finished his phone call, and at that moment the door opened and Theo McCormick came in. He was in his fifties, a burly, forceful man with thinning hair receding above a tanned brow, dark, alert, mirthful eyes, a snub nose, and a powerful, shadowy jaw with strong, even teeth, which was the first thing most people said they noticed about him. His energy and dynamism had become famous on the campaign trail before the election, and it was generally anticipated that he would play a far stronger role in the new administration than was traditional for the vice president. He was holding a copy of the report on Stephanie's activity in California, which he had been reading upstairs. "You did a good job," he told her. His voice was husky, with a hollow tone to it.

"Thank you."

"Talk to us first if you ever want to go full-time." He looked at the other two. "What's the assessment of it so far?"

Landis and Bassen glanced at each other. They had been arguing all morning and still hadn't reached agreement. That wasn't necessarily a bad thing, Stephanie had come to realize. Skepticism and dissent were healthy in this business, just as in science. Nothing hid truth more effectively than unchallenged preconceptions.

"We don't read it the same," Bassen said. "Warren thinks they could be straight. I say it smells."

"What bothers you about it?" McCormick asked.

Bassen massaged his saggy cheeks with his fingers and

thumb for a second—he still reminded Stephanie of a bull-necked basset hound. "They did it all wrong. There was no need to take her to the house and no need to reveal them-selves. Her only contact should have been through Seybelman. If she wasn't genuine, she'd be a direct line back to us." He swept an arm to indicate the papers all over the table and the data on the screens. "We've been able to put together all kinds of things, just because of that. It doesn't make sense. It can only be a setup."

"What for? Any ideas?"

Bassen shook his head. "Right now, I don't know."

McCormick looked at Landis. "What's your side, Warren?"

"I agree that it doesn't make sense," Landis replied. "But only if we assume they don't trust her. Ron's right: we're getting some valuable insights to how the net fits together. We started out from two points that seemed to have nothing to do with each other: Oberwald's recruitment of Brett, and Eva's infiltration of a left-leaning political alliance in California. Now they're starting to look like two ends of the same chain. You see my point—this kind of information is too valuable to be a freebie." Landis showed his palms for a moment. "But if they really do believe she's genuine, the whole picture changes. In that case, the reason that Challin gave becomes credible: to let her see for herself the kind of money and clout that'll be behind her if she does get nailed."

"It would also play to the big-time-ambitious line that Eva was working," McCormick said.

Landis looked less persuaded by that. "Too transparent," he said. "The time for that would be after the mission, not before."

"That, I agree with," Bassen said.

"What are your recommendations, then?" McCormick asked them.

Bassen led once more. "Well, if they are setting us up, the only way we'll find out how is by playing along. So I say we go."

McCormick nodded and looked at Landis. "Warren?"

"If they're straight, and this business with the drugs is really what they want her to do, then we should go, anyway," Landis replied, "because of the opportunity it gives us to make it backfire. We play along dumb until we know all the details, and then blow it to the public. It'll set them back a decade and give us a solid first four years."

Again McCormick nodded. "Fine. So it leads to the same immediate answer, either way." He looked at Stephanie. "Any second thoughts?"

She shook her head. "No."

"Good. Well, start doing your homework, because it looks as if we can take it as final now. We'll be leaving for Cairo in three weeks, and there's the holiday in between."

CHAPTER 43

That evening, Stephanie met Dave Fenner in a small restaurant on Washington's G Street, not far from the Constitutional headquarters. Eva had made a point of seeing Dave if he was in town when she visited Washington, and for the benefit of anyone who might have been following Stephanie's movements now—as was very likely the case—they kept up natural appearances by sticking to the pattern. That she was also supposed to have recently rediscovered her other former lover, Mel, merely provided a touch of added realism. The real reason for the meeting was for Dave to brief Stephanie on her role in the mysterious "Mustapha" affair before his departure for Israel the following morning.

The place was crowded elbow-to-elbow with a typical Washington mixture of lobbyists, lawyers, political figures of every flavor, and open-eared journalists, making it the worst place in the world to talk about anything sensitive. So they talked about the political situation in the aftermath of the election, and the portents for the future—which fitted in perfectly, because just about everyone else there was discussing the same things too.

They started with a carafe of wine, and Dave raised his glass. "Well, you and your people did it. Six years ago I'd never have believed it. Here's to the Tortoise."

They clinked their glasses and drank. "Something like it was about due to happen, anyway," Stephanie said. "There's a time lag of, oh, I'd say around twenty, thirty years between when a new climate of opinion starts to be felt, and when it becomes reality—the time for a new generation to take charge. The people we've had since the end of World War Two were mostly products of the socialist ideological school of the thirties. But what's finally surfaced today is the movement toward individualism that we saw the beginnings of later. That's how the Constitutionals made it. They were in touch with the new ideal. They were an expression of it. An amendment is just words on paper. It doesn't mean anything unless it expresses something that's already there as a latent mood among the people, waiting to manifest itself."

Dave was staring at her wonderingly. "Eva, you never change," he said. It was a big compliment. Stephanie smiled.

There was a Christmas Fair on at the Convention Center on New York Avenue and Ninth Street, which they decided to go and see after lunch. To get some air and stretch their legs, they walked down to Pershing Park, along Pennsylvania Avenue between the FBI Building and the Justice Department, and back up Ninth from there. The stroll outside also afforded them the privacy they'd been seeking.

"We've established that Mustapha is being held captive at a remote PALP camp in northeastern Syria." Dave's breath billowed white in the cold winter air as he spoke.

"You mean the Palestinian group?"

"Right. How we communicate with him doesn't matter. But it seems he has important information for us concerning the space defense system—we believe it's to do with secrets that the Soviets have managed to get hold of. So naturally, our defense people want to know about it."

Stephanie nodded. "So where do I fit in?"

"He'll only talk to the Constitutional party. Don't ask me why—apparently you're the only outfit he trusts." Dave glanced sideways, his hands thrust deep in his overcoat pockets. "See what a reputation you've gotten yourselves already."

"And I'll be going there with McCormick in January," Stephanie said. "So I take it that somehow you want me to be the contact that he deals through."

"Right. Now listen carefully to the exact words I'm going to use. You'll be contacted when you get to Cairo. Someone will approach you in your PR capacity and ask, 'Do you happen to have any signed pictures of Hector Newell—maybe a dozen?' The mistake is deliberate: Hector. Your line is: 'I think we've given the last one away, but I'll check. How can I contact you?'

The contact will give you a calling card, and written on the back of that card there will be a phrase. After the talks in Cairo, you go on to Jerusalem. The day before the party leaves there to come home, McCormick is scheduled to make a speech when he goes on TV with the Israeli prime minister. The phrase on the back of the card is to be worked into McCormick's speech. That will be proof to Mustapha that the channel he's communicating into does in fact go to the Constitutional party. Mustapha will then use that channel to pass his information."

Stephanie frowned. "Why Cairo? Wouldn't it be easier to wait until I get to Jerusalem?"

Dave shrugged. "I'd have thought so. But that's how the Israelis want to play it."

"Okay. And that's it? That's all you want me to do?"

"No. When you give McCormick the phrase, you'll also have to tell him the story about Mustapha, his claim to have important defense information, how the Israelis contacted U.S. intelligence, and his insistence on talking only to your people—the whole works."

"So nobody in the party knows about this yet?"

Dave shook his head. "We agreed with the Israelis that we'll play it exactly the way Mustapha wants. . . . Now are you sure you've got the lines?"

They went through them again a few times until Stephanie had them memorized. "Will I be able to get in touch with you somehow if I need to?" she asked.

"I'll be around," Dave confirmed. "The card you'll be given will also have a number written on it. If you subtract each digit from nine, the result will be a Tel Aviv phone number. If you need to get in touch with me, call that number and ask for Benjamin. Give your own name as Gypsy. But don't use it unless you have to. Emergencies only. If I have to contact you for any reason, I'll use the same codes. Okay?"

Stephanie was relieved to learn that the task for Dave would intrude so little into her time. With her official PR duties and whatever Clines's group wanted—she had agreed to do it, of course, although she wouldn't know the details until she got to Jerusalem—she had worried about getting overloaded.

In the last week there had been a lot of media focus upon the drug issue again, with critics of the proposed amendment arguing that a mandated free market would necessarily mean the full legalization of all drugs. Some had gone so far as to imply that the Constitutional leaders stood to profit immensely as a consequence. It had been a strange, unreal experience to watch the public being conditioned for precisely the kind of revelation that the conversation in Malibu had given her a forewarning of. Eva used to say that the system's function was to program people with *what* to think, instead of enlightening them on *how* to think.

"This still doesn't seem real," Stephanie said after they had walked in silence for a while. "Three months ago I was just a physicist, doing a job. What have I been dragged into? I mean, murders, Soviet espionage . . . now Arab terrorists in the Middle East. Things like that don't happen."

Dave grinned. "Well, obviously that's where you're wrong."

"Have you seen Mel since Pensacola?"

"No."

"I think he's having the same problem. I don't think he knows what's hit him, either."

Dave pursed his lips for a second, then glanced at her. "You know why he's doing it, don't you?"

"Well, it's what he believes in . . . things like that, I suppose."

"No, more than just that."

"What?" It was easier to pretend that it hadn't crossed her mind too.

"You. He's in love with you."

"Oh, come on, Dave. . . ."

"Okay, not quite. He's in love with a woman who doesn't exist—a composite of you and Eva that he's created in his mind. Maybe it's his defense against admitting to himself that she's really dead. I don't know. But he never accepted the real Eva back in Florida. And when the illusion was about to break down, he left to keep it intact. And deep down he's never lost it. That's why he used to go out and visit her in LA at first . . . but there was always something more he needed that wasn't there. What he really wanted was an impossibility: Eva, plus somebody else that projected out of his own fantasizings. But the two were incompatible. The woman they added up to couldn't exist in the real world . . . until now."

"What do you mean?" A pointless question.

"You're the complement of Eva. But because of this situation, you've become her too. See what that means? You *are* the illusion: the composite that could never exist in real life, but does."

Stephanie kept her eyes straight ahead. "Why are you bringing this up, Dave?"

"Because I'm not certain how it might affect him. He's been under more strain than he shows. He was trying to find out who he was back in Pensacola, and I'm not sure he has the answer yet." Dave extracted a hand from his pocket and gestured briefly. "I guess what I'm saying is, be aware of it. I like the guy. I always have. But he can be his own worst enemy when it comes to giving himself a hard time. Don't make it any worse for him, eh?"

Stephanie's features softened into a faint smile. "It's nice to know you feel that way," she said.

One of the big attractions at the Christmas Fair was the Toy Bazaar, which took up one whole end of the building. There were model railroad layouts, talking dolls, radio-operated robots, tanks, trucks, and planes—bringing delight to hundreds of wide-eyed tots and teens who wanted everything in sight, and nervous smiles to the faces of their apprehensive parents, mentally computing bank balances. Colored balls rattled through an incredible Rube Goldberg contraption of spiraling channels, mechanical hoists, and trapdoor bridges that stood six feet from the floor; a conjurer was making bowls of fish disappear and turning bunches of flowers into puffs of purple smoke; there were puzzles and games galore, and a computer that could talk back for hours. And a Santa, of course; a tree festooned with lights and decorations that rose past three storys of stairs; and carols playing from everywhere. Stephanie slipped an arm through Dave's, let herself laugh, and found herself enjoying it.

"Look around," Dave said. "See, most of the world is just ordinary people who simply just want to live their lives, enjoy their children, and be left alone. They don't want to be controlled by anybody. That's what it's all about."

He bought her a teddy bear, and afterward they stopped for ice cream. Then they took a cab back to the hotel where Stephanie was staying and talked and laughed over several nightcaps before Dave left. It was the first time that Stephanie had let herself go since Brett was killed.

Her stay in Washington would be brief. To preserve the appearance of normality, she would go on up to Boston to spend Christmas with Mel. Afterward, she would fly "home" to California. She wasn't looking forward to that part of it—without Mel there this time, it promised to be an ordeal.

But it would afford a last-minute opportunity to gather anything more she could about the Opposition's plans before she
left for Egypt. She had been invited back to Bertram Slessor's
house in Malibu for a New Year's party.

CHAPTER 44

It was only when Mel opened the drawer of his desk after
returning to his apartment in Boston, and then looked more
closely at the papers he had left sorted on top and on the
workshelf to one side, that the cold, prickly realization dawned
on him that somebody had been there: the place had been
searched.

In one of his out-of-the-blue observations, Winthram had
commented once on how, in general, men tended to be
comparatively neat in their personal habits when they were
single and to get sloppy after they married, but with women it
was the other way around. Mel had often been struck since by
the instances he noticed of this being borne out, and while he
didn't consider himself fastidious, he granted that it was to a
large degree true in his own case also. He had certain ways of
arranging things that had become habitual, and he *knew* as
soon as he set eyes on them that his papers had been
disturbed. It had all been very subtle, and considerable care
had been exercised in trying to put everything back as it had
been . . . but whoever had been responsible hadn't gotten it
quite right.

In the course of his work, Mel had occasionally interviewed
victims of burglary, who had all told him that the worst part
was not so much the material loss, but the feeling of indignation and impotence that came with the thought of having their
homes, their belongings, things that related to their most
private thoughts exposed and laid bare to the scrutiny of
strangers. He now knew exactly what they'd meant.

He was still smarting when he told Winthram and Evron
about it at the firm the next morning.

"Was there anything that might have been useful to them?"

Winthram asked across his desk. Evron was by the window, watching the muffled figures on the frozen sidewalks below, scurrying to catch up on all the things they'd put off until the last week before the holiday.

Mel, in the wingback armchair below the bookshelves, shook his head. "Not really. It was all regular case work. I collected it all and brought it in with me this morning."

"Good."

"Aren't you forgetting something?" Evron asked over his shoulder.

"What?" Winthram said.

"You can't be sure it was the Opposition that did it. Mel wasn't just a former boyfriend of Eva's. He was also a friend of Stephanie, who was supposed to have been murdered, and a close buddy of Brett, whom we know the FBI are investigating."

"You think it might have been them—the FBI?" Mel said.

Evron turned away from the window and shrugged. "Stranger things have happened. Anyhow, there's nothing we can do to change it. But I do have something for you that I dug up while you were in California. Let's go into my office."

"Yes, and I've got a client due any minute now, so you'll have to excuse me," Winthram said, drawing a case file across his desk. "I suppose we're working as unofficial allies of the Constitutional party now. Are they aware of it, I wonder?"

"Oh yes," Mel assured him, getting up from the chair. "And they appreciate it, believe me."

"Hmm." Winthram rubbed his chin thoughtfully. "Perhaps we should try billing them after it's all over. After all, have to pay the rent, what? Worth a try, maybe, don't you think? . . . Oh, and Melvin, it is good to see you back and all in one piece. *Do* take care of yourself, my boy. I think that what you're doing is splendid, I really do."

Mel followed Evron to his office two doors along the corridor. Inside, Evron unlocked his desk drawer and took out a file of notes and clippings. Mel took it and began thumbing through casually. There was an article from *Time* magazine entitled GIVE! GIVE! GIVE!—THE BILLION DOLLAR FUND-RAISERS . . . Tables of statistics that looked like breakdowns of mailing lists . . . Samples of religious direct-mail letters and literature . . . Brochure—sober and dignified, evidently intended for a few selected clients rather than a mass market, describing the services of what appeared to be a promotional agency called Carlowe-Merton Consultants, Inc., located in Kansas City.

"What's this?" Mel asked.

"Remember that guy Sheldon Quintz—the one you thought was Oberwald's informant back in Florida? Well, he wasn't among the alumni who vanished into obscurity." Evron nodded toward the file. "That's the outfit he's with now. It's one of the agencies that works behind the scenes to design the big fund-raising media campaigns. In fact he's all set to fly high—buying a lot of stock in the business. I'd give him another five years to make the board."

Mel stared at a picture of a lean, sandy-haired man in a business suit, laughing and looking casual and happy, with a row of computers and printers in the background. "This is him?" Mel asked—needlessly, because the caption said so. He peered more closely. The features were familiar in a vague kind of way. "I know this guy from somewhere. . . ."

"You were at the same university. Probably saw him around."

"So now he's putting campaigns together, eh? What kind of campaigns?"

"That's what interesting. Some of their big clients are from the far conservative Right. One of them, for instance, is the Reverend Jessias Greaves."

Mel stared at the picture curiously. Greaves was one of the better-known TV evangelists. His New World Gospel Brotherhood electronic church was reputed to take in over a hundred million dollars a year in contributions. "It seems strange. . . . Half of what you hear from those people is tirades about godless communists and how Russia is the big evil empire that the Bible talks about." It seemed an odd business for somebody to be in who was supposed to be connected with a Soviet spy operation.

"Well, at least we know where to find him," Evron said. "But not until after the holiday. I did some checking. He's away until the new year."

A pattern was there, but tantalizing in its incompleteness. It connected the new political regime in America, and its covert intelligence operations, via the Israelis, to this base in Syria that also seemed to be the focal point of a systematic purloining of high-performance Soviet military hardware. But why? The pieces belonged together, Lieutenant Colonel Chelenko was certain as he sat staring up at the situation board, with the latest decoded transmission from the KGB's American residency still resting loosely between his fingers. But no matter how he tried to fit them together, the pieces still didn't tell a coherent story.

Perhaps this mysterious lawyer from Boston wasn't as innocent as he had first appeared to be. Chelenko traced over the web of connections again with his eye. It now seemed inarguable that the organization that was collecting the weapon components was linked to whatever was going on at the camp in Syria, where the Israelis had a contact; the Israeli controller of that contact communicates covertly to the U.S. through the American couple, who are also associated with the girl, the agent, Fenner, and the lawyer; the girl will shortly be visiting Israel, ostensibly as part of a political deputation; nuclear shells were missing, and the lawyer visits a nuclear facility in Colorado.

But something vital was missing from it all, yet.

To delve further, he would need to put somebody in, somebody good, closer to where the action was happening—or at least, where all the arrows were indicating that it soon would be. And that was in the Middle East, not here in Moscow.

Chelenko turned to his desk, picked up a telephone, and called the secretary of the section in her office along the corridor.

"Yes sir?" she answered.

"Find Major Brazhnikov and get him here, would you? Tell him I have a job for him. A challenging one. The kind he likes."

CHAPTER 45

Stephanie flew north to Boston early on Christmas Eve to avoid the rush that would be clogging airports everywhere by evening, and Mel met her before noon. They had lunch in a waterfront wine bar in Quincy market, and afterward toured the rows of small shops and stalls, crowded with last-minute shoppers heavily muffled against the New England cold, which had settled in with an icy grip that would last until April. Then they went back to Mel's flat. By early evening they were sitting in the living room, she in the leather armchair by the wood-fired stove built into the fireplace, he on the couch, with the lights working this time, but the kerosene lamp near at hand as a precaution.

They exchanged accounts of their experiences since parting in Washington after their return together from Los Angeles. Mel had brought in a bottle of Gordon's gin and some tonics for Stephanie, a half liter of Whyte and Mackay scotch for himself, and a twelve-pack of Coors for them to share. It was difficult to believe that only a little over six weeks had passed since they had last sat together in that same room, the night Stephanie had arrived from Denver. So much had happened, and there was so much more to burden their minds. As the room warmed and they grew more mellow, the setting brought back memories of that previous occasion, and their thoughts turned again to Eva.

"She was always so positive about everything," Stephanie said distantly, leaning back in the chair with her elbows propped on the arms and her legs stretched straight, watching her glass while she swirled the liquid in it first one way around the ice cubes, then the other. "About people. She had faith in humanity and the power of human reason to solve its problems. I wanted to be like her when we were younger, but politics seemed so boring. I think that had a lot to do with why I went into physics."

"Why nuclear in particular?" Mel asked. He was alternating sips of whiskey with a beer chaser and starting to feel pleasantly hazy.

"Because nuclear processes will be the key to the new technologies that will dominate the next century." She waved a hand before he could reply. "Oh, I know there's been a lot of bad press. But we've seen that kind of thing before with lots of things, such as antiseptics, anesthetics, inoculation, railroads, electricity in the home. . . . Eventually it goes away. People talk about 'alternatives,' but there isn't an alternative. There can't be, from basic principles."

"How come?" Mel asked.

"What matters if you really want to do things better and cheaper is not so much the *amount* of energy you can get from this source or that source—there's a lot of energy in all the chicken dung dropped on Oklahoma in a year, but you can't do much with it—however the energy *density:* how concentrated it is. You could never build a wood-burning airliner, for example—the mountain of logs would never get itself off the ground."

"You need jet fuel."

"Exactly. And the energy densities associated with nuclear processes are thousands of times greater than anything you get from rearranging the outer electron shells of atoms, which is the basis of all chemical combustion. Hence you need thousands of times less fuel. And despite the things you hear, you generate thousands of times less waste. In the end it's the only way to go. You can fool people and you can fool yourself—for a while. But in the end, facts always win through. You can't fool the laws of physics and economics."

"I remember Ed Gilman saying something like that," Mel said, nodding. "So is that what the fission-fusion project there's all about?"

"Yes—eventually." Stephanie sighed. "But Ed's so much of a romantic in some ways . . . taking it on and getting funding for it the way he did, when none of the big energy companies would even look at it. That's what enthusiasm can do for you, I guess."

"How did you come to get involved in it?"

"I saw science as coming to be the same as everything else: turning into a Big-Government-dominated monopoly that can hand out favors to the people it likes and bury anyone it doesn't like. It was degenerating into a competition for bigger handouts at the public trough." Stephanie sipped her drink and shrugged. "In my naïveté of youth, I thought I could escape back to what I imagined science used to be."

"So how does the program at GPD fit in?" Mel sipped his drink while he thought back. "From what I recall, Ed told me that the main project is pioneering a fission-fusion hybrid system. Basically it's a way of getting an economically worthwhile energy gain from a low-grade fusion process, isn't it? It multiplies the energy output somehow, which means you can operate with less strenuous criteria than pure fusion would require."

Stephanie nodded approvingly. "You've got it. And that gives you a stepping-stone to a pure fusion economy one day."

"A fusion economy? You mean not just generating electricity?"

Stephanie pulled in her legs and sat up to pour a splash of gin into her glass and top it up with tonic. "No. That's the whole point. What we're talking about is something that will obsolete just about all of today's industries as totally as steam and electricity obsoleted the technologies of the Middle Ages."

"Ed said practically the same thing, but he never went into details. What would be some examples?"

"Take metals," Stephanie said. "Every shovelful of dirt from your back yard contains trace amounts of iron, copper, molybdenum, manganese, chromium, titanium . . . you name it. With such low concentrations it would be hopelessly uneconomic to try to extract them—*by conventional methods*. But at the temperatures of nuclear plasmas, all atoms are stripped of their electrons and become raw nuclei. Raw nuclei are highly charged. Electrically charged particles can be manipulated and separated very easily and cheaply by magnetic fields. Now all that useless material—even seawater—becomes a valuable resource. You don't need geologically concentrated ores to make it worthwhile any more. You see—we've just obsoleted all of our primary metals extraction industries. And we've got a total recycling method for all forms of waste.

"Or take chemicals. The typical way to produce a chemical compound is by putting the ingredients into some kind of vat, supplying heat, and letting them react together for hours, days, or even weeks. The heat provides the energy to drive the reactions in which the molecules you want are formed. But heat is a broadband source—it provides energy over a wide range of wavelengths. Hence it generates lots of different kinds of molecules. So only a fraction of the ingredients turn into the product you wanted—which makes it expensive—and the rest is sludge that you hope your marketing people can find a use for.

"But on a lab scale, tuned lasers are already being used to energize reactions that are a hundred percent efficient, and in milliseconds. So imagine that we scale it up to industrial dimensions, with the reactants combining from the plasma state, and the plasma radiation tuned to the appropriate wavelength . . ."

"You mean you've just wiped out the chemicals industry, too, now?"

"Right. Plastics, fertilizers, all the funny smells and pollution along the Gulf coast. You can make your own gasoline. . . ."

"Make gasoline?"

"Sure. It's only carbon and hydrogen after all, which are both abundant elements, put together in the right way to lock in a lot of energy. All you need to make it economic is a sufficiently concentrated energy source. Well, we've got one. It won't be worth anyone's while to drill the natural stuff up out of the ground any more. . . . And while we're at it, we can desalinate seawater cheaply and pump it anywhere it's needed. So we revolutionize agriculture too. We can turn millions of square miles of deserts into farms and gardens and cities.

"Or take space transportation. How about anywhere in the solar system and back in a couple of weeks? Never mind spinning ships around like wheels to simulate gravity, the way you always read about in stories. The smart way, given the right propulsion system, is simply to accelerate the ship at one gee for half the voyage, then turn it around and decelerate for the other half. That's in sight now. We're already talking about voyages on the same time scales as ocean crossings. That's why all this talk about the planet being overpopulated is garbage. It's growing human populations that make investments in new technologies worthwhile. If we want to get out and become a space-going civilization, we need at least ten billion people. And we can easily support that. It's all . . . What are you staring at?"

"Was I? Sorry. It's just that you look kind of wonderful when you get intense like that."

"I do get carried away, don't I? It's just that . . . well, it's something that I think is important."

Mel could feel the alcohol releasing his inhibitions. "It all sounds too good," he said, blinking in an effort to break the fascination that was taking hold of him. "So why aren't we doing it?"

Stephanie sighed and slumped back into the armchair. "You know that as well as I do: there's too much invested in conventional technologies that haven't yielded an optimum return yet. You saw the report that Eva found."

"Yes, I know. It's not just the environmentalists."

"They're just the dupes in the middle. They're being used as a front, because their aims happen to coincide for the time being with the policies of the people who really decide, and it provides an acceptable public image. The top levels of the social order always stand to lose the most from from change.

And the changes we're talking about will dwarf any previous revolution in history."

"It will happen, then?"

"Oh, sure. You won't stop it. It's evolution. Nothing's been able to stop it for fifteen billion years. Nothing will."

Mel was becoming more spellbound as he listened. The incongruous thing about it all was that *she* should have called Eva's attitude positive. Their two philosophies complemented each other. Neither vision—the individual liberty that Eva had espoused, nor the freedom from poverty that Stephanie was describing now—could become a reality without the other. The only meaningful safeguard against domination by others was economic independence. But only technology could create the abundance that would mean economic independence for all. Eva's individualism could exist only in Stephanie's world; but that world could be created only by free individualists. Like Escher's picture of two hands drawing each other, the two ideals could only coevolve. Neither could stand without the other.

"What are you thinking about?" Stephanie asked.

"Oh . . . Eva and you. You and Eva. . . . Did you know you were both flip sides of the same coin?"

Stephanie smiled faintly and stared into the distance over her glass. "One thing that Eva never had any time for was people who wouldn't try to help themselves. Maybe that was something that rubbed off on me from her. But she'd do anything to help the ones who would. I remember once—not long before Eva went to university in Florida—there were a couple of little girls from farther along the block where we lived, who went to the same school as Andrew. One was about twelve, the other ten. They were there in the house one morning, and we had a Mozart concerto or something playing in the kitchen while we were talking over breakfast. Then we realized that the twelve-year-old—Nancy, her name was—had gone very quiet. And when we looked at her, she was enthralled. Eva asked what was the matter, and she said, 'What's that music?' Eva told her, 'Mozart,' and Nancy asked, 'What group is that?'"

"What group is that?" Mel repeated, stifling a guffaw.

"That's the point. Eva was so incensed—not because she thought it ought to be rammed down every kid's throat, but because in twelve years Nancy had never been exposed to it. We talk about the information explosion, with all the satellites, computer nets, and so on, but Eva used to say it's a misinformation explosion. Here was a kid with a natural appreciation of classical music, yet she'd never known it existed. After that she used to come around and spend hours just playing record albums with Eva. Eva took her to live concerts in the city. See what I mean—she'd help anyone develop their abilities if they showed a desire to develop them themselves."

"She used to say that Chinese foot binding was nothing compared to Western mind binding," Mel said, raising his glass again. He was aware at the back of his mind that his voice had thickened.

"It's long past dark," Stephanie said. "I'll close the drapes." She pulled her cardigan closer around her shoulders and stood up to reach across the table. From the depths of the torpor that was creeping over him, Mel felt a surge of excitement at the sight of the long sweep of fair hair tossed back from the shoulder, and the way her back curved as she stooped to feel for the cord. The ember that had been glowing alternately dark and bright somewhere inside him all evening flamed suddenly. . . . He was only half-aware of himself getting to his feet and reaching out to touch her.

Stephanie turned abruptly as she felt his hand on her waist. For a moment he stared into her eyes, searching. Something there started to respond, just for an instant . . . then it was swept away by confusion.

The delusion burst abruptly, and Mel faltered. He withdrew his hand and stepped back, flustered and embarrassed. Unable to find words, he retreated to the bathroom and splashed cold water on his face. He looked at himself in the mirror, reviling his stupidity. But he would have to face her.

When he came back, Stephanie had put on some music, and was making coffee. "How about playing Scrabble?" she said. "Let's see if I can still beat you."

It was as if nothing had happened. His heart went out to her, and he forced a grin. "What do you mean? When could you ever? Okay, sure, if you want to try."

"But no legal terms that aren't English."

"Okay. No nuclear physics, then, either."

The incident was forgotten for the rest of what turned into a nice evening.

But Mel was quiet and moody over breakfast. At last he began, "Steph, look, about last night, I—" But she shushed him with a motion of her hand."

"You don't have to say anything. It's been a tough time for both of us. Now why don't we just leave it and concentrate on enjoying Christmas?"

Mel had bought things the day before for a Christmas dinner. They exchanged gifts they had bought, too. Stephanie gave him a set of gold cufflinks and tie clip—it didn't do for a lawyer to look impecunious, she said. Mel gave her a new purse. It was white, ornamented with a distinctive pattern of inlaid silver braid. "At last," he said, grinning. "It took me four years, but there you are. . . . It wouldn't do for a lawyer not to keep his word, either."

CHAPTER 46

There had been a monster loose in Mel's stomach all night, churning and gnawing. Since getting up, he had sat in his room or paced restlessly about, brooding and hatching one impractical scheme in his mind after another for resolving the situation. He had avoided Brett before Brett went out about an hour previously. The day before, Mel had opted out of going to the beach and gone off on his own later and gotten drunk again. But at least the cops hadn't brought him home this time. Small mercies.

Finally he went out into the lounge, stared uncertainly for a while out at the yachts on the bay to steel his resolve, then went back into his room and called the number of the apartment that Stephanie shared with two other girls. A female voice answered.

"Steph?"

"Mel! I've been worried about you, but I didn't want to be a pest. How are you feeling?"

"Oh, I'm okay. Sorry to let down the party yesterday."

"Don't worry about it."

Mel became more serious. "Look, I want you to do a favor for me. About what happened . . . I need to talk to Dave. And I was wondering if you'd call there and see if you can fix something with him. . . . See, I don't really feel comfortable about Eva answering. It's just that—"

"You don't have to explain, Mel. Where are you, at home?"

"Yes."

"I'll call you back."

"Thanks a lot. You know . . ." There was a pause.

"Yes?"

Mel hesitated. "It's just that . . . you're terrific. What did Brett do right that I did wrong? I found you first, remember?"

Stephanie laughed. "Strange, isn't it, how things work out. Talk to you soon." She hung up.

The next five minutes seemed like five years. Mel wandered back out into the lounge and stood there, looking around. His graduation diploma, with Brett's, was on the table—still in their fancy cardboard cylinders and not immediately framed and put up on the wall like most people's. What did that mean? In Brett's case, simply that as always he was immersed in whatever new thing he was into and hadn't had time. He was proud of his achievement, but not intoxicated by it. It was a private, inner satisfaction, not something to be flaunted for the admiration and envy of others. It meant that Brett was aware of how little he knew. His mind was still open, and he would continue learning. He would do well.

And in Mel's own case? He wasn't so sure. Perhaps he was becoming cynical. The application papers for going on to the postgraduate course were still there, uncompleted, on the shelf above the table. Above it, the shelves with the computer monitor and the eternal ensemble of partly dismantled gadgets. Outside, the yachts. Another year of it? Was that what he really wanted? And then what? Another lab somewhere, another terminal, schematic diagrams, computer listings, more of the same. And Eva? He realized to his own surprise that he wasn't sure. Perhaps, deep down, he was hankering toward a new scene, new environment, something different all-round. Maybe that was what he needed to solve the whole problem.

The phone rang, and all such thoughts fled from his mind. He went through into the kitchen and took it there. "Hello?"

"Mel?" A man's voice.

"Yes."

"Dave Fenner." Mel's brain seized up. Seconds of befuddled silence. "I was told you wanted to talk to me."

Mel found a remnant of his voice. "Well, yes . . . privately. I didn't actually mean like this."

"I understand." The voice was firm and even, yet somehow

reassuring. Mel realized with relief that he wasn't going to have to blurt out a clumsy explanation. "I have a flight out of Pensacola at seven-twenty tonight," Dave went on. "Why don't I show up an hour ahead of schedule, and we could have a drink there." He made it sound like the most natural thing in the world.

"That would be okay, I guess," Mel said.

"Okay. I'll meet you in the bar there at, let's say, six?"

"Six," Mel repeated. "Yes, that's fine."

"See you there."

The place was busy with Sunday-night travelers returning to and from wherever after the weekend. It was tired-looking compared to what it once had been, with the black-leather-padded booths worn, and the glass-topped tables in need of replacement. Cincinnati was playing St. Louis on the TV monitor above the bar.

"You've got her all wrong, pal," Dave said, staring fixedly at Mel across the booth and shaking his head. "Look, I think you're a nice guy, and I wouldn't want to spoil your outlook on life. But what you're seeing is a creation from someplace inside your own head. Sure, she's as beautiful as they come, sexy, perceptive, independent, knows how to handle herself, and probably has one of the smartest heads on her shoulders that either you or I are likely to meet—all the things that every guy thinks he's been waiting to find wrapped up in one package, and it can only happen once in a lifetime."

Which came pretty close to summing up how Mel felt. He thrust his chin out obstinately. "So, what's wrong with that? . . . I mean, if you don't think that's particularly special, what are you doing? Just playing a game?" It wasn't coming out the way Mel wanted. He gestured awkwardly. "What I'm trying to say is, it's kind of insulting to her, isn't it? I mean, I appreciate her for what she is . . . for herself. I . . ."

"Care for her," Dave completed.

"Yes."

Dave hesitated for a second, then smiled in a reluctant, I-didn't-really-want-to-say-this kind of way. "But that's the whole point—what I'm trying to tell you. That's how you see her. But what does she see back?"

Mel shuffled uncomfortably. "I'm not sure I follow. Are you saying she doesn't like me or something?"

"Hell no. She thinks you're great . . . as guys go. But that's it."

"What do you mean, that's it?"

"Let's face it, man, she's a ball-buster. She's a great friend and good to know. But she's not what you're seeing." Mel stared down at his glass. He didn't want to start an argument he couldn't win, but was just as reluctant to concede it. Dave went on, "If you want to know, she likes your body, she likes your mind, and she likes you as a person. But that's all you're going to get. That's all any guy is ever going to get from Eva. I guess the reason she gets along with me is that I can handle it. It makes her feel in charge of her life, totally. To her that's important."

Mel picked up his cocktail and sipped at it. It was the bar's special creation, called a Tortoise. His thoughts were mixed and confused. He'd thought he had found what he wanted and had tried to challenge Dave in the only way he knew how. Dave was telling him there was nothing to fight over. What Mel thought he stood to lose was an illusion. Nobody ever would have it. It didn't exist.

All of a sudden he felt weary of it all. He didn't want to discuss the subject further. He just needed time on his own to think it all through. He looked back at Dave, seeking a way to change the subject. Finally he said, "It's not just a friendship with you and her, though, is it? You have a professional relationship with her too."

"That's the biggest part of it, if you really want to know," Dave said.

"So what do you actually do up in D.C.? Are you with the Constitutional thing that seems to take up most of her time?"

"I thought you knew, I'm a purchasing consultant."

Mel looked at him dubiously in a way which said he wasn't sure if he believed it. Dave stared back impassively in a way that said he didn't care what Mel believed. Then a voice from a public address speaker in the ceiling announced, "Passengers for Eastern flight one-one-two for Washington should now proceed through security to gate nine. Flight one-one-two for Washington D.C. is now boarding at gate nine."

"Well, that's me," Dave said, finishing his drink. He stood up. "Don't take what I said too rough. It wasn't meant that way."

"No . . . I'm glad we could talk. I appreciate it," Mel said.

"So, no hard feelings, eh?"

"I guess not." On impulse, Mel extended his hand. Dave stopped and shook it firmly. Then he left.

Mel sat awhile longer finishing his own drink, his mind a confusion of conflicting emotions. Over at the bar, two men roared approvingly as Cincinnati scored. Mel got up and went back to the parking area where he had left his car.

He drove to the university and around the campus, he wasn't sure why. The clusters of buildings that had once seemed protective in their familiarity were now cold and unappealing. He knew what was inside all of them: every room, every corridor. Nothing new, nothing unexpected, nothing to discover. He thought of Dave, at that moment airborne, bound for a distant place, a different scene, a fresh environment. And he envied him just for that.

Hometown, where he'd grown up. Every street and block a book that he knew by heart. He crossed over to Palafox and forced himself to drive past The Viennese, just to prove to himself that he could keep on going; and when he did, he felt a pulse of exhilaration at scoring a small victory over himself. He remembered Eva's words about the prisons that people create for themselves, and the weapons they use to turn others into mutual captives to share them with. Was that what he had been doing?

West and past Obee's, closed on a Sunday. Mac's the convenience store next door was open as always. Mel pulled in for a candy bar. He suddenly had his appetite back for the first time all day.

"Hi, Mac, how's things? Mars bar, please."

"Why, hello there, young feller . . . Mel, that's right. Oh, not so bad, y'know. And y'self?"

"Good. . . . Oh, and how about one of those fruit pies? Better add a can of 7-Up, too."

"So, where's that tall friend o' yours with the beard today?"

"Don't know. He went out someplace this morning."

"Probably with that girlfriend o' his—the one with the sister. Never can tell one from another of 'em meself."

"Did you grow up in this town, Mac?"

"Born and raised. Lived here all m'life."

"Never lived anywhere else at all, then, eh?"

"Nope. Never wanted to, neither. Places is places to me. Same sun shines here as it does anywhere else, don't it? People moving from here to there all the time, but all they're tryin' to get away from is th'selves. Don't work, though, hee-hee. When they get there, they're just as stuck with the same selves they had afore they left. Cain't change a leopard's spots, they say. Well, cain't change 'em any better by movin' it from here to there, neither."

"Do you know much about this new Constitutional movement that people are talking about, Mac?"

"Not much, 'ceptin' it's pol'ticians promisin' all the things we've heard afore. No time for that kinda stuff at my age. Tell y' the truth, never had much time for it any other age neither, hee-hee."

"Just take it easy, right?"

"Yep, 'sright. Nice 'n easy. I just 'cept whatever they give me, and make the best of it. All thieves together, anyhow, if y'ask me. Don't make no difference."

Mel drove back to Pace and parked below the apartment. Brett's car was in the middle of having its gearbox modified, but Stephanie's was parked next to it, and the light upstairs was on. But Mel didn't go in. Instead, he sat staring up at the window, imagining the same setting, the same talk, the same routine. He could almost script how the rest of the evening would go. And tomorrow, and the day after . . .

At length, he pulled out again, crossed the bridge over the bay, and drove along the beach road until he found a remote spot far from lights and anywhere. He stopped there and sat for a long time, staring out at the waves rolling up onto the shore, out of the deepening darkness. Waves that had come from the far side of the world.

CHAPTER 47

The New Year's Eve party at the house in Malibu was held as a masquerade. By eleven o'clock, at least two hundred people had arrived: harlequins, Pompadours, kings and queens, Nelsons, Napoleons, denizens of Wonderland, characters of Disney, gorillas, penguins, astronauts, clowns; there were figures in costumes of every description, milling through the rooms and hallways, eating barbecued steaks and chicken around the pool where the band was playing, cavorting on the beach, falling over the rocks, or shrieking in the surf. Four bars had been set up inside and outside; nets bulging with multicolored balloons hung poised for the magic hour; and strings of lanterns draped around the house and across the surrounding palms and shrubs formed a light-filled cocoon for the revelers to party the night away.

After reflecting for a while on what Eva might have picked, Stephanie had arrived in a silky, body-hugging suit and mask as Catwoman of comic-book fame. The secrecy over the house's location had been dropped, and she had driven there herself. Bertram Slessor, the publishing magnate whose house it was—but Henry VIII for this evening—had returned for the occasion and taken it upon himself to escort her among the guests after Philip Challin, in Kaiser Wilhelm regalia, introduced her.

"Say, who have you got there, Bertie?" the tall man in the leopard-skin called approvingly. "Does she purr? Hello! What should we call you?"

"This is Eva. Eva, Bob."

"Happy to meet you, Bob."

"My pleasure. I don't think we've met before. Are you from near here?"

"I'm just visiting."

"How long for?"

"Oh, a week, maybe."

"Say, look, I'll be taking some friends out on the yacht the day after tomorrow. We could use a couple more girls to make up the numbers. Are you free? Do you like the ocean?"

"I do, but I think I might be tied up. Better not to commit myself, I think. Can I catch you later?"

"Sure. I'll be around. You'll let me know, eh?"

"You're not hard to spot."

"Not hard to spot! Did you hear that? Was it a pun? Say, not bad, ha ha!"

She moved on. A redhead in a flimsy slave-girl costume was trying to divert the advances of an Abraham Lincoln who seemed to be taking his role literally. Cleopatra was dancing with King Kong, who had a lamp shade on his head. There were the inevitable drunks, clustered around the bar.

"Okay, I got one. Why does an elephant have four feet?"

"I dunno. Why does an el'phant . . . whatever?"

"Because it'd look kinda stoopid with four inches! Ha-ha, ha-ha!"

But it wasn't exclusively merriment. She found an intellectual Count Dracula airing his views to a mixed circle in a small room, with bookshelves and a grand piano, that opened off the central hall. "You see, the whole problem is with the economic system. It's corrupt. We've got too many machines at too low a price. And ordinary people aren't any happier, because they're incapable of absorbing the culture or the education. Look at the way they jam the roads up with their cars. No, I think that plain, simple, rural community life is what we have to get back to. Honest labor. It's healthier for the majority, it keeps them out of trouble. And if the truth were known, they're happier being busy than being idle."

"I was in Afghanistan and Vietnam this year," a woman in a low-fronted crinoline gown remarked. "That's what they've done. And you're right. The people I talked to seemed happier."

Stephanie wondered when Dracula had last worked a twelve-hour day of stoop labor on the land and then returned to a house with no machines in it, but a wife who had been reduced to old age in her thirties by childbearing and heavy labor that would have caused riots in today's penitentiaries. It didn't seem to daunt the woman in the crinoline gown that the main preoccupation of the majority of inhabitants of the utopias she'd mentioned seemed to be to get out of them at any price.

"As a scientist, I agree with you about the machines," a sailor suit in the corner piped up. "Energy is too cheap. That's the trouble. Rural communities with wind turbines would keep the price high enough for it not to get out of hand. That would also produce a correspondingly reduced population density, much better for everyone." In other words, a lot of people's children would die, Stephanie thought to herself. Other people's, no doubt. Scientist? Of what? Where would he place himself in the system he was describing?

Dracula provided the answer to that. "What I envisage is an egalitarian system in which all the basic necessities of existence are absolutely standardized. No unnecessary waste. No excess consumer products. Everybody would receive just what they need as determined by impartial committee instead of by greed." And who would decide what they needed? By what right? Who would be the dispensers, and who the dispensedto? And what would happen to those ungrateful enough to dissent? Concentration camps?

"As a scientist, I see a rationally planned order, where . . ."

"Oh, hello there," Dracula said, seeing her at the doorway. "A pussycat. Are you joining us?"

"No thanks. Just browsing through."

"Have fun. Meeow."

"What would you do to provide motivation, though? Some form of religion would still be essential to . . ."

In another room, a relative of Slessor's was showing a group of admiring ladies some of the presents that the children of the family had received. One toy comprised a set of transparent blocks containing pieces of scenes created by a well-known artist, which could be fitted together to create pictures of various kinds. "All the colors are so vivid!" one of the audience exclaimed. "What's inside that one?"

"A part of a landscape. See, if you turn it this way."

"I like that one, with all the blue."

"How much does the complete set sell for?" somebody asked.

"About sixty thousand dollars, I think Joseph said."

"How can I get in touch with this artist? . . ."

Stephanie recalled a black couple in the Toy Bazaar that she had gone to with Dave, who had agonized over the choice between a train set at fifty dollars or a plastic toy castle at forty-five.

Passing the bottom of the stairs, she recognized a famous movie and television actress deep in conversation. "But what happens if the amendment goes through? From what I've heard, the union won't be able to do that any more. The industry will be swamped with kids from every Hicksville in the country, and there'll be no way to keep them out. That's gonna bid all the prices down. I mean, we're talking about *big* cuts."

"Let me give you the name of a good lawyer in LA that you might want to talk to . . ."

On the way out to the pool area she passed a court jester talking to Superman, Annie Oakley, and the Queen of Hearts. "When I set out to make a documentary, the first thing I ask myself is, what is my point of view? What do I want the people out there to come away feeling? Because that's the business we're in, right—shaping perceptions, molding the way people think. And once you've got that clear, then you know what kind of material to look for. For example . . ."

"It's pure propaganda. The Constitutionals will never abolish taxes. You can't. And in any case . . ."

"The Japanese will flood the place. How can . . ."

"This guy goes into a pet shop, see, and he says, 'Have you got a canary going cheap?' And the other guy says, 'Wadda hell d'ya expect it ta do, bark?'"

"Harry, stop staring at her like that . . ."

"Newell has to be a communist. It's the only explanation."

"Why don't we split now and go on back to my place . . ."

"I'd recommend state securities because there's no tax on the earnings and . . ."

Two morons were pushing another into the pool, where more were screaming and splashing. Another had tried to climb the vines on the side of the house and fallen, and was hanging upside down, thrashing frantically while some tried to extricate him and others laughed. The band played on, dancers packed the terrace, steaks sizzled, and the booze at the bar flowed freely. Stephanie wandered through it all, dazed and bemused.

This was it, the top of the heap? This was where all of the clawing and gouging and rat-racing and back-stabbing was to get to? This was the noblesse, the cream, the elite who knew best, and who would dispense wisdom, justice, and largess to the grateful masses? She had never before grasped with such clarity what the simple idea of people being free to run their own lives meant. Whatever their weaknesses or their ignorance—and nothing taught faster than experiencing the consequences of one's choices—how could they do any worse for themselves than depending on the likes of this? The parasites were in control of the hosts—and they had convinced the hosts that it was for their own good.

"Ah, there you are, Eva. Are you enjoying yourself?" A knight in plastic armor was beside her. The visor of his helmet was half closed, but she recognized him as Seybelman from the wispy mustache and the lips stretched back to show his teeth.

"It's . . . very interesting. I didn't know there would be so many people."

"And are you managing to meet many of them?"

"Enough."

"You have a number of other admirers here, incidentally. I've heard several comments. When you get back from abroad, perhaps we should think about doing something to, how should we say . . . broaden your social life somewhat."

"That sounds wonderful."

"Oh, make no mistake, you've done the right thing. You're destined to go places—and I don't just mean this week, hah-ha. . . . Oh, I've just spotted someone I must talk to. Do excuse me. . . . You don't have a drink. Why not get one at the bar? Hey, I say, Joyce, I've been looking for you everywhere. I wanted to tell you about . . ."

Why not? Stephanie thought. She walked over to the bar by the pool, caught the attention of the harassed bartender, and asked for a martini.

"Hi, who are you?" A slurred voice asked. It belonged to a blonde, maybe twenty, dressed like a French chorus girl, in bodice, garter belt, and black net stockings. Her hair was disheveled and she was swaying.

"Eva."

"I'm Susette. I'm an actress."

"Really."

"See him, over there. That's Barry Wedhorn. I'm with him. He's gonna put me in a movie."

"How nice for you."

"Yeah. Then one day you can come to my party, when I'm a big name and I've got a place like this. Wouldn't that be great, huh?"

"I'll bear it in mind."

"Don't forget. Then when I'm a big name, I'll tell everyone I remember you. You're Eva, right . . ."

Stephanie took her drink and moved away across the terrace. That was when she saw Arnold Hoffenach, watching her from one of the doors into the house. He was not in costume, but wearing plain evening dress with black tie. On duty as always: cool, detached, alert; an island of sanity in a sea of banality. She didn't know what to expect or how she was going to handle it, but there was nothing for it but to go over to him.

"Hello, Arnold," she said. She had no idea whether to smile or keep a straight face, so tried to compose an expression midway between.

His eyes flickered over her, making her feel as if she were being scanned by an X-ray machine. "It's been a long time," he drawled. His voice was strong, clear, but restrained. "You caused quite a flap when you decided to take a break. But I guess you know all about that. At one point Louis didn't think we were gonna see you again. I never saw him so bananas."

"He got over it. Everything's fine now."

"I figured it'd work out." Hoffenach studied her face dispassionately for a few seconds. She tried to read something in his eyes, but they were one-way. Was this simply his manner? Was he suspicious? She had no way of telling. Then he said, "I, ah . . . heard about your sister. I'm sorry it happened that way."

So he was human after all. "Thanks," she said. There was a short silence. She looked around. "Quite a party."

Hoffenach leaned a shoulder against the side of the door, folded his arms across his chest, and took in the scene. "Yeah, quite a party. . . ." His gaze came back to Stephanie's face. "Well, congratulations. You made it after all. This is it. The Big Scene. You're about to arrive. How does it feel?"

Stephanie looked at him uncertainly. He remained unmoving, propped solidly against the door frame, at ease, yet poised, his eyes shifting ceaselessly over everything that was happening. She saw the trained fighting machine, the killer, the pick of the best that the military could produce. But seeing him not through her own eyes but through Eva's, she saw also the ruthless acceptance of reality as it was, stripped of the pretensions and illusions, that made the excellence possible; she saw the pride in competence, and the self-assurance that came as a consequence of those qualities. The lion protecting the sheep. Rome's legions standing fast on the northern borders while the capital crumbled from within. And in that instant she realized that he despised all of it—not just all of them individually, but the entire system that conferred power upon them and obligation upon him. The natural instincts of the predator and the conditioned loyalty of the soldier were in conflict. And she sensed then the natural rapport that this man and Eva could have shared.

"I hear there's an old boyfriend of yours back in town. Phil gave me the word to cool it. Is that right?"

Stephanie nodded. "He showed up at my sister's funeral. It goes back a long time. We . . . well, you know how it is."

"I never thought that was like you."

Stephanie shrugged. "Neither did I. You don't, I guess, till it happens."

"How long have you known him?"

"About six years—since we were at university, back in Florida."

"What does he do?"

"You won't believe it."

"Try me."

"He's a lawyer."

"Jeez, that's all I needed. Are you off on a respectability kick all of a sudden? What's next, country club, kids, house in the country?" Hoffenach nodded his head to indicate the general company all around. "You're on your way, baby."

Hoffenach straightened up from the door frame, unfolded his arms, and strode unhurriedly back into the house.

CHAPTER 48

"We have ignition. . . . We have lift-off!"

"Lift-off at zero plus two seconds."

"It's a good'n!"

"Fly, baby, fly!"

The structure seemed to vibrate to a force that could be felt through the floor from the stupendous power being unleashed on the launchpad a half mile away outside the Vandenberg space center. On the screens, the booster carrying the heavy-lift shuttle slid upward through its service gantries, slowly at first, balancing on a column of flame that lifted it clear of the mountainous smoke clouds boiling around it, then faster, upward and away into the beckoning sky. Soon, nothing was left but its exhaust trail, twisted and contorted by high-altitude air currents in the view being picked up by the long-range cameras from an ever-lengthening perspective.

In the center of the group of civilians in business suits and heavily starred officers who had been watching the proceedings from the rear of the control room, Dr. Hermann Oberwald took in the information from the summary data screen overlooking the floor, gave a satisfied grunt, and turned away.

"How long will you be in California?" the Air Force general next to him asked as the party began moving toward the door.

"Another two days. I've decided to combine some pleasure with coming here this time, and take in some sights. Do you know, in all the times I've been here I've never seen Yosemite. I vowed I would last year, and didn't. Now it's the first day of a new year, and this time I'm not taking any chances of repeating the performance. Is the valley open at this time of year, do you know, or closed in by snow?"

They moved out into a brightly lit corridor with glass windows along one side and lots of signs. "It varies," the general said. "Best to check. But if you get the chance, do go up to Glacier Point and see it from the top as well. There's a road that takes you all the way up there. There's an almost vertical hike down to the floor, too, but I don't know if I'd recommend it."

"I suspect I'm getting to be a few years past that kind of thing. Now, twenty years ago—"

Another voice called from behind them. "Oh, Dr. Oberwald. I was trying to catch you before lunch."

They stopped and turned to see General Nathan from Orbital Defense Command leave another group that had been talking outside a door farther back along the corridor to come over to them. "Ah, yes, I was supposed to get back to you, wasn't I," Oberwald said. It was about the report that Nathan had sent on the still unexplained malfunction of the XDS–6 defense satellite over five weeks previously, which Oberwald was required to approve. The subsequent firing tests had been successful, and the satellite had continued to perform flawlessly ever since. But some people were pressing for an explanation.

"There are some figures that I still need to see an analysis on," Oberwald said vaguely. "Can we say another week?"

Nathan didn't look happy. "It has been put back twice already," he said. "I'm being pushed from up top for an answer."

"Refer them to me."

"Can I tell them you're working on it?"

"By all means. Tell them we're going as fast as is humanly possible."

"Do you have any clues yet?"

"As soon as we do, I'll contact you, General. Now, if you'll excuse me, I'm about to lose contact with my party. Good day to you."

Oberwald hurried away to catch up with the others. Nathan

watched him uncertainly for a few seconds, and then walked slowly back to rejoin his own group. His instincts told him that it was going to be a long wait.

That evening, Oberwald received an anonymous call at his hotel. "I have a message from Ivan," the voice said in an East European accent. "He asked me to tell you that the machinery meets its specification." It meant that the other missiles—the special ones—had been test-fired successfully in a bench run.

"Thank you. Thank you very much," Oberwald replied. "Tell him that is most satisfactory."

"Good day." The caller hung up.

Oberwald replaced the receiver and stared at it expressionlessly. "Most satisfactory," he repeated.

The Lynx had treated herself to two new playthings as a New Year's Eve present. One was a lithe, athletically proportioned youth in his twenties by the name of Tony, with dark curly hair and a handsome, Roman emperor's head; the other, a similarly young, shapely, raven-haired brunette called Julie. They had serviced the Lynx's various whims and fancies, sometimes individually, at other times both together, and she had let them go late in the morning, paid off at five hundred dollars each. Now, she lay back among the silken sheets in her penthouse above Madison Avenue, relaxed, satiated, and revivified, smiling and masturbating lazily while she relived some of their more interesting adventures in her mind. More than the purely physical, she found there was a certain spiritual excitement in sex that she paid for. In dehumanizing her partners and reducing them to bought things, it enhanced her domination over them. In some ways it was like being paid to kill people.

Finally satisfied, she rose, slipped into a Japanese ukata, and went into the kitchen to put on some coffee, then through to the bathroom to fill the jacuzzi—sunken, with a black marble surround, built-in TV, and ivory-handled faucets. While the tub was filling, she lit a cigarette at the bar by the window, went back to the lounge area, and sat down on the couch at one end. Using the touch panel connected to the companel unit, she entered a code to access the national news service, and then specified "Local" for the Philadelphia area over the past seven days. When the request was processed, she called up the "Homicide" subsection of the "Crime" index onto the screen.

The holiday had been a fairly quiet one in Philadelphia, she noted as she scanned through the few entries that were listed. She found the name "Shambler, Eric," that she had been looking for, and tapped in a request for details. The item was a brief one. It stated that a man called Eric Shambler, whom it described as "a millionaire real-estate investor with suspected underworld connections, alleged but never proved to have been one of the prime movers behind the 'Blightscam' urban development scandal of four years ago," had been found dead in bed at his home by the Schuykill river. A verdict of a heart attack had been recorded, although Shambler had no previous history of cardiac problems. The report also added delicately that there were ". . . indications that Mr. Shambler had entertained a female companion." There was no clue to her identity, but the police were anxious to contact her.

The Lynx smiled and switched the set off. Rising to her feet again, she went from the lounge into the private room at the back of the suite that she kept locked, and took a brown envelope from a safe behind a false wall panel. She took the envelope out to the kitchen and consigned it to the incinerator. "Alas poor Eric," she murmured. The obvious completion was superfluous.

Then she returned to the den, but instead of closing the safe, she took out another envelope, which had arrived by courier the previous day. She had studied the contents several times, but there were still some parts to be memorized. She carried the envelope out to the kitchen, where she collected her coffee, then proceeded back into the bathroom, set the items down beside the jacuzzi, and turned a knob to inject a bubble mixture into the swirling water. She slipped off the ukata, looked approvingly at her nakedness in one of the mirrors, and then stepped down and stretched herself back amid the warm, pulsing currents.

She sipped her coffee and reached for the envelope. "Ah yes," she said, settling into a comfortable position to read the first assignment for the new year. It would be a good time to get away from New York's frozen, windswept canyons for a sunnier clime. This time her plane ticket had come with the instructions. A winter vacation and sight-seeing tour in Greece. Very pleasant. To avoid leaving a trail that would point all the way to her final destination, she was to purchase an onward ticket to Cairo herself, after she arrived in Athens.

* * *

Somebody had decreed that to contribute to earning his keep, Brett should join a work detail in digging a trench for a pipe from a new water tank recently erected in the camp. On the second day, Hamashad was supervising. "Time for a break," he announced when it had reached the middle of the morning. He sat down on a mound of excavated sand and rocks and proffered a water bottle toward Brett. "Getting thirsty, Blondie?"

Brett sat down next to him and took a long swig. "Thanks." It tasted cool and sweet. They were some distance from the others, who were talking heatedly among themselves over something. Hamashad's voice dropped to a murmur.

"A way also has been suggested for satisfying you that we have a channel to the Constitutional party."

"What?"

"You are aware that the vice president, McCormick, will be visiting Egypt and Israel this month?"

"I saw it on the news, yes."

"Before returning to the U.S. for the inauguration, he is scheduled to appear on television with the Israeli prime minister. You will be able to watch it live in your rooms. If you tell me a phrase, a quotation, anything, consisting of any words you choose, and it is inserted into McCormick's speech, would that convince you?"

It sounded foolproof. In any case, Brett had no choice but to go for it—two of the guards were approaching, looking at Hamashad. Brett thought for a second. "Tell them . . . 'Wherever else you wander, there's no place like home,'" he said.

In the Moscow headquarters of the KGB, Lieutenant Colonel Chelenko stubbed out his cigarette and gestured at the folder lying in front of him. Its contents summarized the most recent reports from the field operatives working the U.S. end of the investigation. "There's simply too much for all this to be coincidental," he said to General Goryanin, on the far side of the table. "After his return from the nuclear facility in Colorado, the lawyer was visited by the girl Carne, who flew to Boston from Washington after meeting with the agent Fenner two days previously. You see, there's a pattern of constant communication between them."

"What about the lines of inquiry nearer home, concerning

the missiles themselves?" Goryanin asked Chelenko. "Where are we on that?"

"We've eliminated all of them except Glinka," Chelenko said, referring to the PALP base in Syria. "Everything points there. In fact, that was why I asked to talk to you. The center of gravity of the whole operation seems to be shifting rapidly into that region, which makes me think that something is going to happen there soon."

"How do you mean?" Goryanin asked.

"The latest surveillance reports are that contact with Fenner has been lost. We suspect he's left for the Middle East, probably Israel. Carne will depart in eight days time, on January nine, with McCormick's party."

"You really think that this political visit could be tied in with the missiles somehow?"

"We have to allow for the possibility."

"Very well. . . . And what are you proposing?"

"That we move our investigation closer to the spot, also." Chelenko inclined his head to indicate the young, smartly-turned-out major who was also sitting at the table. "Specifically, I'd like to send Major Brazhnikov and a support group to the embassy in Damascus, to continue his work from there. He'd be close to where we think the action will be, and in a position to elicit prompt action from the Syrians if we require their intervention."

Goryanin considered the proposal. "How do you feel about it?" he asked Brazhnikov.

"I'm anxious to go, sir."

"Hmm. I don't blame you. Who in Moscow wouldn't be at this time of year? I'd go there myself if I could find an excuse." He looked back at Chelenko. "Yes, I agree. Get the necessary papers prepared, and I'll sign them right away. Let's get them on their way as soon as possible. Was there anything else?"

"That's it for the moment," Chelenko said.

"Very well. Let me have those papers. Good day, gentlemen."

When Chelenko and Brazhnikov had left, Goryanin leaned back and gazed somberly at the window. The previous evening his uncle had confided that he was to become Supreme Commander of the HQ, or Stavka, of the Chief Military Council, which directed the Soviet military apparatus as a subordinate body to the Defense Council, the inner core of the Politburo. Androliev was pleased and took it as a token honor prior to his retirement, which couldn't be far away now. But Goryanin, more acquainted with the patterns of intrigue and misdirection from his position within the KGB, saw things in a different light.

Traditionally the Supreme Commander of the Stavka was either the General Secretary of the Party, in which case the position of First Deputy was held by the Defense Minister—as had been the case until now—or the Defense Minister himself. The moving of Androliev would leave the position of First Deputy open, and it didn't need a lot of imagination to guess that Kordorsky was in line for it, which would consolidate power between the Party and the KGB, leaving Androliev as the focal point of the military command structure. All that would be necessary then would be to replace him with someone of their own choosing—on his retirement, or prematurely if circumstances so warranted—and their control over the Army would be complete. And what the consequences of that might be, Goryanin didn't like to think about.

CHAPTER 49

Carlowe-Merton Consultants, Inc., occupied the eighteenth and nineteenth floors of the Sherbrooke office tower in the Kansas side of Kansas City. Built integrally with one of the largest downtown hotels and an adjacent enclosed shopping mall, the site was one of the city center's prestigious business locations. Sheldon Quintz had been away for the first few days of the year, and Mel was unable to get an appointment to see him until the end of the first week in January.

There was no particular reason to expect that Quintz would be agreeable to answering questions about his activities of years ago to somebody he didn't know, from a law firm he'd never heard of—and since they were somewhat sensitive questions, every reason to suppose he wouldn't be. William Evron had been doing some research that had involved, among other things, a couple of visits to old associates of his in New York, in the course of which he had uncovered some interesting information on what went on behind the scenes with some of the agency's more select clients. Winthram suggested that Evron might want to accompany Mel to Kansas—in case a little pressure should be called for as a supplement to friendly persuasion.

They emerged from an elevator on the nineteenth floor and were greeted by a professional-looking receptionist. She took their coats and informed them smilingly that Mr. Quintz was taking a call. They waited, taking in the setting of deep carpeting, sleek furniture, and modernistic tiled murals.

Quintz appeared less than two minutes later. He was tall and lean, with fair, neatly groomed hair, affable and easygoing, wearing a dark suit with a hint of stripe, and carrying a notepad and folder. They exchanged formalities, and Quintz ushered them through to a small conference room looking out over the city on two sides from a corner of the building. They sat down, Quintz at the end of the table, the others on each side. He placed his hands flat on the table, relaxed back into his chair, and smiled disarmingly from one to the other. "Gentlemen?" Mel guessed that he had already sensed trouble and was offering no targets for ranging shots.

"Quite a pad here," Evron said, casting an eye around to indicate the whole two floors, not just the conference room.

Quintz spread his hands briefly. "'Trust in him at all times. . . .,'" he quoted."

"Psalms," Evron supplied.

"Sixty-two, eight. I see you are versed in more than just secular law, Mr. Evron."

"But some of the electronic churches put a lot of their trust in the agency, isn't that right?"

"Who are we to question the ways of Providence? Do I take it that it is a potential interest in our professional services that brings you here?"

"I'm interested in investing money," Evron said.

"Ah, then perhaps you've come to the wrong place. We are not a brokerage."

Unperturbed, Evron returned a smile every bit as broad as Quintz's. "Speaking hypothetically, suppose I had, oh, say, a hundred million dollars that I wanted to dispose of," he said. "But for various reasons, I wasn't too anxious for questions to be asked about where it had come from. What do you think I should do?"

A look of mild reproach crossed Quintz's face, little more

than a narrowing of the eyebrows, but his smile didn't slacken. "What a strange question, Mr. Evron. Our business is promotion and fund-raising, as I'm sure you're aware. I may have misunderstood, but I'm not even sure that what you're referring to would be legal."

"My information is that you do quite a commendable job for your clients, Mr. Quintz," Evron said, tacking from a different direction.

"We are paid not ungenerously, so naturally we try to please. I'm gratified to learn that our reputation is a favorable one."

"Take the New World Gospel Brotherhood of the Reverend Jessias Greaves, for example," Evron went on evenly. "His receipts last year were put at over five hundred million dollars, according to my figures."

"You are very well informed, Mr. Evron."

"How much of that sum, would you estimate, is attributable to the agency's efforts?"

Quintz made an empty-handed gesture. "How could one estimate? The ways of the Lord are subtle and complex. We simply take a modest pride in acting as one of his instruments among many."

"A more tangible figure, then, which I'm sure is known precisely. What percentage of it flows into here as the agency's fees?"

"That, of course, is confidential."

The fencing continued behind the smiles. Evron was being outrageous, and Quintz's equanimity in accepting it was tantamount to an admission of skeletons behind doors, which Evron was telling him just as tacitly he didn't want to open. To Mel, listening, it was an education in double-talk.

What Evron had discovered, but wasn't saying because it wasn't necessary, was that the New World Gospel Brotherhood was in fact largely camouflage for an operation to process into legal money a part of the four billion dollars that flowed annually from the U.S. heroin and cocaine traffic. Some of the revenues were from true believers and penitents seeking salvation, certainly—and this helped maintain the cover—but the bulk of what poured in came from sources far beyond the Bible Belt.

Five tons of heroin were estimated as being consumed in the U.S. every year, of which 60 percent was refined from opium produced in the world's largest growing region, the

"Golden Crescent," extending from the Khyber Pass and Hindu Kush, through Afghanistan to northern Pakistan. Ninety percent of the heroin entering Europe—three quarters of which did so through the communist bloc via Bulgaria—came from the same source. The cocaine conduit into the U.S., handling almost a hundred tons a year, was primarily from Peru through a complicated web of connections that followed three broad routes: via water through the islands and into the southeast U.S.; over and through the Central American states and across the Mexican border; and by air at a quarter of a million dollars per flight into Canada, and then south.

Twenty percent of the forty billion dollars held in Swiss banks was thought to be drug money; their deposits from Caribbean nations amounted to four times that from West Germany, which was supposed to be incomparably wealthier. There was a pressing demand from the initiators of those accounts for methods that would transform it into clean money that could be reinvested legitimately in enterprises throughout the world. A commonly managed string of fund-raising enterprises each operating in the hundred-million-dollar-and-up region met all the requirements.

"Just imagine," Evron went on dreamily, "five hundred million dollars. "Who'd have thought that *all* that could come from little old ladies buying themselves a patch in heaven, hippies who've found Jesus, and anonymous millionaires cured of cancer and thanking the Lord? Amazing, when you think about it, isn't it? . . . Just out of curiosity, does much of it come from anonymous donations, I wonder—untraceable, tax exempt, immune from scrutiny by the government? . . ." He raised his eyebrows and pursed his lips silently, and after a few seconds began drumming his fingertips nonchalantly on the tabletop. It was blackmail, pure and simple.

"It's astonishing how these things can add up," Quintz agreed. His smile was still there, but it had taken on a frozen quality.

"A situation that some people could find it tempting to abuse," Evron remarked.

Quintz stared down at the table and considered his options. Finally he said pleasantly, "I don't think this conversation should go any further until our attorneys are present. Now, if you'll excu— "

"Come on, you're dead and you know it," Evron said. "Let's

get real. You're no holy roller. You're just here for pure private enterprise, right?"

Quintz dropped the pretense. "Okay, you've got me by the balls. But look, whatever you want, you're talking to the wrong person. I don't own this outfit. I don't decide policy. I just plan campaigns and design letters. Where the money comes from and where it goes isn't my department."

"That's okay," Evron said. "We haven't come on official business that concerns the firm. We're here on a private matter." He glanced at Mel for him to take it.

Mel sat forward, clasping his hands in front of him. "What we've come about concerns you personally, Mr. Quintz. Specifically, it relates to a period some years ago, when you were at the University of West Florida."

Quintz leaned back and looked at Mel curiously with narrowed eyes. "Were you there then, too?"

"Yes, I was."

Quintz nodded. "I *thought* I recognized you from somewhere, as soon as I saw you out there. You had a buddy . . . big guy, fair hair, had a beard."

"Brett Vorland."

"I think that was his name. I only really met him once . . . But anyway, what do you want to know?"

"Do you recall the time that the defense adviser, Dr. Hermann Oberwald, came down to Pensacola as a guest speaker for the Chamber of Commerce one year?"

"Vaguely."

"The next day, Oberwald had lunch with the university Socratic society. He gave a speech there, and afterward talked to some of the members."

Quintz nodded. "Yes. That was when I met your pal. It was the only time I ever talked to him."

"The only time?"

"Yes. I introduced him to Oberwald."

"Whom you already knew."

"No. It was the first time I met Oberwald, too."

Mel bit his lip. Something wasn't quite right here. He reset his sights. "Okay, let's talk about Oberwald, which is what this is all about. I submit that you not only knew Oberwald, but that you had dealings with him that went back a long time."

Quintz shook his head. "You've got something wrong somewhere. I just told you, that was the first time I ever met him."

"Let me be more general, then," Mel said. "You were

working in conjunction with people associated with Oberwald. Now don't get me wrong, I'm not saying that you knew what kind of work they were in, or even exactly who they were. And if it helps, I don't want to know now. But it *is* important for us to know the kind of work you did for them, and particularly as far as Brett Vorland was concerned."

Quintz stared at the table, sighed, sat back in his chair again, and looked at them. But not in the manner of somebody who had been cornered; it was more the natural, exasperated look of somebody who was genuinely bemused. Evron caught it too and glanced at Mel uneasily. Quintz smiled uncertainly and then said in a steady voice, "Look, I would really like nothing better than to be able to tell you whatever you want to hear to get you out of here. Now would you believe me if I told you frankly that I just don't have the faintest idea what in hell you're talking about?" He opened his palms, looked helplessly at them, and shook his head.

"Do you remember a Joan Flassner there?" Mel asked him.

"Joan Flassner? Sure, I remember Joan. The organizer. She was always writing letters and doing stuff for the Socratics. I was on the committee, too, for a while."

"It was she who contacted the Chamber of Commerce and suggested that they might be able to get Oberwald down as a guest."

"Was it? Okay, if you say so."

"That is, it didn't begin as the Chamber's idea. Somebody at the university came up with it. We think it was somebody who was already connected with him, maybe indirectly."

Quintz shrugged. "Maybe. So what?"

Mel held his eye steadily. "Joan Flassner says it was you."

"You're crazy! I never . . ." Quintz's voice trailed off. He frowned across at one of the panorama views of Kansas City for a few seconds. "Wait a minute. . . . Yes, that's right. I passed the suggestion on to her, but I was only the go-between." He nodded as the light dawned. "Ah, okay, *now* I see where you're coming from. No, I'm not the guy you want to talk to. There was one of the professors there that I used to help out with odd things, and run errands for and stuff. That was where the Oberwald idea came from."

"But didn't you introduce Oberwald and Brett?"

"Only as a committee function. As I said, I'd just met both of them."

Mel sat back, stunned. It hadn't been Quintz at all. They'd

been following a false trail. The Oberwald-Quintz connection had never existed. And the new information they were hearing made more sense, too, as Mel thought it through: A university professor with the right leanings would be ideally placed to keep an early watch out for potentially useful talents. Which left only one question. . . .

But before Mel could ask it, Quintz, who had been looking at him oddly, said, "I remember you, now. You're the guy who used to go with that girl who lived up over the restaurant on Palafox, right?"

"That's right, The Viennese," Mel said. "Her name was Eva. . . . But getting back to this professor, who was he?"

"It was a she, not a he. That was what made me think of your girlfriend, Eva. She and Eva had a big fight once. Apparently she had a husband—the professor did—who was kind of popular with the students, and she always had this idea that he was fooling around. Well, one time she accused Eva of letting him inside her pants, and there was this almighty scene—I guess Eva wasn't the kind you say things like that to and get away with. I'm probably the only person who knew about it. I don't think it ever went further, even to the husband . . . but I know Eva never went near their place again. Before that, Eva used to visit them all the time. A lot of the students did."

Mel was listening, dazed. He already knew now who the informant had been. He had known her himself all along, all those years. "Who was it?" he asked mechanically.

"She was an American-history professor who lived out on the Island. Her husband taught at UWF too—politics and economics. They were both into the Constitutional movement in a big way, back in the early days. That's why there were always a lot of students there. Brodstein, her name was. Martha Brodstein."

And the Brodsteins had been involved, unofficially, in the mission that had taken Dave Fenner to Israel. If Martha was a conduit to an organization that had Soviet connections, it meant that he could already be completely compromised.

"I think I'm beginning to understand why Mustapha will only trust the Constitutional party itself," Robert Winthram said when Mel and Evron told him of their fears upon their return to Boston. "There's only one thing to do, Melvin. You have to take the whole thing directly to Henry Newell. Who else is there to go to?"

CHAPTER 50

With all his journeyings up and down, and back and forth across the U.S.A., Mel was beginning to feel like a shuttlecock by the time he arrived at Washington National Airport after making arrangements to see Bassen and Landis. It didn't especially feel like what he had imagined clandestine work of a nationally sensitive nature would be. The man waiting to meet him among the horde of people holding signs and placards at the arrivals as they came off the jetway from the Boston shuttle was at least six feet six, exaggerated even more by his lean, hollow look and protruding upper teeth, and wearing an ill-fitting raincoat with the collar turned, and a black fedora, all of which made him blend into the surroundings about as inconspicuously as a pork pie in a synagogue. He talked about football, next week's weather prospects, Beltway congestion, and other topics that were of no interest to Mel whatever, all the way into the city.

Despite the pressures that came with recently having won the presidential election, Newell wanted to be present to hear what Mel had to say. He had been in the Capitol all morning, and Mel was taken to the Senate Offices Buildings across Constitution Avenue, where a private room had been found for them to talk. George Slade and Larry Molineaux were absent this time, George having gone to Egypt with McCormick's party to handle security arrangements, and Larry remaining at his normal desk in the West Coast office.

Since the whole purpose was to warn Dave Fenner somehow of what Mel had discovered about Martha Brodstein, Mel had no choice but to reveal Dave's working arrangement with first Eva, and then Stephanie, which so far had not been mentioned to the Constitutional people. Because of the uncertainties attending the Washington environment, Dave's intention had been for Stephanie to broach this with McCormick directly, after they got to Israel. On the plane down, Mel had prepared himself for some recriminations over this. Bassen sounded the most displeased. In defense, Mel said, "Ever since I got mixed up in this, everybody has been cautioning me against saying anything that doesn't have to be said. We couldn't see that Dave's involvement affected the job that Stephanie agreed to do for you in any way. We pressed him on it. He was adamant. He was the professional. We went along with doing it his way."

"I can see Mr. Shears's point," Newell said. "In any case it's all water under the bridge now. Let's save our time and energy for the future."

"Is that everything, now?" Landis asked Mel. "Is there anything else at all, however inconsequential it may seem, that we still haven't heard about?"

Mel shook his head. "No, now you know everything I do. That's it."

There was a silence while their thoughts returned to the immediate problem. At length Landis said to Mel, "Stephanie must have some way of contacting Fenner over there."

"She'll be given a Tel Aviv phone number sometime before she leaves Cairo."

"You don't know exactly which department, or whatever, Fenner works for?" Bassen checked.

Mel could only shake his head. "Sorry."

"Hmm."

"Can we trust our satellite link to Theo through the embassy there?" Newell asked. "Is it secure enough to risk sending a message for her to pass on?"

Bassen looked dubious. "With the things we've been finding out, I wouldn't guarantee it," he said.

"We might have to send someone out there," Landis said.

Bassen bunched his mouth as he wrestled for a moment with whatever was going through his mind. Finally he said, "I hear what you're saying, but is it our problem? Fenner doesn't work for us . . . we don't know who the hell he works for. We didn't send him there. He's a professional. He knows the breaks."

"Yes, but we did send Stephanie, Ron," Newell pointed out. "If she's mixed up in whatever Fenner's doing, then whatever affects him could involve her, too. Even if we didn't know about it at the time, we can't wash our hands of the responsibility."

"Hmm." Bassen didn't seem happy, but he wasn't going to

make an argument of it. "Who can we send?" he asked. "All my people are having to be in two places at once as it is. And we don't have many with the right background information on this, anyway."

"With the inauguration due shortly, it's difficult," Newell agreed. "What about Larry out in LA? Could we spare him if we got him across here?"

"Why don't I go?" Mel heard a voice saying, then realized it was his. Three heads jerked around to look at him in surprise.

It had been automatic, from somewhere deep down inside him, driven by reasons he didn't understand. There were too many confused emotions boiling around and intermingled for him to have had a hope of explaining them; and besides, they were not germane, nor even rational.

He floundered for a few seconds while the others continued staring at him, then tossed up his open hands. "You've just agreed that you don't have anybody else who knows the whole story. And even if you found someone that you could clue up in time, what would happen if Stephanie failed to make contact, and he had to go on to Israel to try finding Dave directly? He wouldn't even recognize Dave if they passed each other in a hotel lobby. You don't have a picture of him." He stopped and looked from one to another, inviting them to disagree if they knew something that he didn't. Evidently they did not. Mel went on. "Whereas I've known both of them personally for years. I possess the one thing that nobody else you could send could have: a knowledge of the whole situation, and of the people involved. That has to count for something." He sighed and threw in his only other card. "And besides, it might not really be your problem, but it is my problem. They're both from a very special group of old friends, two of whom are dead already. How do you think I'd feel if something happened and I hadn't tried? Put yourselves in that position."

Bassen was the first to speak. "I hear what you're saying Mel, but it's not just any job. It's one that needs experience and skill of a kind you don't have. It takes years to train one of our people . . ."

"But on the other hand," Landis came in, "let's not forget that we owe a lot of what we know to Mel's initiative already. I'd go so far as to say that he's demonstrated a certain natural aptitude."

"He might be the best choice, in spite of what you say, Ron,"

Newell mused. Mel blinked as he listened. Him, a natural? The thought had never crossed his mind.

Bassen could see that Newell was taking to the idea. "Maybe," he conceded guardedly.

Newell stared at Mel for a few seconds. "If we're going to decide to do this, let's decide right now . . ." He paused, still distant in thought. "But if you are going to confront our enemies, at least you should know something about who they are and what you are proposing taking on."

"Do you mean out there, where McCormick is?" Mel asked.

"Oh no, much more than that. The entire Constitutional movement and what it really means. You should know, anyway, since some of the information which you and Stephanie uncovered has helped us bring together the pieces of a pattern that has been emerging for some time. If you do go over there for us, you should have some idea of what this is all about." Mel nodded, although he didn't quite follow. Newell glanced at Landis. "How much time do we have, Warren?"

Landis looked at his watch. "We're due to meet Collins across the road in thirty minutes."

Newell shifted his gaze back to Mel. "I take it you know about the people Stephanie met in California, and the further connections that Eva uncovered?"

"Yes," Mel said. "Stephanie spent Christmas with me in Boston."

"Some impressive and influential people, would you say, Mr. Shears?"

"They seemed to be. Stephanie thought so. I don't know that I'd describe her as being impressed by everyone she saw, though."

The briefest of smiles flashed across Newell's face. "Yes, compared to the average man with his few thousand in the bank—if that isn't more than offset by debts and credit. In terms of owning wealth—not consumer products, which cost money to purchase, to maintain, and to replace, but real wealth, in the form of income-producing assets—the average American is little different from the Soviet peasant. The comparison is not without significance, as I'll come to later. . . . But compared to the ones who really matter, the people that you know about are just second league—small fish. . . . You look surprised, Mr. Shears."

Mel scratched an ear. "It's just . . . well, a little strange to hear somebody like Groveland Maddock being described that way."

"Maddock? Very well, let's take him. He has a paper fortune built on oil holdings. But that isn't something that translates readily into dollars. It's an industry which is vulnerable to price fluctuations, the revoking of politically arranged tax privileges, and in some parts of the world, confiscation. And remember that to a large degree the numbers you hear derive from *estimated* reserves below ground, which may turn out to be wildly in error. When his father died a few years ago, the press played back an estimate for his estate that *Fortune* magazine came up with of . . . what was it, Warren?"

"Five hundred million," Landis said. "But the probate of his will showed somewhere around eighty million. And there was no record of any gifts large enough to have ever put him in the bracket that *Fortune* claimed."

"Eighty million doesn't sound too unhealthy, all the same," Mel couldn't help muttering.

Newell waved a hand to and fro in the air. "Not bad, granted, but still chicken feed. Maddock is of that part of the society that we might term 'neoconservative.' Their ambition is to join the true top rank—the Property Party, which is the only one that has really run this country for the past century, despite its superficial split—but the big fear is that they mightn't make it, and so they feel insecure. These are the ones who lead the howls against communism and try to cling to the old order, because with every measure of socializing legislation that is introduced, they feel their grip slipping and their chances being eroded away. This is the 'far Right' that the public sees. And on the other hand, men like Duncan Forstner, whom Stephanie also met, are the counterpart on what is perceived as the 'liberal' Left: frustrated and resentful intellectuals and professionals, necessary technicians because of their specialized skills and knowledge, and yet underpaid menials on the economic plantation. Craving influence and recognition but debarred by lack of wealth from positions of power, the only recourse they have is to seek direct control by mass propaganda and manipulating the democratic process." Newell raised a hand briefly. "And there you have the classical confrontation: good versus evil; black hats and white hats; godly and ungodly. The conflict has provided a spectacle that has distracted and enthralled the world."

Mel put a hand to his brow. "What exactly are you saying? That it's all a charade, that it isn't serious?"

"Heavens, no!" Newell exclaimed. "They're sincere all right. Look at some of the things that have happened in places like Spain, Germany, Russia, China in the last hundred years. They murder each other wholesale, in millions. You can't get more serious than that."

"But in this case the amendment threatens both of them," Mel said.

"Yes, and they can come to a temporary truce, induced by a shared survival instinct," Newell said. "But the real control emanates from a more rarefied region, above the level at which those vulgar factions operate, where existence is serene and unthreatened—a world far beyond the hired hands and henchmen who were supposed to impress Eva. She wouldn't even have gotten close to the people I'm talking about, never mind into their homes and their social circles. Neither would I, for that matter."

Landis smiled wryly at the doubtful look on Mel's face. "Seriously," he interjected. "Some of the eastern metropolitan private clubs are so exclusive that neither the pope nor most U.S. Presidents could qualify for membership."

"I'm speaking, of course, about where the concentrations of true wealth and power in this country lie," Newell said. "A quarter of the wealth of the nation is held by just a half of one percent of its citizens. And if you narrow that down to corporate stock, a hundredth of one percent. Old, entrenched, hereditary wealth—in contrast to the comparative newcomers that we talked about a minute ago, who rank as lightweights— can stand unaffected by what appear to be sweeping social reforms, and isn't worried by them. The costs are simply passed on through prices and taxes to the public, whom the act is staged to appease. In effect, they preserve their position by buying off the revolutionary potential that traditionally exists at the bottom of the societal pyramid with the middle section's money. Not being threatened themselves, they have no interest in opposing the ostensible redistribution process, which in fact works to their advantage by emasculating the potential rival class that might rise to challenge them. Hence the cries against 'East Coast Establishment socialism,' which come not from the top, but from the next layer down that would like to be there."

If this was the Opposition, Mel realized as he listened, they were up against a lot more than he'd imagined. Something of a dazed look must have shown on his face, for Newell sat back and picked up his coffee, giving Mel a moment to absorb what he had said.

"Have you heard of Jordan Vandelmayne, for example?" Warren Landis asked.

"Isn't he a banker?" The name had been mentioned in connection with a case Mel was involved in six months before.

"Most people wouldn't have known that much," Bassen commented.

Newell picked up the remains of a chicken sandwich and waved for Landis to continue. "Groton and Yale, currently one of the principals of the Vandelmayne family, whose collective assets were put by the last *Fortune* survey at between one-point-two and two billion dollars." Mel raised his eyebrows, but Landis went on. "However, that report omitted to list at least five hundred lesser Vandelmaynes and extensions to the clan acquired through marriage. Although they may not count for much individually, together, through a network of holding companies and trusts, they constitute a unified, coherent family enterprise that weighs in, I'd say conservatively, at five billion."

"Impressed now?" Newell threw in through a mouthful of sandwich.

"But that's only actual worth," Landis added. "If it's in the form of sufficient stock to give you voting control over a corporation that's capitalized for much more, then your operative clout in terms of the assets you can direct is correspondingly larger. And so, of course, is the political voice you command. In the case of the Vandelmayne fortune, the big slice comes from international investment banking and the perquisites which that brings. You see, whenever a budding entrepreneur or somebody with a bright idea comes to financiers for backing, the first thing they want is a piece of the action—which is how bankers come to sit on the boards of so many lucrative enterprises. That was how the Vandelmaynes obtained their primary holdings, which are in energy, urban development, and chemicals in this country, and steel, plastics, and industrial construction overseas. In addition, there has been a lot of mutual reinforcing of ties into practically anything you can name through marriage."

"That's what the whole amendment is aimed at, isn't it? . . ." Mel said distantly. "Decoupling wealth from political power." Despite his involvement with the party, he had never grasped it so succinctly before.

"That, and more," Newell said. "Most people think of it as rendering the power of government unavailable for making money. That's true, but as you have just recognized, it works the other way, too: making governments unavailable to be bought by money. And that's important, because controlling government is the way to obtain monopoly privilege. But monopolies tend to grow fat and inefficient, and a monopoly on a national scale eventually falls prey to foreign competitors. Traditionally, you then try to eliminate them by war. But what do you do when war has become too destructive to be worthwhile any more?" Newell waited a second for Mel to reply, then prompted, "To get a national monopoly, you control a national government. To get a *world* monopoly, therefore, you have to control a . . . ?"

"World government," Mel completed. The implication was already stupefying him.

"Precisely, which you sell to the people as the road to world peace after using their money to fund an arms race to terrify them into believing that war is otherwise inevitable. But first you have to concentrate the powers of various nations into one point over which you can exercise control. And the perfect instrument to achieve that presents itself in the form of socialism, which started out as a set of ideals with universal appeal, but which in practice has been distorted beyond all recognition—by its alleged adherents as well as its opponents. And here you have the answer to your conundrum of where and how the two apparently irreconcilable ends of the spectrum come together. You have to have some form of bait, because overt dictatorships are difficult to sell idealistically. Socialism provides that through its hopes and aspirations—and don't mistake me, many of its advocates across the world are sincere. That's good, because it makes everything all the more convincing.

"But the real architects of the Grand Design have no intention of sharing out the loot, as their actions through recent history show too well, but to control and consolidate the wealth on a scale that is utterly beyond the comprehension of most sane, ordinary people, who are incapable of conceiving this kind of power-lust. The goal is to preside over a world community of money, freed from the inconveniences of nationalism and competition, first by establishing centralized governments over the various nations, and then consolidating them through a series of grand mergers into the global Superstate."

Newell leaned back in his chair but continued staring at Mel. "And that, Mr. Shears, is what it's all about."

There was a long, heavy silence. Mel had thought he was being drawn in out of his depth with a murder and espionage. Then Landis smiled his cynical smile again. "Now you know what we're up against."

Mel looked down at his hands and exhaled a short breath, not knowing what to say. "Do you still want to go?" Newell asked. " You see, we're not just talking about people who kill. World wars, revolution, and genocide are more in this league's line."

"Which you knew, of course, when you sent Stephanie there," Mel said.

"Yes."

"I don't . . ." Mel checked himself and shook his head. "It's just . . . I mean, that drug plant or whatever they plan on doing, that they told her about at Malibu . . . It just seems too tame. If the stakes are this high, wouldn't they be aiming at something bigger?"

Bassen broke his long silence. "Oh, you can forget that fairy tale. That was just something concocted for the benefit of what they thought was a silly girl with more ambition than brains, to get her out there. What they really want her for is something else."

"What do they want her for?"

"We don't know. That's what this whole thing is aimed at finding out."

Mel was already looking at Newell. "Of course, I still want to go," he said.

"To be honest, I'd never doubted it," Newell said. "Very well, it's decided." He stared at Mel curiously for a second. "You know, I would like to think that anyone doing this knows how to take care of himself. . . . Are you any good with a gun? I'd strongly recommend having one. You won't be able to travel with one, of course, but George Slade will be able to fix you up when you get there."

Mel blinked. "I've never fired one," he said. Bassen closed his eyes momentarily.

"That's something we'd better put right, then," Newell said. "How long do we have? Let's see, we're all right as long as you get there before they leave Egypt. So that gives us tomorrow. Ron, can you arrange for Mel to get a crash course at a range somewhere? And while Ron's taking care of that, maybe you can work out some travel arrangements, Warren." He looked at the clock on the wall. "We have to be moving. Perhaps between now and when Mel leaves, you two can fill him in on some of the background to what we've been saying."

"Should I really be told any more?" Mel asked uncertainly. "I mean, is it safe . . ."

"Oh, I don't see why not," Newell said breezily. "You can't leak it to anyone that matters. I can assure you that the people you really need to worry about know all about it already."

CHAPTER 51

Dressed in his shirt sleeves, Mel stood in a small booth with an entry door and glass observation window behind him, and aimed at the man-sized target that had been raised fifty yards away along the range. "Don't bend that arm. Keep your elbow locked," Jerry, the instructor yelled, raising his voice to be heard through the yellow ear-protectors Mel was wearing. Mel had the feeling that it was his normal way of speaking, anyway. "Grip the gun-hand wrist firmly with the off hand. . . . Okay, head-shot again, five rounds rapid fire, go!"

Mel emptied the clip in five smooth, evenly spaced shots. The electronic indicator at the far end showed three grouped closely near the center of the target area, one drifting, one miss.

"Not bad. Don't blink when you fire. It impairs your aim for the next shot. How's the wrist? Starting to ache a little?"

Mel smiled wryly. "A bit."

"Well, let's take a break for thirty minutes. You can get some coffee upstairs. I'll see you back here at, oh, let's say ten-forty." Just then there was a tap on the door. Jerry opened it to reveal Warren Landis. "You couldn't have timed it better," Jerry told him. "We're just about to take a breather."

"How's he doing?"

"He's good. . . . Got the right eye, and fast reflexes. Get in some regular practice, Mel, and you'll be top line."

Mel grinned as he took off the ear protectors. "Glad to hear it." As a matter of fact, he was thoroughly enjoying himself.

They checked the gun back into the equipment room across the corridor behind the firing booths, and Jerry went to attend to some chores. Landis and Mel began making their way to the small coffee lounge upstairs. "Okay," Landis said. "There isn't time to arrange any kind of cover for you, so you're traveling simply as yourself, Melvin Shears, taking a vacation. To throw off any surveillance you might be under, we're routing you via Toronto. You get a midnight flight out of there tonight, changing to British Airways in London tomorrow for the connection to Cairo. Your Toronto flight leaves at seven this evening."

"Not exactly what you'd call a lot of time for watching the flowers grow," Mel said.

Landis shrugged. "You talked yourself into it."

They arrived at the lounge and poured themselves coffee from a pot. There was nobody else there. "Where's Ron?" Mel asked.

"He'll stop by later to check through a few things with you."

They settled down on leather couches on opposite sides of the narrow room. "How's Newell doing today?" Mel asked.

"He's on his way to Chicago. It's hectic."

Mel sipped his coffee and winced. It was hotter than he expected. "I've been thinking a lot about the things he said yesterday."

"Quite a story, isn't it? Can you imagine the explosions it's going to set off when it all gets out?"

"It's going to, then, is it?"

Landis looked surprised. "Oh, sure. That's what they're panicking about. Once the inauguration's over and Henry's officially in charge, it's beans all over the floor, and they know it. They may have lost the election, but they're not going to stop there. The real fight's only just about to start, and now you know what the stakes are, you don't get three guesses to figure out that it's gonna be mean and dirty. From here on, anything goes."

Mel thought back over some of yesterday's conversation. "You were supposed to fill me in more on the background," he said. "Newell seemed to be saying that people like Vandel-mayne are the real controlling influence behind both sides of what the public sees—left and right; east and west. How is that possible?"

Landis paused and contemplated his cup for a moment, then drank quickly from it and looked up. "All through history, in all nations, all cultures, if you want to know who really runs the roost, don't worry about what the titles say, or who wears the tallest hats. The real giveaway of who hands down the orders and who follows them is where they live: the big wheels own the big houses."

"How about the White House?" Mel asked "Does the president qualify?"

Landis snorted derisively. "Who's he? That's just assigned while he holds the job. He's subject to dismissal anytime, and out on his ear after eight years anyway. I said who *own* the big houses—not who just get temporary rights to shack up in them."

"Give me an example, then," Mel suggested.

"Jordan Vandelmayne would be a good one."

"Okay."

Landis elaborated. "The main family drag is a multiple estate of over a thousand acres in Maryland that contains a score of separate residences for the head-honcho family groups and a few hundred staff—a far cry from the beach hut in California that Stephanie went to. That was typical habitation for the supporting nobility and priesthood, but hardly the ruling caste. Jordan himself occupies a forty-room mansion, modernized Georgian, with all the obligatory paraphernalia of art collection, Oriental rugs and so on that you'd expect—it even has an entire paneled room imported from a European chateau. He also has town houses in New York, London, and Paris, and a ranch in Paraguay. To list the real estate owned by the whole tribe of lesser Vandelmaynes would take us all day."

Mel was nonplussed. "How could one small group have created that kind of wealth?" he asked.

"No way that I know. You have to own a piece of a lot of people breaking backs for you out there."

"How did it happen?" Mel asked. "I mean, at one time most people in this country owned at least a patch of land and could look forward to a future with some measure of self-sufficiency. It seems as if they've been systematically stripped threadbare and reduced to a propertyless class of wage earners."

"That's exactly right," Landis agreed. "As liable to dismissal from their means of livelihood as the peons of any banana republic. Any surplus is siphoned out of their pockets every year by your friends and mine, and anything substantial they manage to hang onto in spite of that is confiscated when they die. So their kids end up being sucked into the same trap of debt and dependency. The results could hardly have been different under a dictatorship. Do you think that's what Jefferson wanted?"

"I guess a lot of people have been asking something like that," was all Mel could say.

"All the vast hereditary fortunes were made with the connivance or outright collusion of agents of the state," Landis went on. "Oh, sure, they can muster processions of house-trained professors to make noises about freedom, but what they mean is *their* freedom to eliminate any risk of competition. The only new, smaller enterprises that are allowed to survive are the approved ones—the ones that don't threaten the system—precisely à la Russe."

"You're making it sound as if we had a second revolution," Mel said. He started to smile, and then saw that Landis was looking at him with an expression of absolute seriousness.

"But we did. The original one was betrayed. So was the Russian one, for that matter. By the same interests. They were both inspired by the same thing: the expression of individualism, and the realization of human potential. Marx didn't say what people are told he said. What's pointed at as socialism today isn't the original at all."

Mel shook his head. "I'm not sure I follow."

"I'm saying that the essential control of this country was taken over by a small inner circle of the financial elite in a bloodless and practically invisible revolution that was pulled off in the first two decades of the twentieth century," Landis said.

Mel stared back, unsure of how to respond. Finally he smiled uneasily. "That's . . . one hell of a proposition. Would you care to explain?"

Landis nodded, having expected it. "One of the best paid ways to make a living is by funding the debts of governments. That's how the international banking system arose. People think that when governments need money they borrow it from the people, but that's largely a myth. The return in interest can be huge, obviously, but as may have crossed your mind already, there's a problem. . . ."

Mel thought for a second. "Well, what's the collateral? I guess. How do you collect if the king doesn't want to pay?"

"Right, first time—and especially when he has an army and you don't. Well, basically there are two ways to do it. Henry said yesterday that when a business borrows money, the creditor gets a voice in management to protect the investment, right? Well, in the same kind of way, the guys who lend hundreds of billions of dollars to countries around the world have a lot of pull on their policy-making. In fact, that's the key to controlling governments to your advantage. If you have a government in your debt, then as creditor you can demand, and get, what we were talking about: *monopoly privileges.*"

Landis smiled, but in a strange, humorless way. "It always comes down to creating monopolies, doesn't it? But this one's the bonanza. Governments that need money have granted all kinds of monopolies, for example in natural resources, oil concessions, and transportation. . . . But the really big pay-off is when you get control of a nation's money supply. And everyone who's gone after that kind of control has understood the necessity of power being concentrated in a central bank. Lenin knew it. He said that establishing a central bank was ninety percent of taking over a country."

Mel thought back to Landis's mention of the turn of the century. "Are we talking about the Federal Reserve Act?" he asked. It had been set up to exercise centralized control over the U.S. money supply and interest rates in December 1913.

Landis nodded vigorously. "Quite."

"But wasn't that after a series of scares that undermined confidence in the decentralized private system?" Mel said.

Landis nodded again. "Which have since been shown to have been manufactured. It was publicly hailed as a victory of democracy over the 'money trust.' In fact it was nothing of the kind. It was engineered by the very people whose power it allegedly curbed. . . . So, the instrument was created to launch the national debt into orbit—obviously you want big debts, because it means big interest payments. But what good is being able to run up the debt unless you have a mechanism for collecting the dues?"

"Go on."

"Two months before the act was passed, the amendment was enacted to impose a progressive income tax on the population. It was sold on a soak-the-rich hook, but in fact some of the wealthiest supported it. Probably some of them were being

genuinely altruistic, but the main reason was that the escape
hatch for superwealth had been provided by legislation that
enabled the creation of tax-free foundations. Thus, the big
monopolies, such as in oil and steel, that the antitrust acts
were supposedly passed to break up, could continue to
consolidate their holdings without hindrance, while the competition took the brunt of the tax system. Neat, eh? So that
gave us the instrument for raising the debt, and the means to
collect. All we needed then was a reason to escalate it. And the
fastest way to get a country up to its ears, of course, is war."

Mel's eyes widened. "War?"

"Of course. The same circle that we're talking about had run
the central banks in Europe for centuries. World War I has
been called the most unnecessary big war ever. Wilson was
reelected in 1916 after a campaign based on promises that
American soldiers would never be sent to foreign wars. And
yet inside five months, we were in it."

Landis shrugged. "And the rest is a matter of record. Since
1913, the national debt has increased by—wait for this,
Mel—four hundred thousand percent! Can you imagine what
the payments have been on that? The Reserve was foisted on
the public with a lot of chicanery including an absolute
guarantee that there would be no more boom-bust cycles. But
that was as much a fraud as the rest of it. Between 1923 and
1929 the money supply was inflated sixty-two percent and the
small investors lured into an orgy of speculation before the rug
was pulled for the big killing. It wasn't the inside club who
were jumping off the ledges. They all sold out at the top of the
wave, and bought everything back later at bargain-basement
prices. Now, do you think that all these things can be
coincidences?"

Mel found himself afflicted by a kind of paralysis, unable to
react. He had accepted the Constitutional movement as
representing essentially the reaction against Big Right and Big
Left that the rest of the country had applauded, too—and like
most, had seen the election result as its gleeful way of
pronouncing a pox on both the houses. He had appreciated
that there was a deeper side to it which didn't lend itself to
electioneering. . . . But he'd never dreamed that it involved
things like this.

But Landis hadn't finished yet. "We said there were two
ways to ensure collection on a national debt. The first was that
you get some seats on the national board. The second is that if

the king starts falling behind on his payments, you can always fund his rivals. In fact it turns out that the same group of interlocked financial interests that I've been talking about have been responsible for funding both sides of all the wars of recent times, including our own Civil War. All the shufflings and realignments of alliances in Europe in the eighteenth and nineteenth centuries that you read about seem pretty confusing until you study the pattern of who owed money at different times. Then it all makes sense, and you can see who was getting his overdue notice." Landis paused for a moment, and his voice took on a curious note. "And if the king doesn't have any natural serious rivals, then maybe you have to make one."

Although Mel had been half-prepared, he could only stare in astonishment. Landis nodded. "A hundred years ago, this country had risen to a position of having no serious rivals in the world. Today, of course, it does, which would suit the bondholders of our four-trillion-dollar debt very well. Could that be a coincidence, do you think? Before you say anything, let's just review a few facts.

"The Revolution in Russia was certainly a turning point in world history. The majority belief today is that it was a successful movement of the downtrodden people under the leadership of the communists against the tyranny of the czars. That's not what happened. The Bolshevik takeover took place in November 1917. The Czar had abdicated in March, seven months earlier. A provisional government was established by Prince Lvov, who wanted a system modeled on ours, but his regime didn't get the backing, and he gave way to a democratic socialist called Kerensky. It was Kerensky who declared an amnesty for all the Red revolutionaries that had been exiled after the uprising in 1905 that didn't come off. A quarter of a million of them poured back into Russia. Lenin was nowhere around when the czar fell. He was a has-been in Switzerland, where he'd been for eighteen years. Trotsky was in New York, running a newspaper. The Bolsheviks simply weren't a viable political force. They didn't come back at the call of the masses to assume power from the bottom up; they were sent in to impose it from the top down—Lenin arrived with six million dollars of German gold. Now, the Germans had a reason to try and topple the Russian government—it might have gotten Russia out of the war. But who sent Trotsky from America—and got him released when the Canadians grabbed him en route? And the whole thing gets real interesting when you find that the German banker who engineered Lenin's transfer was the brother of one of the central figures who'd done the pushing to set up the U.S. Federal Reserve."

"Are you saying that we created the Soviet Union?" Mel asked incredulously.

"We not only set it up. We poured money in to save it in the early twenties when Lenin's New Economic Policy had ruined it. But it got too big and looked as if it might run out of control, and Hitler had to be manufactured out of a nobody to check it. Since then we've resumed the old power-balancing act and bailed it out several times with huge technology transfers and other material assistance from the West, which have included building oil and synthetic rubber plants for them, the world's biggest truck factory, several aircraft aluminum plants, and even supplying the precision grinding machines to make ball bearings essential for their strategic missiles, which their industry couldn't produce! And then Americans get screwed for seventy-five billion to pay for a defense industry to counter it. You see, it conserves parity. Postwar American prosperity could have gone so far out of sight as to make it a no-contest. Now do some of our insane economic decisions over recent years start to make more sense? In short, USSR has got 'Made in U.S.A.' stamped all over it. And it's owned and run by its own luxuried elite of upper management in just the same kind of way. No wonder. They're both divisions of the same company."

Mel could see now where the connections were pointing. "Are you saying that this is where the links from Oberwald lead to?" he asked.

Landis started to say something in reply, but the door opened at that moment, and Jerry stuck his head in. "Okay, Mel, let's get started again. We've only got until noon."

Mel finished his coffee, got up, and followed the other two back out in something of a daze. Somehow the stopping power of a handgun didn't feel quite as reassuring as it had half an hour earlier.

Maybe he would have done better to keep his questions to himself until after this was all over, he reflected as they checked out the gun in the equipment room again. It was possible to know too much. He remembered something he'd heard Brett say once: "Confidence is what you feel when you don't really understand the situation."

CHAPTER 52

In the course of a century, Tel Aviv, situated in the southeast corner of the Mediterranean on the ancient biblical coast road between Egypt and Damascus, had grown from a village suburb of Jaffa founded on sand dunes, to become Israel's center of commerce and fashionable living. From the beach-fronted hotels and shopping precincts on Hayarkon, with the ranks of office towers arrayed around the El Al building along Ben Yehuda Street behind, and the Oriental flavor of the Carmel vegetable and flower market just to the south, the metropolis spilled eastward in a bustling confusion of restaurants for every taste, cafes, sidewalk kiosks, supermarkets and street stalls, thronged daily by tourists from all nations and a native population of over two million Arabs, Jews, Druze, Bedouin and other groups, as well as immigrants from everywhere. The administrative buildings and industrial areas were nearer the eastern limits, around the Hashalom Road, leading to the David Ben-Gurion International Airport, nine miles away. A few hundred yards off the main thoroughfare, between the sports fields of a high school and a repair plant for agricultural machinery, was the headquarters of the Fifth Parachute Brigade, currently attached to Central Regional Command of the Israeli Defense Forces. On the morning of January 12, Dave Fenner met there with three men in a small room at the rear of the two-story administration building.

The map on the wall at one end of the table was of an arid, mountainous region in northeast Syria. The enlarged photographs alongside had come from Israeli intelligence satellites put up by ESA launch vehicles, and showed a fenced camp of several rows of barrack blocks and other buildings, and an airstrip concealed in a valley a short distance away. Yigal Uban, the deputy head of Mossad, who had driven down from Jerusalem to join the others, summed up, "It's not one of the standard PALP units. As far as we can ascertain it's part of the general PALP structure, but under an independent command." Uban was a small, worried-looking man in a striped suit, with a broad brow, rounded, snub-nosed features, and balding head. "Beyond that its origin and precise function are obscure. Even Pierrot has been unable to uncover more than that." "Pierrot" was the field code for the agent that Mossad had working inside.

General Shimon Lurgar of the airborne forces looked down at the notes he had been scribbling. He was a former tank commander, and as is allegedly the case with dog owners, seemed to have acquired some of the attributes of his charges. He was a solid, craggy-faced man with a shadowy chin that looked as tough as armor plate, and a mat of wiry black hair clinging to a squat turret of a head. With him, wearing an open-neck khaki shirt with pips on the epaulets and combat fatigue pants, was Colonel Shlomo Hariv, who commanded a unit that specialized in covert special operations. With his long, slack face, rubbery mouth, and thick-rimmed spectacles, he looked as if he would have been more at home behind a desk or a grocery-store counter somewhere, but Fenner had worked with him before and had no reservations.

"And we don't know who Mustapha is," Lurgar said half to himself as he scanned over the notes he had been scribbling and organized his thoughts.

"He claims to be an American with technical knowledge pertaining to the strategic space-defense field," Uban answered. "The 'American' part of it is consistent with his insistence on dealing only through the Constitutionals. He won't reveal more until he's sure he has a channel to them."

Lurgar looked up, thought for a second, and nodded. "Ah, I see. I take it, then, that you're going to use the American delegation somehow, when it gets here." McCormick and his party had arrived in Cairo two days previously and would be departing for Israel two days hence.

"Exactly," Uban said. "Mustapha was asked to give Pierrot a code phrase which McCormick will include in the public speech that he will be giving before he goes back—Mustapha does have facilities to see the speech live."

"Not a bad life by the sound of it, being a prisoner these days," Lurgar commented, rubbing his chin.

Uban went on. "The information will be given to McCormick through one of his staff, whom we call Gypsy." That was Stephanie, alias Eva.

"How did you approach her?" Hariv asked. "They're not even in the country yet?"

Uban inclined his head in Fenner's direction. "Benjamin took care of that before she left the United States. We have an agent in Egypt, known as Dervish, who will give her the code phrase today."

"I have a question about that," Fenner said, sitting forward. "Why go through a complicated procedure to give it to them there? They'll be in Jerusalem in two days. Why couldn't it be done then?"

"I was wondering the same thing," Hariv said.

Uban steepled his fingers in front of him and contemplated them for a moment. "That is a delicate matter to do with internal politics," he said. "This insistence of Mustapha's on dealing only with your Constitutional people is very odd. It suggests that perhaps Mustapha knows something about unreliability at the top, possibly among highly trusted people, that we don't."

Fenner nodded. "Okay, I'll buy that."

"Therefore we have decided to honor his request to the full, by revealing his existence in the first instance only to McCormick."

"You mean you haven't taken it to our own people officially?" Lurgar said, meaning the Israeli General Staff, and the Ministry of Defense via which it reported to the Prime Minister and the Knesset.

"Quite," Uban said. "In view of the unusual circumstances, we decided to leave it to McCormick to broach it to the upper echelons, as and how he sees fit, when he arrives in Jerusalem." Lurgar sat back, nodding that he understood. Uban looked at Fenner and Hariv, and explained, "As a precaution to protect ourselves, we want to keep our dealings with McCormick out of this country. Then, if McCormick does choose to bring it to the attention of our cabinet officials, he can present it purely as a piece of American-originated intelligence, with nothing to be seen here that could connect it with us. That way there will be nothing to give anyone the idea that we might have withheld information from our superiors." Fenner acknowledged with a half-raised hand and nodded. It all made sense now.

General Lurgar was beginning to see now why Uban had asked him here, and what Mossad wanted from him. He looked up at the ceiling. "How important might the Americans consider this Mustapha to be, do you think, when they find out about him?" he asked, massaging his chin absently.

Uban pretended to mull over the question, as if he were considering it for the first time. "Oh, I don't know. . . . Very important, maybe."

"Important enough to want to get him out, do you think?"

"It's possible, I suppose."

Lurgar looked down at the table gravely. "I haven't seen any orders asking us to look into anything like that . . . but then nobody could have issued any, could they, if they don't know yet that Mustapha exists?" He gave Uban a sidelong look. Uban's face twitched into a quick, nervous smile. "Yet if such an order were to come down, it would in all likelihood be one of those panic, do-it-yesterday affairs, wouldn't it?"

Uban dropped the charade and his face became serious suddenly. "Would you look into it for us?" he asked.

Lurgar looked at Colonel Hariv. "What do you think, Shlomo? Could we give some time to it?"

"Oh, I think we could manage that. It sounds like a fairly small-scale operation, just to get one man out." He turned to Uban. "How much help could we get from the inside man of yours?"

"Pierrot. He will cooperate totally."

"What about the risk of blowing his cover?"

"His job there is almost over," Uban said. "He has been trying to get details of an aircraft hijack that we now know will take place eight days from now, on January twenty. We don't know where or when. But if Pierrot hasn't been able to find out by then, it won't matter. So, it would be nice to make some further use of him before we bring him out. He's overdue for a rest, anyway."

"He could come out with Mustapha, then?" Hariv said.

"Yes."

"Which would make January twenty the earliest date for an operation." Hariv turned to General Lurgar. "Yes, I think we could have something ready by then."

"And if nothing comes down from on high, we'll just burn the papers, forget it, and write it off as a planning exercise," Lurgar said.

"There is one more thing," Uban said. He indicated Fenner with a nod. "If it proves impossible to get Mustapha physically out for any reason, the next priority must be to communicate back the information in his possession. That might require some on-the-spot reassurance that it would in fact be going to where Mustapha has been told it would. To that end, we would want Benjamin to go too. It would provide an American complement to the mission, which might be desirable in the circumstances."

Hariv shrugged, looked at Lurgar, and nodded. "I see no problem with that. He came with us on another job once before."

"No objection," Lurgar confirmed.

"The operation will be referred to as 'Haymaker' in future communications, Uban said. "The code for the camp itself is 'Domino,' and Mustapha will be referred to as the 'merchandise.' I don't think there's anything else for now?" He looked around. Nobody had anything. That seemed to be it for the time being. He gathered his papers together, looking pleased.

Hariv pushed himself back from the table. "Well, it's good to see you back," he said to Fenner. "Have you been keeping fit?"

"The holidays didn't help much," Fenner admitted.

Hariv grinned behind his spectacles. "Oh, that's no problem. We have ways of curing things like that."

CHAPTER 53

Mehemet Kabuzak, currently the Egyptian foreign minister and favorite to become the next head of state, hummed to himself as he stood, knotting his tie by the open window of his suite at Cairo's Omar Khayyam Hotel. He was staying there for the duration of the talks with the soon-to-be U.S. vice president, having traveled down from his residence sixty miles upstream along the Nile from the city. There was still a refreshing touch of night chill in the air from the desert to the west, and he could see the Giza Pyramids above the tops of a long avenue of tall, old eucalyptus trees. The plush modern hotels were all very fine with their clifflike facades of concrete and glass, but he preferred the Omar Khayyam's atmosphere of unashamed Byzantine opulence. The edifice had actually been built as a palace by Khedive Ismail for the French

Empress Eugénie when she visited Egypt in 1869 for the opening of the Suez Canal, and stood not far from the old Giza royal palace, whose grounds were now the Cairo zoo.

Kabuzak moved back to the mirror by the wardrobe to check that the knot was straight, and paused to look his reflection up and down. Not bad for a man past the middle of his forties, he thought, patting his tummy. He was solidly built and of medium height, with a mustache that he kept neatly trimmed, a full face, though not to the point of pudginess, which a flattering number of women seemed to find handsome, and a rich head of hair turning gray at the temples. He liked to think that his eyes still held a youthful sparkle. When life ceases to be amusing, Kabuzak often said, is when getting old begins—at all ages.

The door from the adjoining suite opened and his private secretary, Talaat Ali, came in. "Ah, good. You're almost ready," Ali said. "The car is on its way around." Kabuzak had already eaten an informal breakfast with some of his staff while reviewing the agenda for the day. Ali took Kabuzak's jacket from the hanger on which it had been returned by the hotel's valet service and held it up.

"We'll see what today brings, then, Tal," Kabuzak said, slipping his arms into the sleeves. "Do you know, I must say that these Constitutional people impress me with their honesty. I don't smell the pull of Big Money behind them. I'm beginning to think that for once we might really all be on the same side."

"I hope that doesn't mean you're going soft," Ali said.

Kabuzak smoothed his jacket and buttoned it. "Of course not. But you can always terrify Americans with the word 'socialist' because like 'God' and 'freedom' it has as many meanings as there are people on earth to argue about it." He went over to the desk and began sorting through his papers. "The last time we were in Indonesia, I met a Chinese who claimed he was a socialist, which surprised everyone because he was one of the wealthiest businessmen in Singapore. It turned out that what he meant was being left alone by the government." He selected some documents and put them into his briefcase. "Oh, and have a word with that new assistant who was wearing the shirt with the glittery pattern in it yesterday, would you Tal? It looks too flashy."

"Probably exhibiting to the world his rise to the ranks of power and wealth," Ali said. "I will have a word with him."

"Well, tell him that if he wishes to look rich, dressing in a way that looks expensive is the wrong thing to do. You see, people dress to project what they'd *like* to be. *Poor* men buy expensive clothes—on credit—to look as if they had money. But rich men wear quiet, sensible clothes—to look as if they had brains."

Kabuzak considered himself a true socialist in the spirit of the National Charter of the United Arab Republic, which aimed at achieving social justice and a sound democracy—but grounded in solid Islamic tradition and rejecting the atheistic Soviet model. It also called for the overthrow of imperialism, toward which end it had achieved a huge step with the expulsion of the British in 1952, and for an end to monopoly and exploitive capitalism. And that sounded very close to the new American line that he was hearing. Perhaps times did change, after all.

He believed sincerely in dedicating his powers of office to advancing the cause of opportunity and freedom for the ordinary people by whatever means it took, Soviet or Western. In bygone days, the moneylender traveled on the heels of the tax collector and saved the peasants from the lash by advancing loans to pay their dues; and then the foreign traders would buy the crop at forced giveaway prices to enable them to pay the moneylender. Kabuzak saw the descendants of those peasants now, living in high cities, sending their children to modern schools, and on their way to becoming proud, self-sufficient citizens of the twenty-first century. Allah made only one gift of life, after all. It was only proper and holy to see that the gift was appreciated, and the way to achieve that was to help people enjoy it.

"Tonight we have dinner at seven with McCormick's party," Ali said.

"Hmm," Kabuzak grunted. That was duty, to be expected. Ali knew Kabuzak's tastes well enough by now not to have left the evening's arrangements at that.

"Afterward, I've arranged for you to have a talk privately with their public-relations woman," Ali said. "There appears to be a lot of misunderstanding of your position in the Western press, and it seemed a good opportunity for you to set the record straight."

Kabuzak hesitated in the act of closing his briefcase. "Eva . . . what's-her-name?"

"Eva Carne. Yes."

"Well she's certainly nice and pretty, Tal, but does she? . . . I mean, would it be wise?"

"I thought her company might also provide something of a stimulating aperitif," Ali said. "Naturally there will be a more substantial main course to follow back here, afterward."

Kabuzak smiled with relief. And why not? What was good for the people was surely good, too, for their hard-working representatives. Even ministers needed a break sometimes. "A hint?" he said lightly as they walked toward the door.

Ali made a circle in the air with his thumb and forefinger. "Oh, a choice *spécialité* that combines the best of the Old World with the spice of the New. Slim, blond, German-American."

"She sounds delightful, Tal. Very well, let's be on our way and put in a good day's work. To really enjoy the little pleasures in life, one has to feel that one has earned them, eh?"

The talks that morning were held at the Cairo Governate, east of the river near the various handsomely housed ministries. During the midmorning break, Talaat Ali withdrew from the general company for a while to attend to certain pressing items and to make some telephone calls. For one call, not included on his official list, he went to a public pay phone in the lobby. The call was answered by a man with a French accent.

"'Allo?"

"Jacques?"

"Qui, c'est Jacques."

"Pasha here. Everything is arranged. The details are all as you requested."

"Very good. Your invoice will be cleared."

Which meant that by three o'clock that afternoon, one hundred thousand Egyptian pounds—worth almost the same number of U.S. dollars—would have been transferred to a numbered account opened in Ali's name in Zurich. The rest would follow upon successful completion of the operation.

The public were excited and curious, and it was reflected in the attention that the media were giving to the occasion. In the room at the Cairo Governate where the interim press conference had officially ended fifteen minutes before, Stephanie, bathed in the glare of arc lamps and with microphones being thrust at her from all sides, was still answering the questions of at least two dozen journalists and TV reporters.

"Our position is that in the longer term, any kind of giveaway program suffers from the same drawbacks internationally as it does domestically. Ultimately it creates dependency and prolongs backwardness."

"What alternative will the Constitutional party substitute?" a woman asked, scribbling in a notepad without looking up.

"Unrestricted free trade. With a nation like the U.S., that has to be the best thing that could happen. In fact if the amendment goes through, it would become law."

"Would the U.S. continue to supply Israel with military equipment?"

"I think that would best be left until after the visit there later this week. In any case, it's a policy matter that the president should comment on after his inauguration."

"Could I have another two copies of the release that was handed out?" a man in a green jacket asked.

"Sure. Here." Stephanie reached into a box and passed them over.

"Thank you."

"You're welcome."

A woman in a red dress said, "In his statement earlier, Mr. McCormick said that one of the most important effects of the amendment would be to prevent the use of government force to eliminate business competition."

"That's correct," Stephanie said. "Government's proper function is no more to protect a privileged business than to impose a favored religion."

A huge, rotund, jovial-looking man with a dark face, wearing a loose seersucker jacket and a bright red fez, moved to the front on one side of the table. "Excuse me," he said. "Do you by any chance happen to have any signed pictures of Hector Newell—maybe a dozen?"

"Pictures? Well, no, I'm afraid . . ." Stephanie began answering automatically, and then her voice trailed away as his words registered. She looked up in sudden shock. The man in the fez stood beaming at her. "Er, I think we've given the last one away, but I'll check," she said. "How can I contact you?"

"I would be so grateful, if it's no trouble. My card." He handed her a calling card that read, HAMDI KEMMEL *Antiques, Ornaments, Rare Books, Curios* with an address and a Cairo phone number. Stephanie knew she should wait until later, but she was unable to resist lowering it below the edge of the table and turning it over to peek at it. Handwritten on the reverse side were the words, "Wherever else you wander, there's no place like home," with another number. She looked up again, but Hamdi Kemmel had already disappeared.

"Ms. Carne?" a man in a white shirt was saying.

"Er . . . excuse me?"

"I said, why does the Constitutional party reject the notion of a centrally planned economy?"

"It would have the same problems—of catering to self-serving interests."

"Could you explain that please?"

"Well, look at it this way. What planner would permit a system that didn't need any planners?"

When Stephanie finally got away to grab a snack lunch, it was after three in the afternoon. The time was two hours earlier over southern England, where a British Airways flight was climbing from Heathrow Airport, London, bound for Cairo. Aboard, having made a tight connection from Toronto, Melvin Shears slumped back in his seat and let himself relax for the first time since his departure from Washington. After a night flight across the Atlantic, his first impulse was to sleep. But the cabin crew would be serving lunch as soon as the plane made cruising altitude and leveled out. He would eat first and then sleep, he decided. As his mind unwound, his thoughts drifted back over the things he had learned in the last two days, the enormity of which he still hadn't absorbed fully. Perhaps minds, like anything else, took time to adjust to big upheavals.

A ruthless and systematic exploitation of the mass of humanity, perpetrated for the most part without care or compassion by the very powers that the people trusted most, and in the name of their own good. Mel was unable to comprehend the kind of mind that it took. Newell had said that it went largely unseen because such power-lust was beyond the comprehension of ordinary people, who became not only unwitting victims of the process, but its instruments also. Yet, at the same time, he was convinced that in the end, the forces arrayed against the tide of human evolution could no more check it than a summer breeze could reverse the tide. This was what Stephanie had meant when she said that nothing had been able to stop it in fifteen billion years.

He thought of Stephanie and how long it seemed already. He thought about Eva. He thought about Brett. . . . Brett dead because of a teacher. Had Martha Brodstein known she was consigning students to be killed when she passed their names back as "potentially valuable"? Probably not. In all honesty Mel couldn't hold that much against her, whatever else he felt. Brett's first meeting with Oberwald had taken place almost three years before the accident.

Why had Martha done it? Mel wondered. He remembered how she had been in the early days, involved with Paul's work, helping the cause, being a part of the scene. Then she had seemed to fade into the background, eclipsed by more pressing things in Paul's life as the movement gathered momentum toward the election. The resentment, the jealousy, had been there then, Mel could see now, which through some Freudian sleight of mind Martha had transferred to the female students, such as Eva. It was true, as Quintz had said, that Paul's bubbling enthusiasm and open personality had made him very approachable and popular with them. And in all this time, Mel had known nothing of Martha's confrontation with Eva. . . .

He hauled himself slowly upright in his seat, fully awake suddenly with that foreboding that comes a moment before something that has been lurking just below the surface finally penetrates consciousness. He picked once more through the last threads of thoughts that he could recollect. Sheldon Quintz had said that Martha had accused Eva of having an affair with Paul, and that after the subsequent row between them, Eva stayed away from the house. It wasn't the kind of thing to be forgotten in a hurry. . . . And yet Mel and Stephanie, posing as Eva, had gone breezing in, full of smiles and good cheer, just as if nothing had happened. Only then did the significance dawn on him of the strange way Martha had behaved when he and Stephanie went to Florida.

Oh God! Mel felt himself turning cold as the realization of what it meant sunk in.

Martha had known she wasn't Eva. Therefore Martha knew she was Stephanie. Mel was on his way to warn Dave Fenner, via Stephanie, that Martha might have compromised him. But couriering for Dave wasn't the only aspect that involved Martha. The people that she communicated to were also the ones that Brett had worked for. They were the ones who had already tried once to kill Stephanie. Never mind warning Dave in two days time; it was *Stephanie* who needed to be warned! And right now! It might even be too late already. Mel's hands were already clammy from thinking about it.

"Would you like something to drink, sir?"

"Pardon?" Mel looked up. A cabin attendant was standing in the aisle with a refreshment cart.

"Would you like a beverage?"

"Oh, coffee, please. . . . Ma'am, how long will it be before we reach Cairo?"

"A little under six hours. We're due to land just after nine in the evening.

The red-bearded man on the other side of Mel grinned across over the paper he was reading. "It's a long flight, eh? Hi. Name's John. I do it all the time."

"It's a long flight," Mel agreed bleakly.

The mildness of Cairo's January was a pleasant contrast to New York's. Wearing a silk headscarf and a beige raincoat over a plain, pastel blue dress, the Lynx departed in the middle of the afternoon from the Nile Hilton, which stood in the row of hotels facing the river by the Tahrir Bridge. She had plenty of time to spare before her appointment, and strolled at a leisurely pace, map and tour guide in hand, eastward from the river toward the center of the city. At the wide, open expanse of Tahrir Square, she stopped to buy a Coca-Cola and a hot fried donut at one of the curbside booths, and then sat on a bench while she munched and sipped, watching the tide of every description of humanity ebb and flow around the fountains, flowerbeds, and stalls, where noisy men in colorful djellabas pestered passersby to buy peanuts and roast corn-cobs, hot dogs, and candies. There were garish plastic belts, cheap, mass-produced souvenirs, busts of Nefertiti in all sizes, and newspapers in Arabic, English, French, and Italian. On the far side of the square, the tawny frontage of the Old Egyptian Museum hunched like a fading grandfather against the white, upright modernity of the Nile Hilton, blocking the view to the river.

Following her map, she walked from there along Kasr el Nil Street, and crossing opposite Groppi's, a large and old, famous cafe at the convergence of two long avenues lined with shops and arcades, made her way to Opera Square. Swinging her purse casually and enjoying the sights, she traced her way between shady clusters of ilex trees and beds of scarlet and yellow cannas, and found the open-air cafe in the center that her instructions described. There, she took a seat at one of the sunshaded tables by a pool with a waterfall, ordered a Turkish coffee and baklava, and relaxed back in her chair to wait.

According to her guidebook, the intricately embellished nineteenth-century Opera House had been built for the visit of a French empress—half of Cairo seemed to have been—and Verdi had been commissioned to write an opera in honor of the occasion. He wrote *Aïda*, but the Franco-German war delayed production, and the first performance at the Opera House didn't take place until two years later. As with everything else, the Old was giving way to the new, and the Opera House had ceded its dominance of the square to a white, modern skyscraper. The guidebook said it was the Telegraph Building. The huge equestrian statue in the middle of the square was of Ibrahim Pasha, son of Mohammed Ali—not a black heavyweight boxer, but a prince.

The sound of a chair leg scraping on the ground made her look up. A tall, distinguished-looking man in sunglasses sat down at the table. He was in his early fifties, with tanned, aristocratic Gallic features and hair a shade too dark for his age not to have been tinted. He wore a yachting blazer with handkerchief showing in the breast pocket, red cravat and white shirt, light tan slacks, and white canvas shoes. In his hand he was carrying a small package in gift wrapping with a pink ribbon.

"Punctual to the minute again. I'm getting to know your habits, Jacques," the Lynx said.

Jacques took off his sunglasses, folded them, and put them in his breast pocket. His eyes were gray, deep-set and weathered, and sparkly. "Some of us are busy people, my dear. For you this is more of a vacation than work."

"Oh, really? Care to trade places?"

A waiter appeared, and Jacques ordered a Pernod. Then his manner became more serious and his voice dropped. "Everything is arranged as planned. There are no last-minute changes."

"Good."

"Let us just recap on the main points briefly. Kabuzak will meet the American girl privately in the main bar at Shepheard's Hotel after the dinner there tonight. Thus, they will have been seen together, which is enough. Afterward, he will return to the Omar Khayyam for his date with you. Talaat Ali will have taken you in through a side entrance earlier in the evening and left you in Kabuzak's suite. The security people know his ways and are used to looking the other way when women are brought in."

"Do I still meet Ali outside the Palmtree bar?"

"Yes. He'll pick you up there at eight sharp."

"Okay."

"Ali will then go to Shepheard's and collect Kabuzak. When Kabuzak arrives, fuck his brains out and put him out of it by eleven. I'll give you a drug for him that will last all night. It's widely used as an aphrodisiac, and soporific overdoses are not uncommon. It's important that the lethal stuff isn't administered until later, after the American girl is there. Otherwise an autopsy might reveal inconsistencies. Got that?"

"Jacques, don't talk to me as if I were an amateur."

"I apologize. The American girl will be induced over to the Khayyam on a pretext. Ali will bring her in the same way and leave her in his suite, which adjoins Kabuzak's. She'll be there by eleven o'clock." Talaat Ali, Kabuzak's secretary, had agreed to set things up, but he wanted no part of it beyond that.

"Okay," the Lynx said.

"How you handle it then is up to you. When you've put her out, move her through into Kabuzak's suite, and then take care of both of them." Jacques pushed the package across the table. "This contains the drug, dose premeasured, and the coup de grace: ricin in a DMSO carrier. It's absorbed through the skin and lethal in under ten minutes, so for God's sake be careful handling it. You wouldn't be the first to terminate yourself instead of the target. That's why it was picked for this job."

The Lynx nodded. "I've used it before."

Jacques shrugged. "And that's how they will be found in the morning. Use your know-how to set the scene. The way we want it to be reconstructed is that the plan was for her to get into his room, screw him silly, apply the juice, and slip away without anyone being the wiser. But they overdid it with the drug and knocked themselves out. She tried to finish it when she came round, but was too groggy, bungled it, and got both of them. So I'd suggest soles of the feet for him, but splashed clumsily on palms or arms for her. Knock some furniture over. Leave her near the door, maybe with half her clothes back on. There should be semen traces—you know the kind of thing. When you're through, let yourself out. There will be no need to see Ali again."

The Lynx nodded and had no more questions. She sipped her coffee and sat back, staring at the Frenchman curiously. "So what's the angle? Are you out to shoot the Constitutionals down?"

"Now, I think, you're getting into aspects that don't concern you," Jacques said. "Just worry about enjoying the rest of your vacation. Have you thought about taking one of the boats up to Aswan afterward? . . ."

CHAPTER 54

Shepheard's was an old name among Cairo hotels, but the original building had been burned down in 1952 and completely rebuilt in the sixties. It was after eight in the evening, and the dinner, which had been scheduled earlier than was customary, to cater to the American guests, was over. Stephanie was sitting with Mehemet Kabuzak in a booth on one side of the main bar opening off the lobby, sharing a pot of tea as they talked about Kabuzak's image in the West, the eternal Arab-Israeli problem, and the differences and similarities between people the world over. He had indulged and laughed freely at dinner, and now as he talked easily and fluently, Stephanie couldn't help becoming just a little captivated by his deep brown, lively, intelligent eyes. She had heard rumors about his amorous exploits, and could see how they could easily be true. In the present situation, however, apart from paying some glowing personal compliments that had seemed sincere, he had remained perfectly gentlemanly and confined his attentions strictly to business.

"Nasser was a very misunderstood man in the West, you know," Kabuzak said. "The prejudice against him can only be described as pathological. He was called a dictator, a Hitler of the East. Yet how many of his detractors ever bothered to read anything he'd written? His *Philosophy of the Revolution* reveals admissions of profound sensitivity, soul-searchings, and misgivings that no Western politician would dream of admitting to publicly. Try it when you get a moment, Eva. I recommend it."

"I will get a copy," Stephanie promised.

"Better, I'll send you one." Kabuzak sipped his tea and waved a hand briefly above the table. "No, he was not a man of violence. He tells a story of when he was a young revolutionary, he was involved in planning an assassination—of a very bad man. Well, it was all carefully organized and went as planned. The victim appeared in the right place, on time. The death squad fired and withdrew, protected by a cover party." Kabuzak raised a finger for emphasis. "But not before they heard the wailing of the victim's wife and the screaming of his terrified child. Those sounds echoed in Nasser's mind all night, and he stayed awake praying to Allah that the man would not die. In the morning, he rushed out for a newspaper and was overjoyed to read that the man whose death he had plotted was destined to live. And his revolution, when it came, was bloodless."

Stephanie hesitated for a second, not wanting to be argumentative, but at the same time not too much of a patsy either. "But wasn't it he who created the Fedayeen and trained them for terrorist raids against Israel? And it was his mobilization, surely, that provoked the 1967 War."

Kabuzak sighed wearily. "Israel itself was a state founded in terrorism. Terrible things happened to the Arabs in Gaza in 1948. . . . The British never believed it would survive after they pulled out. The true tragedies of history don't arise from conflicts of right versus wrong; they are soon resolved. The big tragedies come from right versus right, where neither side will give way, and it goes on for ever. . . . But why are we talking about things like this? Anyone would think you and I are the heads of state. The day's work is over and we should be relaxing."

"I'm finding it interesting, really."

Kabuzak waved a hand. "No, enough. The next time you're in Cairo, you should make some time to come and see the older part of it. The hotel I'm staying at down on the river, not far from the zoo, which is opposite Roda Island." His eyes twinkled. "You know the story, of course. That was where that pharaoh's daughter, no doubt with a very wicked smile on her face, said she *found* a baby in the rushes by the Nile. . . ."

As Stephanie laughed, Kabuzak looked up and saw Talaat Ali, who had been standing at the entrance to the bar, waiting to attract his attention. Kabuzak nodded, and Ali disappeared back out to the lobby. Kabuzak finished his drink, leaned across the booth, and took Stephanie's hand. "I'm afraid my pumpkin coachman has arrived. I have to go now. Thank you for the company, which has been every bit as charming as informative. I have learned a great deal. My only hope is that it has proved equally useful for you."

"Very. And delightful, thank you. We'll see you again tomorrow, then, Mr. Kabuzak."

"It will, how do you say, make my day." He released her hand and stood up. "Good night, Eva. A busy day tomorrow. Nothing like an early night for an early start, they say, eh?" And with that he left.

So did the two plainclothes Egyptian secret-service men who had been keeping an eye on things from two tables away.

"Welcome to Cairo International Airport, ladies and gentlemen. The local time is ten minutes after nine. Please remain seated until the captain has turned off the seat-belt sign, and refrain from smoking until you are inside the terminal building. Remember to check around your seats and in the overhead compartments for any items you may have brought on board. Thank you for flying with British Airways. We look forward to having you on board again in the future."

John with the red beard, in the seat next to Mel, already had his books and magazines packed, jacket over his arm, and was ready to go. "I always think the worst thing about flying is being squawked at by loudspeakers wherever you go, from the time you walk into the terminal until the time you get out. And then in some places they get you outside, too. I mean, there's no escape from it," he said.

"Right," Mel said.

"If they changed it around and made it a bit different sometimes, it would help. But they always have to say the same thing. No imagination, that's what it is. Same everywhere these days."

"I couldn't agree more."

Passport control was somewhere in the next county from the gate, as usual. Sure enough, the lines at the booths on either side moved on through, while Mel stayed rooted to the spot. He watched in disbelief as a fat woman at the booth in front of him carefully positioned her collection of purses and bags, spread her elbows for comfort, and launched into an explanation of her life history to the immigration officer. Mel shuffled from one foot to another, unable to suppress his impatience.

"Don't worry about it if you've got bags to collect," a voice said from behind him. It was John. "You'll have a long wait at Baggage Claim when you get through, anyhow . . . if they

show up. And then there'll be Customs." He patted his
carry-on bag knowingly. "Me, I always take one change of
clothes and toilet stuff with me. It's nice to feel clean while
they're finding your bags and getting them to your hotel. They
usually show up by camel."

"Let's hope you're wrong this time."

The fat woman eventually passed through before expiring,
and Mel moved forward to the booth. There were no hitches.

The bags from Flight BA207 would materialize, the monitor
said, out of Carousel 5, which jammed before disgorging
anything. Everybody moved to Carousel 3. Mel called Shepheard's Hotel and tried to contact George Slade, but Slade
couldn't be located and didn't respond when he was paged.
Mel told the hotel to keep looking, and to give Slade the
message that he'd be arriving shortly. It was urgent. Then he
went back to await his suitcase.

"Which way are you headed if we ever get out?" John asked
beside him.

"Shepheard's. It's in the city, by the river, I think."

"Nice place. In fact I'm staying not far from there myself.
Care to split a cab? I have to make a couple of phone calls first,
though."

"Thanks, but I'm in a rush. I'll get my own."

"Okay. It's been nice meeting you, anyhow. You don't find
too many good conversationalists around these days. People
don't have any imagination. I enjoyed listening to you."

"My pleasure."

"Wait until you get out. The traffic will be terrible."

Doris, one of McCormick's secretaries, intercepted Stephanie halfway across the lobby. "Eva, there you are. I've been
looking for you. How would you like to join us for a nightcap?"

"Who's 'us'?"

"Everyone. The group. Theo and George have just got back.
They went for a walk by the river and ended up going a lot
farther than they intended. So now they're getting a few drinks
in Theo's suite to cool off. Everyone's invited. Interested?"

Stephanie thought for a second. "I haven't had a chance to
clean up yet. I'm going up to my room to shower and put on
something fresh. I'll be there in, say, thirty minutes. How's
that?"

"Fine. I'll tell the others." Doris drew Stephanie closer

behind a potted palm at the base of one of the pillars lining the lobby. Her voice fell to a whisper. "What's he like?"

"Who?"

"Kabuzak. You hear all these things. Did he try to . . . well, you know."

Stephanie shook her head, at the same time smiling exasperatedly. "He's gone back for an early night and behaved himself perfectly. I also think he's one of the most thoughtful people I've talked to since we got here."

"Oh." Doris seemed disappointed.

"So if you laid any bets, you all lose. Talk to you later." Stephanie crossed the lobby to the front desk. One of the clerks looked up inquiringly. "Could I have my key, please? It's seven-one-six."

"Certainly." The clerk turned to the pigeonholes behind and took out the key. There was a small white envelope with it. He took it out. "Ms. Eva Carne?"

"Yes."

"There is a telephone message for you."

"Thank you." Puzzled, Stephanie took the envelope and retired a short distance to open it. The slip inside read:

> *Change of plan. Am in Cairo. Must talk tonight.*
> *Will send cab to side door at 10:15 sharp.*
> *Dave F.*

She glanced at her watch. Forty-five minutes. She stuffed the note in a pocket of her dress and walked slowly across the lobby to the elevators, wondering how best to work it.

After her cozy-looking talk with Kabuzak, and especially with the kind of talk going around that Doris had intimated, she could hardly tell the others upstairs that she had changed her mind and then disappear without its looking more than a little suspicious. And then there would be the problem of getting out. All of the delegation were in a block of rooms on the same floor, and George Slade kept two of his security men posted at opposite ends of the corridor day and night. Also, it was chilly out, and she would need a coat.

She arrived at her room and took a shower while she thought about it. A possible way suggested itself. When she had dried herself, she called McCormick's suite.

"Is Doris there? This is Eva."

"Eva! We were wondering what's happened to you. Are you on your way?"

"No. Look, I'm sorry about this, but I've had a terrible headache come on, and on top of that I'm exhausted. I'm going to give it a miss tonight."

"Oh gee, that's too bad. Can I get you anything?"

"No, I have some stuff, thanks. What I'd really like is just a quiet early night to sleep it off. Apologies to everyone. I'll see you tomorrow, okay?"

She hung up, then walked over to the closet and put on a dark top with a low neck, a skirt, and the bathroom slippers provided for guests by the hotel. Then she put the voluminous bathrobe that came with them on over everything else and pulled the lapels close around her neck while she checked herself in the mirror. None of the clothes showed. She took a short green topcoat and rolled it up tightly around her outdoor shoes, added her purse, then nestled the items in the crook of her arm and draped a large bath towel over them. Then she let herself out into the corridor and walked toward the elevators. The security man on duty looked up from his table.

"Hi, Mike. Just going down to the hot tub."

"Wish I could join you. Not partying tonight?"

"Maybe later. I just called and told them I was feeling out of it, but I might change my mind later."

"Maybe the tub'll help."

"That's what I thought."

"Take care."

"You too."

She got off at the second floor and found a ladies' restroom in a corner at the end of a row of meeting rooms. She went inside, put on her shoes and coat, and left the hotel's things. Then she emerged once more and went on down to the lobby. The concierge was standing nearby when she came out of the elevator. She walked a few paces, then stopped and looked around uncertainly. "Er, which way is the side entrance?" she inquired. "A taxi is supposed to be picking me up there."

"This way, madam." He escorted her past plants and shops, around a corner and through a series of connecting halls to a carpeted vestibule, where he called over the doorman and said something in Arabic. The doorman took Stephanie outside, and a cab that had been waiting a few yards back drew forward. The doorman opened the rear door, she climbed in.

"Carne?" the cabbie said.

"Yes."

He nodded. The doorman outside closed the door, and the driver pulled away without another word.

Theo McCormick watched as his senior aide poured scotch into the glass over a pile of ice cubes. "Whoah, that's plenty! What are you trying to do, destroy me for tomorrow?"

"Just a little unwinder. You deserve it. It went well today."

"Well, let's remember that this is just a little social gathering," McCormick said. "It's not supposed to be a party. Save that till we get back."

"I'll have to come back someday when there's more time," the group's economics adviser said. She was standing with two of the secretaries. "I had no idea Cairo was such a lovely place."

"People should make more time to get out and see the world," McCormick agreed.

"It's a pity that Josef didn't make it," Doris said.

"Josef?" Clare, who was next to her, queried.

"Joe Kirkelmayer." Doris looked uncertainly at McCormick for a second. "Do you think what they said about him is true, Mr. McCormick—about why he was replaced by Eva?"

"I don't think this is the place to try and decide that," McCormick said.

"Are we in good shape for when we get to Israel?" somebody else asked from across the room.

"Oh, I think so." McCormick took a sip of his drink and popped some peanuts into his mouth.

"What's the thing to remember with Israelis?" Doris asked. "Is there a rule?"

"Oh, they like practical jokes. That's why they're always switching countries on everyone. If you really want to make them laugh, tape some railroad flares to an alarm clock and hide it in your baggage. They'll love it."

Everyone laughed. The phone rang in the next room. "I'll get it," George Slade said, rising to his feet over by the door. He went through.

"Will we see the Pyramids?" someone asked.

"Well, I know it's only supposed to be a quick working visit, but I'll let you in on a secret," McCormick said. "The reason tomorrow afternoon is left blank on the schedule is to get in some sightseeing. Not a lot, but it's the best we could do. If things hadn't gone so well and we thought we needed the time, I wouldn't have told you."

Approving murmurs came from all around. "I haven't even seen a camel yet," one of the group said.

"Is the Nile the longest river in the world?"

"I thought that was the Amazon."

"Isn't that supposed to be the biggest?"

"What's the difference?"

Slade appeared in the doorway of the adjoining room again, caught McCormick's attention, and beckoned him over. "Excuse me for a moment," McCormick said. "George wants me for something."

"What about those ones that flow north in Siberia?"

"I don't know. Do you know anything about them, Harry? . . ."

Slade motioned McCormick through into the next room with a nod and eased the door shut. The phone was still off the hook. "It's Melvin Shears," he murmured. "He's here."

"Here?"

"Downstairs in the lobby."

"What the hell's he doing here? Why didn't anyone tell us?"

"There's some kind of trouble concerning Eva. It sounds serious. I'm going down there now to talk to him."

"Okay. Call back up if you need me."

Slade went back to the phone. "Okay, Mel, you stay right there. I'm on my way down."

CHAPTER 55

"Jesus!" Slade breathed as Mel finished summarizing the situation. Mel had drawn him aside into a quiet alcove off the lobby and simply shoved his suitcase behind a chair. "They *know*? This is bad. Why in hell didn't anyone radio it to us via the embassy?"

"They think it's only Fenner who needs to be warned. I didn't figure the rest out until after I was on the plane. It's all been too hectic. I tried to call you from the airport but you were out."

"We ought to wake her up and let her know now," Slade said. "She went to bed early."

Mel shook his head. "I already tried. There's no answer from her room."

Slade strode grimly over to the desk, brushing aside another guest who was complaining about something, and summoned the assistant manager. The assistant manager sent for the hotel security manager, who picked up a passkey, and the four of them went back up to the seventh floor. Mike, at his table looking along the corridor, stood up as they came out of the elevator. "We need to check Eva's room," Slade said. "There could be trouble."

"She's not there. She went down to the pool. Said she was going to take a hot tub."

"How long ago?"

"Ten, fifteen minutes, maybe."

Slade turned to the assistant manager. "Could you have someone check the pool area?" The manager nodded and hurried away. "We'll try the room anyhow," Slade said to the security manager. They went along to room 716, and the security manager knocked loudly, waited, then again. He opened the door and stood back with Mike while Slade and Mel went inside. Stephanie wasn't there. The shower was wet and steamy, and there were some crumpled clothes on the bed. Slade looked around, his mind racing. "Why would she take a shower if she was going down to the hot tubs?" He went over to the closet and looked along the rack inside. "She has a green topcoat. I don't see it."

Mel was checking the pockets of the dress thrown on the bed. He found the slip of paper with the phone message on it, read it, and showed it to Slade. "'Dave F.'," Slade said. "That's his name isn't it—the guy you just told me about downstairs?"

"Yes."

Slade shook his head. "This message is a fake. He'd have used a code if it was from him." For a moment Mel thought he was going to be sick, but Slade was already on his way out of the room. "There mightn't be a lot of time."

Mel kicked himself into motion and followed, catching Slade by the sleeve just before he reached the door. "If we're going after her, I'd feel a lot better if I was able to protect myself," he muttered. "Henry Newell said you'd be able to fix me up."

Slade's eyebrows knotted. "I thought you couldn't use a gun."

"Ron Bassen put me through the range. I know which end to point now."

Slade held his eye searchingly for a split second, then gave a brief nod. "Mike can handle it. I'm going back down to the lobby to try and find out if anyone saw her." They went out into the corridor. Slade took Mike aside and murmured a few words in his ear. Mike looked across at Mel and nodded faintly. While Slade and the security manager hastened away toward the elevators, Mike led Mel to another door a short distance away, opened it, and ushered him through. Inside, he took a sturdy leather case from one of the closets, unlocked it, and produced a Walther .32 PP, shoulder harness, and an ammunition clip and several spares from a compartment inside. Mel took off his jacket and Mike helped him secure the harness. He watched as Mel pushed a clip into the butt, and slid the weapon into the holster. As Mel adjusted the straps for comfort, he found to his mild embarrassment that he couldn't hide the shaking of his hands.

"New to this, eh?" Mike remarked.

"Don't ask."

They went back into the corridor and found McCormick looking along from the doorway of his suite to see what was going on. "I'll take care of it," Mike said to Mel. "You get downstairs after George. Good luck."

"Thanks."

Mel arrived in the lobby to find a general confusion of jabbering and waving of arms going on, as doormen and bellhops were located and quizzed, making guests coming and going turn their heads curiously. The assistant manager reappeared and joined in the throng to say that Eva wasn't in the pool area and hadn't been seen there. Others poured in their contributions: yes, she had caught a cab from the side door; no, the doorman didn't know where she'd gone in it.

"Which cab company was it from?" Slade demanded. "They can put out a radio call."

The security manager translated the question. The doorman couldn't remember.

"How many cab companies serve this place?" Slade asked.

To one side of the confusion, the hotel concierge stood, wrestling with his dilemma. The attractive American girl had been drinking tea earlier in the evening with Mehemet Kabuzak. Later, she had slipped out the side entrance and left in a cab that had been sent for her. It was quite obvious where she had gone. . . . But there was such a thing as professional discretion to be considered. . . . On the other hand, the situation did seem to be serious.

In the end he stepped forward and drew Slade to one side, just as Mel arrived from the elevator and came within earshot. "The young lady whom you seek went to the Omar Khayyam Hotel," he murmured. That was where Kabuzak always stayed.

"How do you know?" Slade asked.

"It is my job to know everything, sir."

At that moment a couple of the local secret-service men appeared to see what was happening. A detachment of them was stationed in the hotel, under orders to keep a low profile. It was all turning into a circus, with everyone in charge. But nobody as yet had made any connection between Mel, who had drawn back from the commotion, and Slade, who was trapped in the center of it. Slade looked across at him, and in the brief instant that their gazes met, he motioned in the direction of the hotel entrance with his eyes. It was a signal for Mel to go on ahead and do what he could.

Everything had taken on a strange quality of unreality. Responding like a zombie in some kind of trance, Mel returned a faint nod and moved away across the lobby to the doors. A cab was already at the curbside, with an elderly man in evening dress and a heavily bejeweled woman about to climb in. Mel darted around to the front and slipped in beside the driver. "Omar Khayyam Hotel!" he snapped.

"Hey you, what do you think you're doing?" an indignant voice shouted from behind.

The cabbie shook his head protestingly. "Sir, you can't—"

Mel reached over the seat and slammed the rear door. "Triple fare. Make it fast."

"Yessir!"

The cab was already up to forty when it reached the end of the drive and cut across three lanes of highway. It U-turned amid blasts of horns and swerving vehicles into the traffic going the other way and accelerated again, heading south. Inside, Mel slumped against the back of the seat and felt his chest pounding and his shirt sticking to his body. For a moment his mind flashed back to the quiet, sedentary, lawyer's life that he'd known in Boston. Then he looked out at the lights of Cairo streaming by as the cab wove in and out through the traffic, and became conscious of the solid, unfamiliar bulge under-

neath his left arm. He'd been off the plane less than two hours.
Welcome to fucking Egypt, he thought resignedly.

Stephanie had tried to find out from the driver where they
were going, but his incomprehension of English was total—or
else he had been told to make it appear so. They arrived at a
huge, splendidly ornate building, floodlit from the grounds
and looking magnificent against its setting of tall palm trees.
Stephanie presumed it to be a hotel, but to her surprise,
instead of continuing to the front entrance, the cab swung off
the main driveway and took her to a smaller, side door. Her
confusion increased when she climbed out and recognized the
man waiting for her there as Talaat Ali, Kabuzak's private
secretary, whom she knew from his comings and goings at the
talks of the past few days. Then her confusion turned to alarm.
Perhaps she had misjudged Kabuzak completely after all—and
he, even more completely, her!

Ali read the look on her face and raised a hand reassuringly.
"Please, it is not as you imagine. There is much that you don't
know. We are working with Fenner. Come this way." He
opened the door and gestured. Stephanie hesitated, but the
cab had disappeared by now anyway. They went in.

Ali led her to an elevator at the rear of the building that
required a special key to enter. It went directly to the top
floor, without provision for making intermediate stops. "For
the special guests who stay on the penthouse level," he
explained. "There is a security check where you get off the
regular elevators on the top floor. So demeaning." From the
elevator they entered a corridor. The fittings and furnishings
were luxurious with an elegance of days long gone, but
Stephanie's mind was in too much of a whirl to take much
notice of the details. Ali stopped at one of the doors, opened it,
and let them in. Inside was an L-shaped room of a large suite,
with the section at the rear leading around a corner to another
room. There were bottles and glasses, bowls of fruit and
candies, a desk with papers strewn on top and a man's
briefcase beside.

"May I take your coat?" Ali asked.

"Thanks. I'll keep it on."

"Something to drink, perhaps?"

"I don't think so."

"There might be a short wait. Lots of things are happening."

"Very well. Just a grapefruit juice." Stephanie sat down on one of the chairs and put her purse on the table.

"Ice?"

"Please."

Ali half filled a glass with ice, topped it with juice from a pitcher, and handed it to her. "Now, you must excuse me," he said. "There are things I have to attend to." He seemed tense, and had crossed back to the door before Stephanie could reply. His departure, she thought, seemed unduly hasty.

"An American girl. She has long, fair hair, almost blond, down to here. About this high, probably wearing a green coat. She came here by cab. . . . it must have been within the last fifteen minutes. You're sure you haven't seen anyone like that at all?" Mel looked from one to another of the clerks behind the front desk of the Omar Khayyam Hotel. They looked at each other and shook their heads.

"Nobody like that has been through here," one of them said. He called the bell captain over from the desk across the hall. A two-way torrent of words ensued, ending with the bell captain shaking his head, shrugging, and going back to his desk. "I'm sorry," the clerk said again.

Mel stared across the desk helplessly, hoping for some advice or suggestion, but the clerk had already returned his attention to the chart he had been filling in. "Look, could you— "

At that instant a hand with a grip that felt like a bear trap clamped itself around his upper arm, and he was propelled like a toy out through the door into the night again. For an instant the thought flashed through his mind that hotel security was throwing him out, and then he found himself staring up at a round-bellied giant of a figure with a dark face, light-colored jacket, and a fez on its head, red in the light from the floodlamps. His face was smiling broadly, showing white, even teeth; but it was the kind of smile that said its owner could kill you quite cheerfully and not mind a bit. "What are you to do with the American girl?" he asked.

There wasn't time for verbal dueling. And if this guy turned out to be on the wrong side, he was dead anyway, Mel told himself. "She's in danger. I'm here to help," he said.

"Who are you?"

Stephanie had told him the details of her conversation with

Dave Fenner in Washington. Mel tried the only line he could.
"A friend of Benjamin."

"Who are you with?"

How could he say, a law-firm in Boston? What was he here
for in the middle of the night—to serve a writ? He replied,
"U.S. intelligence." And then, "Who the hell are you?"

The giant released his grip, and his manner changed.
"Mossad asked me to keep an eye on her. She went upstairs
with Kabuzak's secretary. I didn't know if the arrangement
was . . . agreeable."

"I don't understand."

The big man shrugged. "Many beautiful women visit
Kabuzak."

Mel shook his head. "She's in trouble."

"Bad enough to warrant intruding?"

"They've already tried to kill her once."

The other nodded. "There is another door around the side.
Come this way."

Stephanie's nervousness had been increasing ever since the
party left the United States. All day long, alone with her
secret, she had been feeling more unsure of herself and
isolated. So when the message turned up unexpectedly with
its promise of a chance to talk to Dave, she had pushed
everything else out of her mind. Now, as she sat thinking back
over it, she was growing uneasy. Why was it signed with
Dave's own name, and not his code, Benjamin? She had
registered the fact fleetingly even as she read the message, but
her need just at that time had been such that she had forced
the thought aside. And now that one simple irregularity was
taking on steadily larger significance in her mind.

She got up and walked nervously to the far end of the room.
The door around the corner was open and led to what was
presumably the bedroom of the suite. She went over and
peeked inside, but there was nobody there. A door on the
opposite side looked like the communicating door to the
adjoining suite. She went back into the lounge. Her impulse
was to leave now, go down to the lobby, and get a cab back to
Shepheard's. Then she tried to control her fears. How could
the Opposition have known of her connection with Dave?
Only he and Eva had known of that, surely. Maybe "Benjamin"
only applied after they got to Israel. She pictured herself
fleeing like a rabbit, and then Dave appearing in the next few

minutes. She stood in the lounge of the suite, torn by indecision. . . . But after the dinner, followed by drinks with Kabuzak, there was one thing she had to do first, whatever she decided afterward. She put down her glass and went into the bathroom.

Next-door in the bedroom of Kabuzak's suite, the Lynx finished dressing and tidying herself up. She collected together the things she needed and checked Kabuzak, snoring soundly in the bed. No problem there. Just then the phone rang, right on time. She reached out to the end table by the bed and picked it up.

"Ja?"

"She is next door, alone," Talaat Ali's voice said, and he hung up.

The Lynx replaced the receiver, smiled to herself, and rose to her feet. She crossed to the communicating door into Ali's suite, turned the key, and let herself through. "Hello?" she called softly. "Eva, are you there?" No reply. She went on through into the lounge. There was a woman's purse on the table, and a three-quarters-full glass of juice. "Eva?" she called again.

"I'm in the bathroom," a voice said through the door. "Who's this?"

"Oh, a friend of Dave's." The Lynx looked at the glass again and smiled to herself. This was going to be much easier than she'd thought. She took a phial from a pocket inside the shoulder cape she was wearing, unscrewed the cap, and tipped three drops into the glass. "Sleep well, sweetheart," she murmured, then replaced the cap and put the phial away again.

"Is Dave there?" the voice asked from the bathroom.

"On his way. He'll be another couple of minutes."

"Just tidying my hair."

"That's all right. There's plenty of time."

Downstairs, Talaat Ali put down the house phone and came out of the alcove, turning to head in the direction of the side door. He had made other arrangements to keep himself away for the rest of the night, with plenty of witnesses. When he returned to the hotel in the morning, he would call security and let them find the bodies when Kabuzak failed to answer his wake-up call or open the door.

A man-mountain wearing a broad smile and a red fez

stepped in front of him from nowhere and slammed him back into the alcove again, cracking the back of his head against the wall and knocking all the wind out of him.

"The American girl. Where is she?"

"I don't know who you mean."

Ali's arm was being pushed up to somewhere near the back of his head by a force that could have snapped it off like a dry twig. "Is she upstairs with Kabuzak?"

"No! I don't know what you're talking about. . . . Stop it. . . . Arghh!"

"Then let's go and see, shall we?" Ali was bundled along a short corridor to the private elevator like a sack, his toes barely touching the floor. There was a second man there, younger, a Caucasian. They obviously knew the hotel layout. "Your elevator key," the big man said. Ali groped frantically at his pocket with his free hand. The younger man fished out the key and unlocked the door. They pushed Ali inside.

"How many others are in there?" the big man with the fez demanded.

"Nobody. I told you, I don't know—"

"How many?" The big man scraped the edge of the sole of his shoe hard down Ali's shin and stamped on the instep. Ali screamed. "Kabuzak—he's there, right?"

"*Arghh!* Yes. . . . Stop, please! He's unconscious. . . . Just one other. A woman."

"Which suite, yours or Kabuzak's?"

"Mine."

"Give him the key."

They knew which suite was Ali's. The big man grabbed the back of Ali's collar and pushed him ahead, at the same time drawing a gun from inside his jacket and nodding at Mel to open the door. Mel swallowed a lump in his throat and took the Walther from its holster. He thumbed off the safety, turned the key quickly in the lock, and threw the door open. The big man shoved Ali through and went in after him like a charging boar.

The woman who had been standing inside whirled around, her eyes wide with shock. She had long platinum hair and a short shoulder-wrap cape. "You see, I told you there is no American." Ali cried. The big man stopped and looked around.

Mel saw the purse on the table. He would have recognized it anywhere. "That's hers," he said.

The woman was unarmed. "Keep an eye on her," the big

man said to Mel. And then, urging Ali forward again, "Let's look around, shall we?" He yanked him away around the corner and into the bedroom. Mel's gaze followed after them unthinkingly as the sounds receded farther, through the communicating door and into the next suite.

He didn't realize his mistake until he caught the movement from the corner of his eye, and suddenly found himself staring into a gun that had appeared magically in the woman's hand from under her cape. "Not one movement," she hissed. Mel had let his aim drift with his attention, and she had the edge. He froze, helpless. She moved back to get the wall behind her and edged toward the door. He could read her mind, assessing the odds. Should she kill him there and then and reduce the opposition, which would bring the big man back and probably wake up the whole hotel? Or disarm him and make a quiet getaway, playing for the extra time? At that instant, a door to one side opened and Stephanie appeared. She saw Mel with a gun, the woman covering him, and stood paralyzed.

But she was not the only one to be transfixed by shock.

The Lynx never forgot a face. Remembering faces was part of her profession. It was one of the things that made her good. Another was the iron control she had over her concentration. Never once had she allowed it to slip or waver at a crucial moment . . . until now. It was just for the briefest instant, when she saw the girl who came out of the bathroom. Because she *knew*, beyond any shadow of a doubt, that she had killed that girl ten weeks previously in Denver.

And that was when Mel shot her.

He did it instinctively, unconsciously. Some automatic self-preservation mechanism, from deep below the thinking processes that had seized up, took control, and he had fired before he knew it. The bullet hit her in the chest and threw her back against the wall. She wasn't dead, but the impact had made her drop her arm.

Everything then seemed to happen in a strange, hypnotic slow motion, even though Mel was aware somewhere in a part of his mind that his sense of time was distorted. He watched himself watching her in numb fascination as she struggled to bring her gun up to bear on him again, while blood spread into the fabric of her sweater, trickled down over her skirt, and splattered on the floor. Reflexively he fired again. This time her arm fell limply. Mel could see her hand clutching to keep its hold on the gun, but getting feeble; but still her eyes were blazing hatred at him, the eyes of a trapped, wounded, wild animal.

And that was when he knew. Possibly it was from some subconscious reading of the recognition that showed in her eyes when she saw Stephanie, but in an indefinable flash of certainty that he would never be able to explain, he knew then that it was she who had killed Eva.

He stared deep into those eyes, prolonging the moment until he saw the flicker of disbelief that came with the realization that she was about to die. Dispassionately, with no feeling of emotion, he fired once more. On the fringes of his perceptions, he was aware of the big man coming back around the corner, and of the man they had intercepted downstairs raising his hands to his face.

The gun fell from the Lynx's hand as she leaned there against the wall. Her legs buckled and she slid slowly down into a grotesque sitting position, leaving a smear of blood down the wall where two of the bullets had exited and lodged in the paneling. Still she was looking at him, still hating. Mel raised the gun and aimed deliberately between her eyes. . . . But before he could squeeze the trigger, her eyes glazed emptily, and her head lolled over onto her shoulder. Her mouth fell open, and a trickle of blood ran down the side of her chin.

Mel lowered the gun and returned it to the holster. Stephanie was standing petrified, and Ali was on the verge of hysteria. It could only be a matter of moments before the security people appeared, but Mel was spent, for the moment past caring what happened next. Only the big man was on top of the situation. He thrust Ali back against the wall and pushed the barrel of his gun up under his chin. "Listen to me and hear what I say," he muttered. "Nobody saw Eva Carne come in, and nobody will see her go out. You haven't seen her here at all. Is that clear? One squeak out of you, and you're as dead as that one over there. Do you understand?" Ali nodded his head violently, gibbering in terror. The big man tossed him down on the couch. "This way," he said to the other two. Mel grabbed Stephanie's arm, but she stood rooted. The big man turned back, looked at her, and then slapped her sharply across the face.

Her eyes cleared. She shook her head, gulped, and then nodded. "I'll be all right."

They went out into the corridor and ran to the private elevator. Just as the doors were closing, the sounds of excited voices and hurrying footsteps came from the stairway at the other end of the building. They descended and came out of the elevator on the ground floor. As they were leaving the building by the side door, the wails of approaching sirens came from the direction of the front, and moments later police cars with flashing lights began arriving at the main entrance. The big man bundled them into the back of a white Fiat van—looking ridiculously small for somebody of his stature—hurried around and climbed in the front, and drove out through a rear gate from the parking lot while Mel and Stephanie made room for themselves among a litter of boxes full of books, vases, framed pictures, and oddments of furniture.

Meanwhile, back in the front lobby, where Slade had just arrived with the police, another scene of pandemonium was being enacted. City police and secret-service guards were milling around, and within minutes staff and security personnel from the hotel were getting involved, too. There had been a shooting upstairs. . . . Somebody had been killed. . . . A woman, Caucasian, with long fair hair. . . . A matter of minutes ago.

Slade closed his eyes and released a shaky breath. Along with it went the hope he had been nursing through the wild ride from Shepheard's. They were too late. "Okay," he murmured to the police inspector who had brought him. "Let's get it over with." Steeling himself, with a feeling in his chest as if there were a cannonball lodged there, he went with the others to an elevator. The doors closed, and he felt the car move. Oblivious to the chattering that continued around him, he thought of the sister who had been killed in November . . . and now the one they had put in her place. The one he was supposed to have been protecting. When they got home, he decided, he was through with this whole lousy business.

They emerged on the top floor of the building. There were more security men up there, more shouting and gesticulating, guests being ushered back into their rooms, police radios squawking. Somebody was tracking bloody footprints off his shoes. They took Slade along the corridor and into one of the suites—Kabuzak's secretary's suite, somebody said. What in God's name had Stephanie been doing here? . . . And then he stopped, staring in total bewilderment suddenly. The body hadn't been moved. It was a gruesome sight, certainly, but . . .

The inspector turned to him gravely. "Is this her, Mr. Slade?"

Slade could only shake his head, still staring disbelievingly. "No, Inspector. . . . No it isn't. That's not her."

"I'm sorry . . . I don't understand."

"Neither do I." Slade's relief at that moment was such that he was beyond understanding anything.

"Mr. Kabuzak is asleep next door," someone reported. "We can't wake him, but he appears unharmed."

Talaat Ali, Kabuzak's secretary, had been sick in the bathroom and was now sitting on a couch with his head in his hands. "And there was no other woman here at all tonight?" a police detective was asking.

"No, none. Just her. . . . I heard the shots and ran back, but whoever it was had already gone. That was how I found her."

"You didn't see anyone else—a large man in a red fez, for instance?"

Ali shook his head adamantly. "No. I saw nobody."

Slade had no idea what had been going on, and if he was honest with himself, he no longer cared all that much. There was nothing more for him to do here. His main concern now was to extricate himself as quickly as possible and avoid any risk of the American delegation becoming publicly linked to what had all the signs of becoming an ugly affair. He looked back at the policeman. "I'm sorry, but it looks as if I might have been wasting your time, Inspector. Obviously it wasn't our woman who came here at all. The concierge at Shepheard's must have been mistaken."

The inspector looked down at the corpse. White woman, slim, long hair, fair . . . Yes, it was understandable. "Well, we have a problem on our hands," he said. "But at least I'm glad that it hasn't turned out to be your problem. Don't apologize, Mr. Slade. I appreciate that you have your job to do, also. One can't be too careful. Let's go downstairs. I'll find a driver to take you back to Shepheard's."

CHAPTER 56

The big man drove at a leisurely pace, like a tourist seeing the sights or a family man out on a Sunday afternoon cruise. His name was Hamdi Kemmel, Mel learned. Stephanie had already met him, briefly. He was her Mossad contact, and had passed her the code phrase for McCormick's speech earlier that day. It was fortunate that his duties hadn't ended with that.

"Who was she, do you know?" Kemmel asked over his shoulder as he drove.

Mel could only answer from his conviction that it was the same woman who had killed Eva in mistake for Stephanie. "She worked for the Soviets back in the States," he said.

"A professional?"

"Yes."

Kemmel nodded. "Well, it's one less to worry about. You were absolutely right, of course. We couldn't have left her as a witness."

"No," Mel said.

In the intermittent lights of passing vehicles, he saw Stephanie's face staring at him from the shadows opposite with a mixture of incredulity and lingering shock. He smiled tiredly at her, but was too exhausted to want to talk any more just then, and the conversation petered out.

They crossed to the east side of the river and took the corniche northward to an older part of the city that lay below the heights dominated by the immense fortification known as the Citadel, built by Saladin. Here they entered a maze of narrow streets and arched alleyways, with dimly lit coffee shops and dingy restaurants huddled around mosques thrusting up their domes and minarets. Finally the van came to a street of buildings of assorted shapes and sizes with wooden balconies and outside stairs, backing onto the riverfront itself.

Kemmel parked outside one of the shops, unlocked the

door, and led them inside. The interior was one huge clutter, piled high to the ceiling with antique furnishings, good, bad, and indifferent, innumerable clocks, display cases containing jewelry, chinaware, stamps, and coins, shelves of dusty books, copperware, brassware, old guns, sword, hats, helmets, and a real sarcophagus. Mel thought that some of the things must have been there for years.

Behind the shop was a small, carelessly littered office with a roll-top bureau, and some rickety stairs going up. Kemmel led them on through and showed them into a parlor at the rear, where he turned on a small electric heater. It was a small, overfurnished room, with heavy drapes and tapestries; solidly built wooden dresser, cabinets, and sideboard of massive proportions; and a table in the center, covered with a richly embroidered cloth. There was a basket containing a sleepy cat and three small kittens on the bracing bars under the sideboard. Kemmel spread his hands to indicate two of the chairs. As Mel and Stephanie sat down, the sound of a door opening came from upstairs, and a woman's voice called down. Kemmel called something back in a jovial tone and smiled at them. "My wife, Sarah. She is very competent. You need have no worries about her. Excuse me for one minute, and I'll get some coffee started." He went back out and into the kitchen.

It was the first time that Mel and Stephanie had been alone. She stared at him, still with bewilderment on her face. "Would you tell me what's going on? When did you get here?"

"About three hours ago . . . less than that."

"What on earth are you doing?"

"I came to tell you to warn Dave that he might be compromised. Then on the way over, I realized that they know about you, too . . ." He couldn't help adding, "in case you didn't know." Stephanie's expression did all the questioning necessary. Mel went on, "Quintz wasn't the informant. That was a wrong lead. It was Martha Brodstein all the time."

It took a while for Stephanie to register what that meant. "Oh my God," she breathed as it sank in. She shook her head dazedly. "Where did you get that gun?"

"George Slade . . . as a precaution. It's lucky for us that these people are all paranoid."

"So you've been to the hotel."

Mel nodded. "I must have missed you by minutes. We found the message from Dave. It was a fake. You should have spotted it."

Stephanie nodded bitterly. "I know. I realized afterwards. How did you know where I'd gone?"

"One of the staff at the hotel knew."

"How?"

"I don't know."

They heard the door upstairs open again, and footsteps descended. Kemmel came out of the kitchen in time to conduct her into the parlor. She was a tall, dark-skinned woman with handsome features and hair coming down over her shoulders. She carried herself with a quiet dignity that projected itself even in a dark blue nightgown, minutes after being woken up in the middle of the night. "This is Sarah," Kemmel said. "Eva, the American woman we saw on television yesterday. . . . And someone whose name I don't even know yet."

Mel didn't know whether he should give his own name or not. Deciding that it was something that he could always correct later if he was being to melodramatic, he replied on impulse, "Mohican." Stephanie raised her eyebrows for an instant, but said nothing.

"Welcome to our house," Sarah said. She inclined her head and permitted a shadow of a smile. Mel got the impression that she had long ago come to accept strange goings-on, such as unexpected visitors showing up in the middle of the night, as something that happened all the time.

"I've started some coffee," Kemmel said.

"You sit down, then. I'll see to it," Sarah said, and went back out.

Kemmel took a box of cheroots off the sideboard and sat down on one of the empty chairs. He smiled broadly at the other two, offered the box, and when they shook their heads, took one himself and settled comfortably. "It was a good thing that you turned up when you did," he said to Mel.

"I could say the same about you."

There was a pause. "You said you were with Benjamin," Kemmel said, rummaging in a jar for some matches. "How is he connected with what happened tonight?"

"We found out after Eva left the States that one of the people involved in arranging Benjamin's contact was an informant, which is why I was sent over," Mel replied. He indicated Stephanie with a motion of his head. "It also turns out that the same informant has certain information about Eva . . . which we don't need to talk about."

Kemmel struck a match, drew on his cheroot, and nodded. "I understand."

Mel looked down at the tablecloth and sighed. He had been trying to fit Seybelman and the people who had given Stephanie the drugs-plant story with the ring that had killed Eva, but he still couldn't see how they connected. True, they came together at the worldwide commonality of superwealth interests that Newell and Landis had talked about, but that was up in the stratosphere; it didn't extend down to the operational levels of recruiting programmers to pass on defense secrets, or promoting socialist politics in California.

He went on. "The job that Eva is doing for Benjamin and for your people is just one of several tasks. Her work with the Constitutional party goes beyond her official public duties. She's infiltrated one of the party's opposition groups back in the States, but they believe that she's turned, and is really working for them, against us."

"You live a complicated life," Kemmel remarked, glancing at Stephanie.

"You don't know the half of it," she couldn't help muttering.

Mel continued, "We knew they were setting her up for something when she got over here, but it wasn't supposed to be until she got to Jerusalem. What happened tonight must have had something to do with it."

Kemmel puffed smoke contentedly for a few seconds. "So you really don't know what the purpose of that was?"

"I've only just arrived here. All I know is I got off the plane, McCormick's security man—"

Kemmel nodded. "George Slade. Yes, I know."

"He pointed me to the Omar Khayyam, you grabbed me at the desk there, and the next thing we're up at the room, Eva's there, and a woman who's about to kill both of us. There wasn't time to ask questions."

"I think I can answer that now," Stephanie said. They looked at her. "It was a scheme to discredit the new administration—even to bring it down completely, maybe. Kabuzak has been getting a lot of distorted press in the States, saying he was going to take Egypt back to the Soviets, which would have been a disaster for Newell. I think they were going to kill him and pin it on me somehow: a political assassination by no less than one of the future vice president's personal staff. I'm not sure what the repercussions might have been. Maybe they'd have had to call off the inauguration, somehow. Can they do that?"

Kemmel nodded that he followed her reasoning and looked at Mel. "What do you think?"

"Well, I have to take Eva's word on that for now, because I don't have enough background yet," Mel said. He stared hard at the table, going over what she had said and trying to fit it into some kind of perspective with the other thoughts that had been going through his mind. Kemmel said nothing, but watched him with a steady, unblinking stare.

If the intention had been to rig a political assassination in the way that Stephanie was saying, then presumably she would have been eliminated, too. Anything the Constitutionals might have claimed about nonexistent drug-scams to try and clear themselves afterward would easily have been dismissed as fabrication. And it wouldn't have mattered whether she had really been Eva or not. So that explained quite a lot.

What didn't fit was that Martha hadn't worked for that side of the operation. And Eva's murder in mistake for Stephanie hadn't been arranged by that side either. Both those factors were linked in with the Oberwald operation, and that connected to the Soviets. Would the Soviets have wanted to assassinate a pro-Soviet minister? Mel asked himself. Yes, conceivably—if undermining the Constitutionals was considered more important. In fact it could work to their advantage by directing the world's suspicions away from themselves. But if the Soviets were behind it, then the overall direction must have come from the upper levels of the global tie-in after all. And the more Mel thought about that, the less he could accept that something as elaborate and involved as this was turning out to be could all have been merely to engineer the discrediting of a political party. When all was said and done, Kabuzak was a relatively junior figure on the international scene, and the repercussions could only go so far. There had to be, Mel was convinced, another layer to the onion yet. And the remaining loose ends all seemed to be converging on one place.

He looked back up at Kemmel and shook his head. "Even if what you say is true, I'm still not comfortable about it. It's not total enough. I think that what they tried to pull off tonight was a diversion."

Stephanie was looking amazed—but then she hadn't been there to hear Newell and Landis. "Not total enough?" she repeated. "They wanted to kill a foreign minister, kill me, pin it all on the party? You don't think that would have caused enough trouble?"

"Oh, it would have caused trouble, all right," Mel said. "Imagine the consternation everywhere in the next few days if it had succeeded. It would have occupied everyone's attention, distracted us all from everything else. And I think that was precisely the idea."

"What is their real intention, then?" Kemmel asked, puffing his cheroot.

"I don't know," Mel replied. "But it's something that ties in with Mustapha and whatever's going on in Syria. And it'll happen in the next week or so, maybe in the next few days."

Sarah came in with a tray of small cups of strong coffee, some sliced fruitcake, and honey cookies. "Will this be enough?" she asked. "I didn't know if you had eaten. There is more if you are hungry."

"I'm fine," Stephanie said.

Mel raised a hand. "I ate twice on planes."

Sarah passed out the cups and sat down at the remaining chair to join them. Kemmel reached under the sideboard to lift one of the kittens onto his lap and began fondling it with the fingers of a hand that could have squashed it to pulp. "So you've only just arrived in Egypt," Sarah said.

"Yes."

"You won't have seen much yet."

Mel caught Stephanie's eye. "Well . . . as a matter of fact I'm already finding it quite exciting," he replied. Sarah met Kemmel's eyes with a knowing look. Kemmel beamed back at her good-naturedly and shrugged.

"I didn't mean to interrupt," Sarah said. "Please carry on."

"To get to more immediate matters," Kemmel said. He looked at Stephanie. "You, Eva, must go back to Shepheard's tonight, to reappear fresh and bright for work in the morning as if nothing had happened." He turned to Mel. "Do you know if she was missed?"

"Missed? It was like Fort Knox had been robbed. That's probably why all those police cars showed up just as we were leaving." Across the table, Sarah raised her eyes momentarily toward the ceiling.

"So," Kemmel said to Stephanie, "we work out an alibi for you, and you stick to it. You weren't seen leaving Shepheard's, and you won't be seen going back. Where were you supposed to be?"

"I told the security guard I was going down to the hot tubs."

Kemmel shrugged. "They probably looked in the pool area, but so what? You changed your mind and went into the sauna. They must have missed you. You went back up and went to bed, and that's all you know."

"Er, I think the concierge saw her leave," Mel said. "So did the doorman."

Kemmel shrugged again. "How could they have done? She never left. Mistaken identity. They must have seen one of the high-class hotel hookers. They're in and out all the time."

Mel nodded. "How do we arrange it?"

"I will telephone Mr. Slade and arrange to meet him somewhere," Kemmel said. "I want to find out the rest of the story before I reveal where you are. If things sound okay I bring him back here, and he takes Eva back to Shepheard's and gets her inside invisibly."

"Sounds good," Mel said. He looked inquiringly at Stephanie.

She nodded. "What about . . . " she hesitated for a moment and glanced at Mel, "Mohican?"

"You must stay out of sight," Kemmel told him. "You were seen at Shepheard's and at the desk at the Omar Khayyam. Although little of this will probably get into the papers, there will be eyes on the lookout for someone of your description all over Cairo by tomorrow. Also, you'll be a dead duck the moment you try passing through an airport."

"You were seen too," Mel pointed out.

Kemmel smiled. "True, but I am used to it. I know the city, where to go and where to stay clear of."

"So what do you suggest?" Mel asked.

"As you know, I have connections with Mossad. I think we keep you lying low until we work out a way to get you out of the country unofficially, and into Israel. Then you can rejoin your own people in Jerusalem and become their problem. That's one of the things I want to talk about with Mr. Slade, and why he should come back here tonight." The kitten purred loudly as Kemmel tickled it under the chin. "What do you think?" he asked. "Have we overlooked anything?"

Mel sipped some of the hot, rich coffee, nibbled a piece of the cake and went over it in his mind. "Just one thing," he said at last.

Kemmel looked surprised. "Oh, really? What?"

"My suitcase. It's still in the lobby of Shepheard's somewhere."

"Oh, I'm sure we can take care of that," Kemmel promised.

CHAPTER 57

Kemmel left shortly afterward to telephone Slade and arrange a middle-of-the-night appointment. He warned that he might be gone for a couple of hours. Sarah had some business to take care of on the other side of the city early the next morning, and Stephanie urged her to get back to bed and not lose any sleep on their account.

"Perhaps you two should try to get some rest also," Sarah said. "Something tells me that you have had a trying evening." Not once had she pressed to find out what had happened. Her mouth twitched in a faint, Gioconda-like smile. "Sometimes Hamdi's 'couple of hours' can be a little more than that. Come."

She led them up the stairs and showed them into a back room, as jammed with furniture as the rest of the place, and as nineteenth century looking. It had a miniature but splendid four-poster bed, red-cushioned Ottomon couch, and heavy, carved wardrobe, chests of drawers, low coffee table, small round table, and two upright chairs. "Hamdi has many guests," Sarah explained. She squeezed between the bed and the chest of drawers to get to the other side of the room and drew aside the floor-length drapes. Behind was a set of French windows, which she opened, revealing a wooden veranda overlooking the Nile. "A little air," she said. "Close them if it gets chilly." She crossed back to the door. "I'll be back in a moment."

Mel moved into the room and stood looking around. "I didn't know people lived in museums," he said. Stephanie didn't answer. He stepped around the table and stared out over the veranda. The river was wide, its slowly rippling surface glittering with reflected city lights from the far bank.

There were many boats moored closer in to the shore, and a large, sleek motor yacht, its windows lit up and mast strung with colored lights, was moving slowly downstream farther out in the channel. "It's prettier out here," he said. "How far would you say it is across to the other side there?"

"I don't know." Stephanie's tone said she didn't especially care.

"I wonder what kind of a job you have to have to own a boat like that. It sure doesn't come with being a lawyer, whatever else they tell you."

At that moment, Sarah came back in. She had some linen and blankets draped over her arm and was carrying two small glasses in her hands. "Perhaps you would like these," she said. "I think you call it a nightcap, yes? Cognac. I'm told it steadies one's nerves. We don't drink alcohol, but we keep some for visitors." She put the glasses down on the small table and the blankets on the ottoman. "Those are there, if you want to use the couch . . ." She left the sentence unfinished, giving a slight shrug and a tossing of her head in a way that said it seemed silly to her, but one never knew with foreigners. "There is a bathroom up one more flight of stairs, on the right. Is there anything else I can get you?"

"I don't think so," Stephanie said. "Thanks for everything."

"I will say good night then. And in case I don't see you again, Eva, good luck."

"I guess I'll probably still be around tomorrow," Mel said. "Good night until then."

Sarah left, closing the door. Mel picked up one of the glasses and turned to take it out onto the veranda and let Stephanie get settled. Equality being what it was, he assumed he was on the ottoman. He rested one hand on the rail and sipped from his glass in the other as he stared out across the river. The liquid ran down his throat, warm and mellow with just the right kick. He felt the tension draining out of him, and downed some more.

He was still waiting for the reaction to hit him, now that the adrenalin charge had died away. Knowing fully what he was doing, and quite deliberately, he had just, bloodily and violently, killed another human being. It violated what was supposed to be one of the great taboos of his cultural programming.

The mysterious rationale was something that he and Eva had talked about. Soldiers went through the same programming, supposedly, for eighteen years, and were then expected to be able to switch it off at will, simply because somebody pronounced the mass killing of people they had never seen before "just," after consulting an all-merciful, all-powerful God who had botched the job by creating imperfect men, and then had to have his only son tortured to death to remedy it. It was just as well that humans made better parents, Mel had often thought. But exercising discrimination and killing for a reason was not okay—except when it was carried out ritually to extract vengeance on behalf of the same all-merciful God.

So, what form would the reaction take? he wondered. Would it develop as a trauma that would haunt him for life now? Remorse? Guilt? Self-loathing?

But he felt none of those things. He felt curiously liberated. He felt calm, at peace, and perhaps truly for the first time ever, fully in command of himself and his faculties. It was as if all of the other taboos and delusions that had been weighing him down all his life had shattered along with it; as if he had broken out of a prison that he hadn't even recognized, and only now, from the outside, could look back and see as a product of his own mind. It was their willingness to accept guilt that put men in bondage to others. There could be no form of slavery without there first being slavery of the mind. He felt whole, somehow. Now he understood what Eva had tried so many times to tell him.

He sensed a presence close to him and turned his head to find that Stephanie had taken off her coat and was standing just inside the French windows. "Hi," he said, surprised. "I thought you were getting tucked in."

She said nothing, but moved out to him, slowly but deliberately, watching his face, talking with her eyes and her movement. He could feel her warmth, smell her nearness. He turned fully to face her, alive now to what she was saying. He touched her shoulder, and she moved unresistingly into his arms. They kissed lightly at first, both in a strange, curious way as if neither of them was sure this was really happening; and then harder, hungrily, as the tension which the events of that evening had left in both of them craved for release in each other's bodies. He tightened his arms around her and pulled her against him, feeling her breasts pressed eagerly on his chest, himself thrusting against the firm mound beneath her skirt, and her responding.

Yet at the same time there was a part of him that said it

shouldn't be like this: a hurried, stolen hour. It should be when all this was over. He drew his head back, held her shoulders, and stared into her face in the lights from across the river.

"I want to . . ." she whispered before he could say anything. "So you'll know that it doesn't make any difference to anything . . . what happened tonight." She was telling him that she wanted to accept him as he was, in the only way that would set him apart from what he had been. She lowered her hands and unfastened her skirt, letting it fall to her feet, then stepped out of it and pressed herself to him again. He ran his hands up over her body underneath her top, and slid it up over her arms.

And for this one time, it was *she*: the wantonness of Eva, the tenderness of Stephanie, fused into one person. He finally consummated his impossible love for both of them. It was complete. And he, too, now, was complete.

They were still clinging to each other in the four-poster when a tapping on the door woke them and let them know that Kemmel was back. He had been gone for three hours. They dressed and went downstairs to find that Slade was there with him as planned, and had brought Mel's suitcase.

Back around the table in the downstairs parlor, they reviewed the situation with him, much as they had gone over it among themselves earlier. There seemed to be no reason to change the plan that Kemmel had proposed. The news was that the police had not linked Stephanie to the killing at the Omar Khayyam, and the concierge and doorman at Shepheard's had agreed that they might have been mistaken about the girl they had seen leaving. If Stephanie reappeared as normal in the morning, everything would soon smooth itself over.

From other inquiries that Kemmel had made, the police were taking the official line that the woman who was killed had been a womanfriend of Talaat Ali's—it had happened in his suite—and that the minister next door had been sedated all through and had nothing to do with it. In fact, the police had their own private doubts about that, but nobody was interested in delving further. Descriptions of Mel and Hamdi Kemmel were being circulated, however. It was all virtually just as Kemmel had anticipated.

Mel told of his conviction that it had been the woman at the

Omar Khayyam who had killed Eva. Stephanie, it turned out, had felt the same thing.

Finally, Stephanie left with Slade in a cab to return to Shepheard's. She and Mel would not see each other again until he joined McCormick's group in Israel.

Exhaustion overcame Mel at last, and he slept soundly until late the next morning. The bed smelled of Stephanie. When Sarah returned from across the city and woke him finally, it was almost noon. She nodded approvingly to herself as she carried out the blankets from the couch, still folded. Mel washed and went downstairs to find that she had prepared a breakfast of sausage, bread, and a spicy egg dish. He ate hungrily but without rushing, thinking back over everything that had happened. Then he went out onto the veranda and stood leaning against the rail, watching the river.

Kemmel reappeared late in the afternoon. He had left his red fez at home, Mel noticed, and was wearing a flat black cap. "Have one thing that stands out, which everyone will remember," Kemmel said when Mel remarked on it. "And then when it's not there, they'll be unable to recall anything else. Anyway, everything went okay at Shepheard's this morning. Eva is back at work today, and there have been no questions. Everyone there accepts that she never left the hotel."

"Is there anything in the papers about the Omar Khayyam?" Mel asked him.

"Just a brief mention that there was a fire alert, which turned out to be a false alarm."

"Okay. . . . Any more on how I get out?"

"Yes. They're going to take you out by sea. I will drive you down through the delta to the coast, but that can't be until tomorrow at the earliest, I'm afraid. So it looks as if you're with us for at least another night."

Mel browsed through the books in the shop and found some in English to pass the time with. One of them was an English law manual from 1898. After dinner, he and Kemmel spent the rest of the evening playing backgammon. When he went to bed, he thought again of Stephanie. The delegation had left Egypt that evening, and she would already be in Jerusalem.

CHAPTER 58

Damascus is built amid deserts, in a two-hundred-square-mile oasis of trees and orchards fertilized by soil carried down by rivers from the mountains of Lebanon. It styles itself the oldest existing city in the world. Certainly men came there before their coming could be recorded, and if Jericho counted merely as a small town, then the claim could well be just, for Babylon and Nineveh were its siblings. The millenia have seen it conquered repeatedly by East and West—Egyptians, Ammonites, Philistines, Mesopotamians, Greeks, Romans, Persians, Saracens, Crusaders, Mongols, Turks, French, British—and without being changed much by either, until latter-twentieth-century bad taste began submerging its defiantly irrational piles of architecture and twisting anarchies of alleyways beneath disciplined ranks of concrete cinemas, offices, factories, and parking lots.

The Soviet embassy, and the Damascus residency of the KGB's First Chief Directorate, which it housed, was situated in the more fashionable district stretching to the northwest of the old city, near the Parliament and other government buildings, below the slopes of Mount Kassioun, where the better-to-do built their homes above the summer heat. The layout was to the standard Soviet pattern found the world over, comprising two plain, eleven-story buildings standing side by side inside a walled compound of lawns, trees, and shrubs. The embassy building contained regular rooms and offices in its lower nine floors, with the top two being highly secured, accessible to authorized personnel only, and reserved for KGB activities. The other building held the staff residential quarters and recreational facilities, and most of the occupants ventured out of it infrequently, and then usually on supervised sightseeing tours.

But Major Yuri Brazhnikov had no thought in his mind of going to see the Great Ommayad Mosque, the Nureddine

Tower, or the house where Cain was supposed to have killed Abel, as he crossed the compound to the main building on the morning of January 15. There was a strange concurrence of things happening at once in different places, which his instincts told him was more than coincidence. Chelenko had felt the same thing even sooner, which was why he had approached General Goryanin to have Brazhnikov sent to Syria. First, the enigmatic American, Shears—whom agents in the U.S. had continued to keep an eye on, even though Brazhnikov had tended to dismiss him as the primary lead at the moment—had vanished suddenly three days previously. The Israelis were thought to be hatching something, although their security was first-class as usual, and nobody had any idea what. Satellite observations had shown activity around the mysterious PALP base to be increasing. And was it mere chance that right in the middle of it all, the American political deputation that was visiting the area should have arrived in Jerusalem last night? Something, somewhere, a feeling in Brazhnikov's bones told him, was about to happen.

He acknowledged the salute from the sentry at the main entrance and crossed the vestibule to the elevators. A huge, framed picture of Lenin watched as he pressed the call button and waited for the car to arrive. He was still shivering from the walk across from the residential block. The winter here wasn't much warmer than Moscow's.

On the tenth floor, he came out into the lower level of the residency. A special key opened the armored outer door, and beyond it an inner door was opened from the other side by a security guard after checking Brazhnikov's identity—Brazhnikov's was a new face, and he could turn out to be more of a stickler for rules than some of the regulars. Inside, he went past the room where the case officers worked in their separate booths, and along a corridor to the small office that had been assigned to him and his two assistants on direct instructions from Moscow. Lieutenant Kugav, who had called him over from the residential building, was standing over a littered desk wedged into one corner with a data terminal, beneath a corkboard covered in pinned notes and messages. The other wall carried a large-scale map of the area between the east shore of the Mediterranean and western Iran. A red circle indicated the location of the enigmatic PALP base in eastern Syria, code-named Glinka, around which the whole operation pivoted.

"What's the news, Aram?" Brazhnikov asked.

Kugav handed him a transcription of a signal that had come down from the communications room upstairs. "It was passed down about fifteen minutes ago," Kugav said.

The information had come via Moscow, where it had been routed across Chelenko's desk. It was from a source in Tel Aviv, undisclosed but given a confidence rating of over 80 percent by Moscow, and stated that an Israeli special-duty paratrooper unit was planning an operation aimed at lifting some unidentified "merchandise" out of a remote location in Syria. Chelenko had attached a note instructing Brazhnikov to contact him via a high-security satellite link.

"Merchandise?" Brazhnikov repeated aloud as he reread the transcript.

"It has to be the missiles," Kugav said. "Either as parts, or assembled. That's where they've been brought together."

Brazhnikov crossed to the map and stood staring at it. It seemed unlikely, to say the least, that the Israelis would be working in conjunction with the Palestinians. The more likely explanation—which Chelenko agreed with—was that some Arab faction had organized the thefts somehow, the Israelis had found out about it in the same way that they seemed to find out about everything, had waited to let the Arabs labor to bring the parts together for them. Now they intended to steal the fruits. They had pulled off more audacious stunts than that in the past.

Chelenko, with the blessing of Goryanin and whoever gave approvals above him, did not intend to simply sit back and watch it happen. If the presence of the missiles at Glinka was established beyond reasonable doubt, he would send in his own force to take them back again—they were Soviet property, after all. And even if their existence was not certain, but any of the Western powers seemed about to intervene there, he would give the order to go, anyway, in case they knew more than he did. Accordingly, he had arranged for the Third Battalion VDV, special assault-trained airborne troops, based in southern Armenia, only four hundred kilometers away, to be held in readiness. It seemed to Brazhnikov that the second of those conditions was close to being fulfilled.

He called Chelenko as instructed a few minutes later. "I agree that it is time to move," Chelenko said. "We will proceed with phase two of the Blue plan as a precaution now, without waiting further. So you can make your preparations to move out, Major."

That meant that a small force of Vysotniki—the Russian equivalent of the British SAS infiltration and sabotage troops—would be put down on the ground to reconnoiter the area, observe the disposition and strength of the potential opposition, and generally prepare the way for a possible assault group. Because of his knowledge of the overall situation, Brazhnikov would be flown up to Armenia to go in with the reconnaissance force. Chelenko would come down to coordinate the operation locally from Damascus. One of the reasons for sending Brazhnikov ahead to Damascus had been to enable him to set up a base and operations group for Chelenko to work with when he arrived.

The telephone rang in a room above a carpet-mender's shop in a narrow, nondescript alley in Tel Aviv. Dave Fenner reached an arm out from the iron-frame bed where he had been lying, staring at the ceiling and thinking. "Yes?"

"Who is this who speaks?"

"This is Benjamin."

"There is a message from Gypsy."

Fenner took a pad and pen from the table by the phone. "Go ahead."

"The message is as follows: *Sheldon Q. never talked to the doctor. It was the wife of the professor who lived on the beach.* Message ends."

Fenner frowned, stared at it, and then, slowly, a stunned look came into his eyes as the meaning sank in. All these years, and he'd never suspected. He would have to go over everything again in his mind now, looking for anything that could have been compromised. It made it doubly important that he remain out of sight and stay away from Jerusalem and the American group.

"Is there a reply?" the voice inquired.

"Not for now. I'll let you know if that changes." He hung up.

There was no need for any reply. He knew what he needed to know.

CHAPTER 59

Hamdi Kemmel drove Mel out of Cairo in the Fiat van, and then northward for three hours through the flat country of the delta, crisscrossed by a bewildering network of irrigation channels and waterways, past innumerable villages, plantations of maize, rice, cotton, and fruit trees, and fields of cattle. Eventually they came to a small harbor village on an inlet of the sea, which Kemmel said was close to the port of Damietta, on the northeast side of the delta.

He drove through outskirts of reasonably modern-looking shops and bungalows to the older core of crumbling traditional yellow-brick dwellings stacked in a disorderly heap on the waterfront. There, he pulled up outside a store that sold marine equipment and had several boats moored to a jetty at the back. Kemmel introduced Mel to "Akhmet," who had been expecting them. He was a small, gnarled, crouching man of an age impossible to guess, with disintegrating teeth and a face like a simian walnut. Akhmet would take Mel out that night, to be picked up by an Israeli vessel twenty kilometers offshore. Akhmet said that the latest weather forecasts weren't promising, but agreed to give it a try. After staying for a meal of fish salad, fish soup, a fried fish-and-millet preparation, and fish, Kemmel said his farewell, wished Mel good luck and a favorable nod from Allah, and left to drive back to Cairo.

With two other men to help, Akhmet and Mel boarded one of the boats, a tall-masted *felucca*, traditionally a sailing vessel but assisted by an engine, and put out a little before midnight. A light rain was falling by then, and the wind had been rising for several hours. Mel found that he didn't have a sailor's stomach, and consigned his fish feast back whence it had come. Conditions got worse, they missed the rendezvous, and arrived back in harbor shortly after dawn. Mel went to bed to sleep or die, not caring especially which. When he woke up in the early afternoon, there were no books or backgammon partners to help pass the time. He sat in a dingy back room watching the harbor, while Akhmet made innumerable comings and going to the only telephone in the vicinity, the location of which seemed to be a closely guarded secret, somewhere along the street. At last he announced that they would try again that night. Later, he produced a steaming concoction in a large dish, which he said was a fish-and-octopus casserole. It smelled dreadful. He invited Mel to share some dinner before they set out again. Mel declined as politely as he could.

The sea was calm that night, however, and Mel felt no discomfort this time. It was well into the early hours of the morning when Akhmet gave a shout and pointed, while one of the other hands signaled with a lamp. Mel stood up and saw the sleek, black outline of an Israeli Navy patrol launch turning toward them, silhouetting guns mounted fore and aft and moving almost noiselessly, cutting a white wave from its bow. The launch cut its engines and hove alongside, and moments later strong, sure hands were helping Mel, still with his suitcase, aboard. He was taken below and offered hot cocoa and beans with toast, which he accepted gratefully, his appetite now restored.

Then they gave him a sweater and a hooded topcoat to wear. He went back up and stood for a while on the bridge, exchanging intermittent words with the captain and watching the sea race by and the straight, foamy wake rolling away into the night behind. But sustained talk was impossible over the roar of the wind, plus four engines with a combined output of sixty-five thousand horsepower, and eventually he went back below. One of the sailors gave him some blankets and showed him to a spare bunk in the forward quarters, which also accommodated three of the crew. They chatted with him for a while and seemed suitably impressed when he took off his jacket and removed his harness and shoulder holster before settling down. Mel rather enjoyed the feeling it gave him. Then, lulled by the steady drone of the engines and the powerful, eager thrusting of the ship through the waves, he dozed off.

A drop in the note of the engines awakened him. The boat was slowing down. He put on his things and went back up to find that it was daylight, and they were just off a coast. There was a headland to the right, formed around a large central mountain with streets and buildings gleaming in the sun all the way to the top, and merging ahead of the boat into a city that was etched into mountainsides and overflowing in every direction around a vast, sweeping bay. His watch told him it was 9:15 A.M. They were at Haifa, Israel's main port. The mountain behind the headland, one of the crew informed him, was Mount Carmel.

Mel wasn't sure what he should expect next. He had vaguely anticipated some kind of questioning by officials, followed by transportation to Jerusalem, where McCormick and his party should have arrived late the evening before last. He was surprised, therefore, to be met at the quayside by two Israeli paratrooper officers with a staff car and driver. It didn't seem to matter much where Mel might have had thoughts of going. They were heading for Tel Aviv, fifty miles south. To his mild bemusement, which if he'd thought more about it would have crossed the borderline into apprehension, they addressed him respectfully as "Mohican."

A corporal sent by the officer of the watch in the duty room delivered a message to the group gathered in a briefing room at the headquarters of the Fifth Parachute Brigade, and handed it to Colonel Hariv. Hariv read it and announced, "They've landed at Haifa. He should be here in about an hour."

There had been a lull in the talking, which had been going on since early morning. Dave Fenner got up from his chair to stretch his legs. Although he had committed the information to memory long before, he walked to the head of the room to study again the map showing the details of operation "Haymaker." It was just habit, something to do while they waited. It was now the sixteenth of January, and McCormick and his people had been in Israel for two days. Stephanie would have told McCormick about Mustapha, and the role she had agreed to play of acting as a link between him and the Israeli intelligence group. Also, she would have given McCormick the line to include in his broadcast, signaling that such a link had been completed.

"Dervish," the Mossad agent in Egypt who had passed the line to Stephanie and been detailed to keep an eye on her, had also radioed a coded report on the incident at the Omar Khayyam Hotel, which had taken everyone by surprise. The frightening thing was how near the plan had come to succeeding. If it hadn't been for the sudden materialization of some superprofessional whose existence even Dave hadn't been told of, the whole thing would already have been a disaster. It looked as if maybe the "Colonel," back in his dungeon beneath the Pentagon, was even shrewder than Dave had given him credit for. Or had it been someone put in by the Constitutional people? He had no way of knowing. But at least it was nice to think that there was a department left somewhere that knew what it was doing.

"So, who is this mysterious Mohican, who appears out of nowhere at the last minute and saves the Egyptian foreign minister's life?" a voice inquired.

Dave turned to find that Yigal Uban, the Mossad representative, was standing beside him. "I don't know," he replied. "I was just wondering the same thing. It sounds as if he was flown straight in from the States to do the job. I don't think it can be anyone I've met."

"Dervish rates him highly," Uban said. "And Dervish is good. This man must be quite somebody."

"Who was the woman that he killed?" Dave asked. "Is there any more news on her yet?"

"We have a contact in the Cairo police department, but it doesn't sound as if they've made a lot of progress," Uban said. "She was staying at the Nile Hilton, and she entered from Athens on a false passport. Her belongings indicate that she traveled from the States. That's about all anyone really knows. But from some of the things in her possession, she was no amateur. She was going to use ricin and DMSO. There can be little doubt that she meant to take out both of them."

"Both?"

"The minister and the American girl. Obviously they wouldn't want her able to talk."

That fitted, Dave thought to himself. Planting drugs was something she could have agreed to go along with plausibly, even if she hadn't meant it; but never something like an assassination. But according to Dervish's report, Mohican suspected that even that in turn had been intended as a diversion from something else. A triple-level deception. Mohican sounded like the only person who really understood what was going on. As Uban had said, he must be quite somebody.

"But he got her, eh?" Dave murmured, half to himself. He found himself thinking that perhaps he was just beginning to realize how much Stephanie had taken on. This was Eva's line of work, not Stephanie's. He put out of his mind any thought of what would have happened if Mohican's plane had been late getting in. Some things just didn't bear thinking about.

The staff car carrying Mel and the officers entered the outskirts of Tel Aviv and headed for the eastern fringes of the city. They passed some industrial building set well back from the road with a lot of tractors and other farm machinery lined up in a fenced area outside, and then turned off the main road by some fields where schoolboys were playing soccer. Mel had quickly realized from the conversation during the drive from Haifa that some garbled account of his doings at the Omar Khayyam must have preceded him, doubtless from Hamdi Kemmel. If so, this wasn't the place to try and straighten it out, he decided. So, he sat back and watched the scenery, wondering in his mind at the strange string of events which in the space of a month had transformed him from a respectable young Boston lawyer into an unshaven gunman being smuggled out in the middle of the night to rendezvous with a Navy boat off the coasts of the Levant.

They came to a military barracks, with a high wire fence and armed sentries at the gate. One of the officers in the car said something to the duty officer in the guardhouse, who picked up a telephone. They passed through, and drove across a parade ground, and then between a two-story office building and a transportation depot to some buildings at the rear. They got out, and the two officers conducted Mel through a door, into a corridor with brick walls painted glossy lime green to half height and cream above, past brown doors and red fire extinguishers, everything looking scrubbed and clean. They went up a flight of steel stairs to a junction of two more corridors, and followed one of them to a door with guards outside. One of the officers said something in Hebrew, and showed a pass, the guard knocked on the door and opened it, and Mel was ushered through.

There were a dozen or so men sitting and standing around the table inside, a couple in civilian clothes, the rest wearing the dark khaki of the Israeli military, with insignia and badges of rank that Mel was unable to interpret. They all looked bronzed, capable, confident. A large map was pinned to a board on one wall, some pictures that looked like satellite photographs, and a chart showing columns and numbers, which could have been a timetable. Mel saw the intrigued looks that greeted him from every side and sensed that they had been waiting for him. A tall, gaunt-faced officer with thick-rimmed spectacles introduced himself as Colonel Hariv, "Shlomo to everyone here." One of the civilians was Mr. Uban, from Mossad, and another of the officers, Captain Rachmin . . . but Mel lost what Hariv was saying at that point, when he saw Dave Fenner, standing across the room in a plain uniform without Israeli insignia. Mel shook his head in astonishment.

But it was nothing compared to the gaping, wide-eyed disbelief that Fenner seemed to be experiencing at seeing him.

"You two already know each other?"

Fenner recovered first. "Yes . . . it goes back a long time." And then to Mel, "I never expected to bump into you here." Hardly a necessary statement, mainly for everyone else's benefit. Mel was still having to bite his lip to stop himself from breaking into laughter at the look on Fenner's face.

"Good to see you," Mel said. "Er . . . what do I call you here?"

Fenner shrugged. "How about Benjamin this time?" Some of the others in the room exchanged knowing smiles. Cool, cool . . .

Hariv completed the introductions, most of which Mel failed to register, and then concluded, "Gentlemen, Mohican." There was a general murmuring that sounded approving, and someone near the front clapped his hands in applause. Mel, dazed by it all, was shown to a seat by Fenner. Hariv looked at the officers who had brought Mel from Haifa. "Is General Lurgar joining us?"

"We had the guardhouse call him when we arrived. He'll be about ten minutes," one of them replied.

General? Mel thought. Christ, what had he gotten into now?

"I trust your voyage was pleasant?" Hariv said to Mel.

"Fine, compared to when they tried last night."

"Mohican didn't come in yesterday, then?" one of the Israelis said to Hariv.

Hariv shook his head. "They missed the rendevous in the storm the other night. He's come straight here this morning."

"Oh, I see."

"I'm sure he doesn't look like that all the time," Hariv said. "You've been watching too many American gangster movies,

Moshe." He paused, then looked around the room and raised his voice. "Gentlemen, could we have silence, please? . . . Thank you. If we have a few minutes, I'd like to run briefly through the plan for those of you who haven't been involved so far, and for Mohican's benefit, before Shimon gets here."

Did Mohican know about Mustapha? Hariv asked. Mel glanced at Dave, uncertain of whether he was supposed to know or not, but Dave gave nothing suggestive of a warning signal. Mel said that he did, which seemed to raise his status even further, and Hariv went on to explain that they had been considering a plan to get Mustapha out. The plan would involve some help from an agent referred to as Pierrot, whom Mossad had managed to put inside, and Fenner would be going along too. Good luck, Dave, Mel thought as he listened. The plan was only tentative at this stage, however, pending orders that might or might not come down from the high command. Hariv was evasive about the background to that.

He continued. "The airstrip suggests an immediate way in and out, but that makes it the first thing that would occur to anyone else, too. Also, when we look into things further, we find that the approaches from the south and west are covered by overlapping ground radars, many of which we're not supposed to know about. The camp itself is fenced, guarded, and swarming with armed Palestinians, and we don't have the kind of international situation that would justify an overt military strike—as at Entebbe. The only way we'd ever get him out is with inside help, and that's why we must use Pierrot. He will get Mustapha out inside one of the trucks that travel between the camp and the airstrip. The details of that we leave to him. The break will be at dusk, allowing maximum distance to be covered by daybreak."

"So we're going in and out overland," somebody checked.

"Yes." Hariv looked at a soldier sitting to one side, in shirtsleeves with paratrooper's wings. "Ehud, since you'll be in command on the ground, why don't you go over that part of it?" Ehud was the one who had been introduced to Mel as Captain Rachmin at the beginning of the meeting.

Mel remembered reading somewhere that the Israeli military apparatus had originated from a citizens' army, and its universal conscription of women as well as men gave it an essentially civilian nature, making it perhaps the most informal army in the world. The casual use of first names between all ranks was widespread, and stiffness and saluting rare. It was also one of the most professional of armies, known for its emphasis of initiative and penchant for the bold and unexpected.

Rachmin got up and walked over to the map. He was athletically built, with dark curly hair, blue eyes, and a ready smile. "We land here, to the north of Domino, two days before H-hour," he said, pointing at a spot. "The ground force will be nine men. The terrain is broken enough for a chopper to fly in low and make the drop from the north, in other words from behind the radar screen that Shlomo mentioned, without detection. That puts us close enough to get to Domino in two nights march, laying up by day. The force will comprise three squads. The first, A squad . . ." he nodded at someone near the back, "you, Rafael, and two men, will detach after the first night to select and secure a point suitable for helicopter pickup somewhere in this area." Rachmin drew a circle around a portion of the map with his finger. "The rest of us will make a second night's march to the target. B Squad will be Zvi," another nod, "Haim, and Benjamin. You will rendezvous with Mustapha and Pierrot at point Green, and then head north, moving cross-country. And that, of course, leaves C Squad— myself and the other two men. We are there because our friends at Mossad couldn't let the opportunity go by." He glanced at Yigal Uban as an invitation to elaborate.

Uban responded, "If we're going to have men on the ground there, it would be a pity not to try and find out what they're doing at that airstrip." He pointed at one of the photographs by the map. "There's something going on under camouflage nets that we can't get from satellite pictures. They've tightened up on their security and won't let anyone from the camp go up to the airstrip. But Pierrot has a friend on the guard detail there who says that an aircraft arrived there recently. He thinks it's a Soviet Ilyushin—but definitely a commercial jet. From the appearance, it sounds like one purchased secondhand, maybe from India or somewhere. Apparently they're painting it."

There were mystified looks around the room. "Could it be connected with the hijack somehow?" Someone asked.

"Maybe," Uban said. "But it doesn't seem to make any sense. Anyway, we want Captain Rachmin's section to take a closer look."

Rachmin resumed. "We should arrive in the area of the camp before daybreak. I'll conduct a ground reconnaissance of the airstrip after we've rested up. B Squad will collect

Mustapha and Pierrot at nightfall and then proceed to a prearranged rendezvous with A Squad, while we follow as rearguard, creating diversions if necessary. The pickup will be predawn after the night's march, before any search parties or aircraft have a chance to set out. The chopper will fly from a temporary landing strip established just across the Turkish border. A C–130 will be waiting there to lift us all out, with the chopper."

"Do we have clearance with the Turkish authorities?" an officer asked.

"The arrangements are, shall we say, somewhat informal," Rachmin replied, smiling. In other words, no.

Then one of the guards outside opened the door again, and a broad, dark-haired, craggy-faced officer in shirtsleeves strode in, wearing a peaked cap with a respectable amount of braid. Hariv introduced him to Mel as General Shimon Lurgar, who would be ultimately responsible for the operation. "My compliments on the job in Egypt," Lurgar said as he settled himself down. "Our man there was impressed by the way you handled it." Mel nodded his head in an acknowledgment, feeling it would be wisest to keep his mouth shut. Beside him, Dave brought his hand up to his brow and shook his head in an involuntary gesture of disbelief. The general opened a thin red folder that he had brought with him, which contained several sheets of computer printout and some typed notes. He studied them briefly to cue his memory, then looked up at Mel again. "This American girl that we have been calling Gypsy . . . She is on the Constitutional staff."

"Yes," Mel said.

"We understand that she was asked by the party's political opponents to embarrass the party by agreeing to be caught with a large shipment of drugs. But that was just a smoke screen. The real plan all along was to implicate her in this assassination in Egypt."

"Party intelligence never really bought the drugs story," Mel said. "They guessed she was being set up for something else. Where they got it wrong was in thinking it wouldn't happen until McCormick got here, to Israel."

"Hmm . . . but whoever you are with got it right, fortunately," Lurgar mused. He waved a hand before Mel could respond. "But those details are not our concern. . . . What interests me more is this. According to Dervish, you said that this isn't the end of the affair, but a more elaborate diversion to distract attention from something else in turn. Am I right?"

Now Mel was beginning to see where he came in. He took a second to collect his thoughts, then nodded. "It still doesn't seem sufficient to justify what's been going on behind the scenes," he said. "I think there's more to it, and that it involves people who are a lot more powerful than the ones who planned the thing in Egypt. Those were just the second-string team. The deception was designed to mislead *them*, as well as us."

"You mean their own people?" Colonel Hariv said. "Only a small inner clique knows the true plan?"

"Exactly," Mel said. The rest of the room listened in respectful silence. Even Fenner was staring in a strange kind of way that said maybe he'd been missing something all along.

"Could you be more specific as to your reasons for supposing this? General Lurgar said.

Mel drew a long breath. He could hardly hope to reproduce the speech he'd had from Newell, and besides it would have been out of place. This wasn't the time for political theory. He said, "The assassination attempt was set up by a political opposition group whose horizons end with hostility to the constitutional party—don't get me wrong, I mean violent hostility, as evidenced by the extremes they were prepared to go to." Lurgar nodded. Mel went on. "But they are being manipulated by more powerful interests whose goal is complete political and economic control not only of the United States, but of the Eastern bloc too. The people who set up the affair in Egypt aren't directly a part of the broader scheme. They're probably not even aware that it exists."

"Now I'm beginning to see why they would need to mislead their own side," Hariv murmured.

"It operates at a higher, global level." Mel nodded toward the map on the wall. "And I believe that the other arm of it extends into the Soviet hierarchy, and that's where it connects somehow to Mustapha." Which, of course, was what interested the Israelis.

"Do you know what this something else is that they are planning?" Lurgar asked.

Mel shook his head. "No, but I think Mustapha might."

"Do you know when it will happen?"

"If the business in Egypt was to divert our attention, which is what I believe, then it has to be imminent."

Lurgar thought hard for a while, then got up, walked across

the room, and turned to face the table again. "Our problem is this," he said, looking at Mel. "We have been considering this operation on a tentative basis only. For political reasons that we needn't go into, it is not certain that we will be ordered to go ahead, or if we are, how long it might take for those orders to come down. But from what you're saying, Mustapha's information could be of global importance, and any delay in getting it might be fatal. So my question to you, Mr. Mohican, is: In your opinion, could the situation be sufficiently important to justify a decision by me to proceed anyway, without the authorization of my government?"

Mel whistled silently. He realized that Lurgar was just asking for an opinion, but it was evident from his attitude that he would attach a lot of weight to it. Mel couldn't bring himself to back off at this point and say that it really wasn't his department after all. If anything like that needed to be said, Dave could say it. Dave, however, unable to fathom just how much Mel did know, wasn't saying anything.

Mel stared up at the map, aware of every eye in the room watching him. He could sit here for the rest of the day, he realized, trying to balance imponderables. It wasn't going to change anything. Then he thought about Eva, dead, Brett, dead, Stephanie, almost dead—not to mention himself—what had brought it all to pass, and how it was that he came to find himself sitting here. What was it all for, after all? And he gave the only answer he could have. "Yes, sir," he said, looking at the general steadily. "In my opinion it would be justified."

Lurgar looked at him for a few seconds longer, then came back to the head of the room and stood staring at the map. Finally he turned to face the room and announced, "McCormick leaves tomorrow evening. We will wait until then for the official order. In the meantime, complete your preparations. Should we decide to proceed with Haymaker independently, the responsibility will be mine alone. Yigal, make sure that Pierrot is alerted accordingly."

"I'll see to it," Uban confirmed.

Lurgar looked at Mel again. "Since you are key in this, and in view of your strong opinion on the subject, I assume that in the event that we do go ahead, you'll have no objection to joining Benjamin as an addition to the American complement." He nodded to the rest of the room, "Good day, gentlemen," and strode toward the door.

It took a few seconds before what Lurgar had said hit

Mel. . . . God, he thought Mel was a professional at this
kind of thing! Mel didn't know how to load a Uzi, never mind
keep up with trained paratroopers moving fast over rough
country at night, and then taking on Palestinian terrorists. He
turned toward Dave in an appeal for him to intercede somehow, but Dave clearly wasn't going to, and Lurgar was almost
out the door. The assembly around them was breaking up into
knots of twos and threes, gathering notes, swapping comments, getting up from their seats. "He can't be serious," Mel
muttered as the general noise level rose.

Fenner looked at him, not without a hint of amusement.
"Why not? You look in pretty good shape to me," he murmured. "You'll do okay. Don't worry about it."

"*Don't worry!*" Mel hissed through his teeth. "Are you out
of your fucking mind? I could get everyone killed out there."

"I don't think so," Fenner said. "You've done okay so far, and
you seem to know more about what's going on than anyone."
He paused for a second and gave Mel a curious look. "And
besides, you need to be there because of who really matters."

Mel frowned, puzzled all of a sudden by Dave's tone. "What
do you mean?"

Fenner's voice dropped even lower and he leaned across in
his chair, looking at Mel intently. "Pierrot describes Mustapha
as tall, with fair hair, a beard, and about your age. He's
knowledgeable about U.S. strategic defense software. Now
think about it. Who do *you* think Mustapha could turn out to
be?"

CHAPTER 60

Theodore McCormick braced his hands on the podium and
looked directly at the TV cameras across the press auditorium
of the Israeli Knesset building in Jerusalem. Behind him, the
Israeli prime minister and the cabinet members who had come
to be present at the address looked happy. The talks had been
constructive. "In conclusion, I'd like to thank you again for the
hospitality we've been shown in your country, and to say how

much I look forward to coming back—in the not-too-distant future, I trust—as the official representative of the United States. I've been told innumerable times that you've welcomed our determination to 'tell it straight,' as we Americans say. Well, in that tradition I'll say that it has been wonderful here, but it's always nice to be going back to where you belong. As the song says, wherever else you wander, there's no place like home. Thank you all, once again." There was applause, McCormick stepped down, and the Israeli prime minister came forward to take his place and deliver a response.

Stephanie was sitting near the end of one of the rows near the back. Mike, the party's security guard, was next to her, and his partner, Don, in the row behind. There were also Israeli security men in plain clothes at the doors and scattered around. Some people were going to have to answer a lot of awkward questions based on her testimony, when she returned to the States. Nobody was taking any chances.

George Slade came in the door at the rear, saw Stephanie, and came over to take the empty seat on the opposite side of her from Mike. "I've had some news through the Israeli intelligence people on Mel," he whispered, leaning close to her ear. "He's in the country, and he's okay. But for various reasons, he's being kept out of sight."

Stephanie nodded. "Thanks for letting me know." No doubt to avoid embarrassment if he were to be identified in connection with the affair in Cairo, she thought.

Slade went on. "And there's something else. Look, they want you to stay on here in Israel after the rest of us fly out tonight. I've made your accommodation arrangements. The Israelis will be handling security, so you should be okay. It'll only be for a few days. I don't know a lot more than that myself. But can you catch me afterward when this is over?"

"Sure . . . I guess so."

Slade nodded. "Fine. I'll talk to you outside." He got up, nodded to Mike, and left.

Brigadier General Shimon Lurgar arrived in Jerusalem from Tel Aviv just over an hour after receiving an urgent summons from the Ministry of Defense. He was driven to an annex of the Knesset building, and received in a closed-session meeting by Lieutenant General Yosef Bahal, chief of staff of the General Staff of the Israeli Defense Forces, Major General Chaim

Almagi, chief of the Intelligence Branch, and Michael Charon, the head of Mossad.

"There is a guerrilla base up in the other end of Syria, used by an offshoot of the PALP faction," Charon informed him.

"I see," Lurgar said, nodding, appropriately attentive at the revelation.

"We know very little about it, even though we've had one of our agents working on the inside there for a considerable time now," Charon went on. "His name is Pierrot. He has been trying to uncover details of an air hijack that we've been getting wind of, but so far without success."

"Yes."

"As a matter of routine, he has also informed us of a captive who's being held there, believed to be an American."

Yosef Bahal took over. "However, according to confidential information that the American vice-president-elect disclosed during his visit, he is thought to be an expert on computer software used in the Western space defense system. Also, he is believed to be in possession of information that the Americans consider vital to our interests, as well as to theirs. What we want you to look into as a matter of top priority is the possibility of getting him, and the information, out."

Lurgar blinked and made an effort to look suitably surprised.

Almagi pushed across some files and papers. "Here are details of everything we've got on the place currently. You can assume full cooperation on the inside from Pierrot, naturally. We'd like preliminary estimates of manpower, skills, and equipment needs, along with time to prepare and time to execute, by noon tomorrow if at all possible."

"That's . . . cutting it a bit fine," Lurgar ventured.

Almagi nodded. "I know, Shimon, but it is most urgent. That was why we sent for you."

"It would be impossible to stress the importance of what lies behind this." Charon said.

Lurgar took the files, scanned inside them briefly, and nodded. "I'll do my best. I'll need a Mossad officer assigned to the operation."

"Of course," Charon said.

"How about Yigal Uban?" Lurgar said. "I've worked with him before, he's clear-headed and fast, good at details, and we get along well."

"That's exactly who I would have offered," Charon said. "In fact, he is Pierrot's controller."

"Who should we put in charge of it, do you think?" Bahal asked, obviously relieved at the way the conversation was going.

Lurgar went through the motions of thinking. "Well, it would depend on the nature of the operation, naturally, so I'd have a better idea after I've read this, but tentatively I'd say someone like Shlomo Hariv."

Bahal nodded. "Good choice."

"Er, what kind of jump-off date are we talking about?" Lurgar asked cautiously.

"As soon as you can realistically manage," Bahal said.

Lurgar nodded gravely. "Very well. Could I go away and have a preliminary look at this now, while you are all here together? Maybe there's an office somewhere I could use?"

"Good," Bahal said. "We have some other matters to discuss anyhow. Shall we say, thirty minutes?"

"That would be fine."

"I'll find you some space somewhere," Almagi said, getting up.

Lurgar kept a poker face as he left the room with the intelligence chief. Inside, he was relieved and thankful at no longer having to make a decision.

As he closed the door, he heard Bahal saying to Charon, "What I don't understand is how the Americans knew all this, when you've had a man in there all the time. And . . ."

They were going to get another surprise, too, he thought to himself. If his guess was right, he was about to set a speed and efficiency record for operations planning.

The movie was Swedish, and reaching its climax with an orgy of coeds after the graduation dance. Brett had lost count of the number of orifices and protuberances in use. He wasn't especially interested, but it held everyone else's attention, and the encouraging suggestions and bawdy comments being shouted from around the room covered his muttered conversion with Hamashad.

"Did you watch McCormick's speech this afternoon?" Hamashad asked him.

"I did."

"And?"

"Obviously I'm satisfied. You went to a lot of trouble."

"That is my job. You were right to be cautious."

Brett glanced at him quickly. "So, what should I do to get this information out through you? I'll need to write it down?"

"That will no longer be necessary."

Brett looked worried. "How come?"

"They want more than just the information. They want *you*. An Israeli commando unit is being sent in to get you out."

For a few seconds, Brett was speechless. "When?" he murmured when he had recomposed himself.

"Three days from now, on the evening of the twentieth, immediately after sundown. I will be coming with you."

"Okay, I'm listening. What's the plan?"

"We leave separately and meet up outside the camp. There is an airstrip near here, which trucks make trips to regularly. . . ."

CHAPTER 61

An advance party had been dropped by parachute several hours earlier to mark out a landing strip and clear it of rocks and other obstacles. Mel sat on a cramped seat in semidarkness, staring at the dark bulk of the helicopter secured in the cargo bay and listening to the drone of the four Allison engines as the C-130 Hercules transporter flew low through the mountains on the southern fringe of Turkey. Like the other shadowy figures sitting silently or dozing around him, he was wearing a jump-smock over combat fatigues, rubber-soled boots, a woollen cap-comforter on his head, camouflage cream on his face, and cuddling an Uzi 9mm submachine gun against his knees.

An attempt to fool the kind of soldiers he was among wouldn't have lasted long, and they wouldn't have appreciated it. He had agreed with Dave that the best policy would be to rely on his existing prestige to carry him, and to make no bones about it. Accordingly, they had announced to the others simply that Mel's professional skills were in other areas— which was true—that he wasn't from a military background, and that was that.

"What kind of background are you from?" one of them had asked.

"I sit at a desk," Mel had told him.

The reply was so incongruous that everyone had taken it as a joke. Obviously his line of business was security sensitive, and Lurgar had made a mistake. They interpreted Mel's readiness to go with them, nevertheless, as a noble gesture to avoid embarrassing the general, which enhanced Mel's popularity with them even further. So two of the NCOs had spent a couple of hours the previous day giving Mel a crash course on handling military hardware, and Mel had been pleasantly surprised to find that he wasn't bad at it.

He still hadn't fully absorbed the suggestion that the person they were going there to bring out might be Brett. Yet the more he thought about it, the more sense it made. Besides the similarities that Dave had listed, it seemed too coincidental that no body had ever been recovered from the car that went over Devil's Slide. And thinking about it more, why would a hostile power that had somebody with Brett's kind of specialized knowledge in its possession want to kill him, when he could be so much more potentially useful in other ways? Some of the things he recalled Stephanie saying made him wonder if, deep down, she had ever really accepted it, but perhaps been unwilling to say so for fear of sounding too much like somebody merely trying to convince herself. He thought back to the five people of six years ago, and of the strange twists of circumstances that we're bringing them all together again now. All, that was, except one. . . .

The plane banked, and Mel could feel it dropping, then straightening out again. Captain Rachmin came back from the forward compartment and moved along the row of forms hunched in the shadows. "Five minutes to touchdown," he told them. "Be ready to move."

Mel checked his pack, equipment, straps, weapons.

The plane landed on rough terrain, bounced, and lumbered to a lurching halt. Its loading ramp was down almost immediately, and the troops began untying the helicopter. Mel squeezed past them and walked down the ramp beneath the aircraft's tail. It was cold, and the sky clear but with no moon. While the helicopter was being rolled out and its rotor unfolded, he saw in the starlight that they were in a desolate valley with steep sides of broken rock and boulders that appeared ghostly white. Rachmin was talking with the commander of the party that had been dropped earlier. There had been no intrusions, and nothing had flown overhead. Everything was fine. Within a few minutes, the helicopter was ready to fly.

"I bet you didn't think you'd be joining the army when you got on that plane out of Boston," Dave's voice murmured next to him.

The C-130 would wait until the helicopter got back after putting down the ground force, and then fly out with the parachute team. It would return to send out the pickup helicopter the night after next.

The helicopter started smoothly, raising a cloud of white dust from among the rocks underfoot, and the ten-man team—the original nine, plus Mel—climbed in with their weapons and packs. It was a lot more cramped than the Hercules had been. More time dragged by, of darkness, vibration, and hypnotic engine noise. Another leg farther away from the familiar, all-electric world of city streets, warm houses, and people who wore clothes that were picked to look nice.

The flight into Syria lasted less than half an hour. The helicopter landed on crumbly, slatelike rock, and lifted off again as soon as the last man was on the ground. As Mel's eyes adjusted to the distance, he saw that they were in a depression between two ridges which converged toward a low peak dimly outlined against the sky. As the sound of the motor died away, an uncanny stillness descended, disturbed only by a faint wind. Mel had never felt so far away from everywhere in his life. While Rachmin and the other two squad leaders conferred briefly over maps and compasses in the light of a torch shaded by rocks and a cape, the others adjusted their packs and weapons and waited without talking, eyes and ears probing the surroundings. First priority would be to get clear of the drop zone as quickly as possible.

They moved out in single file, following the valley southeast, spaced well apart but not enough to lose contact in the dark—Ehud's squad leading, Zvi's next with Zvi in front, then Mel, then Dave, followed by Haim, a lance corporal, and finally Rafael's squad bringing up the rear. The pace was brisk but not grueling. The Israelis seemed to glide effortlessly over the broken ground, making no sound other than the occasional crunch of a rock being squeezed down against another. Every time Mel kicked a loose stone and sent it clattering a few inches, it sounded to him like an avalanche.

They edged gradually toward the ridge on the left, and then angled upward toward its crest over steeply tilted rock slabs and crazily piled boulders, which caused his heels to rub in his boots. Then they crossed the ridge and went down the far slope, still bearing southward, which chaffed his toes. After another mile he was perspiring despite the chill, and his breathing felt labored. His big fear was that he would lose the faint shape constantly retreating at the limit of vision ahead, and then have to flounder helplessly, or worse still, take everyone behind him off in the wrong direction.

But gradually he got his second wind, and as the rhythm insinuated itself into his subconscious, his pace became firmer. Swinging a leg the way one would on a sidewalk was no good. Each foot had to be deliberately *planted*, in a smooth, catlike motion which in darkness combined the functions of feeling one's way and moving. Slowly he was getting the hang of it, at first having to consciously direct every step, but feeling it becoming more automatic with repetition. They climbed another slope, steeper this time, a treadmill of fine, deep dust that feet sank into and slid down almost as fast as he tried to push himself up. At the top they stopped for five minutes in a crevice between shattered rocks to empty bladders, wash the dust from their mouths with swigs from water bottles, unwrap chocolate, chew dates. Mel was surprised at how high they seemed to have climbed.

"I said you'd do okay," Fenner murmured as they shared a nut bar. "How d'you feel?"

Mel's teeth stood out against his blackened face as he grinned in the starlight. "Just fine."

That he'd probably have sore feet by morning—and certainly after the second night—he knew already; and there would be more than a little stiffness in places, too. Paratroopers were expected to go through far worse than this for weeks on end, and to arrive in a fit condition to fight. Mel wasn't sure at this stage if he'd arrive in a fit condition to ride a bicycle. But one fear had left him. He was going to make it.

A hand was shaking his shoulder. "Mohican, wake up." Sudden daylight. A sun-bronzed face beneath a woollen cap was staring down at him.

"Uh? . . . Waddisit? . . . " It took Mel a few seconds to

remember where he was. He shook his head and sat up. Zvi was squatted next to him. The others were asleep among the boulders in a cleft below a rock wall, huddled in capes and smocks, their packs strewn around them and weapons near at hand.

"Ten o'clock. Your turn to stand watch. Take the lower post above the cliff. Jacob will take the upper one. Haim and Meir will relieve you at noon."

Mel hauled himself to his feet, shivering and flexing his arms to get the circulation moving. His calves were cramping, and he could feel aches in his thighs and waist. "How is everything?"

"There is nothing to report. It has been quiet."

"Have a good sleep."

"That will be no problem."

Zvi took off the binoculars hanging at his neck and handed them to him. Mel took some chocolate from his pack to chew, a carton of orange juice, then picked up his Uzi and clambered down twenty feet over reddish, gritty rock to a niche behind two boulders, with a higher block behind. The position commanded a view of the approach to the bivouac along the ridge, without offering an outline against the sky. He rested the Uzi on the ledge of rock in front of him and blew into his hands and rubbed them together as he surveyed the surroundings.

The ridge rose gently away in front of him and slightly to his right, toward a rounded, barren summit about a mile away—an indifferent pile of shattered rock and tumbled boulders piled haphazardly on each other amid slides of pebble scree, that could have been a piece of the moon and have sat there just as changelessly for just as long.

He was looking along the side of the ridge, which plunged abruptly in a series of knobbly cliffs to a jumble of crags and house-size boulders several hundred feet below, on the upper slopes of a wide valley. Mel swallowed involuntarily as he looked at it. That was the direction they had come from last night. A detour around the ridge would have taken them too far off route, and so they had climbed the cliffs. He was glad they had done it in darkness. Looking at it now in daylight, he wasn't sure he would have tackled it with such determination had he known what he was doing. Brett's observation came to mind again: "Confidence is what you feel . . ." Best forgotten about, now, he decided.

Across the valley to his left, the hills were troubled and chaotic, seeming to bump against each other in constant strife to claw their way to the skyline, with the shadows of clouds rippling across them like waves of creeping scrub. Beyond, in the far distance, a more massive mountain broke free from foothills smothering its base and rose to a snowy summit feathered with clouds. As he looked and his senses attuned themselves to the emptiness and stillness stretching away from him in every direction, a profound feeling of the vastness of it all overcame him. It was difficult to believe that places like Boston, Los Angeles, Cairo, and Tel Aviv existed on the same planet. Stephanie was right. The earth wasn't overpopulated at all. Far from it. It was simply that people packed themselves by the million into tiny corners of it, and then lost the ability to see beyond the boundaries to their perceptions which they had created.

A movement caught his eye and made him turn his head. A lizard had emerged to see what was trespassing in its domain, and was looking at him inquisitively with one eye from a nearby rock. As he moved, it vanished into a crevice like a piece of trick photography—suddenly there, then gone. And then he noticed other movement. There were flies and slender black beetles; saffron and brown-speckled butterflies fidgeting among clumps of tough, leathery grass that he hadn't noticed before either. Suddenly there was life all around him: a cluster of pale yellow plants with spiky leaves; tiny violet flowers clinging to hairline cracks in the rocks, surrounded by moss; wild lavender frothing from a chink filled with sand; even the colorless thistles and brittle thornbushes, defiantly preserving themselves against the ravages of the sun and the wind. A shadow wrinkled its way across the folds in the rock, and he looked up to see a hawk spreading sail and rising on some invisible current of air.

He had visited the Grand Canyon with Eva once, in one of his pilgrimages to LA. She had never been there before, either. They had arrived late in the afternoon, intending to see what there was to see and then be on their way, but one look across it had been enough to cause them to check into a hotel. They'd got up early the next morning and walked down to the rim as the mists were clearing, before anyone was around . . . and just sat there, staring at it. It had taken him two hours just to comprehend what he was looking at. Then a bus had pulled up noisily behind them to digorge a noisy tour

group of Australians with cameras and cowboy hats. For five
minutes, at the most, they had chattered, jostled, formed up
in grinning lines to be photographed—facing the camera, not
the Canyon—drunk sodas . . . and then piled back inside
again and disappeared as suddenly as they had come, leaving
the silence to close again behind. Eight thousand miles, for
that? Mel had often thought. "Oh yes, and that's me and
George at the Grand Canyon." But it wasn't. They were never
there. They had never seen it.

And what of these hills and deserts that he was staring out
over now? History was being written in them that was old
before the white civilization existed, and they no doubt looked
much the same now as they had then. What did they think of
these men who came, snatched a few hours of sleep, and then
were gone? How much more was there to see and hear and
comprehend out there that he had no inkling of? Perhaps
there was something to mysticism after all—it was as good a
name for such a sensitivity as any other. He could see how men
invented their gods. Not the death-cult God, who was locked
up in gold-plated boxes and interred in dingy, tomblike
cathedrals. But gods of life and regeneration and perpetuation.
The same god as Eva's.

Solitude distorted time as well as distance. Noon arrived so
much sooner than he expected that he almost missed it. He
went back up to the bivouac to find that some of the others
were awake, sitting, conserving energy. Haim was already
moving off to the upper post to take over from Jacob. Meir was
munching a hot breakfast of tomatoes, beans, and pressed
meat from compo ration cans. "My watch?" he said as Mel sat
down.

"I guess so."

As Meir got up, he waved toward the mess tin on the stove,
sheltered between two rocks. "I fixed some for you too."

"Wonderful. Thanks." Mel set the Uzi aside and sat down,
rubbing his eyes with his fingers.

"How is it? Is anything happening?"

Mel stopped and stared over his hand as he considered the
question. But there was nothing else he could say. "It's quiet.
Everything's dead out there."

CHAPTER 62

The sun was getting low, turning the hills and peaks to the west into jagged silhouettes. It was the evening of January nineteen. Ehud's and Zvi's squads would be moving out in an hour, leaving Rafael and his two men to pick a landing zone and guide them to it on their return, which was scheduled to be two hours before dawn at the end of the next night. Mel had a blister on his right big toe, another on his heel, and a tender patch on his left ankle, and he spent some time padding them with Band-Aids. The bivouac was located high up, with the only approaches to it visible to a considerable distance from the two sentry posts, and normal nighttime discipline had been relaxed a little. After a day of following the example set by the lizards and lying among the rocks and soaking up the sun, the troops were rested and refreshed. There was more life and banter among them as they sat cleaning the dust out of their weapons and checking slides and catches, getting a last meal inside them of soup, cheese and biscuits, jam pudding, and coffee, and packing kit.

"Did you see any UFOs while you were on watch, Har?"

"You can laugh. They're up there. You'll see one day."

"Come on, let's be serious."

"We'll go to the stars one day, sure, but it will be spaceships that we build ourselves. We don't need little green men to take us there."

"I wish a UFO would drop some girls here. Think of what it would do for the place."

"Listen to him. One day out and he's horny already."

"The girls in Marseilles are supposed to be good, I'm told."

"What good is that to me? I don't have a dick that will reach to Marseilles."

"You don't? Really? Listening to you, I always thought you had."

"He told me that when they circumcised him it weighed two kilograms."

"That was because they threw the wrong piece away."

"I met an American girl in Tel Aviv in October. Did I ever tell you about her?"

"Only a hundred and twenty-seven times, I think."

"She was a nurse. . . ."

Ehud Rachmin came over and squatted down by Mel. "How is it going?"

"Pretty good."

"How are the feet?"

"I taped them up. They should be okay now."

"We have seven hours of march tonight, and the same back again tomorrow night. Do you think you're up to it?"

"I'll manage."

"You know, it wouldn't be too late to change the roster. You could remain here with Rafael's squad if you wish. Nobody would think any the less of you. You've done very well, especially getting up the cliff."

"Is that a polite order?"

"No. Just an offer."

Mel looked up and shook his head. "I was included because I might be useful to have around when you collect Mustapha, and especially if there's any problem getting him out. If I'm here at all, that's where I need to be. I'll be okay."

Ehud clapped him lightly on the shoulder and nodded. "Good man." He got up and moved away to join Zvi, who was checking the radio reception.

Meanwhile the talk had turned to America and its recent election.

"How do you feel about the Constitutionals, Mohican?" Jacob asked. "Are you for them?"

"Absolutely."

"So Henry Newell will do a lot of good, you think?" Meir said.

Dave Fenner, who was checking magazine clips nearby, saw no reason not to give Mel's image another boost. "Mohican has met him," he threw in. "I mean personally."

"Really?" Haim said. Everyone looked impressed.

"How was that?" Jacob asked.

Mel thought for a second, perplexed, and then said, "He was the one who sent me over here." The others smiled and accepted it as a polite way of telling them to mind their own business.

"I hear so much about prices and taxes and wages, but I'm still not sure what they're trying to do," Haim said. "How would you sum it up, so that someone like me understands it?"

"It's actually very simple," Mel answered. "People are better qualified to run their own lives than governments are. And if they're not, they soon will be if they're allowed to get some practice. In other words, individual freedom and free enterprise."

"I thought that leads to capitalist monopolies."

"If it does, then you don't have free enterprise. But the answer to too much private power isn't to have too much state power. Too much power concentrated anywhere is bad. Period. People don't want their lives planned and regulated to be efficient as if they were parts of machines. They want to feel they've done well by their own efforts. They might not have everything or be everything, but they like to be able to say, '*I* did it.'"

"You sound like a professional talker," Meir said. "You're in the wrong place here."

Mel shrugged. "I've already told you that. I live behind a desk."

Meir grinned at what had become a standard joke. "Oh yes, of course. And what do you do behind your desk?"

"I'm a lawyer."

"Right," Jacob said. "And you bring them to trial, and then you're the judge, and after that you're the executioner too, yes?"

Everyone laughed.

They moved out shortly after dusk, seven of them now, and descended the reverse slope of the ridge. Then came another ascent, not steep, but long and tiring. At first Mel's stiffness was worse than he had realized, and for a while his anxiety increased that perhaps his optimism had been misplaced. But after a couple of miles his muscles loosened up, and he fell into the rhythm again. The sore spots on his feet continued to nag, but at least he no longer had the sensation of them being rubbed raw and sticky in his socks. If he'd thought about it, he could have taped the vulnerable areas before leaving base, he reflected ruefully.

Now that the notion had had time to sink in, he could accept that Mustapha might be Brett. For over two months, ever since Stephanie had told him her story in Boston in early November, although they'd had immediate doubts that what had happened to Brett could have been accidental, they had accepted that he was dead. The brutal murder of Eva hadn't been a figment of anyone's imagination. It had brought home to them that they were dealing with people who didn't hesitate to kill, and the knowledge had skewed their thinking.

If it did turn out to be Brett, then another belief that Mel had been clinging to would have been vindicated, too. He had been unable to reconcile what he knew of Brett with a deliberate betrayal of the nation, and had remained convinced that Brett must have been tricked into it somehow. And that appeared to be the case, for if Brett were a knowing ally of the Soviets, why would they have needed to kidnap him? This raised the further question of why they should have chosen to keep him at a remote Palestinian guerrilla base, when they presumably had plenty of more secure and convenient places of their own. The only thing Mel could think of was to make sure that he remained invisible, at least for a while, since he was supposed to be dead. But that would all be resolved shortly.

They stopped to rest for five minutes, silently, all senses alert now they were nearing the objective. When they resumed the march, the terrain became less broken, the hills bleaker and more rounded. The ground took on a more desertlike quality of stone embedded in hard-packed sand, making the going easier. An endless procession of scattered scrub and thorn plants passed by in the starlight. Then they began climbing again, toward a saddle between two hills rising away ahead into the darkness. Mel found that his mind detached and lost itself in its own thoughts while his body continued to probe ahead, move, and listen under its own reflexes. He lost his sense of time, and was surprised that so little of it seemed to have passed when Ehud called another halt in a small depression beneath a clump of boulders. There was a whispered exchange between him, Zvi, and Rafael, over the map, and then Ehud came over to where Mel was crouching with Dave Fenner and Haim. He informed them that Domino was in the valley that lay on the far side of the saddle.

They moved on for another twenty minutes, halting again when they reached the saddle crest. The far side of the saddle

looked down from a line of low hills over shallow slopes
receding to the south. There were lights in the darkness
below. Beyond the lights was the black outline of another
ridgeline, and to the left, just gloom. Mel found it impossible
to judge the distance. Ehud said that the camp was a little over
three miles away, and six hundred feet below them. The
airstrip was located beyond the camp, on the far side of the
ridge. That was where he and C Squad would have to get to by
daybreak.

They set off again, moving westward to the right, following
the hill line and maintaining their height. After about thirty
minutes they found a suitable place for "Point Purple," which
was where B Squad—Zvi, Haim, Dave, and Mel—who would
meet Pierrot and Mustapha, would lie up for the day. It was a
small hollow with a reverse slope fringed by a natural parapet
of rocks to conceal it from direction of the camp, with the mass
of the hill rising to a summit behind. A rock slab that had fallen
against another formed a natural recess at the back of the
hollow, promising shade as the day warmed up, and cover
from above, in the event that anything from the airstrip passed
too close.

There was a final conference to run through the procedure
one last time, confirm map references and passwords, and
synchronize watches. Then Ehud and his two men slipped
away into the darkness. According to the plan they would not
be seen again until the predawn hours of the next morning, at
the rendezvous with Rafael's group for the helicopter pickup.

The rest of them stayed awake until dawn to get an early
view of the surroundings. As the first light crept down from the
ridgelines and across the valley, it uncovered the camp, lying
at the bottom of gentle, undulating slopes of scattered rocks
and withering thornbushes below them. The ridge behind it,
which in the dark and been just an indistinct black mass, was
revealed as an abrupt insurrection of red rocky crags and
crumbling cliff faces, marching down and nearer from hills
away to the left to form a backdrop to the camp. Past the camp
to the right, the ridge ended in a spur, jutting out onto a plain
carved into irregular blocks by deep, dried-up watercourses.

Through binoculars, Mel could see the camp buildings and
huts behind the wire perimeter fence, guards at the gate, and
a truck bumping its way along a dusty road that followed the
foot of the ridge away into the distance. There was another
track, too, leaving the camp in the opposite direction to go

around the spur, into the valley behind, where the end of the airstrip itself was visible. He followed one of the deeper gullies and found the point where the track disappeared down into a fold in the ground, with a glimpse of the first couple of oil drums painted white to mark the bends. Down there would be the bridge underneath which they were to meet Pierrot and Mustapha.

Mel didn't do any musing over nature and mysticism in his spell of watch that morning. Now he had seen the objective, he was tensed up and restless to go. He had the feeling that today was going to be a long one.

CHAPTER 63

Lying prone in a rock crevice high on the spur overlooking the airstrip from the north, Captain Ehud Rachmin murmured into a tiny, voice-activated tape recorder clipped to his collar in front of his mouth. "The large structure at the far end of the strip is an aircraft hangar. It's bigger than was previously thought, because the back is dug into the hillside. The doors are partly open, and the nose of an aircraft is visible inside. Estimated size of doors, sixty meters wide, fifteen meters high. There is a tractor outside, and two trucks. The huts immediately to the north appear to be workshops. The constructions five hundred meters to the east consist of pipes and machinery underneath camouflage nets. My guess is that it is a pumping point for fuel tanks buried underground."

He lowered the binoculars from his eyes, while beside him, Jacob completed the series of pictures that he had been snapping. "Seventeen through thirty-eight," Jacob murmured.

Rachmin turned his mouth toward the recorder again. "Series two, frames seventeen through thirty-eight refer, taken from approximately one and a half kilometers. Reference alpha-romeo-six-two-five, oh-eight-oh-nine hours, January twenty. Now moving down the slope and closer, to view from point Echo Three." He flipped it off. "Ready?"

"Just a couple of seconds." Jacob added a few final details

and notes to the map he had sketched and returned the pad to the chest pocket of his smock. "Okay."

Rachmin turned on his side and looked over his shoulder at the scarp above and behind them, where Moshe was positioned with an Armalite. Moshe signaled frantically for them to stay down. Ehud tapped Jacob sharply on the shoulder. "Don't move."

"What?"

"Moshe has seen something." Ehud read the hand signals: seventy degrees to their left, a little below them, three hundred meters. He raised his head cautiously behind a rock and scanned through his binoculars in the direction indicated. It was no good. Whatever Moshe was indicating was in dead ground from where they were, hidden by a rib of rock. He would have to get onto the rib to see down the other side of it. He signaled his intention up to Moshe. "Stay here," he muttered to Jacob. "There's something over those rocks. Cover me while I take a look."

Lodging the binoculars inside the neck of his smock and taking up his Uzi, he rolled over the lip of the crevice into the cover of a sand gully, and from there wormed his way on his stomach across to the rib. Then, very carefully, he moved up to a gap between two rocks from where he could look down the other side, and raised his head. They were not alone, it appeared. There were two other figures down there, also armed, and observing the airstrip from behind cover. Ehud brought his binoculars out for a better view of them.

Their weapons were AKS74 assault rifles, the Soviet replacement for the AK47M. The caps with ear flaps were standard Soviet pattern, and so were the parkas. He identified details of the packs, boots, webbing, and a patch just visible on the shoulder tab of one of them. He watched them for a while, then retraced his path cautiously to where Jacob had been watching.

"What is it?" Jacob asked as Ehud rolled noiselessly back into the crevice.

"We have company, two of them."

"Who?"

Ehud frowned to himself for a moment before answering. "I'm certain they're Russians."

"What are they doing?"

"From the look of it, the same as us." Ehud's face took on a puzzled, faraway look.

"What are you thinking?" Jacob asked.

Ehud looked at him. "Doesn't something strike you as very odd?"

"What?"

"This is supposed to be a PALP base. The Soviets back and train PALP. Why should they be hiding from them?"

Jacob chewed his lip, then nodded. "I see what you mean. Yes, it is very odd. . . . What do you make of it?"

"I don't know," Ehud confessed.

There was a silence. Eventually Jacob said, "There's only one person around here who seems to know what's really going on."

"You mean Mohican?"

"Yes." Jacob waited for a few seconds. When Ehud didn't respond, he went on. "One of us could go back to Purple and tell him the situation. Let's see what he makes of it."

Ehud considered the possibility but didn't seem to like it. "It's an hour away. Then it would be another hour at the least before anyone could get back here." He indicated the direction of the rib with a nod of his head. "And I can't believe that those two aren't part of a larger force. They won't sit there obligingly for two hours and wait for us."

Jacob looked at him suspiciously. "What do you mean, Ehud? What's going through your mind?"

Ehud shrugged. "Those Russians are who ought to be talking to Mohican. They could make a lot more sense about why they're out here than I could right now. So let's grab them and take them back to him."

"Grab them?"

"Why not? It's three to two right now, and surprise is with us. But that could change at any time. I say we do it now, while we've got the odds."

The introduction of unducted-fan engines in the mid-nineties had reduced the fuel costs of commercial flying by almost 30 percent. One result was an increase in the number of nonstop flights being offered over longer ranges. This had been particularly true among the nations aligned with the Soviet bloc, who had taken advantage of the improved economics to establish more direct links between them.

"Good morning ladies and gentlemen. We'd now like to begin boarding Syrian Arab Airlines Flight twenty-eight, nonstop service to Havana. Would anyone who needs extra time to board the aircraft come to the gate now, please. . . ."

A stir rippled through the departure lounge at Damascus Airport as the passengers who had been waiting closed books and magazines, stood up to put on coats, and collected together cabin bags and children. Among the first-class passengers at the gate was a tall, middle-aged, sophisticated-looking man with white hair, wearing a navy blazer, who was accompanied by a fashionably dressed woman in a white hat. The man smiled at the attendant as he presented their boarding passes, and wished her a cordial good morning. The attendant returned the smile, and they passed through.

Sitting out in the lounge, waiting their turn, were two men in their late twenties, both swarthy-skinned, dark-haired, and wearing light, waist-length jackets and blue jeans.

Back at the security checkpoint, a man with a mustache, wearing a tan cord jacket and open-neck maroon shirt, was stopped at the machine where carry-on bags were being X-rayed. "I'm sorry, sir, but there's something in there that we can't see through at all. Would you open the bag, please?"

The man smiled sheepishly. "Oh, of course, my disk. I forgot." He unzipped the bag and exposed a large, gray metal object, about the size of a shoe box, with electrical connectors and a power cord.

The security guard stared at it nonplussed. "What's that?"

"It's a computer hard-disk—pretty ancient, but it works. There's delicate machinery inside. I didn't want to risk it being thrown around."

"What does it do?"

"You connect it to a computer. It stores data, like a tape. . . . I'm an author. That's what I write my material into."

"Can you open it?"

"Open it? I wouldn't know how to. Look, it's all screwed together. You'd ruin it."

The guard made a sign, and a supervisor ambled across. "He says it connects to a computer. It's bolted everywhere."

The man in the cord jacket was starting to look worried. "Hey, look, I mean, I've got almost a year's work inside that thing. If you—"

"That's all right," the supervisor said. "Those are standard." He nodded and waved the man on.

"Gee, thanks. I think my flight's boarding."

"Have a good trip."

Two girls were giggling over something as they waited to pass through the metal-detector frame. "Next please," the guard said to hurry them.

The first of them handed a ring of keys and a belt with a heavy metal buckle to the guard, then walked through without incident. The guard returned the items. The second girl handed the guard a large, sealed tin of dates and passed through also. They walked on to the gate, still laughing and giggling.

As the boarding process continued, the passengers who had shopped in the duty-free store stopped to pick up their purchases, which had been brought out for collection at the jetway in stapled plastic bags. The bags had not passed through a security check between the store and the aircraft. One of the passengers picking up the bags was a man wearing an Iraqi Air Force uniform. The bag that he picked up was different from the others, however. It didn't contain anything that had been bought at the duty-free store.

Men in dark coveralls slid the hangar doors completely open and hitched a tractor to the nosewheel gear of the aircraft inside. Major Yuri Brazhnikov watched through field glasses as the tractor slowly hauled the plane out fully into view. He lowered the glasses and stared over the top of them, not knowing what to make of it. The aircraft was a regular Soviet Ilyushin commercial jet, painted in Syrian Arab Airlines colors.

"What the hell is one of their planes doing here?" Leo Dorkiev breathed, lying beside him.

Brazhnikov shook his head. "I don't know." He thought for a moment. "Maybe it's a cover. That could be how they're going to get the missiles out. But it seems a needlessly elaborate way of doing it."

"Then we're too late. That baby's ready to go. Look, there's already a flight crew in the cockpit."

Brazhnikov snapped a series of photographs while the tractor hauled the plane clear of the doors and was decoupled, and Dorkiev made notes of its markings and registration code, SY4362F.

If this was the missiles or the missile parts being shipped out, then as Dorkiev had said, they were too late, Brazhnikov thought bitterly. The strike force that had been assembled to fly in and snatch them was still sitting at alert in the VDV base in Armenia. All he could really do was get back to the post farther along the ridge where they had left Maitsky and Gorvorin with the radio, and get an update on the situation off to Chelenko in Damascus. Just as he was thinking this, the engines of the Ilyushin roared into life, and the aircraft began moving forward under its own power, lining itself up with the center of the runway.

"That's it," Dorkiev muttered. "It's away already. They're not wasting any time."

The sound of the engines rose, and the plane began moving slowly, then gathering speed toward them, lifting off just as it came opposite the point where they were concealed. Its undercarriage retracted, and it banked to port in a turning climb toward the west. There was something very unusual about this, Brazhnikov thought to himself as he watched it disappear over the skyline. If the Palestinians were supposed to be on the Soviet side, why were they cooperating in stealing Soviet missiles for the West? Dorkiev noticed the puzzled look on his face. "What is it?" he asked.

The aircraft's taking off had provided the perfect diversion for Ehud and Jacob to move. Before Brazhnikov could reply, a voice from somewhere nearby called out in Russian, "Freeze! You are covered by machine guns and surrounded." The voice was low but sufficient to carry.

Dorkiev looked wide-eyed to Brazhnikov, who had rolled back to look over his shoulder. Whoever was talking was out of sight. But from an outcrop of rock overlooking them from behind, a figure in a soft cap and khaki smock was training a gun on them and allowing itself to be seen deliberately. There could have been a dozen more, easily, hidden up there. The voice nearer them called, "Raise your hands very slowly, away from your weapons." They were caught cold. Trying anything sudden would be out of the question. "We will fire on the count of three," the voice warned. Brazhnikov gave Dorkiev a quick nod. They raised their hands and sat up. "Don't turn around. Keep looking forward. Now, you to the left, with one hand only, throw your gun well clear and to the back of you. . . . Now your pistol. . . . You on the right, do the same. . . . The pistol. . . . Now remain as you are and don't move."

There was a movement close by, then the sound of somebody slithering down over the rocks, followed by a couple of footsteps immediately behind him. A hand frisked Brazhnikov expertly, found his knife and removed it, then did the same to Dorkiev. "Okay, you can turn."

Brazhnikov sat up and turned around to find himself looking at an Israeli paratrooper. The Israeli had picked up both their rifles and backed off a few feet to cover them with the Uzi he was holding in his other hand. Another Israeli was covering them from a mound slightly farther back. The first nodded toward Dorkiev. "Stay low and out of sight from below. You see where he is up there? Okay, we go that way. Move." When Dorkiev had moved up to become the charge of the second Israeli, the first one nodded at Brazhnikov. "Now you. I'll be right behind."

The Israelis shepherded them up to the outcrop where the one that Brazhnikov had seen first was stationed. Then, still making use of cover, they moved away around the tip of the spur, toward the valley where the Palestinian camp was. To his surprise and chagrin, Brazhnikov realized that there were only the three Israelis. There had never been any machine guns.

They crossed the plain beyond the end of the spur, keeping to the gullies to stay out of sight from the camp and following a course that curved round and to the north, well clear of its vicinity. When it became apparent that the Russians were not going to try anything foolish, the Israelis relaxed a little and the tension eased.

"Where are we going?" Brazhnikov asked the swarthy, blue-eyed one who seemed to be in charge.

"You'll see. We just want you to talk to someone."

"You wouldn't have gotten away with it so easily if we'd known there were only the three of you."

"Well, that doesn't matter now, does it, because we've got the guns and you haven't."

CHAPTER 64

Aboard Syrian Arab Airlines Flight 28, a half hour out from Damascus, bound for Cuba, the man in the Iraqi Air Force uniform reached down into the duty-free-purchase bag by his feet. He drew out a flat package wrapped in plain white paper and transferred it to his jacket pocket. Then he closed the bag again, picked it up from the floor, and turned to the woman in the seat next to him, who was dozing. "Excuse me. Could I get out, please?" She opened her eyes and stood up to let him pass. He smiled apologetically. "I'm sorry to disturb you."

"That's all right."

He went forward and passed the row where the two girls were sitting who had laughed as they passed through the airport security check. The one who had handed the tin of dates to the attendant was sitting with a blanket wrapped around her knees. Underneath the blanket, she had broken the seal of the tin, lifted out the shallow tray of dates, and passed one of the two 9mm automatics that had been hidden below it to her companion, retaining the other for herself.

The man in the Iraqi uniform went into the first-class compartment and handed the duty-free-purchase bag to the white-haired man in the navy blazer, sitting with the well-dressed woman. "I might as well give this to you now," he said.

"Yes, thank you. Did you find the ones I wanted? . . ."

While they continued a casual conversation, the author in the tan cord jacket, who had been seated in the smoking section, went into one of the lavatories at the rear of the aircraft and locked the door. Above the sink was a small closet where additional stocks of paper towels were stored. He opened the door and placed beneath the towels two of the three automatics that had been concealed inside the computer disk-drive case. Then he waited for a few minutes, rinsed his face and combed his hair, and returned to his seat. A few minutes later, one of the two swarthy men in jeans used the same lavatory and retrieved the guns, concealing one inside his jacket and folding the other in a magazine. When he came out, his companion had also left his seat, and the magazine changed hands in a second when they met midway along the aircraft at one of the cross-aisles. Farther forward, the two girls were also out of their seats, one visiting a forward toilet, the other rummaging in an overhead bin. Thus, when the man in the Iraqi Air Force uniform finally left the couple in first class, there were six armed people on their feet at strategic points along the aircraft, and two more immediately aft of the flight deck.

The takeover went so smoothly and quickly that the silver-haired man in the blazer was inside the cockpit with his pistol leveled before most of the passengers even realized what was happening. He waved the radio engineer away from his panel and settled himself into the seat, while his female companion covered from the door. There were some screams and one or two shouts of indignation back in the passenger cabin, but nobody tried to be a hero. As what was happening dawned on the rest of the passengers, the other hijackers ordered the cabin crew to sit down and began moving the men into the window seats and the women and children to the seats by the aisles.

The man in the navy blazer smiled amiably as he tuned to a frequency in the local band and drew the hand mike across. "I'm pleased that you're behaving sensibly," he said to the flight-deck crew. "There really isn't any need for unpleasantness." He spoke into the microphone. "Caliph calling Trojan. Trojan do you read?"

A voice answered at once from the panel speaker. "Trojan, roger."

"Advise squawk, over."

"Our squawk is alpha-four-six-five, repeat, four-six-five."

It sounded clear enough to be very near at hand, the captain was thinking—maybe it was the Jordanian training flight that traffic control had just warned him to keep an eye out for because it was getting too close.

The man in the navy blazer leaned forward to read the transponder code that traffic control had assigned to the Syrian plane. "Squawk here is alpha two-two-six," he said into the microphone. "Repeat, two-two-six. Changing setting now." He reached forward and changed the number to the other aircraft's.

"Setting clocks to count of ten. Synchronize on zero," the voice said over the speaker.

"Roger."

"Starting count at ten, nine . . ."

"And don't try changing it," the man in the blazer warned the captain. Quietly changing the setting to send back the wrong identification code was the standard way of indicating that a plane had been hijacked.

". . . two, one, zero."

The man in the blazer pressed a button on the transponder. The two aircraft had now switched identities. Upon interrogation, each would return to traffic-control radars the transponder identification code that had been assigned to the other.

"Trojan set, over."

"What are your flight directions, Trojan?"

"Heading nine-zero, descend to flight level one-zero-zero."

"Roger, over."

"Proceed as directed, Caliph. Over and out."

The man in the blazer gestured toward the navigation panel with his gun. "Now, set your nav VHF1 to one-two-eight decimal six, and nav VHF2 to five-zero-five decimal nine," he told the captain. "Turn onto a heading of zero-nine-zero and reduce height to flight level one-zero-zero."

"Where are we going?" the captain asked resignedly.

"Oh, not that far really. I hope you didn't have any swimming planned for this evening. You won't be seeing Cuba today, I'm afraid."

Commercial jets have no rear view at all. As the Ilyushin banked and came around onto an easterly heading, the captain was surprised to see that the other aircraft had been close behind them. But far from being a Jordanian Air Force trainer, it was another Ilyushin of the same type, and also with Syrian Arab Airline markings. As the SAL flight turned away, the other aircraft continued on the northwesterly course that would take it over Turkey and the Balkans, across central Europe, and out over the North Atlantic.

On a radar screen in the sector air traffic control center at Nicosia, the two sets of flashing dots and associated flight-data flags that had merged together over the sea to the north of Cyprus separated again, the Syrian commercial flight continuing on course, and the Jordanian military plane turning toward the east. A few seconds later the flashing alert for an imminent conflict situation ceased. The controller who had been following the encounter breathed easily again and turned his attention to other tasks. Very probably, neither of the pilots would file an air-miss report. They never did. Too much trouble. But it would be everybody else's fault, as usual, when one of them did blow it one day.

Mel stood at the bottom of the shallow hollow that had been designated point Purple, staring at the cave beneath the fallen slab where the packs and equipment were stacked, trying to make sense of the situation. Dave was a few paces behind, equally bemused, and Ehud nearby keeping silent, letting them think. Haim and Moshe were standing watch on the rocky lip of the hollow, while Zvi and Jacob kept an eye on the two Russians, who were sitting with their backs to a rock. Mel's first attempt to elicit any information from them, using Ehud as interpreter, had met with total noncooperation.

Something was tugging at the fringes of his awareness, screaming to be recognized, but he couldn't pin it down. There was something that didn't fit, something so obvious and fundamental that nobody had thought to question it. He tried to analyze his own structure of beliefs about what he thought was true and separate it into its assumptions and deductions. The deductions, he was fairly happy about. He had gone through them a thousand times, both in his own mind and with others, and he could find no flaw. The problem had something to do with the assumptions. He found himself thinking that this could turn out to be the most important case he had ever handled.

He forced his thinking processes back to their basics and went through the chain again. Why didn't Ehud's account of how they had found the two Russians make sense? Because the Russians had been operating covertly. Why was that strange? Because this was PALP country, and the Soviets ran PALP. Why should they be clandestinely spying on their own operation?

Okay, he thought to himself, back up a step further. How did they know it was a Soviet operation? Because Brett had been tricked by Oberwald into working for them, and then kidnapped by them when he tried to get out. And the Soviets had killed Eva, thinking she was Stephanie, to protect what they'd thought she knew. Very well, then, how did they know that Oberwald was in with the Soviets? Well, it was obvious. . . .

A professional reflex pulled him up sharply, right there—as soon as he found himself about to dismiss something out of hand because it was too obvious. How did they *know* that Oberwald was involved in a Soviet espionage ring?

It was simple: Who else would want to know about U.S. strategic space defense secrets? *No!* he told himself. A simple process of elimination like that didn't work. The logic was the same as claiming that a four-legged animal had to be a horse because you didn't know of any other kind. At that point he became aware of a rising feeling of discomfort that all of their thinking had been erring in precisely this way all along. Because previously they hadn't known of any other animal that was hostile to the Western way of life. And now there was another one that he knew of. When he examined the remaining evidence in that light, it turned out to be very flimsy. In fact there really wasn't any. Everything that they had taken as proof had been nothing more than their own preconceptions all along.

Stephanie had said that mail had arrived for Brett from the Western Peace Initiative, known to be a subsidiary of a KGB-managed propaganda front. But that had been *after* Brett disappeared—when he couldn't have disputed it. Anyone could have sent it. Not good enough to stand in court.

The FBI had come looking for Brett, Gilman had said. Didn't that say that Brett had been mixed up in something that threatened national security? Not necessarily. Again, anyone could have fed false leads to the FBI—especially someone with Oberwald's contacts. And once more, that had begun *after* Stephanie was supposed to be dead, and unable to refute any allegations of Brett's activities.

But PALP was run by the Soviets. Yes, *PALP* was. But that didn't make them the people who controlled this place. Dave Fenner had said that this camp was run by PALP. But that had been on the basis of information gathered through Mossad, and from American sources. Well, they could have been victims of deliberately planted misinformation too, just like the FBI.

Which brought them back to the only positive evidence available—the behavior of the Russian soldiers themselves. And they had been acting as if they had no more business there than the Israelis had.

In short, there wasn't one single hard fact to show that the people manipulating Brett had had anything to do with the Soviets at all. There was much, however, that was consistent with the idea of *somebody wanting to make it look like the Soviets*! . . . Such as choosing a Soviet client state to locate this base in, complete with a population of Palestinians as cover. . . .

A lot more things made sense, too, in that context. Of course Brett would have been brought here and not to somewhere more convenient in the Soviet Union—if the Soviets had nothing to do with it. And no wonder Pierrot hadn't been able to find out very much in the camp itself. The whole place was just camouflage for . . . for what? It could only be the airstrip.

All the pieces fitted. Mel couldn't yet make out the design

that they formed, but at least now it was free of contradictions. He was on the right track. But he would never get any further until he knew what the Soviets knew about that airstrip that he didn't. They each had half the key.

Meanwhile, Major Yuri Brazhnikov, sitting on the ground with Dorkiev under the watchful gaze of two Israelis with Uzis, was still wondering how he had stopped his shock from showing when they arrived here and he saw who it was they were being brought back to talk to. After weeks of seeing his photograph in the reports he'd studied in Moscow, and later in Damascus, he had recognized the American immediately. No wonder the agents in the U.S. had lost him without trace a week ago. Shears was here, in Syria!

Mel sighed, realizing that this wasn't going to get anyone anywhere. He came back to the others and drew Dave and Ehud to one side. "Look, I'm going to say something that probably sounds like heresy and violates everything about the way you've been trained to think. But these guys obviously know something that we don't, and I think it's crucial. I've also got a hunch that they don't know a lot that we do. Nothing's going to add up unless we put it all together, and somebody has to make a start."

"You mean you want to level with them?" Dave said.

Mel nodded. "Exactly." Dave winced.

"There are methods of field interrogation," Ehud said grimly. "If it's that important, we can get it out of them."

"That's not necessary," Mel said. "We'll have to hang on to them until tonight, anyway. Once Mustapha is out and we're ready to go, the only choices will be to let them go, take them with us, or shoot them. Whichever we pick, anything we've told them about what we know now will have ceased to matter."

Dave heaved a sigh and nodded. "Whatever you think's best. You seem to have a bigger picture than the one they told me. One day you and I are gonna have to do a lot of talking."

Mel looked at Ehud. "Are you asking me?" Ehud said.

"You're in command."

"Of the ground operation. This is politics. What Benjamin says is good enough for me, too. I'll support whatever you decide to do."

They went back over to the two Russians. From tags, insignia, and equipment, they had established that one was a lieutenant in the Soviet VDV, or Vozdushno-Desantnyye-

Voyska, airborne shock troops, from a specialist group known as the Vysotniki. The other, Nordic looking, with fair hair, was carrying credentials that identified him as a major of the KGB. Mel beckoned the latter to his feet and took him aside, again calling Ehud over as interpreter.

"What would you say if I were to tell you that I think we've both been set up?" Mel asked the Russian. "You thought this place was ours, and we thought it was yours. But obviously it's neither. Whatever's going on here, for once we're on the same side."

The major looked openly contemptuous. "I'd say it was a trick." Yes, he thought, sure they were on the same side. They both wanted to steal the same missiles. The only difference was that the Russians would be stealing them *back*, whereas the Americans wouldn't.

"What do you know of an American defense scientist who is being held in that camp down there?" Mel asked.

"Why should I know anything?"

"He was supposed to be passing information to your side."

"Are you trying to tell me that is why you are here?" the Russian asked.

Mel took a long breath. "Yes. Tonight we are getting him out."

Brazhnikov snorted. Lies. He knew full well why Shears was here, and why he had come all the way from the U.S.A. It was a line to find out why *they* were here. But as he thought about it, Brazhnikov grew less satisfied with that explanation. For if the presence here of the Israelis and the two Americans was connected with the missiles—whether or not the missiles had been flown out in the Syrian airliner—then they would know perfectly well why the Soviets were here. What would all the mystery be about?

"If what you say is true, then the Palestinians here would be controlled by us," Brazhnikov said.

"Yes," Mel agreed.

"But that is obviously not the case. If it were, we would be able to walk about the place openly, would we not? But we don't. Therefore what you say is not true. Therefore there is no scientist of yours down there."

"Unless he was being held by someone else," Mel said.

Brazhnikov shrugged. "If he exists, it is your problem, not mine."

"I'm not so sure."

"What do you mean?"

"Look at it this way," Mel said. "If *we* were wrong about who controls this place, *you* could be, too. And the only way either of us will get it right might be by knowing what the other knows. I can't put it plainer than that."

The Russian stared at him, obviously in a dilemma. Mel had nothing more to say. Ehud waited impassively, while Dave watched from a short distance back. The hardness in the Russian's eyes flickered for just a moment, and Mel thought he had gotten through. But before that spark could catch, Moshe's voice called from one of the guard positions at the rim of the hollow, "Aircraft approaching, heading directly this way." The distant drone of its engines reached them moments later.

They squeezed back under the cover of the rocks and motioned for the two Russians to do the same. The aircraft was a large one, coming over low from the northwest, an airliner. As it came nearer, the form resolved itself into an Ilyushin with Syrian Arab Airlines colors. "It's the one that took off earlier," Jacob said. The plane straightened into an approach, wheels and flaps down, and swept down and past them to their right, and touched down on the end of the strip just visible beyond the tip of the spur. The roar came of the engines reversing thrust to brake, and the note dropped.

Ehud checked something in the notepad that he had taken from the other Russian, and then looked up, puzzled. "No," he said. "It's not."

"What's not what?" Mel asked him.

Ehud nodded toward where the plane had just disappeared from view. "That plane's registration code was SY7719A. The one that took off this morning was SY4362F. It isn't the same one."

Dave shook his head, baffled. "Exactly what in hell is going on in this place?" he demanded.

"I don't know," Mel said. "But it's getting more and more mysterious."

CHAPTER 65

Major Yuri Brazhnikov of the KGB was getting weary of it. For over two hours the two Americans, Shears, who went by the name Mohican, and the one they called Benjamin, had been arguing relentlessly. The lawyer was the worst. In fact Brazhnikov had begun to suspect that perhaps he really might be a lawyer, and that whatever else he did was really his cover. He had saturated Brazhnikov with every tactic of logic, suggestion, and persuasion. At one point Brazhnikov had appealed to the blue-eyed Israeli paratrooper who was doing the interpreting, "Get on with the thorns under the fingernails or the cigarette lighter to the foreskin if you're going to. I can understand that—I'll even hold it for you. But get *him* off me!"

And yet, at the same time, there was something about this young American's quiet but impassioned sincerity that touched a sympathetic note somewhere. Brazhnikov had read that the new American administration was heralded as one of honesty and bluntness. This Shears seemed an embodiment of it. In other circumstances, at another time, perhaps they could have been close friends.

In the end, Brazhnikov agreed to something that "Benjamin" suggested. The Israelis had apparently been expecting an aircraft hijack, and it seemed evident that the business with the two Ilyushin aircraft was connected with it. That had been as mystifying to the Russians as it was to the others. Brazhnikov used the Israelis' radio to contact Chelenko in Damascus. They allowed him to send a short message giving the two aircraft identification codes and asking for details of their current whereabouts. The Israelis themselves had maintained a strict radio silence.

It was almost four in the afternoon when Zvi, who was crouched by the radio pack, called across to Ehud and Mel. "It's Hydro. We've got a reply." They brought Brazhnikov across from the cave, where he and Dorkiev had been given a

411

meal and some coffee. Ehud stood by with an automatic and Mel stood behind while the Russian squatted down next to Zvi.

"Hydro, this is Snowball One. We read you, over," Brazhnikov advised.

"Hello, Snowball." It sounded like Aram Kugav's voice. Chelenko was doubtless with him. "I have the information you requested."

"Go ahead, over."

"SY7719A is the registration of an Ilyushin 127 of the Syrian Arab Airline fleet. It is currently flying as flight two-eight, Damascus to Havana, which departed at ten hundred hours today. SY4362F is a nonexistent registration."

"Thank you, Hydro."

Another voice came on, more guttural. "Hydro One here." That was Chelenko's personal call-sign. "What is going on there? Where are you? Snowball Four has been reporting that—" Ehud leaned forward and switched off the set.

Brazhnikov sat back and looked inquiringly up at his captors. "Well, what now?"

Mel sat down opposite him and looked at him earnestly. "Think about what this means. Your people have just said that 7719A is on its way to Cuba. But we know it isn't. It landed here almost six hours ago. An aircraft belonging to the state airline of one of the Soviet Union's allies has been hijacked, and the world doesn't know about it yet. Whatever's going on can hardly be in your country's interests, can it? But if it was supposed to be in our interests, we'd already have known about it, surely. I put it to you again, Major, other things may be as they may, but on this issue we both stand to lose. Your silence is only helping *them*, whoever they are. It's not helping you, me, America, or the Soviet Union."

Brazhnikov looked at him. Again he found himself wanting to believe. Zvi looked at his watch and then at Ehud. "It's getting on," he said. "We should decide who's going down to meet Pierrot." With the captives to take care of, the original schedule would have to be modified.

"I think just you and Haim, with Benjamin," Ehud said.

"So you really have come to collect a scientist?" Brazhnikov said. "You were serious."

"I've never been more serious," Mel told him.

Brazhnikov drew a long breath deep into his chest, held it for a few seconds, and then exhaled it sharply. "We have information that certain missing airframes and components have found their way to this location to construct two complete SA–37 air-launched missiles, complete with low-yield nuclear warheads," he said. "Our mission here is to reconnoiter for a possible assault to seize them back again. I assumed that the Americans were behind it, and that you are here for the same reason." The astonishment on Mel's face told him all that he needed to know about how correct that assumption had been.

"What made you think we were mixed up in it?" Mel asked.

"Well, wouldn't the Americans be the first people one would suspect of wanting a working Soviet missile?" Brazhnikov looked at him, hesitated for a moment, and then allowed himself to smile. "And besides, we know something about the circles you move in . . . Mr. Melvin Shears, lawyer from Boston."

Possibly an indiscretion, Brazhnikov conceded inwardly; but the look on Mohican's face was worth it. So was that on the Israeli's as he translated.

Ehud, watching, took in what was happening and motioned to Zvi. He indicated the two Russian soldiers with a nod of his head. "Return their weapons to them, Zvi," he said quietly. And then to Brazhnikov, "I take it you have others here."

"There are four more," Brazhnikov said. "They're probably wondering what the hell has happened to us."

"And they have a radio?"

"Yes."

Zvi came over and handed the two Russians their assault rifles, sidearms, and other items. "Zvi," Ehud said to him. "Let the major use the radio to contact the rest of his unit. Make it brief. Give them the map reference of Purple. They can make their way here."

While over to the side, Dave Fenner turned toward Mel, ashen-faced. "I've just realized what day this is," he whispered.

Brett was by now accepted as a regular at the Saturday evening movie show, without having to fix anything or give English lessons to earn it—although he still did such things, partly to break the monotony and partly because he had no particular reason not to.

Tonight, he was even less interested in the offering than usual, as he sat near the door at the back, where Hamashad had placed him. It was an appallingly amateurish Indian romance set in the days of the British Raj, with the hero a prototype mix of every revolutionary hero from Lenin to Ché; with a strong, incongruous dose of Gandhi, and the British recognizable as the bad guys everywhere by virtue of their inferior barbers and launderers. But the worse the movies, the more the audience seemed to enjoy them, and the noisy enthusiasm abounding tonight was just what Brett wanted. The day had passed agonizingly as he waited for dusk, his tension mounting as hour dragged after endless hour. He had stood for much of the time at the window of his quarters, staring out at the desert. It was a strange feeling to think that the Israelis were out there somewhere, watching the camp invisibly; that they had come this far and were out there because of him.

It was well after six when Hamashad returned and whispered something in the ear of the guard who was at the back with Brett. The guard nodded and disappeared out the door. Hamashad looked quickly around, then waved Brett quickly toward the door. Brett slipped out as smoothly and with as little fuss as that. They went quickly through the canteen area adjoining, to some store rooms along a corridor by the kitchens. It was dark outside, and the truck that was due to go up to the airstrip was parked near the door. It had been a busy day for some reason, with more traffic than usual making the trip. Hamashad said that large quantities of food had been taken up there, including one shipment consisting of nothing but crates of soft drinks. He had speculated jokingly that perhaps the government was going to open a supermarket there. "It would be typical socialist economic planning!"

Brett stood inside the door, with the truck just a few feet away outside. Again, everything was quick and simple. Hamashad came out of another door and said something to the two Palestinians who were loading the truck, drawing them around to the other side. Then Brett came out, ducked underneath the vehicle, and lodged himself up on top of the rear axle housing and transmission shaft. The truck was fitted with high suspension for desert duty, and there was adequate room even for someone of his size. Now there was nothing to do but wait. Hamashad would report him as being back in his quarters after the movie, which meant it would be daybreak before he was missed. But by that time he hoped to be airborne and on his way to Israel.

* * *

In Washington, D.C., the time was approaching 11:30 A.M. It was a fine, if cool, day, and because of the significance of this, the accession to office of the first administration of the new millenium, and especially with the slow realization that was dawning on the public of exactly what the new philosophy of government was going to mean, the capital had drawn a larger than usual crowd for the inauguration ceremony, due to take place at 1:00. While final preparations were being made for the parade, and officials buzzed importantly this way and that on last-minute errands, many people were already milling around below the Capitol steps, and scores of senators and representatives were already in evidence.

Among the people who had made a special effort to come to Washington for the event were Robert Winthram and William Evron. Over the years they had worked in their own way to uphold principles that made civilization worthwhile, and in that way had contributed to the outcome that was being made visible today. It hadn't been a revolution of bombs and bullets, or mob riots, or liquidations; but it had been a revolution, nevertheless, and perhaps a more meaningful one for those very reasons. For it had been a revolution in the name of reason, fought, not by demagogues thirsting for power, but by those who would renounce power in order that it revert to where it rightfully belonged. How well it would be used now would depend on the people. It was an astonishing expression of confidence and trust, and it seemed appropriate for the two men to be here today to see their faith in the ultimate decency of humanity being vindicated.

Also from Boston in the crowd was Alan Dray, from Platek, whose patents were attracting interest from all kinds of unlikely investors now that the state Compliance Board had backed down—guesses were that it wouldn't be around for much longer; his legal difficulties seemed to be abating, and business prospects improved.

And Ed Gilman was there from Denver. His woes hadn't gone away yet. Financial backing for the fission-fusion project was still being blocked, but now that he knew the real opposition was political, and the technical and economic objections a sham for public and media consumption, he had hopes that the situation would improve rapidly once the new administration got itself fully in gear.

The Constitutional representatives and senators who had

flooded Congress over the previous six years were all here, naturally. The president and his entire cabinet, of course. And so, almost to the last one, were the thousands from the state-level legislatures who had taken the Constitutional philosophy out to the nation, and who would spearhead the call for a convention to pass the new amendment as one of the new government's first official tasks. It wouldn't have been true to say that the entire body of the Constitutional organism was here, for it was too vast; but its head and its motivating force was. What drove it and inspired it was gathered in one place for the first time ever. Deprived of what was concentrated in Washington today, the rest of what had taken years to nurture and grow would quickly disintegrate, wither, and die forever. It would never be rebuilt.

Syrian Arab Airlines Flight 28, by that time flying southwest, a few hundred miles off Nova Scotia, Canada, reported a fault indication in one engine. The captain requested a revised flight plan, closer to land, in case he had to put down in an emergency. It was standard procedure in such circumstances, and Air Traffic Control at Halifax complied. The plane's new course would take it virtually down the eastern seaboard of the U.S.A.

CHAPTER 66

Brett was through the main gate and out of the camp. The road was bumpy and littered with rocks, and the lurching and pounding threatened to throw him off at every yard to be crushed beneath the truck's doubled rear wheels. The axle box and transmission-shaft casing were slippery with grease, and there seemed to be nuts, bolt heads, and sharp edges everywhere, cutting and bruising him whichever way he tried to twist as he fought to keep a grip. He should have thought to equip himself with some pieces of rope for improvising slings to hang onto, he told himself belatedly. Yet despite the discomfort, he had to concentrate on counting off the sequence of left and right bends that Hamashad had described. The trouble was that the truck swerved so much to navigate between the bumps and depressions that he had difficulty telling just where the bends were.

At last, if he had counted correctly, the truck reached the straight stretch after which there would be one left-hand turn, followed after a short distance by a right-hand one, which would be the start of the drop down to the bridge where he was to jump off. He readied himself. And then lights appeared behind. He turned his upper body painfully to peer back beneath the tailboard, and something missed in his chest. There were headlights behind them, gaining fast. He lost them as the truck entered the left-hand bend, three hundred yards from the bridge. But as the truck straightened out, the lights emerged from the bend immediately behind it. They flashed several times, signaling urgency, and there was a series of blasts from the vehicle's horn. Brett felt the truck slow down, and then it pulled over. His impulse was to drop down and make a break for it, but he fought it down. It would have been hopeless—he would have come out fully in the glare of the headlights of the vehicle behind.

But the vehicle didn't stop. It bounced on by amid dust and flying stones—something small, like a jeep with a canvas top, Brett saw as it passed through the lights from the truck. It wasn't somebody from the camp coming after them, but simply someone in a hurry. The truck pulled out again and continued on its way.

It came to the sharp turn and the dip down, then made a turn the other way to cross the ravine. Brett braced himself, ready. The wheels made a hollow sound as the truck crossed the bridge, and then the truck ground almost to a halt as it came to the steep upward bend and the driver slammed into bottom gear.

Now!

Brett launched himself downward and as far sideways as he could, bumped and scraped himself on the ground, and without daring to hesitate a moment, rolled clear, pulling his arms in tightly just as the wheels began turning again. And then the truck had gone. Brett lay motionless, listening as it ground its way up the turns out of the ravine, then changing to a higher gear and receding. Gradually, the quiet of the night asserted itself. He sat up, waited, listening for a few seconds, then got to his feet and walked back to the end of the bridge.

He lowered himself down into the darkness beneath it and huddled himself up against one of the concrete supporting piers to wait.

He didn't hear anyone approaching, but sooner than he had expected, a voice from along the gully called his name softly—there had been no reason for using pseudonyms in the camp. "Here," he replied. There was a scuffling, and Hamashad materialized beside him.

"Any problems?" Hamashad whispered.

"No. Everything went okay. Just a lot of bruises. How about inside?"

"Everything went as planned. You are officially locked up for the night."

"Great."

Having two groups blundering about in this terrain trying to find each other in the dark would have been asking for trouble. The Israelis were due to collect them right here. And just a few seconds after Hamashad arrived, a voice from the other direction, but surprisingly close, murmured "Bluejay," which was the challenge that Hamashad had given Brett to use if Hamashad failed to appear for any reason.

Hamashad called back "Redfish" in a stage whisper, and three figures that must have been there all the time detached themselves from the shadows and joined them.

"Is everything okay?" one of them inquired.

"Fine," Hamashad said. "I'm Pierrot. This is Mustapha."

"You've gone to a lot of trouble," Brett muttered.

"We must move quickly. A lot is happening. My name is Zvi. This is Haim, that is Benjamin."

Brett nodded in the darkness. "Hi."

The third figure, the one who had been called Benjamin, peered closely at Brett, as if straining to make out his features in the weak light. Then he said, "You'll never guess who else I am." The voice was American."

Inside the KGB residency at the Soviet embassy at Damascus, Lieutenant Colonel Sergei Chelenko was troubled and suspicious. Something had gone very wrong with the ground operation at Glinka, and although Brazhnikov, who was in command there, was capable of communicating, he wouldn't say what. Meanwhile, the strike force in Armenia was still standing by, and its commanding officer was demanding to know what was going on. While Lieutenant Kugav busied himself with updating logs and report files, Chelenko paced over to the corkboard to peruse the sequence of messages again.

First, at around noon, Stavisky, Brazhnikov's second-in-command, had radioed a worried report that Brazhnikov and Lieutenant Dorkiev had disappeared and not been heard from for over two hours. The circumstances that Stavisky had described sounded mysterious: a Syrian airliner had taken off from the airstrip at Glinka, and later returned. Chelenko had no explanation.

And then Brazhnikov himself had come through suddenly—not on his own radio, since he wasn't with Stavisky—asking for information on Syrian aircraft registrations; and then he had signed off after giving an unauthorized call frequency, before Chelenko could talk to him and without giving any further information at all.

Baffled but with no real choice, Chelenko had obtained the information from the aeronautical authorities, and then transmitted it to Brazhnikov. But again the Major had signed off abruptly—he had cut Chelenko off in midsentence! Brazhnikov hadn't responded to further calls, and a check with Stavisky had shown that Brazhnikov and Dorkiev still hadn't been seen.

And now the latest. Stavisky and the three men with him had heard from Brazhnikov and were moving to rendezvous with him and Dorkiev at a point that Stavisky had given Chelenko the coordinates of. Chelenko had checked on the map, and found it to be out on a line of hillsides about five kilometers on the other side of the guerrilla camp, out in the middle of a remote area that Brazhnikov had no business being in at all. Chelenko could only conclude that either Brazhnikov had taken leave of his senses, or something very odd was going on. And to somebody of Chelenko's turn of mind, "odd" meant "wrong"; and anything that was wrong was dangerous.

He turned away from the board and walked back to where Kugav was sitting. "Get the communications room to give you a channel to Moscow and keep it open," he ordered. "Have them find General Goryanin and put him on. They're to tell him that we have a peculiar situation that I wish to discuss with him."

"Yes sir."

Chelenko went over to the map and stared at it. He might have to order the force in Armenia to move quickly, he decided, but just at this moment he had no idea why or against what. It was always a good idea to get blessings from higher up in situations like this—or at least, some kind of tacit understanding. That was something that Brazhnikov needed to learn. It wasn't going to do his career prospects any good, running off and trying to be independent. He was in the wrong army for that.

After all that had been happening, Mel hadn't realized how much the uncertainty had been gnawing him inside. It hit him with a relief that seemed explosive, when Jacob called a challenge from the guard point on the rim of the hollow, a voice responded, and a few seconds later five figures dropped down inside. Mel felt his breath catch and his eyes mist over in the shadows. It *was* Brett! It was, it was. . . . He threw an arm around Brett's shoulder and hugged him, lost for the moment for words. It took a moment for Brett to realize who it was.

"*Jesus goddam Christ!* What in hell are *you* doing here as well?"

"Dave didn't tell you?" Feeling as he did at that moment, Mel forgot all about code names and such.

"No."

"He was having trouble enough getting over seeing me," Dave said.

"Does everyone in America know everyone else?" Ehud asked curiously.

Dave noticed that there were more forms scattered around in the darkness than there should have been. "Who else is here?" he asked.

"Russians—Yuri's other four guys showed up," Mel told him.

"Okay."

Brett was staring uncomprehendingly. "Russians? I don't understand. What are they doing here? It's just taken me months to get away from them."

"It's not the way you probably think," Mel said.

"What are you talking about?"

Mel paused to collect his words. "Look," he said, "this is going to have to be quick, but we'll explain it all later. Just answer the questions for now, okay?"

Obviously Mel knew more than he did. Brett nodded. "Shoot."

"It was Hermann Oberwald who recruited you, right?"

"I didn't know he was working for the Soviets at the time. I thought—"

"What did he tell you?"

"That the world situation wasn't safe enough to be left in the hands of crazies . . . on both sides. And you know how I used to feel about things like that—it was what I wanted to hear."

"Okay, and? . . ."

"He said he was part of an international organization of people who were above all that. Rational, sane . . . you know the kind of thing. So being the dumb shit that I am, I bought it. It was only later that I figured out it was a front. . . ." Brett's voice trailed off as he saw the point that Mel had been making. "You mean it wasn't a Soviet front?"

"That's right," Mel said, nodding. "You made the same mistake we all did: you *assumed*, with a little bit of help, that it was the Soviets."

Brett looked nonplussed. "But who else are you saying it could have been?"

"Believe me, that's a long story. I'm not even gonna try and get into it. But what I need to know is *why* they needed you to supply space-defense secrets. I mean, somebody like Oberwald could get anything he wanted. Why did he need you?"

"That's the whole point of what I've been trying to communicate out through Hamashad," Brett said, his voice straining now with urgency.

"Who?"

"The guy who's with Mossad—the one I just came out with."

"Okay."

"With people like Oberwald in it, I couldn't risk tipping off the wrong side. The Constitutionals were the only people I felt I could trust."

Mel nodded. "Yes, I see that. But what was it? What was it that you wanted to tell them?"

"Supplying information isn't what Oberwald wanted me to do. Hell, I'm a programmer, not a goddam mailman. He got me to *alter* it!"

Mel shook his head. "What do you mean, 'alter it'?"

"His line was that space-based beam weapons are too powerful, totally destabilizing. In the hands of an evangelical government, that would be all they'd need to bring down the Armageddon and cry hallelujah."

Mel nodded rapidly in the darkness. "Sure, I know the line. So what did you do?"

Brett spread his hands. "I thought it was an organization of rational-thinking, high-principled people with influence, who'd bring some sanity into the mess. I—"

"Yes, sure, sure, I understand all that, Brett. Nobody's blaming you. I just want to know what you did."

"They convinced me that the only way the world would be safe once the U.S. space-weaponry system was deployed would be if *they* had the option to override it—to veto a fire command. In other words, to switch it off." Brett drew a long breath. "So that's what I put into it for them."

"You *what?*"

"There's some code that I buried inside the fire-control executive software that they can activate remotely. It recognizes a pattern that goes in through the target-tracking radar, not through the command links where all the security precautions are."

Mel was looking bemused. He tried to think back to his own software days. "But how could it go undetected? I mean, a chunk of illegitimate code that isn't supposed to be there would be the first thing the debug would pick up."

Brett was shaking his head already. "It depends how the debug is written. *I wrote* the debug routine that was used to test that part of the software. It only tells you what it's been told to tell you is in there. If there's something in there that it's been told not to tell you about, you'll never know."

The only way to find out what was in a program was to write another program to look at it and tell you. But the second program could be written to have blind spots.

Mel gaped at him, glassy-eyed. What Brett was saying was that the people who controlled both sides of the world had the ability to switch off the West's space-defense system at will. And the full meaning of it all finally became clear in its horrifying completeness.

Apart from the inner core of the elite who were responsible, this tiny group of Americans, Russians, and Israelis in a remote part of Syria were, right at that moment, very probably the only people anywhere who possessed all the information.

The two halves of the key had finally come together.

CHAPTER 67

In Tel Aviv it was almost 8:00 P.M., corresponding to 1:00 in the afternoon, East Coast American time. At an address used as a safe house by the Israeli intelligence service, Stephanie sat in a comfortably furnished lounge with balcony looking out over the city, watching the U.S. inauguration ceremony coming in live from Washington. With her were two women from the Israeli secret-service team that had been detailed to watch over her while she remained in the country.

No reason had yet been given for asking her to remain behind after McCormick and the rest of the party returned home. She could only assume that it had something to do with Mel or Dave Fenner. However, she had seen and heard nothing of Mel since her middle-of-the-night departure from Kemmel's house in Cairo a week previously, and there had been no response from Dave to the message she had left by telephone for "Benjamin" upon her arrival in Israel. McCormick had broadcast the code phrase from Mustapha as requested, which meant that Dave would now be involved in whatever was happening as a consequence; and after what had happened in Egypt, God alone knew what Mel had gotten himself mixed up in. So until one or the other of them chose to make his presence known to her, there was nothing she could do.

A more worrisome thought was that perhaps she hadn't been extricated from the business in Egypt quite as cleanly as she'd been led to believe, and somewhere behind the scenes wheels were turning slowly but inexorably that would eventually catch up with her. If so, she concluded resignedly, there wasn't anything she could do about that, either. She was now totally a pawn of events outside her control. For once, trying to guess what Eva would have done was no use at all.

On the screen, the crowd was filling the square in front of the Capitol steps. Henry Newell and Theo McCormick were visible to one side of the group congregating at the top, the Chief Justice had appeared, ready to receive the oaths of office, and in the background it seemed that every congressman, woman, state official, and party worker from the United States must have gathered to witness the culmination of all their efforts. It made her feel all the more out of it not to be there, and without even knowing why.

She realized that the two Israeli secret-service women had been talking while she was thinking. "What do you think, Eva?" one of them asked her. "Will this amendment that everyone has been talking about make so much difference to the world?"

"It's not the amendment that matters," Stephanie replied. "That's just words on paper. What matters is that it expresses the collective mood of a people." She nodded toward the TV screen. "That's what you're seeing there. And yes, I think *that* will make a difference."

On the screen, a hush had come over the crowd, and Henry Newell stepped forward and raised his hand. The shot switched to a closeup, and in that moment the expression on one man's face embodied the will of a nation passing from adolescence to maturity, a nation that was taking charge of itself.

"I do solemnly swear that I will faithfully execute the office of president of the United States, and will to the best of my ability . . ."

At that precise moment, the Ilyushin that had been flying on a southerly bearing twenty miles off the Maryland coast completed a starboard turn which brought its nose around to point directly at Washington, one hundred and thirty miles westward. A pair of long doors extending for half the length of the fuselage hinged open on its underside, and moments later a black cigar-shaped object fell away, its stub wings already unfolding. A finger of flame leaped from its tail as the motor ignited, accelerating the missile up through supersonic speed in a few seconds. As the first streaked away, a second missile dropped from the aircraft's belly, fired, and followed after it.

Within ten seconds the computers of the North Eastern Air Defense Region had extracted the anomaly from the datastreams pouring in from the surveillance radars on the East Coast, sounded an audible alarm, and presented flashing warning signals on the display screens to alert the operators.

Alerts also went out automatically to USAF Defense Command Headquarters, the Operations Room of the recently created Strategic Defense Command, and the Situation Office in the Pentagon.

One of the air-defense radar crew was the first to realize what was happening. *"Holy Christ, they're missiles!"* He began flipping switches frantically. "Get me CP on that! Alert Stingray, Code Red." Activity erupted on all sides, lamps flashing, bells clanging. Bodies jerked upright in chairs at consoles; somebody sent a styrofoam cup of coffee flying across the floor. "Bravo Two, we have gremlins, range two-zero, bearing one-two-one decimal three, altitude thirty thousand, descending, speed increasing at nine-zero-zero on course two-six-five decimal one. . . . Update on five, Charlie Two. . . . Wilco, go to red on Dagger. . . . Holy shit! . . ."

"Bring Angels three-two-nine to alert and advise."

"We have confirmation on Zebra Seven, Stingray."

"Give me an ETT on Washington . . ."

The Duty Officer Commanding appeared, white-faced. "What's happening?"

"Fucking missiles, two of 'em—going straight for Washington!"

"How far off target?"

"If it is Washington, less than six minutes."

General Goryanin listened incredulously to what Colonel Chelenko was saying as his voice babbled over the satellite link from Damascus. "They're certain that the aircraft is a camouflaged launching platform. That's what the missiles were for. If it left here at ten o'clock this morning on the same route as the regular flight, it would be right off the North American coast by now. That means that Washington has to be the target."

Goryanin blinked and shook his head. "Brazhnikov has joined up with Israelis? The lawyer is there? . . . I don't—"

"There isn't time to go into the whys and wherefores," Chelenko interrupted. "The inauguration is taking place there at this moment. Don't you see what this means? An act of war is about to be committed against the United States, and we have been set up to appear responsible. Somebody is out to destroy the regime, and they want it to look as if it were us." Goryanin stared numbly at the wall of the map room, where Chelenko's call had found him. "Do something . . . now!" Chelenko's voice pleaded.

Goryanin shook himself back to life. The correct thing now would be to refer the situation to Kordorosky as his direct superior. But he rejected the thought instinctively, even as it formed in his mind. Not with something like this. Kordorosky would be happy to sit back and let it happen. Even though it might get him shot, Goryanin would have to find another way. He picked up another phone that was lying on the desk, on which another officer was standing by for orders on a separate line.

"Get ahold of the defense minister, Marshal Androliev," he instructed. "Interrupt him at once, whatever he's doing. Tell him that it's his nephew, and that we have an emergency."

In the Situation Room beneath the Pentagon, General Sommerfield stood in an agony of suspense, watching the plots and data updates on the screens. Some aides were rushing this way and that in frenzied activity to keep their minds occupied; others had given up and just stood, petrified. It had all happened so quickly. There hadn't been time to summon anyone. The course of the missiles was now unmistakable: straight at the Capitol.

"Two minutes, twenty-seven seconds," someone announced. "Gremlin One has crossed the shore." That was the eastern shore of Chesapeake Bay. Forty-two miles away from the target.

An Air Force general, surrounded by a numbed entourage, turned from where he had been talking frantically at a screen on the dais facing the room. "Not a chance. We'll never get anything off the ground, never mind within range."

"Gremlin Two is over the Bay," someone called. The displays changed to an updated plot.

"What's happening at Bolero?" Sommerfield demanded tightly.

"General Knowle in back now. Screen Six."

Sommerfield strode back to the console he had been at shortly before, which was communicating with Strategic Defense Command. That was the only hope left now.

Knowle appeared back on screen as Sommerfield reached the console. "XDS–7 is primed and tracking. Target illumination radars have found it. We've gone to Red-Red. I've assumed command." Sommerfield felt a little easier, although his brow was glistening profusely. Thank God they had enough birds up now to ensure permanent cover.

"Two minutes," a voice called out.

Sommerfield could hear other voices coming from the screen, in the background behind Knowle.

"Fire inhibit is lifted. Go ahead, Delta."

"Uplink holding steady, switch to seven-five-zero."

"Seven-five-zero, roger."

"On synch, yellow-five. Beam power is good."

"Set count on—"

"*Negative function!* We're losing it . . . the beam's down."

On the screen, General Knowle whirled around.

"Bolero, what's going on there for Christ's sake?" Sommerfield shouted, his rising voice causing heads to turn all around the room.

"SYS Three has aborted. We're dead here."

Knowle shouted a stream of orders off screen, then turned back, looking dazed. "We can't fire. It's not responding. The satellite isn't responding!"

"It's the same thing that happened with Six in November," a voice said somewhere behind him. "It's spooking out the same way, all over again."

There had been no time for Marshal Androliev to leave his office in the Kremlin. He had contacted General Roskovin, the commander of the Soviet Orbital Defense Force, directly via the communications screen by his desk.

"We have a channel to OCC now," Roskovin reported from the headquarters in Riga. "Satellite OBF-3 is within range. But active intervention would require Defense Council authorization."

"Dammit, General, I am the defense minister! There isn't time to call a meeting. The responsibility is mine alone. Do you understand? This is an emergency. You must obey my orders."

"I need confirmation from at least another member. We have alerted the general secretary. He is on his way to your office now, with Comrade Kordorosky."

Androliev's heart sank. "There isn't time. I order it."

Roskovin shook his head. "Washington isn't worth my neck. Sorry."

"I—"

The door burst open and Kordorosky strode in, looking tight-lipped and even whiter than usual. Vladimir Petrakhov, the general secretary of the Party, appeared close behind him.

He came over to Androliev's desk and pivoted the screen around to face him. "Very well, we are in control here, now," he told Roskovin. "What is the situation?"

Roskovin consulted briefly with somebody offscreen. "We now have long-range optical and infrared contact. Two missiles have been launched."

"Remain standing by."

Kordorosky looked at Androliev with contempt. "What do you think you were trying to do, you old fool? This is the best thing that could have happened for us."

Androliev slumped down in his chair and lifted a cigarette to his lips with a shaking hand.

Someone had ordered the siren alarms to be sounded in the city. Newell stood bewildered at the top of the Capitol steps, cut off in midsentence as the noise swelled. Police radios were squawking and babbling everywhere, and some people started running blindly in any direction, impelled by some animal instinct that sensed disaster. Then the entire crowd broke up into massive eddies, swirling turbulently. McCormick came forward, looking from side to side in bewilderment. "What's happening?"

Newell could only shake his head helplessly. "How do I know?"

An assistant rushed out of the doors behind the steps and over to them, clearly panicking. "It's an attack! An aircraft off the coast has fired missiles! They're coming right at us!"

The defense secretary was at the center of a flurry of figures in suits and uniforms. "What's happening with the satellites?"

Somebody proffered a radio phone. "Situation Room on the line now."

"How far out are they?"

"We have to evacuate."

"No way. We've got less than two minutes."

"Oh my God!"

A man with a bald head ran past, clutching his brow. "I'm gonna die, I'm gonna die. Shit, it's real, I'm gonna die. . . ."

"They've got a bead on 'em with the lasers! The lasers have got em'! It'll be okay."

Newell wiped his brow. There was nothing to be said. Running around and demanding answers would only be getting in the way now.

The defense secretary looked up from the handset he was

holding. His face had gone pale. "Something's wrong," he choked. "They can't fire the laser. The satellite's gone dead up there."

In the darkness of the Syrian desert, the Americans and the Israeli and Russian troops were sitting in a tense, silent huddle around the cave, where Zvi and Brazhnikov were crouched by the radio pack. They had already been in contact with the Russians' commander in Damascus, even before Mel realized what the aircraft, the missiles, the date, and the time of day added up to. There hadn't been time to get through to the authorities in Washington via the Israelis. And besides, after the experience with Oberwald, nobody knew if the top levels of the U.S. defense hierarchy could be trusted, anyway. And even if they could, it wouldn't have done any good; Brett had already told them that the U.S. space defense system could be neutralized.

So they had done the only thing they could and let Brazhnikov try to do something through his command chain— as Mel had pointed out, what was happening was no more in the Soviets' interests than the Americans'. And it had turned out that the Russian commander in Damascus was already holding a channel open to Moscow.

The radio crackled suddenly. "Hydro calling Snowball."

Brazhnikov leaned closer and acknowledged. A brief exchange ensued. Then Brazhnikov spoke in Russian to Zvi.

"What's happening?" Mel hissed.

"Damascus is through to the Kremlin via the KGB. But there's a lot of confusion there, and General Secretary Petrakhov himself is involved now. . . ." Then the voice crackled again from the radio, sounding excited and somehow despairing, even in the foreign tongue. Mel looked at Zvi questioningly.

"What was that?" Mel said. He could see the horror-struck expression on Zvi's face, even in the darkness.

"We were too late," Zvi choked. "The missiles have been fired."

It was all over. Sommerfield could only stand looking numbly at the data displays. All activity in the Situation Room ceased as one by one the operators at the rows of consoles and terminals rose slowly to their feet. One man had broken down and been taken out by MP guards. A deathly hush fell, broken only by one operator, reciting mechanically in a trancelike voice, "Twenty-one miles, sixty seconds to target. . . . Nineteen miles, fifty-five seconds. . . ."

Marshal Androliev flicked at the lighter several times. It was empty. He tossed it back onto the desk and opened the top drawer to search for matches. Somebody at the door was calling for the general secretary. Petrakhov went over, and a moment later disappeared outside. The screen was still turned away from him, but Androliev could hear Roskovin in Riga.

"Targeting radars are tracking and locked. What do you want us to do?"

Kordorosky was standing a few feet away, still looking in the direction of the door, away from Androliev and outside the viewing angle from the screen. The situation would last for a few seconds at the most. Androliev looked down again at the Luger automatic lying in the drawer. He lifted it out and raised it above the edge of the desk, aimed in Kordorosky's direction. The KGB chief caught the movement from the corner of his eye and turned his head. His eyes just had time to widen before the bullet hit dead center between them.

Androliev got up and moved around the desk to face the screen.

"We have reached a unanimous decision," he told Roskovin. "Shoot the missiles down."

"Yes, sir."

Androliev pivoted the screen back to point at the empty desk, at the same time turning down its sound control so that anything else wouldn't be heard. A second later, the general secretary rushed back in through the doorway, officers and guards behind him.

"What was that? It sounded like—" He saw the body of Kordorosky, sprawled full length on the floor. "Good God! . . ." The others came to a confused halt behind.

The old marshal rose from his chair and covered them with the gun. "We just wait for thirty seconds, gentlemen," he said. "After that, you may do with me as you wish."

"Seventeen miles to target, fifty . . ." The voice faltered and stopped. The silence persisted for a few seconds.

"What's going on?" another voice asked, sounding bewildered.

"I don't know. It's disappeared from the display. . . .
What's the situation with the second . . . What?"

Sommerfield stared up at the big display screen disbelievingly. Around him the statues were beginning to move and
speak again.

"That one's gone, too. I don't understand it."

"They've both just . . . vanished!"

"That's impossible."

Sommerfield looked at the screen still showing Knowle at
Strategic Defense Command. "Did you do that?"

Knowle shook his head, looking equally bemused. "Negative. The bird's still dead."

"Get an ADS update and confirmation," Sommerfield told
an aide.

"I already have, sir. Radar has lost both missiles."

"Evaluation?"

"None possible at this stage, sir."

"Does anyone know what's going on?" Sommerfield demanded, stepping back and asking the room in general.
Nobody did.

Then a telephone rang nearby. An Air Force major took the
call, listened for a few seconds, and then looked up. "Sector
Five has a visual confirmation," he informed the room. "Both
missiles exploded in flight east of the city. First reports put it
at somewhere near the Patuxent River."

Minutes later, four F-15 interceptors formed up around the
Ilyushin, radioed orders to it to land, and escorted it down to
Langley Air Force Base, Virginia.

CHAPTER 68

It was late the next morning when the C-130 landed at an air
base fifteen miles northeast of Tel Aviv with its complement of
nine weary but relieved Israeli paratroopers, along with Mel,
Dave, Brett, and the agent that they now knew as Hamashad.
The original plan—to lift them out of Syria via the temporary
strip in Turkey in the same way that they entered—had been

scrapped late the previous evening. Instead, with clearance
from the Syrian authorities, the transporter had flown directly
to collect them from the airstrip at Domino the first thing next
morning, and had sent the helicopter out from there to pick up
Rafael's squad from the desert. By the time the plane left
Domino, newspapers and TV reporters were already inform-
ing the world, still recovering from the shock of what had
almost happened in Washington, of the Soviet commando
force from Armenia that had landed during the night and freed
the passengers from a Syrian airliner that most people hadn't
even known was hijacked. Syrian troops had landed there, too,
and the Israelis had left a scene of excited questionings and
interrogations in progress among the Russians, the Syrians,
and the Palestinians, with every sign that it would all be
continuing for some time.

"How does it feel to be back on the ground outside Syria?"
Mel asked Brett as the giant plane slowed and swung off the
runway to taxi to its dispersal area. "Did you ever think that
maybe you'd never get out?"

Brett grinned and shook his head. "No way. You can't sink
me. I'm a rubber duck."

"You mean you still remember that?"

"Sure." Brett frowned. "Say, where did it come from?"

"That party the night before I left Pensacola, remember?
There was some idiot in the pool."

"That's right . . . that was it, yes."

"Do you guys still remember things from back then?" Dave
said, sitting by them. "It seems like a thousand years ago."

"It was in a way," Mel said. "That was back in the nineteen
hundreds."

Dave gave him a funny look. "That's right. I never thought
about it like that."

The aircraft rolled to a halt, and the Israelis got up and
moved back to cluster around the tail door. "A long hot bath
and clean sheets tonight," Ehud said to them as he gathered
his equipment. "Looking forward to it?"

"You could say that," Mel agreed.

"We couldn't persuade you to take this up full-time, then?
Why not? You'd be a natural at it."

"I think I'll stick to lawyering, thanks," Mel said.

"You won't, you know," Dave told him.

Ehud was looking at Mel quizzically. "I still don't know what to make of that," he said. "Are you really a lawyer? You sounded serious when you said it."

Mel leaned close to his ear. "Classified," he whispered. Ehud gave a laugh and shrugged.

The tail ramp swung down. The arrivals walked down it into the sunlight as the airscrews stopped spinning, and ambled in a loose gaggle across to the two pickup trucks waiting to take them to the terminal area. Mel waited for the boots ahead of him to lift clear, then swung his pack and Uzi up over the tailgate and hauled himself up between Dave and Brett. Hamashad was sitting opposite, looking distant, and in a way, surprisingly, somewhat sad. "What's the matter?" Brett asked him. "I thought you'd be on top of the world to be back."

Hamashad sighed and returned a smile. "Oh, it isn't all as simple as people think. Living among the Palestinians as one of them, you learn to understand them. It's a recognized fact among us that some of the strongest spokesmen for their cause are Israeli agents who've infiltrated them."

"Just more people who wanted to be left alone, eh?" Dave said as the truck pulled away.

"Their fathers' land was taken away from them by foreigners, and given to other foreigners," Hamashad said. "How would you feel?"

The trucks passed a line of helicopters painted olive with Army markings, crossed the concrete apron, and drove in front of a hangar with a fire truck and rescue wagon parked outside to the aircrew buildings and control tower. There, by a parked Land Rover, Colonel Shlomo Hariv and General Shimon Lurgar were waiting for them. And there was a third figure with them also, Mel saw as the pickup lurched to a halt and the khaki-clad figures began tumbling out.

She was wearing a white shirt with tan slacks, and her long, fair hair was loose and billowing in the wind. In the message that Mel had asked Yigal Uban to deliver just before the U.S. delegation left for home, he had asked Slade not to tell Stephanie the reason for leaving her behind. There was always the chance that Mustapha might not have been Brett. Mel wouldn't have wanted to raise her hopes that high, only to be dashed. If Mustapha had turned out to be someone else, they would simply have fobbed her off with an excuse and that would have been that.

Mel hadn't realized until late the previous night, while they were still in Syria, that Brett had received information through

Hamashad—official, but wrong—that Stephanie was dead. He suspected that Brett still hadn't recovered from the emotional effect of learning the true story—the way that Brett had been talking about anything else ever since suggested that he was still coming to terms with it internally. Brett was still collecting things together on the floor of the truck and hadn't seen her yet. Mel hadn't said anything about her being at the airfield for the simple reason that he'd had no reason to suppose that she would be.

And Stephanie, for her part, didn't know why she had been brought there because nobody had told her. It was one of those things that had slipped down a crack somewhere amid all the excitement and confusion of the past night. Hariv thought that Lurgar had told her, Lurgar assumed Hariv had taken care of it, and everyone else had been too busy to even think about it.

She was more puzzled than ever as she stood with the two officers and saw that the trucks from the plane that had just landed were filled with Israeli paratroopers. The first ones came up to the officers who had brought her here, and there was a lot of laughing, back-slapping, and joking exchanges in Hebrew. And then her eyes widened incredulously as she recognized the grinning, black-faced figure in a camouflage smock, a pack slung across its shoulder, and carrying a submachine gun, approaching her with a cocky swagger behind them. "My God, it's Mel!" she gasped weakly. And Dave Fenner was with him.

"Hi," Dave said. "We brought him back in one piece. He ends up in the strangest places."

Stephanie was shaking her head, unable to speak. She brought a hand to her brow, her mouth moved helplessly, and she started to laugh. Then she found her voice at last. "It's just . . . I had no idea that . . ."

"You mean they didn't tell you?" Mel said.

"No. I haven't heard anything at all since . . ." And she stared past them, forgetting for the moment that they existed. She had just seen who had climbed out of the truck after them. "Oh my God . . ."

Brett was looking at her, equally thunderstruck.

"And nobody even told you that—" Mel began, but Dave caught his sleeve and shook his head. It wasn't a time for talking. And Stephanie wasn't listening, anyway.

Brett came slowly across from the truck, ignoring the other two, and reached out for her. The spell broke, and she threw herself into his arms and clung, shaking her head and pressing herself to him while he closed his eyes and pulled her close. The tears came then, in a flood, releasing everything that had built up inside her for months.

And as Melvin Shears watched them, something happened inside him, too. It was Brett, the old Brett, just as he had always been. She was Stephanie again, and belonged with him. And the world belonged to Mel. For Eva had finally died.

He and Dave glanced sideways at each other. "I don't think they'll need us around for a while, do you?" Mel murmured.

Dave shook his head. "What would you say to a long, cool, Israeli beer right now?"

"You've talked me into it," Mel said. They turned away and began sauntering toward the buildings behind the Land Rover, where the others were converging. "I always said you were persuasive, Dave."

"I thought that was supposed to be your job."

"Well, you're not doing bad for a beginner."

Dave clapped an arm around Mel's shoulder. "You didn't do too badly yourself for a beginner, either."

"Glad to hear it."

"It's not the best beer in the world, you know."

"You're wrong there, Dave. It'll be the best I ever tasted in my life, I promise you."

EPILOGUE

Four people stood in silence, staring at the grave in California, each absorbed in personal thoughts and recollections. Stephanie was wearing a black dress and hat. The last times he had been here, she'd had to watch from afar, at the gate. This was her way of making up for it—her own private ceremony. Brett, Mel, and Dave had put on suits and dark ties to be here with her.

The grave was laid with fresh flowers. A new headstone had been erected. It read:

EVA SHIRLEY CARNE
1973–2000
FREEDOM'S CHILD

They stood for a while, each having prepared words to say at this moment, all of them feeling now that no words were adequate. The silence and the individual inner communions were more appropriate.

Stephanie had half expected to be tearful, but found that she was not. Somehow, after everything, tears seemed inappropriate, too—unbecoming to the memory of someone like Eva. At last Stephanie nodded briefly. Brett took her arm and steered her back to the roadway leading to the gate. Mel and Dave followed. They had left their cars outside, preferring to walk to the graveside, in a small gesture of homage, rather than disturb the tranquility.

As he walked beside Dave, Mel thought back over everything that had happened since that first week in November. . . .

Setting up the missile attack to look like the work of the Soviets had been the last in the long trail of false clues pointing in that direction. After all the previous deceptions and the preparation of public opinion, with the missiles being

436

launched from a Soviet-built aircraft flying from a Soviet client state, what else could the world have thought? Even the crew of the Ilyushin—drawn from a fanatically anti-Western Muslim sect—had believed they were working with the backing of the Soviets.

If the plan had gone as conceived, the world would also have been reacting to the assassination in Cairo, by the new U.S. regime, of a figure the public had been led to believe was about to shift the Middle-East power balance in favor of the Soviets. The destruction of the regime would have been seen as the Soviet response, the elimination of a leadership that preached humanity while it operated by gangster methods. Although the act would no doubt have been judged insanely harsh and out of all proportion to the provocation, who would have doubted that the Soviets had been responsible? (And any lone voice trying to point out that it couldn't have been organized in a mere matter of days would have been drowned in the furor.)

America would have screamed for war, of course, but its leadership—whatever little of it survived—would have known that with the space defenses useless war was out of the question. In the ensuing political turmoil, the country would have disintegrated into anarchy as totally as Russia itself had in 1917, setting the stage for America to be brought to heel with the same ruthlessness and for the same ostensible reasons—to restore stability and order. And the yoke around the neck of the world would have been complete.

As things were, however, one of the Kremlin's periodic internal feuds seemed to be erupting, and from the few details that had leaked out through the smoke, there were signs that Russia might be undergoing an upheaval. Oleg Kordorosky, the sinister deputy chairman of the KGB, reportedly had died of a heart attack; the general secretary, Petrakhov, was out of favor suddenly, and the more moderate faction among the military was making a concerted bid for power, rallying around the figurehead of the aging Marshal Androliev, who had emerged as a popular hero. Nobody on the outside could be sure what it all meant, but one thing was certain—the new American administration would have all the time it needed to find its feet.

They reached the gate, where the two cars were parked. Brett and Stephanie would be going straight on to Denver now, to pick up the threads of their life together. Brett had already talked to Ed Gilman about some of the advanced programming that the fission-fusion project was going to need—the attitude of the financiers had begun to reverse itself, thanks to the sensational revelations emanating from Washington since the new government had assumed office. Mel had been to Boston to show his face at the firm and tell his story . . . but somehow he couldn't see himself back in his office there again. Evron and Winthram had its place in his past now, like Pensacola, like Chapel Hill, like Eva . . . and that was where, like them, it belonged.

Stephanie hugged and kissed Mel, hugged and kissed Dave. Brett embraced them. They said final good-byes . . . for the time being. Nobody promised to stay in touch. It wasn't necessary. Brett opened the passenger-side door to let Stephanie in, then walked around the car and climbed in the driver's side. He started the motor, U-turned on the roadway, and with a final flurry of waves and a few toots on the horn, they were on their way.

Mel watched until the car disappeared from sight. Then he turned and walked back to where Dave was waiting at his car. They climbed in, and as if compelled by the same instinct, both turned their heads and stared back in the direction of the new white stone gleaming distantly in the sun, with the flowers piled around it.

Dave started the motor, and they pulled away. The heaviness of their mood lifted gradually as they left the San Mateo area and cruised north on Highway 101 in the California sunshine, bound for San Francisco.

"What are you planning on doing next?" Dave asked, eyeing Mel curiously. "Take a break, then back to the desk?"

Mel shook his head. "To be honest, Dave, I can't see it."

"Oh, really? Didn't I tell you that, though?"

"I can't remember. Did you?" They were playing games again.

Dave waited. Mel watched the scenery. "What, then?" Dave asked finally.

"I don't really know."

Dave smiled to himself. After a short pause, as if the thought had just occurred to him, he said lightly, "You know, the people I'm with aren't going to be all out of work suddenly, just because of what happened a couple of weeks ago. There'll always be plenty to do in that line. They're always interested in meeting new people. I, ah . . . I just happen to know somebody who'd be real keen to talk to you."

Mel pretended to think about it. He still didn't know who Dave worked for, he realized. "I guess you do get kind of hooked on the adrenaline kick, don't you?" he said.

"Interested, maybe?"

Mel grinned and quit the pretense. "Sure, I'll talk to him."

"See, I knew it. You're really a cowboy at heart. You like toting an Uzi around. That's no good, Mel. Guys like that bomb out on the first interview."

"That's not it at all. I like the paid vacations to exotic places."

A car passed them in the fast lane doing at least ninety. Its rear window displayed a Constitutional tortoise. Mel relaxed back in the passenger seat and smiled to himself. It was funny, yet at the same time seemed symbolic. He surveyed the prospects for the future, and they looked good. New millennium. New direction. New person. New phase of life. Everything was evolving. It was a good feeling to be a part of it all.

True, one day none of it would matter. But that only made today matter even more.

That was what Eva had understood.

ABOUT THE AUTHOR

Born in London in 1941, JAMES P. HOGAN worked as an engineer specializing in digital electronics and for several major computer firms before turning to writing full-time in 1979. Winner of the Prometheus Award, he has won wide popularity and high praise for his novels with their blend of gripping storytelling, intriguing scientific concepts and convincing speculation. Mr. Hogan currently makes his home in the Republic of Ireland.